FOR MARILYN, JACK, & CHARLIE

THE
CHOWDERHEAD
CRUSADES
by
J. J. Walsh

PROLOGUE

I DIDN'T SEE THE LIVE BROADCAST. IT AIRED JANUARY 20, 2036, and I missed it because I was too busy being a stupid fetus. Needless to say, recordings could never match the shock and awe of the live spectacle. It was an AV feed that hijacked virtually every television station, every radio station, and every internet site. And it was 100 percent crazy town.

It opened on a sprawling convention hall, filled wall to wall with people dressed as iconic comic book superheroes and villains, surrounded by similarly themed exhibition booths, wall banners, and sandwich board signage. Most viewers had no idea what they were looking at. But to some, like my parents, the setting was instantly recognizable as San Diego's Comic-Con: the world's biggest and best convention for all things comic book. (While my folks had been regulars at the show in previous years, they were unable to attend that year because my mom was seven months along with me, and it was an iffy pregnancy. See what a stupid fetus I was?)

The scene set, the frame was flooded by a bright light, illuminating a group of costumed convention goers. As they looked over, shielding their eyes, a shadow crept into view, framed between one fan sporting the star-spangled stylings of Captain America and another decked out in full Wolverine wear. Then a voice called out.

"People of Earth, I . . . am Cateklysm Catholicon!"

At that point, the feed cut to the second of Cateklysm's many miraculous levitating cameras, and viewers at home saw him for the first time as his strangely misspelled name appeared in glowing, holographic letters above his head. He seemed like a normal enough guy – two arms, two legs, the usual assortment of facial features. But outside of Comic-Con, his attire would definitely have raised some questions. He was wearing a red cape, black spandex, and a blue domino mask, as well as metallic gauntlets and boots, which pulsated with luminous red and blue circuitry.

Considering estimated viewership, I think this was the first time in history billions of people had shared the exact same thought at the exact same moment. That thought was: *Who the hell is this crackpot Halloween reject?*

As if in answer, Cateklysm continued, "I am a transcendent intelligence dedicated to improving the potential of lesser life-forms. And I must say, human beings are lesser. Way lesser. I mean really bad. Just terrible."

I guess Comic-Con security had really seen it all because the three guards who approached Cateklysm didn't seem particularly fazed.

One of them spoke up. "Sir, we're going to need to see your exhibitor's pass."

At that, Cateklysm just smiled and said, "Certainly, gentlemen."

Then he took off. I don't mean he ran away. I mean a cloud of fire and smoke erupted from his heels, and he flew into the air, easing to a stop just below the latticework ceiling and hovering gently in place. From there, he spread his palms and a series of brilliant beams of energy blasted out, slamming into the security guards and hurling them twenty feet across the exhibition hall.

I think this was probably the second time in history billions of people had shared the exact same thought at the exact same moment. And that thought was: *Holy crap!*

There was a tense silence as the active camera panned across the crowd of slack-jawed onlookers. Then…a huge round of applause broke out. Everyone who hadn't already been enthralled crowded closer and craned their heads to get a look at what they assumed was a surprise show, staged by Comic-Con's organizers. They had no way of knowing the magnitude of it all—not yet.

Cateklysm descended slowly and touched down, holding up a hand to quell the applause.

"Where was I?" he said. "Ah yes, my very generous offer to help you overcome your massive shortcomings as a species. The fact is, you people are lost. Your religion, your politics, your pop culture—it's all the absolute worst. There is but one exception."

He gestured around the hall with a big "ta-da!" look on his face, but he got back only blank stares.

"Comic book superheroes!" he clarified. "They are your saving grace. They embody the courage, strength of character, and values to which you should aspire. They exemplify the resolve to do right that should be your guiding light. And now, Grant Morrison, one of your pitiable dimension's only true luminaries, will read a passage from his book *Supergods*."

This was definitely one of the most bucknutty moments of the broadcast but one of my favorites. A window behind Cateklysm shattered and two steel-skinned humanoid robots flew in, carrying Grant Morrison between them. With blue capes and stylized yellow and red "S" insignias stenciled onto their chests, the robots seemed to be fresh from guarding Superman's Fortress of Solitude. They were an astonishing sight to behold but the air of reverence that fell over the crowd was owed more to their passenger—who seemed disoriented but not overly surprised. Many of the things the septuagenarian comic book auteur had said over the years suggested he expected something like this to happen sooner or later. One of the robots handed him a bookmarked copy of his book, and after taking a moment to compose himself, he donned a pair of reading glasses, cleared his throat, and began reading in his distinctive Scottish accent:

"Could the superhero in his cape and skintight suit be the best current representation of something we might all become, if we allow ourselves to feel worthy of a tomorrow where our best qualities are strong enough to overcome the destructive impulses that seek to undo the human project?"

"Indeed, Mr. Morrison," Cateklysm broke in, clapping. "The answer is yes! Yes, a hundred times yes." The robots hoisted Morrison back into the air, a metallic hand under each of his armpits suspending him like a toddler, and flew back out the way they'd come. Then, without missing a beat, Cateklysm continued, "So where does that leave us? How shall I help you help yourselves? The answer is: Cateklysm's Challenge. Boom! You're welcome."

After gazing out at a sea of blank faces once again, he elaborated.

"It's a three-stage contest of superhero scholarship! And it's your chance to learn the lessons that will make you all better people. Alas, I do have my doubts about your intrinsic motivation to improve yourselves. You are such a lazy lot—just a disgusting bunch of potbellied lumps planning to forget me as soon as I return to my own dimension, so you can return to your nacho cheese chips and reality smut TV. As such, I'm going to light a fire under you. The first one to complete the Challenge will be granted a piece of unimaginably advanced technology, endowing him or her with the power to change the world! Of course, this is a limited time offer, good only until the year 2055. But that should be more than enough time for you people to get your ducks in a row."

Above his head, his name blinked out of existence, replaced by a URL: CateklysmsConundrum.com.

"Now then, each stage of the Challenge will lead to the next, and you'll find the first stage here," he said, gesturing to the URL. "It's a puzzle worthy of the Riddler. It will test your will, cunning, and valor. But the key is to take a shot of Pentagramite and just go for it."

He winked enthusiastically before adding, "Collaboration is allowed, but comic book publishers and certain industry professionals are prohibited from taking part in the Challenge, or providing others with any kind of assistance. They have been well apprised of the benefits of their cooperation, as well as the consequences of noncompliance."

The active camera pushed in close, and he looked gravely into it, presumably to let his ominous reminder sink in with the people in question, before addressing the crowd again.

"So there you go. Good luck with becoming slightly less pathetic!"

And that was it. Well, except for his exit, which consisted of him leaping into a swirling, sparking blue tunnel of energy that appeared behind him with a whoosh. As the last of the cameras followed him into the tunnel, every screen and speaker around the world returned to their regular programming.

As you can imagine, about two seconds later, a good chunk of humanity was logging on to CateklysmsConundrum.com. What they found was unusual but not all that surprising considering what they'd just witnessed. It was a puzzle: a bastardized crossword, with dozens of cells configured to form a stylized letter C (see Appendix A). There were large cells in which the clues had been placed and smaller cells sized to fit the individual letters that would comprise the answers. Some of these featured the usual numerical annotations in their upper left corner, but some of them were shaded and contained larger semi-opaque numbers that filled most of the cell. Finally, set between the arms of the C was a separate grid of shaded cells with large semi-opaque numbers matching those in the puzzle. Presumably, once the puzzle was completed, the contents of the shaded cells of the puzzle would be inserted into the corresponding cells in the grid to reveal some sort of message that led to the next stage of the Challenge.

Below the puzzle was a list of directories for various comic book publishers. Within each directory were subdirectories containing scores of digital copies of comics from that publisher, ranging from 1938 to the present. With just a few clicks, it was easy to see there were well over a hundred thousand entries.

Keep in mind, all this went down a while before the world turned to shit. The economy hadn't collapsed. Folks weren't killing each other for food. Norman Corp hadn't started strip-mining Mars. Things were still peachy keen. So people weren't too preoccupied to pay attention, and the media went nuts analyzing whether Cateklysm was for real. It was impossible. Ridiculous. He was totally and obviously a charlatan. Except for the hand blasters. And the robots. And the apparent hole in space time. Special effects? Maybe. Maybe not.

People fixated on his name. In plain speak, "Cateklysm Catholicon" translated roughly to "catastrophe remedy," which jibed well with his stated intention to rectify the disaster he considered our species to be. This, and the fact that he was supposedly from another world or dimension, suggested the name was merely a pseudonym. But why had he misspelled it? He was, after all, supposed to be a "transcendent intelligence."

Every frame of the broadcast was dissected, but there were no definitive results. Comic-Con attendees and organizers were grilled relentlessly to no avail. As for the comic book industry, those who had apparently been told not to talk, didn't. (Although Grant Morrison released a statement that amounted to "I told you so" before going dark.) Digital files and warehouse supplies of every issue appearing on Cateklysm's site were locked away, with newly published issues containing minimal references to them. The few comic book stores that had survived the digital revolution surrendered most of their back inventory through compulsory publisher buyback deals and leaned more heavily into manga and other genres inexplicably excluded from the site. Even relevant wiki pages evaporated. Rumors began to circulate about vast sums of compensation in play, but no one knew exactly how much there was or to whom it was going.

That said, as hard as it was to grasp the amount of juice required to ensure the majority of the Conundrum answers could only be found on one site, the site itself was even more confounding. It was built on some incomprehensible, untraceable, seemingly sentient code. It repelled all image or text-recognition programs and defied any efforts to download its contents. What's more, it would not load on any device without an active, functioning camera—and as various people discovered when trying to produce a less secure Conundrum copy through creative means, the site was monitoring user activities, melting down motherboards at the first sign of hijinks.

Bottom line: the only way to solve the Conundrum was good old manual labor. It seemed Cateklysm wanted to be sure we'd learn the broader lessons and not just the answers to the puzzle. But what he wanted only mattered if people were crazy enough to believe he was what he said he was.

People were crazy enough. Granted, the believers were only a small percentage of the broadcast's viewers, but that percentage was all in. Why? Well, Cateklysm had made that "unimaginably advanced technology" thing sound awfully nice, but it wasn't just that. You see, Cateklysm wasn't wrong about superheroes. They had been pretty good role models since day one. The US was sitting on its hands, waiting for Pearl Harbor to happen, when Captain America socked Hitler on the jaw in 1941. Girls were being told they were the weaker sex when Wonder Woman claimed a solo title in 1942. Americans were begrudgingly granting African Americans the basic right to vote when Black Panther (who predated the Black Panther Party) introduced the world to an African nation with vastly superior science and technology in 1966.

Before long, the progressive ideology of superhero lore catalyzed a cult movement, with diehards referring to comic books simply as "the Scriptures." These diehards initially called themselves Superhero Heads, or Supe Heads. But it wasn't long before detractors devolved the homonym Soup Heads into the derogatory Chowderheads, which the Cateklysm crowd adopted with defiant pride.

The Chowderheads' obsession defined them. They spent every spare moment gorging on the contents of Cateklysm's site. They lived and breathed the stuff. They even spoke it. If a guy was popular with the ladies, he was a *stark*, as in Iron Man's playboy alter ego, Tony Stark. If someone was smart, they were *reedy*, as in the Fantastic Four's super genius front man, Reed Richards. The police weren't *pigs*, they were *bullocks*, as in the Gotham PD's slovenly detective, Harvey Bullock. (That one offered a convenient double meaning with its proximity to the British slang for testicles.)

All that said, even for the most dedicated Chowderheads, progress on the Challenge was slow. The Conundrum was just the first of three stages, but it was a monumental undertaking. Lifelong comic book fans had an advantage but less of an advantage than they expected. Any one of the solutions could be hiding on any one of over three million pages, or lurking in some conceptual connection to be derived from a sum of parts.

After a year, only a handful of answers were public knowledge (see Appendix B). Everyone agreed these were the least elusive answers, but even so, they would have stumped most people were it not for the warm, collaborative spirit at work at the outset of the Challenge.

Now, given his intent for each of us to put in the elbow grease to earn our own superhero PhD, it was strange that Cateklysm had allowed collaboration. Then again, it seemed impossible for him to stop it – and he didn't need a lot of insight into human nature to know it wouldn't last anyway. Before long, a wave of realization came over the community, and everyone realized that every tidbit they shared with anybody could be putting the "unimaginably advanced technology" in the hands of that anybody. So people clammed up big time, and a Chowderhead adage was born: give away an answer, give away the world. Sure, some Chowderhead friends and families continued to work together, but there were plenty of fallings-out, and even divorces.

Yet, for all their pathological obsessing, a lot of Chowderheads began turning away from the movement a couple of years later. You may think this exodus was a product of frustration or fatigue. Not so. For many, the infatuation with an all-powerful being granting someone the power to change the world was simply being replaced by the panicked revelation that people were already changing the world – into a living hell. Of course, as bad as Earth would get in the coming years, there were still worse places to be. And that brings me to me.

My name is Clayton Clayborn. I was born on Earth, but I did most of my growing up on a deep space freighter called the Charon – one of dozens of vessels transporting an ore called Normanium from Mars to Earth for the Norman Corporation.

I landed onboard the Charon at age nine, when I was orphaned and Norman Corp bought me from the government as slave labor. Technically, it was a "labor for loan" contract, but government euphemisms aside, my life was pretty damn slavey: abusive guards, unregulated living conditions, and life-threatening working conditions. Things were bad. Really bad. And then my friends and I hatched an insane get-dead-quick scheme that landed us in a Chowderhead showdown with a trillionaire whack job, hell bent on world domination. But I'm getting ahead of myself. So let's start at the beginning.

ISSUE I OF 4
ORIGIN STORY

CHAPTER  01

I WAS DREAMING OF MARY JANE WATSON. SHE WAS STANDING at my door saying, "Face it, tiger . . . you just hit the jackpot." I'd been transported into a panel from *Amazing Spider-Man* #42 (1966), and I was playing the part of Peter Parker in his first meeting with this stunning young woman who had been foisted upon him by his dear old aunt May. It was one of my favorite non-superheroing moments in the Scriptures.

MJ's first-ever words may seem immodest, but any Chowderhead could tell you that the term *jackpot* actually fell woefully short of describing the sweetness and splendor of the woman destined to become Mrs. Peter Parker.

For me, MJ was the embodiment of a vital message: no matter how hopeless life seemed, things could get better. Even after Peter's parents died in a car wreck, even after his beloved uncle Ben was slain by a dirtbag gunman, even after his first love, Gwen Stacy, was murdered by the deranged Green Goblin, things could get better. Because eventually a redhead with a huge heart and a figure molded by God on a pervy day would show up at Peter's door. (Yes, this panacea was mostly powered by my warped teenage perception of what a woman was. But what are you gonna do?)

The fact that I would seek comfort in the Scriptures is no surprise, what with being a devout, purebred Chowderhead. The fact that I would seek that comfort often is also no surprise, what with being a space-based slave whose "happier days" had been spent in a sewer-adjacent concrete cave beneath the Discards—a sprawling shanty town in the urban wasteland that had once been San Francisco's financial district.

My dream skipped ahead to a scene of my own creation. MJ and I were seated on the couch—my head in her lap as she stroked my hair, soothing my worried mind. My subconscious was struggling with the fact that it was New Year's Day, 2054. Cateklysm's deadline was just a year away, and the pressure was on.

I was certain I'd know about it if anyone had completed the entire Challenge, but there was no reason to think I'd know if anyone had solved the Conundrum. It was very possible I was way behind tons of people, but I had to push on. Why? Well, Chowderheading was my way of honoring the memory of my parents, who were both hard-core Scripture nuts. But there was more to it. I was a Pun. This was a term Chowderheads used to identify themselves with one of two main superhero philosophies, based on the Pro/Pun scale. Every superhero from A-Bomb to Zatanna falls somewhere between two poles: protection and punishment. Pros like Superman, the Flash, Captain America, and Professor X fall closer to the protection pole. They have a basically optimistic view of the world, and they're driven mostly by the desire to keep innocent people safe. Puns like Batman, Blade, Spawn, Wolverine, and the Punisher (big surprise) fall closer to the punishment pole. They have a pretty bleak view of the world, and they're driven mostly by the desire to slice, stab, shoot, or batarang bad guys into oblivion.

I'd become a Pun the day I'd seen my parents murdered. I felt a deep need for retribution – a need to take vengeance on the man who had taken their lives. But that was only the beginning because there were more like him. That's why I needed Cateklysm's unimaginably advanced technology (or U.A.T.). After all, I figured "the power to change the world" should enable me to give every last evil bastard what they deserved.

Of course, that all started with winning the Challenge, which started with solving the Conundrum – which wasn't going all that great. Even after all these years, I was still stumped by six clues. MJ looked down into my troubled eyes and recited them:

1 Across: The Marvel with the greatest destiny.

2 Across: The most worthy weapon.

4 Across: Without the gift he gave, the obelisk would have been transformed into trash.

8 Across: A nice little mountain home for bad guys.

9 Across: Green ring teacher.

1 Down: 69, 86, 92, 94. List the link.

After she finished, she said, "Don't worry, tiger. Everything will be okay." And a calm came over me. I'd been stuck for eighteen months, and there were two more stages of the Challenge ahead, which would presumably require me to be on Earth, millions of miles from my current location. But I had MJ. Things could get better. I felt myself drifting deeper into sleep. Until the jarring wail of the morning klaxon bashed me in the head.

I sat up. It was 5:30 a.m., Earth Standard Time. I was on the Charon, on the top bunk of the twelve-by-twelve quarters I shared with Darcy Matua. For the last three months, we had been in the barracks on Mars, and we were just getting reacclimated from the dog-shit living arrangements there to the dog-shit living arrangements here. As the lights cycled to their daytime setting, I scanned the room, taking in its familiar detail. The walls were metal, tinted yellow from a coating of latex insulation. A seam could be discerned around one of the panels on the back wall because that panel could be rotated forward to reveal a small toilet and sink. The only feature that took up any permanent floor space was the bunk bed I was lying on.

Our quarters were on the top level of four mostly identical levels of the ship. About two-thirds of each level was dedicated to Labor Loaner living quarters, cargo bays, and storage facilities. The other third housed stuff like navigational operations and crew quarters, insulated behind a series of blast doors. The ship was home to four hundred Loaners, overseen by four crew bosses, each backed by a staff of underlings.

I removed my company-issue jumpsuit from the drawer below our bunk bed. As I slipped it on, it occurred to me for the thousandth time that the logo embossed on each shoulder was less like a corporate brand and more like a cattle brand. Norman Corp owned me, even if they called it a loan.

Labor Loaners like me were referred to as Orphan Loaners, or Orphs – wards of the state absorbed into the Norman Corp-initiated government program, which had started with the lease of prison labor. There was no real distinction between the quality of life experienced by Orphs and most other Labor Loaners, except for our holo-pods – holographic projection devices used the world over to interact with the internet. All Orphs were issued one, along with a web-based storage account where we could keep digital property: photos, books, games, movies, etc. The holo-pods also gave us access to the web in general, where we were allowed mostly free rein, with only certain correspondence being monitored and censored.

It may seem like this relative freedom to communicate with the outside world would lead to image management troubles for the company, given the stories we had to tell about our living conditions. But there was an army of PR people to handle that. One stroke of genius they'd had was to make our holo-pod account access contingent on our ongoing completion of our holo-pods' interactive education modules. This motivated many of us to advance quite quickly through those modules, and our high test scores provided a PR hook to distract from the reality of what the company was doing to us. They weren't "subjugating children"; they were "giving at-risk youths the chance to travel the stars and get an education along the way!"

Now, to be fair, our lives were a whole lot better than the prisoners on level one. There were fairly well-substantiated rumors that Norman Corp had created a synthetic amphetamine called PDQ that made cocaine seem like Pixy Stix, and they were using level-one lifers to test it as a productivity enhancer. Word was, it was working. Most of the level-one population slept less and worked faster. The downside? Even the ones who hadn't come in nuts were now completely out of their gourds, and the guards were barely able to keep them in check. Needless to say, while Orphs were never eager to go on field trips to any of the lower levels, we were all scared shitless of the first level in particular.

Darcy snarled awake and rolled to his feet, stomping irritably into his own jumpsuit and boots. He was short, round, and Polynesian, contrasting my own less committal tallish, skinny-ish, Caucasian-ish appearance.

"F.L.N.," I said.

"F.L.N.," he replied grumpily.

"F.L.N." was a standard Orph greeting and expletive. It stood for "Fuck Luthor Norman," the head honcho of Norman Corp.

"What do they have you on today?" I asked.

"Bitches put my ass on shit detail," he said.

It wasn't a figure of speech. Every week a group of Orphs had to walk the ship, making repairs to, and cleaning up after, the various ruptured waste disposal lines. Many of the lines needed to be replaced altogether, but the company hadn't seen fit to allocate the budget. The system was so primitive that there were no automated alerts to indicate where leaks were, so the work was not only repulsive but slow and laborious.

"Eck," I exclaimed sympathetically. "Doody duty, first day out? That sucks."

"But better me than you, right?" Darcy groused.

"Well, I mean, if I had to choose."

"Punk-ass bitch."

His parlance was mostly a put-on. Before his parents had been killed in a fire, he'd been raised in a strict Christian household, in a decimated but intact suburban community. I think emulating what he'd seen of urban culture in TV and movies made him feel tough—tough enough to handle Orph life.

We were the same age, and we'd been rooming together for about a year. We'd both had previous quartermates, most of whom had aged out, but Darcy's last quartermate had died of a cancer that was much less mysterious than Norman Corp wanted people to think. The illness hadn't taken anyone close to me, but I'd seen enough from a distance to know how hard it must have been on Darcy. When his roomie underwent an ultimately unsuccessful cancer treatment and lost his hair, Darcy had shaved his head in solidarity. He'd kept it shaved ever since.

A second, softer alarm rang out, and the door of our room slid open with a rickety mechanical clank, revealing the corridor outside with its unfinished metallic panels, grated flooring, and hit-or-miss LED lighting. We filed out of our quarters and into the river of passing Orphs.

Orphs ate in two groups, scheduled twenty minutes apart. Today we were in Group A, comprised of about thirty-five Orphs between the ages of nine and seventeen. The broken, old-before-their-time faces surrounding me as I trudged toward the mess hall always made me feel like I'd stepped into a zombie movie. Of course, there was good reason for us to look the way we did. Our repetitive hard labor, combined with the abuse doled out by our jailers, created an existence that was simultaneously monotonous and terrifying.

For many, the only joy came from our time with our holo-pods—which was limited by our ability to keep ourselves awake after a day of grinding drudgery. That said, some sought solace in sex, stolen during the moments between shifts, in whatever hidey holes were available. This was almost always consensual. Not that rape didn't happen. It did—to girls and guys. But it was rare for two reasons. One, the lack of time and privacy made sex hard enough to pull off even when both parties were ready to rumba. And two, the penalties for rape were severe, as were penalties for any sort of assault. Per the PDQ experiments, the company's primary concern was productivity, and the psychological effects of living in fear of your peers impacted productivity negatively. Anyway, as harsh as the penalties could be, most of us were in favor of them. We were naturally less rapey and murdery than people on the lower levels, but it was good to have some fail-safes in place to keep it that way.

Darcy and I entered the mess hall, and I nodded to a few other Orphs slumped groggily around the eight-by-forty table that ran the length of the room.

"F.L.N.," they muttered.

"F.L.N.," we answered.

The room had the same soulless yellow metal interior as our quarters and was equipped in the same ruthlessly utilitarian fashion. There was the table, a set of benches on either side of it, and a series of cubical nutrient dispensers lining the far wall. The tops of the dispensers had built-in shelf space where glasses, bowls, and spoons were laid out.

The spoons were the talk of the mess hall. They had been absent from the mess hall on Mars for some time. In the weeks prior to that, a lot of spoons had gone missing—a few at a time but adding up to hundreds. Most of us were pretty sure there was no widespread plot. The popular theory was that it was a single person's doing. No one knew what motive could be at work, but we didn't care. The Spoon Bandit, as we'd dubbed the person, had become a cult hero to Orphs—a ridiculous symbol of defiance. Consequently, Charon management had made it very clear that once they got their hands on this anarchist, there would be hell to pay. But when they'd come up empty, they'd just removed the spoons from the equation – until today.

I grabbed a bowl, keyed my ID code into the nutrient dispenser, and placed the bowl below its nozzle. Out flowed a measure of sludge, littered with small, chewy protein bricks. The sludge was a yellowish brown. Good news. We were at the beginning of the batch. Of course, the stuff was puke inducing at this stage but marginally less so than it would be when it went from yellowish brown to greenish brown.

I sat down across from Darcy, who held up his spoon.

"Think it's a trap?" he asked.

"What do you mean?" I answered.

"They don't give a shit if we got spoons. We been drinking from the bowls just fine. I think they're baiting the Spoon Bandit."

"Hm. Think he'll fall for it?"

"She."

"What?"

"She, not he. Heard it was Felicia Larkin."

Felicia was Cassie Greenbaum's quartermate, and Cassie and I were close. So I was concerned about Cassie getting caught in the middle of the fallout if Felicia was actually the Spoon Bandit. But the chances she was were slim, and it only took a few questions to discount the possibility altogether.

"Who said it was Felicia?" I asked.

"Norris," Darcy answered.

"Why does he think it's her?"

"Anderson told him."

"Why does Anderson think it's her?"

"Eh, probably lying. He tried to get with her one time, and she kicked him to the curb. I think he just wants to get the guards to throw her a beating."

"So why would you tell me you thought it was her?"

"Eh," he grunted.

Darcy was a one-man sewing circle. If it entered his ears, it would exit his mouth soon after, with very little intervention from his brain.

Anyway, the novelty of a spoon didn't make the sludge taste any better. I forced it down and rushed out of the mess hall.

I was scheduled to spend the next five hours in the fuel bay, replacing dead fuel cells. I arrived a minute or two late, so I expected to find one or more of the three Orphs with whom I was sharing the shift already there. But I was alone. The tracking chips in the anklets we wore ensured that the guards always knew where we were, and anyone who was more than five minutes late was paid a very unpleasant visit. So my shift mates were cruising for a bruising.

As I began work, removing the first of many spent fuel cells, Rick Boyle arrived. Now the situation made a little more sense. A lot of people called him Rick Van Winkle because he slept through breakfast nearly every morning, only to arrive at shift in the nick of time.

Boyle was kind of a curmudgeon, but he was also the quartermate of my friend Arthur. So we were friends-ish.

"F.L.N.," he said, as he grabbed the next fuel cell down and yanked it loose.

"F.L.N.," I replied. "You know who's supposed to be on shift with us?"

"Nope."

It was six minutes past. Time was definitely up. I was feeling a sense of dread for our missing shift mates when someone grabbed me by the shoulder. I turned to recognize Malcolm Pincher as he slammed me against the wall. My forehead bounced off, and I felt a ringing in my ears.

Malcolm was the sadistic bastard of a crew boss that ran our level, and he handed out beatings left and right. Not working fast enough? That was a beating. Not getting high enough quality ore? That was a beating. No reason at all? That was a beating.

He pinned me in place and leaned in close, his enormous gut compressing my rib cage.

"Hope ya enjoyed yer vacation, ya little shit," he growled with his Brooklyn-ese inflection. "'Cuz it's ova now."

The "vacation" to which he was referring was our time on Mars, where we'd been manually mining and refining Normanium all day, every day, with breaks to eat, sleep, or die. Now back on the Charon, we'd spend our time performing similarly backbreaking tasks, some of them related to keeping the aging shit heap flying and some of them related to preparing the mining shipment for market.

Malcolm leaned back away from me and stomped off, leaving two very disoriented new Orphs in his wake: a girl and a guy. Malcolm had been briefing them on the work detail, which explained and excused their lateness. Sometimes Norman Corp would send a batch of new Loaners with the supply ships that kept the Mars site stocked, to be inducted into our merry crew on the trip back to Earth. These two were obviously in that boat.

As Malcolm departed, I gave them a c'est-la-vie look, and Boyle and I went back to work. The two of them followed our lead, each removing an old fuel cell and placing it into the first of two carts we were pulling with us. I guessed they were both around fourteen years old. They introduced themselves in tentative English as Atsumi Tanaka and Soshi Ono. They both seemed even more bewildered than typical newbs, and that, combined with their Asian descent, suggested they were casualties of the recent expansion of the Orph program to Japan.

As we all collected fresh cells from the second cart, Atsumi looked off in the direction Malcolm had gone and asked, "Where did he go? Will he return?"

"They only come around now and then during shift to keep us on our toes," I said.

She continued with a strange combination of timidity and outrage. "How can they treat us this way? Like animals? We –"

"Nobody wants to hear it, kid," Boyle cut her off. She went mute. I felt for her. But Boyle was right. The sooner she got used to her situation, the better off she'd be.

Soshi asked, "How do they know we are here if they are not? How do they know we are working?"

I pointed to his anklet. "They know where every one of us is, all the time. And they know what we can get done on every detail. They come through to check after shift, and if we come up short of the minimum, bad stuff happens."

"Kuso," he swore, looking down at his anklet. "Can we cut it away?"

"Probably. If you don't mind setting off a section-wide alarm and getting hunted down by every guard on the ship," I answered.

"Kuso!" he repeated more emphatically.

The lack of supervision we received was painful because it highlighted the obedience that we'd all learned. Stepping out of line wasn't worth the consequences. I knew that better than anybody.

"Malcolm seemed to not like you," Atsumi said. "Did you anger him?"

Boyle gave a snorting chuckle.

"You could say that," I answered.

Malcolm was a brutal bastard to everybody, but I was his favorite punching bag. My first week on board, he'd gone after Cassie with his shock stick: a special issue Norman Corp sidearm that was half billy club, half stun gun. I'd never even met Cassie at that point, but I laid into Malcolm with everything I had. Because that's what Steve Rogers would do. And Bruce Wayne. And Matt Murdock. Unfortunately, I was not Steve Rogers. Or Bruce Wayne. Or Matt Murdock. I was a nine-year-old who weighed about as much as Malcolm's foot. That became especially evident when he pinned me down and began alternating between bludgeoning me with the shock stick and gouging me with its electrified prongs. That first week ended with me in the infirmary, bloodied and bruised all over, with a broken wrist and rib. But that was just the beginning. Because with one arguably ill-advised act of heroism, I'd made a rep for myself. People were talking about me. So Malcolm needed to make an example of me.

These days, I tried to stay off the radar, but every once in a while, Malcolm or one of his guys would cross a line I couldn't stomach, and I'd go at them. Of course it always ended the same, and my infirmary file was a thing of legend. Those bastards had broken just about every bone in my body, collapsed my lung twice, and given me more concussions than I could remember–which kind of goes with the territory when it comes to concussions, but you know what I mean.

CHAPTER  02

SO HOW WAS THE WRETCHED LIFE I WAS LIVING EVEN POSSIBLE? Where did the twenty-first century go wrong? Well, the history books never tell the whole story, and that's truer in this case than most, for various reasons. Let me lay it all out for you the way I remember it.

Between 2038 and 2044, things went to shit across the globe. Why? Because people are dumb. Really dumb.

As we entered the mid-2020s, artificial intelligence was becoming a reality. Phones were giving people dating advice. More and more cars were driving themselves. Presidential elections were being predicted by algorithms so accurate, voting became nothing more than a formality. It was a sea change, and people started joking that the robot apocalypse was upon us. However, a few activist groups made a case that the real threat was not that machines would do things we didn't want them to, but that they would do exactly what we did want them to, which was basically everything. Hello, worldwide unemployment crisis.

But this was cast as a fringe theory. Experts explained that we'd learned the same lesson again and again, since automated looms were introduced in the early nineteenth century: while new technology may drive some short-term job losses, a rapidly expanding supply chain would usher in greater prosperity for all. Still, the so-called fringe theorists insisted that this wasn't just another industrial revolution, arguing that this time the machines that were taking over the jobs in question would be equally capable of performing the new jobs they were creating.

But no one listened, and for a while they were glad they didn't. In the years that followed, the manufacturing and retail sectors were revolutionized by AI that brought about an unprecedented boom in productivity and efficiency. (Mind you, the physical embodiment of that AI didn't evolve much past the mechanical limbs found on assembly lines a decade before. Sure there were a few cyber-pets paddling around and some crazy rumors about mad scientists and synthetic humanoids, but not enough to let the robot apocalypse worries get in the way of progress.)

It was a new era. The cost of goods went down—way down. Shoppers received virtually anything their hearts desired within hours, if not minutes, via flying drones. Thousands of low-orbit mini-satellites were launched, and free worldwide internet access became a reality, along with early solar-powered holo-pods that were so cheap they were essentially disposable. Technology was making the world a wonderland.

It was amazing. Until it wasn't.

In 2038, fringe became fact, and we were fucked. There had been warning signs. Most conspicuously, seemingly overnight, everyone who had driven a vehicle for a living was out of a job – from bus drivers to Boeing pilots. But this was written off as the aforementioned "short-term job losses." Every other sign was explained away as well, until mass layoffs struck across every industry, and we finally woke up. Of course, it was way too late. At that point, the infrastructure was relying on AI systems, and the AI systems were being designed and maintained by – you guessed it – AI systems.

The widespread layoffs were followed promptly by a massive crash of the financial markets. Paradoxically, the bullet of financial ruin was dodged only by a few progressive private citizens who had signed a release to give an AI unit called a *broker bot* control over their finances. The bots went far beyond the basic robo-trading accounts of the 2020s. They were granted full authority over all client finances, from investment and retirement accounts to checking and savings accounts to home mortgages and car loans. So they were able to fully leverage every penny – and leverage it they did. They read all the trends and made all the right calls based on countless statistics and probability calculations, earning billions for their very tiny group of clients, who would eventually come to be known as the AI Broker Barons. The Barons watched from the safety of their secluded estates as the world was plunged into an economic crisis that made all previous crises look like minor hiccups. Banks failed, and businesses across the board went belly-up. With unemployment running at an outlandish rate, no one had the money to buy anything, even though everything was cheaper and better than ever.

There was a global ban on AI R&D because no one wanted to know how much worse the next wave of AI could make our lives. But there was less consensus about retiring existing AI to create jobs. Many argued it was beyond impractical. The infrastructure had been redesigned to accommodate machines. Re-redesigning it and providing the new training people would need would mean a catastrophic decrease in productivity and increase in costs, which the already-collapsing market simply would not bear.

And let's not forget climate change. Not that our feeble efforts to slow its progress had made much of an impact, but with all our other problems, those efforts dropped off entirely. The only energy resources fit to feed our needs were dooming us. Glaciers were disintegrating, and ice across the Arctic and Greenland was going bye-bye in a big way. El Niño was here to stay. The Amazon rain forest was singing its swan song. The next few generations would all be shafted to increasing degrees, and if something didn't change, the few after that would be our last. The people of Earth needed a miracle. Then along came Luthor Norman.

★

Luthor Norman was born to Gregory and Louise Norman in 2025. Before the economic collapse, Gregory had been a successful industrialist, and Louise had been a college professor. After the collapse they had become the world's new order of royalty: AI Broker Barons. They were set for life – especially considering neither of their lives would last very long. Louise died of cancer in 2039 and Gregory of a prescription drug mishap in 2042. At that time, their seventeen-year-old son, Luthor, took over the family business, focusing entirely on its fledgling energy interests, driven by a stunning ambition.

As the PR release had put it, "Mr. Norman has searched the world for a better energy source. But he won't stop there." Norman self-funded a dozen unmanned campaigns to Mars. The red planet had been pseudo-colonized earlier in the century, but when things went to hell on Earth, the settlement had been abandoned and the colonists had been shipped home. However, ultrasound scans had revealed rich deposits of minerals below the surface – some with unfamiliar densities. So Norman had landed equipment, built an automated operation center atop the tiny ghost town, and run tests across the planet.

It had cost a fortune, and there was almost no reason to think it would pay off. Wall Street was furious. But Main Street loved it. This kid was risking it all to save us all. Then, in 2045, Norman Corp made the discovery: a strange new ore that could be refined into a miraculous new energy source. It burned cleaner. It burned slower. And its output was off the charts.

The sole bump in the road was the fact that the ore, dubbed Normanium, gave off a strange electromagnetic radiation that fried any complex circuits to which it was exposed. The refinement process negated this effect, but Norman had baked hundreds of mining bots just getting the first few raw shipments back to Earth to carry out that process.

There was no shielding that solved the problem, and Norman continued to pump billions into R&D, presumably to address this issue. However, the energy revolution would not have to wait. The good news, as Norman's PR people could tell you with powerful conviction, was that the radiation had no effect on human beings. This didn't necessarily convince thousands of people to sign up for manned mining missions to Mars. But it did convince them to vote for Norman Corp's Labor Loaner program proposal.

The proposal was simple: Norman Corp would give the states loans to be repaid through prisoner mining labor. This would rehabilitate criminals by giving them a chance to serve the greater good and provide state governments an infusion of revenue, which would trickle down through the entire economy. Did it work? Not really. But a short time later, the PR people convinced the world it was working well enough to expand the program to include orphans who had become wards of the state throughout the US. There were, of course, lengthy and exacting regulations as to the fair treatment and boarding of said wards – and those regulations were enforced by the Department of Nobody Gives a Shit.

Norman Corp rapidly became the world's biggest energy company, and it was on its way to becoming its only energy company. You can bet Norman was back on Wall Street's Christmas card list.

Keep in mind, the good to come from the discovery of Normanium was largely incremental. Over the next several years, a barely discernible stream of jobs began appearing, spurred by growth at every level of the energy sector. Measures to manage climate change were put back in place, along with measures to cope with the fallout from the damage already done. But stepping back from Armageddon was one thing. Returning to a functional society was another.

Meanwhile, Norman Corp was subjecting tens of thousands of people to unthinkable living conditions and/or a painful death at the hands of – surprise, surprise – a nasty new form of cancer. And remember, many of the casualties were innocent kids. But the facts couldn't compete with Norman's PR juggernaut, fueled by the tagline "Norman Corp: saving the world, one shipment at a time." People ate it up, hailing Norman as a hero. I guess those who knew the details figured if you want to make an omelet, you gotta kill a few thousand kids.

Anyway, that, for the most part, is how I ended up getting semi-daily shock stick beatings from Malcolm fucking Pincher.

F. L. N.

CHAPTER 03

AFTER MY SHIFT ENDED, I HEADED BACK TO THE MESS FOR lunch. As I entered, I saw Cassie and made a beeline toward her as if I was being reeled in by some magnetic field. Aside from my parents, Cassie was the only other real Chowderhead I'd ever met. Over the years, a couple of guys had passed through the Charon who thought they were Chowderheads, but they were wannabes. They didn't know shit. Cassie was another story. She knew plenty. Some days, I was sure she knew more than me.

She looked up and waved as I approached. She had a mocha complexion, courtesy of her father's Nicaraguan roots. But her skin seemed pale in contrast to the raven mane that framed her face. By some standards, she might have been considered quite plain. But I couldn't keep my eyes off her, or my mind off the heavenly mystery concealed beneath the featureless lines of her Norman Corp jumpsuit. I was a seventeen-year-old heterosexual male whose sex life consisted of nothing more than fevered fantasies of burdensome-breasted comic book nymphs like Poison Ivy, Vixen, Witchblade, and Black Widow. So the notion of being with a real girl was like a gamma-radiated big bang in my brain. As I've said, there were kids sneaking off for desperate carnal relief between shifts, but I wasn't one of them. I knew Cassie wasn't either.

"F.L.N.," I said.

"F.L.N.," she responded.

I saw she'd already served herself some sludge.

"How bad is it?" I asked.

"Totally foomed," she answered.

"Crap."

She and I had recently established a Chowderhead-based DEFCON ranking for the sludge, with degrees of green ranging from the Green Goblin, to the Hulk, to the twenty-ton alien superdragon Fin Fang Foom, who was obviously the final word on green.

"Wish me luck," I said, grabbing a bowl. "I'm going in."

I headed over to the serving station. The sludge was as foomed as predicted, but there was nothing else on the menu. I served myself and returned to take a seat across from Cassie. As I did, she said, "You know, Stan Lee always intended for Hulk to be gray—like he was in the first issue before the printing problems made them switch to green. Plus, he's been gray since, like in issues #331–#346. I say we sub in Super-Skrull on the sludge scale."

I sighed. "We've been over this. Hulk is nonnegotiable."

"Right, right. I know," she said. "Except . . . how about replacing him with Martian Manhunter?"

"What?!" I couldn't believe what I was hearing. "So now we'll have a scale that mixes Marvel and DC? Are you totally billy[1] in the brain? I wouldn't be surprised if you suggested Savage Dragon next. I mean it. That would not surprise me."

"Whoa. Whoa! Back the truck up," she exclaimed. "What did you just say to me?"

I knew I'd gone too far. Savage Dragon is an Image title. Image had been formed by eight heavy-hitting artists as an independent publisher in 1992. Among its founders were Todd MacFarlane and Erik Larsen. During their time at Marvel, MacFarlane and Larsen had created, as Cassie put it, "the most amazing *Amazing Spider-Man* runs in history." But when they'd founded Image, they'd stated that doing future work for Marvel would represent a conflict of interest, which meant they would never again lead the charge on a Spider-Man title. For Cassie, it was a betrayal that could not be forgiven.

"Alright, alright. I take it back," I conceded. "Heat of the moment. I beg your forgiveness."

"Begrudgingly granted," she said. "But I guess I knew the Martian Manhunter thing wouldn't fly. Let's just do Gamora and call it a day."

I paused. She rolled her eyes and said, "You're going to say you'd like to 'do' Gamora real good, aren't you?"

"I wasn't going to say that," I scoffed. I was totally going to say that. I won't deny I had a thing for Gamora. She was probably my second or third favorite green-skinned woman fantasy. But let's not get into that.

"Gamora's a badass," I said, redirecting. "But she's a regular-size humanoid. She doesn't really up the ante enough from Green Goblin."

"Oy vey," Cassie groaned. This was one of many Yiddish expressions she favored, invoking the Jewish heritage that came through her mother's side. She treasured that heritage because it connected her to the early greats of the comic book art form, though that wasn't the only reason she'd taken her mother's maiden name at age eight.

"We could go all DC," she persisted. "Keep Martian Manhunter in the mix and throw in Beast Boy and Miss Martian."

I snorted derisively. "Martian Manhunter AND Miss Martian? That's crazier

1   *Chowderhead slang, meaning crazy. Origin: Street slang invented by Frank Miller in his Dark Knight saga.*

than a soup sandwich! Look, woman, you need to know I am all in on Hulk. This whole conversation is dots and lines."

She grimaced. *Dots and lines* was Chowderhead slang for a waste of time. In the early days of the Challenge, Chowderheads had noticed a couple of tiny dots in quadrants three and five of the Conundrum solution block, as well as a slightly thicker line on the right border of quadrant twenty-six. They weren't prominent features. They were barely perceptible. So most wrote them off as digital imperfections. But some people wasted years fruitlessly obsessing over their possible significance, inspiring the expression *dots and lines* to describe any pointless endeavor.

"What happened to your head?" Cassie asked, looking at my forehead with concern. Apparently, my "all in on Hulk" declaration was enough for her to abandon our sludge-scale battle, for now. I touched my forehead and noticed a welt had risen there.

"Oh, yeah. Goddamn Malcolm," I said.

The fact that Malcolm's contempt for me had started with my effort to protect Cassie wasn't something we really talked about. That had been a long time ago, and I'd accumulated a lot more bad blood with Malcolm since – bad blood that had nothing to do with her.

"When I get my hands on the U.A.T., that bullock's[2] gonna be one of the first ones I put out of my misery," I said. "With extreme prejudice."

She nodded, clearly a little uncomfortable. While I was a Pun, she was a Pro, through and through. We had very different plans for the U.A.T., and she was always taken aback when I went on about executing the scum of the Earth. So I usually refrained, but now that she'd drawn my attention to it, my head really hurt and I couldn't help but fantasize about some payback.

"Any progress?" she asked. Now she was changing the subject to the Conundrum. No segue was needed. The Conundrum was always lurking in the background for us – especially now that the deadline was less than a year out.

"Zilch," I answered. "You?"

"Zip."

"You'd say that either way, though."

"So would you."

"Obviously."

Give away an answer, give away the world. It was baked into our brains, making secrecy second nature. We were the hardest of hardcore Chowderheads, and we felt more compelled than ever to represent. After all, thanks to nearly

---

2   *Over the years, the definition of this term had been broadened to apply to uniformed officials of all stripes.*

two decades of attrition, there weren't many of us left.

"Well pace yourself," she said. "You'll have plenty of time to get the job done once you get off this crate."

She was being sarcastic. Due to the timing of our birthdays and the ship's docking schedule, we would both be released on the same date, later this year—a measly two months before Cateklysm's deadline. That, combined with a number of other factors, was almost enough to convince us that we'd never be able to win the prize. Almost.

The klaxon sounded, and we shoveled down the rest of our foomed-out sludge, trying to outrun our gag reflexes.

"You're in Group B with me for dinner, right?" I asked.

"No, A. It's Thursday."

"Crap."

She smiled coyly at my dismay at being deprived of her company, then we parted ways and headed to our next shifts in the work rotation.

Cassie and I didn't see each other for more than ten or twenty minutes every couple of days, but those meetings were one of the only things that kept me going. While I ached to know everything about her, I'd learned relatively little over the last nine or so years. That said, I knew enough to know that she'd had as shitty a childhood as I had.

She was only two years old when her mother died in a flash flood. That left her with just her father, and he was a psychotic parasite that abducted people, beat their financial information out of them, drained their accounts, and killed them. Yet, he never hurt Cassie. He told her everything he did, he did for her. The way he saw it, he treated her like a princess. In fact, that's what he called her: Princess. Talk about messing with a kid's mind.

Anyway, like me and so many Chowderheads, she'd found escape in the Scriptures and the lessons within. It was those lessons that ultimately drove her to turn her father in. She was just an eight-year-old kid, and the cops would have ignored her, but they were taking every lead seriously because the people her father had killed had enough money to matter. Crazy as he was, her betrayal sent him over the edge. If they hadn't pulled him off her in the police station, she would have been dead.

At the time of his sentencing, the US had abolished capital punishment—not because the country had evolved beyond the practice, but because there was money to be made through the Labor Loaner system. So Wilson Ramirez was still out there somewhere, serving a life sentence for the crimes he'd committed. And I knew he haunted Cassie's dreams.

The shittyness of my own childhood had a very different flavor. My parents were as far from Wilson as it got, which was why their loss was my lowest low. But even before I lost them, things were rough. In 2038, as the world was beset by a global depression, a C-5 military transport aircraft was remotely hijacked by hackers and crashed into the heart of downtown San Francisco. Among the casualties was our condo, into which my parents had sunk every cent they had and then some. Insurance companies were failing left and right, so we were left with almost nothing, barely hanging on, in temporary housing. Then, a year later, the other shoe dropped, and both my folks lost their jobs within weeks of one another. That's when we landed in the shanty town known as the Discards, which had sprung up amid the twisted rubble left by the terrorist attack.

Actually, technically speaking, we weren't in the Discards. We were underneath them, in the basement of what had been the Flood Building. It hadn't been discovered by anyone else because access involved a fairly lengthy stroll through a particularly fetid section of sewer. That meant we never had to go far to find a suitable place to relieve ourselves, but it also meant our lives were lived between periodic floods of sewer waste. For food, we relied on very occasional government handouts and fished the bay for bass or halibut but ended up catching and eating plenty of other shit packed with polychlorinated biphenyls, mercury, and other stuff you only eat if you're stupid or starving. It was rock bottom, but it wasn't a breaking point for my folks. The love they showed me and each other was like Adamantium, the virtually unbreakable metal with which Wolverine's bones are laced.

I think I associated the strength of my parents' bond with the fact that they were both card-carrying cuckoo-for-Cocoa-Puffs Chowderheads. So when I met Cassie, I naturally thought we were meant to be. Alas, progress had been slow, and that's being generous. Sure, she gave me signals—clear enough for a kid who'd never gotten signals to get. But I hadn't been able to work up the courage to tell her how I felt, much less make a move of any kind. And as if that wasn't bad enough, every time I got close and bailed out, she seemed somehow relieved. I didn't know why. But I did know I didn't like it.

CHAPTER  04

MY NEXT SHIFT WAS CRATING DETAIL. DURING THE REFINING process back on Mars, the Normanium ended up in thousands of forty-pound canisters that looked like scuba tanks. For the sake of the schedule, they were just dumped into massive steel bins and loaded onto the ship to be slotted neatly into twelve-pack crates during the voyage back to Earth. Sure, there were machines that could be purchased for crating, but why bother when you had a ship full of Labor Loaners and two months of flight time as the ship returned to Earth to make delivery?

Two of the Orphs on my shift were new kids – a couple of ten-year-old boys I didn't know. But I was less than thrilled to find the fourth member of our quartet was Ben Decker. He'd been transferred from another ship six months ago, and I doubted anyone on that ship missed him. His empirical good looks and exotic Texas drawl were wasted on him, as his relentless arrogance was off-putting to all but the few misguided girls he'd lured into brief trysts.

He saw me walk in and scoffed, "Well there he is. Clayton Clayborn."

I hated the Texas treatment he gave my name, warping the last syllable to sound like "barn."

"Seen any tenth-dimensional bullshitters lately?" he asked sarcastically.

I gave him the finger. The other two Orphs broke off to work on the other side of the room, as they sensed a brewing showdown. You see, on top of everything else, Decker was a Moorean. I'd never met one before, and I wished I'd been able to keep it that way. Mooreans were people who had believed in the Scriptures but lost faith in them (and Cateklysm) when they found what they considered contradictions no superior intelligence could overlook. They were called Mooreans because most of them were inspired by Alan Moore and his seminal 1986–87 series, *Watchmen.* While most heroes embody the maxim that with great power must also come great responsibility, many of Moore's raping, murdering main characters embody the counterpoint that absolute power corrupts absolutely.

Chowderheads interpreted *Watchmen* and high-octane following acts like Epic Comics' *Marshal Law* as lessons warning us that without vigilance, we can all be seduced by the power to do as we please. But Mooreans saw those titles as ideological missteps, promoting an immoral world view. They started a movement to smoke out every moral shortfall that could be found in the Scriptures – eagerly adding fuel to the fire that labeled Cateklysm a fraud.

Decker took an uninvited step closer to me and said, "For real, Clayborn. How can you just ignore the Wonder Woman codswallop? And Steamboat? Not to mention AC-58 and SPJO-61?"

Mooreans loved to pick on the early days of the Scriptures, when otherwise progressive artists were struggling to shrug off the ignorance and prejudice of their time – and Decker was calling me out in shorthand. You see, Wonder Woman was originally rendered powerless if her hands were bound by a man, and the first Captain Marvel's black sidekick, Steamboat, was drawn more like a monkey than a human being. AC-58 was *Action Comics* #58, the cover of which featured a hand smacking a bucktoothed, yellow-skinned man across the face while inviting readers to buy a war bond and "slap a Jap!" Finally, SPJO-61 was *Superman's Pal Jimmy Olsen* #61, where it may have been suggested that a woman doesn't mind a little domestic abuse, as long as the fella dishing it out is a "real he-man." On the surface, it's all pretty damning, but for me, the shit was so played out.

"I don't have to ignore any of that," I said. "I just look at the rest of the facts, moron," which was what Chowderheads called Mooreans.

"What facts?" he demanded.

"Uh, the fact that Wonder Woman's weakness was retconned, for one."

Retconning is short for retroactively writing something out of the continuity.

I continued, "And then there's Black Panther, Luke Cage, Katana, Renee Montoya, Northstar, Monica Rambeau, and Kamala Kahn, to name a few."

My list was a testament to the fact that as the years passed, the Scriptures had grown up, fully committing to their progressive potential by striving to bridge social divides with heroes of different genders, sexual orientations, and ethnicities. For instance, Monica Rambeau, a black woman, eventually became one of the many Captain Marvels.

"Whatever," Decker said. "Publishers can retcon all they want. It don't mean they didn't do what they did."

"You're a myopic tool, you know that?" I shot back.

"If I'm myopic, you're way past blind," he scoffed. "Worshippin' a bunch of people who wear their underwear on the outside. That really sound like a religion any higher power's gonna endorse? It's ALL dots and lines, my man."

I wanted to be the bigger person, so I decided to extend an olive branch. Just kidding. I said, "Eat shit, fuck face."

He shook his head. "It's sad, really. You're never gonna see it's just a bunch of bullshit–from Batman to Bee-Man."

My expression must have betrayed my thoughts as he spoke, and he read me condescendingly.

"You dunno who Bee-Man is?"

I snorted. "I know who Bee-Man is."

I had no idea who Bee-Man was. That was what I hated most about Decker. His Chowderhead kung fu was legit, even if he was using it for evil.

I'd had enough of him, and I walked off to work by myself in the far corner, which the others were avoiding. There were more alarms beeping there than anywhere else. Each canister was equipped with a warning beacon to indicate when the interior temperature moved above the optimal zone. The canisters were old and tired, and their built-in temperature regulators were always struggling, causing their alarms to start and stop constantly.

Once in a while a canister would emit a screeching flatline, which indicated it was in critical failure–on the way to a fairly nasty blast that could take off a hand or a foot. Luckily, a blown canister was highly unlikely to damage the bulkhead the crating bay shared with the ship's reactor. However, after the Normanium's energy was spent, it was obviously worthless. So if we didn't want to take a beating from Malcolm and his goons, we had to risk our limbs rushing failing canisters to the chamber's emergency refrigeration unit to bring down their core temperature and prevent combustion. Then the canisters would be marked with an *F*, taken out of service, and the contents transferred to a slightly more reliable canister for the rest of the journey.

There were obviously ways this jerry-rigged system could be improved, but it hadn't merited any thought or investment because flatlines were typically quite rare. That said, the logs showed three canisters had actually blown during the two-hour gap between the last and first shifts. The timing was lucky because the guards couldn't blame any of us for failing to stabilize the things. But the trend was very unsettling, and the beeping was especially nerve-racking today. Of course, even on a good day, crating was the most dangerous work detail on the ship by far. Which is why my good friend Malcolm had me in here far more than most. For instance, I was scheduled here for my second shift today and my first shift tomorrow. I think it would have been every shift, every day, were it not for other Orphs pissing Malcolm off and earning their turn.

After crating, it was dinner with Group B. No Cassie, but her quartermate Felicia was there. I grabbed some semi-foomed sludge and slumped down in the seat next to her. She looked angry.

"F.L.N.," I said.

"F.L.N.," she fumed.

"What's wrong?"

"That turd Anderson is telling people I'm the Spoon Bandit!"

"Oh. Yeah. I was gonna give you a heads up about that."

"You heard it too?! Shit! He's just mad 'cause I wouldn't give him a handy."

"I wouldn't worry," I consoled her. "In the last week, I've heard rumors that the Spoon Bandit is Lathem, Johnson, Riggs, and now you."

"Yeah, well, the guards don't need to narrow it to one suspect. Sooner or later they'll round the bunch of us up, and we'll all get shock-sticked up the ass. But that's still better than giving Anderson a handy."

"Neither one sounds fantastic," I offered.

"You know what? I don't even blame Anderson. I mean I do blame him—he's an asshole. But it's not all his fault. You know whose fault it is?"

"Luthor Norman," I said without hesitation.

"Luthor Norman!" she spat. "This whole goddamn hell we live in is on him. The guy is a monster. Why can't the world see that?"

"They're not here, watching it happen," I said charitably.

"Well they don't even have to know what's happening here! They know he's playing Captain Kirk with sixty-five billion dollar ships that don't even work while people starve!"

She was talking about Project Javelin. Some years prior, Norman had commissioned a couple of scientists named Valorie Cunningham and Bart Wilhelm Keyes to build three small prototype spacecrafts. Cunningham and Keyes had risen to fame in early 2037, when they found a quantum reaction through which a natural warp field could theoretically be created and manipulated, sparking excited talk about the possibility of F.T.L. (faster than light) travel. Unfortunately, the reaction required an energy source with an insane mass-to-output ratio. There was a surge of optimism with the discovery of Normanium, and it did allow Cunningham and Keyes to prove their drive worked, but only to the tune of transporting a few molecules. After that, the prevailing opinion was summarized by a preeminent physicist who said, "The Cunningham-Keyes drive may as well be wired to run on leprechaun farts." Still, Norman had commissioned the largely impotent ships, using them for nothing but his personal travel to and from Mars. The eccentricity of it made his epic collection of classic sports cars and his aircraft carrier, the Samuel Sawyer, seem positively commonplace. He'd taken a good deal of flak for it all, but not enough to offset the rep his PR snakes had built.

"You know at first Anderson asked me to go all the way?" Felicia said.

"Really?" I answered.

"Yeah. So I told him the convenient truth: I'm not into dudes."

"Right."

"Then he started nagging me about the handy."

"Well just because you're gay doesn't mean your hand is," I quipped.

"Exactly. Anyway, I kept turning him down, even when he got desperate and said I could wear my work gloves."

"Ow. Those things are like sandpaper."

"Right? I save the guy's junk from the chafing of a lifetime – and now he's gonna get me electrocuted. I hope Luthor-goddamn-ass-face Norman is happy."

She stood, dumped her half-eaten sludge into the waste disposal and gave me a wave.

"F.L.N.," she sighed.

"F.L.N.," I replied, as I watched her walk out. She seemed to hate Norman as much as I did, which was really saying something. As an Orph and a Chowderhead, I had extra beef with the guy. You see, Norman himself had been a Chowderhead in his youth, and there were a couple of reasons the community had come to deeply despise him. First, the dude had two supervillain names, as in Lex Luthor and Norman Osborn. Those aren't single-story arc baddies. They're the guys that give Superman and Spider-Man full-time jobs. Norman might as well have been named Caligula bin Laden. Second, as if his name wasn't bad enough, he'd acted like a real hemorrhoid in the Chowderhead community, starting at the tender age of eleven.

It had begun with him attempting to supplement his Scripture research by offering a reward to anyone who would share their Conundrum findings with him. Predictably, the community instantly lost all respect for him, which badly bruised his young ego. Of course, he might not have minded as much if his efforts had produced results, but most of the people who actually knew anything weren't talking about what they knew, and Norman's money wasn't going to change that. They were just like me. To them, Chowderheading was as legitimate a faith as any other, and no payoff could compare to the holy reward of the U.A.T. This obstinance, combined with the contempt he faced, enraged Norman, who was like a tyrannical boy monarch who couldn't fathom the notion of the townsfolk denying him his heart's desire. When the bribes didn't work, there were several reports of blackmail and even rumors of abductions and torture. Few really believed it all, but the unconfirmed transgressions supercharged the impact of the confirmed transgressions, driving Chowderhead secrecy and paranoia to a new magnitude. In other words, an urban legend about some little psychopath sending out henchmen with car batteries attached to nipple clamps didn't exactly encourage people to brag about the answers locked away in their noggins.

For a time, people hoped Cateklysm would pop in to deal with Norman's perversion of the Challenge, but when he didn't, everyone agreed he'd done all he was going to do for us. If our better natures didn't prevail, we weren't worth saving.

Norman continued to crop up in Chowderhead circles for years. But then, overnight, he suddenly disappeared from the community. Some wondered if he'd solved the Conundrum and found no further use for his fellow Chowderheads. But the question seemed moot because around that same time, his father passed away and everything changed for him.

Norman's relationship with his father had been a stormy one, based in part on his father's belief that Norman had "a truly brilliant mind that was being wasted on a childish obsession with cartoons." There were news stories about his father threatening to disown him on this account, though Norman denied them.

In any case, after his father's passing, purportedly out of guilt, Norman refocused all his energies on the company that bore his name. He would often speak fondly of his Chowderhead childhood, but his once all-consuming obsession with the Scriptures seemed to be reduced to a quirky eccentricity manifested in the form of vintage Marvel or DC T-shirts and baseball caps. He was gone from the Chowderhead nation, and Chowderheads were happy to see him go. For all the good press he'd eventually garner, they would always think of him as a maniacal little shit.

CHAPTER  05

WHEN I GOT BACK TO MY QUARTERS, DARCY WAS WATCHING A movie on his holo-pod.

"Wanna watch?" he asked.

"Nah," I answered. "Research."

He shook his head.

"Man, don't you wanna break from that shiznat?"

"The future is worth it. All the pain. All the tears. The future is worth the fight."

He rolled his eyes and awaited my inevitable follow-up attribution. I did not disappoint.

"Martian Manhunter, DC's *One Million* series, 1998."

"Fuckin' dork," he replied, turning his attention back to the movie.

My zeal was a front, of course. At the moment, I was disgusted by the thought of the Conundrum. My eighteen-month dry spell had left me half wishing Cateklysm had stuck to his own damn dimension.

Regardless, I sat cross-legged on my bed and set my holo-pod in front of me. Unlike the crude shoebox-size plastic number that had been released back in '37, the modern model was a four-by-four-inch hexagonal carbon fiber pyramid with a flat top, housing a plexiglass lens.

I'd never been without a holo-pod. My parents could easily have hocked the janky unit we'd had back in the Discards, but they were obsessed with me getting a decent education, and it was the only means to make that happen. Plus, it was our only window to the Scriptures. Alas, it had eventually been taken from me, along with the rest of that life, but unlike everything else I'd lost, I'd been given a replacement.

I powered it on and entered my Green Lantern-inspired password: "no evil shall escape my sight." My default feeds materialized and hovered in front of me. They were pulled slowly but surely from secure servers back on Earth via a daisy chain of satellites stretching all the way to Mars. This meant significant delays in user experience, but you got used to it. For feeds containing 2D content, interaction was limited to scaling, zooming, etc. But for feeds containing 3D content, the interaction was very immersive–I could manipulate the scale and position of the projections as if they were physical objects.

The first feed was simply a 2D browser window displaying the Conundrum.

The second feed held a 3D model of a hardcover notebook: my parents' Conundrum research diary. I'd been making annotations and adding pages to it ever since I'd inherited it and everything else in their web-based account. The third feed was another 2D browser window, displaying the Morlock Underground, or M.U. to those in the know. It was the only remaining Chowderhead community site. Giving in to procrastination, I grabbed that feed and scaled it up.

The site's functionality had been woefully behind the times when it had been built nearly two decades prior. But it was the first community site for Chowderheads, and it attracted a robust enough following to outlast competitors that appeared later. The most commonly used area was the Hall of Justice, which showed who was currently logged on and allowed members to launch private conversations with one another. There was also a mass message channel, through which people could message all active users. I had my holo-pod calibrated to monitor that stream and provide alerts based on thousands of Scripture-based key words in the ridiculously unlikely event of somebody giving away a Conundrum answer. To date, the alerts had produced nothing but false alarms—flagging messages like "U 2 down to play some MSH?," which was an invitation to play the classic Marvel Super Heroes pen and paper RPG rather than a stunning reveal of 2 Down.

There was no video chat. Conversations could be conducted only via text or audio. Though for me, the latter was not an option. As primitive as the site was, my experience of it was even more so. Orph holo-pods had an audio/video transmission inhibitor. There was a camera to process the user's movements and facilitate interaction with content, which was thankfully enough to access the Conundrum site. But there was no way to share AV info, for the same reason there were no security cameras on the Charon. Thanks to Norman's PR snakes, most people back home were able to discount the stories they'd heard about Orph life as exaggerations, but Norman Corp had no desire to contend with more impactful, harder-to-whitewash AV feeds gone viral.

I checked the Hall list to see if Zodd MacFarlane was logged on. This was Cassie's handle. It was a mash-up of Todd MacFarlane and the Kryptonian überjerk, General Zod—a literal attempt to villainize MacFarlane for his unforgivable abandonment of the Amazing Spider-Man.

She used the site mainly to keep an eye on the mass message channel, though I always tried to get her to chat. Sadly, at the moment, she wasn't online. But CAPTAIN BRITA1N and DANE WH1TMAN were. They were an old gay couple in England whose handles were tributes to British Marvel superheroes. (Unlike CAPTAIN BRITA1N, DANE WH1TMAN used the civilian alter ego of his chosen hero, the Black Knight, to avoid confusion with the three lesser Marvel characters who had used the Black Knight moniker–some of whom were, as he put it, "right proper cunts.")

I was about to ping them with a conversation request when they sent me one. I accepted, and a message appeared.

CAPTAIN BRITA1N: Thwppit!

My handle was Thwppit Good, a play on the trademark sound made by Spidey's web spinners and an old song my parents used to sing when they were being weird.

ME: Hey C. B. What you guys up to?

CAPTAIN BRITA1N: Usual.

ME: Any progress?

CAPTAIN BRITA1N: Loads! We've finished the Conundrum and the rest of the Challenge. We're DD-50³.

DANE WH1TMAN: We're unimaginably advanced technology-ing all over the bloody place. Try not to be a jealous bitch about it.

I was pretty sure they were kidding, as usual. Dane in particular was fond of telling people he was "minutes away from solving the Conundrum," but I knew they were more hobbyists than serious Chowderheads.

CAPTAIN BRITA1N: You alright?

ME: Never better.

"You alright?" was code for "have you been to the infirmary recently?" A while after we'd met, I'd had a bad week and shared some of the details with C. B. Unlike most, he'd believed my version of things implicitly, and he'd been enraged by the glimpse into Orph living conditions. But the fact was, he and Dane were just scraping by, and there was nothing they could do about the sins of the world's most powerful corporation. So I regretted saddling him with the worry and guilt of it all, and whenever he asked if I was alright I gave him the same answer: "Never better." I wasn't technically lying–because while I believed things could get better, they'd never been that way on the Charon. Life had always been a shit burger with no side of fries, and would be until I aged out.

We all received a notification that 1MP3R10US R3X had logged on. I sighed, and was sure everyone else online had just done the same. "Imperious Rex" is the battle cry of the Atlantean Prince Namor the Sub-Mariner, and it had been co-opted by plenty of users, forcing 1MP3R10US to settle for a super jenky spelling. He was a colossal jackass, and virtually everyone denied

---

3 *Chowderhead slang, meaning triumphant. Origin: A reference to Daredevil #50 (2003), in which Daredevil finally beats the tar out of Wilson Fisk, aka the Kingpin.*

his conversation requests, so he hassled everyone via the mass message channel. He belted out his usual salutation:

1MP3R10US: Greetings surface dwelling filth!

No one responded, but that never stopped him.

1MP3R10US: Listen up homos . . .

This wasn't aimed at C. B. and Dane in particular. He called everyone homos. (Many of the Scriptures' lessons had been lost on him.)

1MP3R10US: Which one of you homos wants to trade me the answer to 8 Down?

No response. He undoubtedly had nothing of value to trade. If he weren't such a repugnant tool, I would have felt sorry for him. I hadn't thought there was a Chowderhead alive who hadn't solved 8 Down, Fed with *magic milk, foiled with magic sword.* Per Marvel's retelling of the Norse myth, Ymir, the evil king of the Frost Giants, was nourished by a magic cow before tangling with Odin, who imprisoned him in a volcano with a strike of his magic blade (*Journey into Mystery* #97, 1963). It was amateur hour stuff—arguably easier than the answers that went public early on. Anybody who'd read just the first few issues of Thor knew it.

1MP3R10US: What's a matter, none of you homos has the answer to 8 Down?

Surprisingly, his childish challenge did not compel any of us to type, "Shows what you know, homo! It's Ymir! Ymir is the answer!" Instead, everyone just waited for him to go away.

1MP3R10US: Whatever. You guys suck whale dicks!

This was a pretty standard appearance for 1MP3R10US, and many simply blocked his user tag. But a lot of us left him unblocked because his dumbassery made us feel like Scripture geniuses. Unfortunately, at the moment, he only reminded me of my very ungenuisy progress lately. I realized it was late and I was fading fast, so I typed "Listen guys, I gotta go—Scriptures are calling." C. B. typed back, "Stay safe my boy!"

Even though my heart wasn't in it right now, I had to make an effort to move my research forward. I grabbed my Conundrum diary and flipped through it. It was 357 pages long now. Sadly, most of the notes in it had turned out to be dead ends, and I recalled the fits of cursing those dead ends had triggered from my parents. I remember waking up one night to hear my father shouting, "Professor X is an asshole! An asshole!"

You see, in *X-Men* #42, he'd discovered that the venerable X-Men founder

Charles Xavier was killed in a battle with Grotesk. He thought he'd solved 4 Down, *#2 gave Professor X #1 smackdown*. By my dad's reckoning, being killed had to rank as Professor X's #1 smackdown, and Grotesk's birth name was Gor-tok II, as in #2. But nothing fit the puzzle. He'd tried Grotesk, Gortok, GortokII, Gortok2, and every other relevant permutation. But none of it had worked. Why? Because as my dad discovered no less than twenty-three issues later, Professor X wasn't really dead. He was faking. He'd gone into hiding to prepare for an alien invasion, and he'd had the Changeling impersonating him. But he didn't bother to tell his students. In general, Professor X is a good guy, but in this case, I think my dad had him pegged right.

I'd spent a lot of time thinking about my parents' cold leads lately and reminiscing about the two of them furiously discussing the possibility that Cateklysm might actually be the demented fifth-dimensional prankster and Superman adversary, Mister Mxyzptlk. Such memories were more a comfort to me now than ever. For one thing, my parents' struggles with the Conundrum mirrored my own, and that made me feel closer to them. For another thing, knowing they'd gotten past many of their stumbling blocks gave me hope. For instance, about a year after my dad's meltdown over *X-Men* #42, he found the answer that fit 4 Down in *Plastic Man* #1 (1966). In that issue, Eel O'Brian – son of the Golden Age Plastic Man, ergo "Jr.," ergo "#2" – delivered a smack down to an obscure DC villain, inexplicably named Professor X.

My father had been apoplectic about the fact that the answer had nothing to do with Professor Xavier or the X-Men. But he shouldn't have been surprised. Aside from a few straightforward answers like the magic milk-chugging Ymir, Conundrum solutions always had an unexpected twist. Take 2 Down, *City where Howard Stark's son was born*. Initially you'd think the answer is Long Island, where Tony Stark was born. But that doesn't fit the puzzle. And only after cycling through the entirety of Marvel's Earth-616 continuity and a good deal of the 1610 continuity would you find the answer that did fit, when you met Tony's grandfather, Howard Stark Sr., in *Ultimate Armor Wars* #4 (2010). Bad news for Tony because the old fella sics two giant robots on him. But good news for you because the revelation that Tony's grandpa is named Howard Stark means the son of Howard Stark is Howard Stark (Jr.), who was born in Richford, New York – a perfect fit for the puzzle.

I thought about this and the many other solutions my parents had cracked and felt a tug of guilt about the fact that I still hadn't finished what they'd started. I'd tried to populate the secret message grid with my incomplete solution set on various occasions to guess the message. But so far, it looked like gibberish. I convinced myself that filling in the remaining blanks would clarify it. The only other possibility was that some of my answers were somehow wrong, and that was simply too painful to consider.

So here I was, working my way through the last of the issues in Volume 2 of *The Mighty Thor*, desperately trying to sort out 2 Across, *The most worthy weapon*. Any Chowderhead worth their salt would immediately think of Thor's hammer, Mjolnir. Thanks to Odin's magic, Mjolnir can only be wielded by one who is worthy. But Mjolnir didn't fit the puzzle. Nor did any of the nicknames by which it is known. Of course that made sense. The clue referred to a weapon that was worthy, not a weapon that judged worth. Still, I would have bet my life that Mjolnir would ultimately figure into the solution. I just couldn't see how. Sadly, the final issues of the second volume weren't helping. Eventually, just as it had for the last dozen nights, demoralization crept in and raped my resolve, and I passed out.

CHAPTER  06

I AWOKE TO THE MORNING KLAXON BLARING. I'D HAD LESS than three hours of shut-eye, and I felt like it. I dragged myself out of bed and sleepwalked my way to the mess hall. But I perked up when I found Cassie there. It was Friday, and on Friday I had breakfast with Group A, and she usually had breakfast with Group B.

"What are you doing here?" I asked.

"Guards switched my group," she answered. "Now I have to get up twenty minutes earlier and suffer through yet another meal with you. Talk about adding insult to injury." She smiled.

"You poor girl," I sympathized.

I was playing it cool, but I was ecstatic. My Fridays had just gotten about fifty thousand times better. We both grabbed bowls and hit the nutrient dispenser. The sludge was almost all brown. So far, today was turning out to be too good to be true. The trend continued as Cassie accidentally spilled a glass of water down the front of her shirt.

"Oy gevalt!" she exclaimed.

Our jumpsuits were made of pretty sturdy stuff, but the fabric still clung ever so slightly to her chest. She caught me staring, and I fumbled to hand her a towel. As has been established, it didn't take much to supercharge my sex-starved psyche. Poison Ivy, Vixen, and the rest of them were promptly booted from my brain bed and replaced by Cassie. It wasn't the first time. While I was somewhat old-fashioned-minded about the reality of sex, neither that nor my profound feelings for Cassie as a human being made her immune to the objectification of my depraved and ravenous teenage imagination. She patted herself down with the towel in a way that was not at all suggestive to any normal human. But there was a hint in her manner that let on she knew I was not a normal human. She seated herself.

"What've they got you on for first shift?" she asked, unintentionally bringing me off my high.

"Back to crating," I sighed.

"Wow. Weren't you in there second shift yesterday?"

"Yup. Malcolm won't be happy until I'm dead. Or at least horribly maimed."

"Don't worry, if you get anything important blown off, Fate Force will fix it."

"Sure," I scoffed at her oft-repeated mantra – the tagline from Fate Force. *Fate Force* was one of her favorite series, featuring Atticus Slade and his crew – members of an elite order of Fate Force agents, charged with monitoring the timeline and intervening where needed. Published by the very obscure Kaput Comics, it had earned some surprising recognition when it was referenced in Cateklysm's broadcast by way of his allusion to Pentagramite, the superfuel that powers the Fate Force fleet. But despite the nod from Cateklysm, I still had mixed feelings about the title.

"You know, I'd like to shove that tagline where the sun don't shine," I said.

"Here we go," she sighed, bracing herself for my grievances.

"Seriously, if your job's to fix history, maybe swing by the Titanic during boarding and give folks a heads up? Or pop into the theater in 1865 and tell Lincoln to duck?"

"That's not the way it works," she told me for the millionth time.

"Yeah, yeah."

According to the comics, when the Fate Force needs to "force fate" down a new path, they can't simply jump back in time and tell the world, "Hey, we're from the future, and something bad's about to happen," because humanity would start relying on the warnings and spiral into a pattern of recklessness that even the Fate Force couldn't stay ahead of. So they mostly alter the course of history indirectly through "scenarios." These are elaborate capers, in which they influence events by masquerading as politicians, business tycoons, or mutant veterinarians. Only those few civilians needed to execute the scenarios are put in the loop – sworn to secrecy on pain of death.

All that said, unfortunately for Lincoln, the folks on the Titanic, and many others, there wasn't always a scenario that got the job done.

"It just pisses me off that their history still has most of the shitty stuff ours does," I said.

"You know as well as I do that there are things they can't change," she rebutted.

It was the convenient plot device the series frequently fell back on: intractable clots of events that occurred no matter what.

"Lazy plotting, plain and simple," I said.

"You're a schmuck," she replied. Then she smiled and added, "But Fate Force will fix it."

And there it was again – the feeling that this girl was the one. I thought I should probably do something about that. But all I did was stare at her in smitten silence until the klaxon sounded a moment later.

★

As I entered the crating bay, I saw Steve Schakter and Frank Stibble. Schakter was kind of a dirtbag, and while we hadn't ever had a serious confrontation, we weren't friendly. Stibble was nice enough, but never had much to contribute to a conversation. The last member of our party was Arthur.

Arthur was a quiet, rail-thin Black kid. He seemed normal enough at first blush, but he had a stiff alien way about him and a fairly prominent stutter. He was an odd duck, and aside from me, Cassie, and his quartermate, he didn't have a lot of friends. Nor did he have a lot of memories of his life before roughly a year prior, when he was found wandering the streets in front of an Orphan Care Station in Seattle, Washington. He'd had nothing on him but an asthma inhaler with the name *Arthur* scrawled on it. The folks at the station had to assume that was his name, as his fingerprints and other physical identifiers didn't get hits in any system. This and his disorientation made him a perfect victim for the state.

While he looked to be fifteen or sixteen, Norman Corp still hadn't gotten around to testing his biological age. (The company was notoriously slow about this, as their upside was minimal.) He was one of only a few Loaners assigned permanently to the ship, remaining onboard to perform comparatively easy maintenance labor during each visit to Mars's surface. Such assignments necessitated a special circumstance, and Arthur's was his asthma. The electrostatic precipitators we used at our work sites managed the toxic Martian dust fairly well, but trace amounts of the stuff still got into everything and stuck there. It wasn't great for anyone, but it had been deadly to more than one asthmatic.

Some people envied Arthur's ship-only status, but I wasn't one of them. Sure, our time on the surface might have been miserable, but at least it was a change of scenery. For Arthur, there was no relief from the rusty prison that ferried us back and forth from the red planet. Not to mention, with no ID and no record of him in any system, he'd have to go through a lengthy appeals process to affect his release from the program, even if and when biological testing clocked him at age eighteen.

"Hey, Arthur, how's it going?" I asked him, as I helped him roll a gargantuan bin of canisters over to the stacks of empty crates we were to fill.

"I'm edgy as h-h-heck," he answered.

"Heck" was about as racy as his language got—a quirk that had earned him ridicule over and above the guff he got for his stutter.

"I heard a bunch of canisters have blown," he continued. "The alarms are d-d-driving me crazy."

"Tell me about it," I said. "I'm on my second shift in here in twelve hours."

"Geez, M-m-malcolm really hates you, doesn't he?"

"Yes, he does."

The first half of our shift passed uneventfully. The second half, not so much. The trouble started with Schakter, foregoing the use of the designated toilet twenty feet up the hall and urinating liberally a few paces from where we were working.

"What the hell, Schakter?" I yelled.

"F.L.N., man," he replied, as if his actions were a rebellious affront to the company's namesake.

"Luthor Norman doesn't have to smell your piss for the next few hours," I growled. "We do."

"Well then F you guys, I guess."

Like most imbeciles, when confronted with his own lack of foresight, he fell back on belligerence.

"Let it g-g-go, Clayton," Arthur said.

"Yeah, let it g-g-g-g-g-go, Clayton," Schakter taunted, as he zipped up his pants.

"You are such an asshole," I said, starting toward him. But Arthur put a hand on my shoulder, slowing my roll.

"Grow a sense of humor," Schakter said. Because our inability to get his subtle brand of comedy was the problem here. He walked back over to Stibble, who'd continued working throughout the whole incident and now seemed terrified that he may somehow be drawn into the exchange.

"Ignore him," Arthur said.

I knew he was right. Schakter wasn't the type to back down, and if the guards got word we were fighting, we'd both get shock-sticked. It wouldn't matter who started it. Still, I was struggling to walk away—until I heard one of the canisters somewhere in the vicinity speed up and flatline. We all looked at each other, alarmed. Arthur and I started digging through our bin. Schakter and Stibble ran over and joined us, the enmity between Schakter and me easily forgotten for the moment.

"Does anyone see it?" I asked.

"No!" each of them replied in turn.

"Shit."

Then we heard a second canister flatline, and a third, and a fourth. After that, I lost count. And then I saw it: a faint smudge of ink on one of the flatlining canisters, and I knew what had happened. But there wasn't time to dwell on it.

As more flatlines sounded, Schakter and Stibble backed away from the bin, clearly freaked.

"Screw this!" Schakter cried, then turned and ran out of the chamber. Stibble was right behind him.

"Where the hell are you going?" I bellowed after them.

"The same place we should be g-g-going," Arthur shouted. "We have to get out of here!"

"What? We can't. We have to do something."

"Do something?" he exclaimed, yanking his asthma inhaler from his pocket and taking a hit from it. "Like what?"

"Like stabilize the faulty canisters!"

"How the h-h-heck are we gonna do that? Blow on them?!"

He had a point. The refrigeration module only held six canisters at a time. There was no precedent for this many failing. Still, there was more at stake than the Normanium. The reactor bulkhead was thick, but there was no way to say whether it could withstand a dozen or more canisters going up at once, or the even greater chain reaction that might follow. The entire level could be at risk. Maybe the entire ship. It was drastic measure time.

"The air lock," I said.

Arthur thought for a moment and got my meaning.

"Good . . . that's g-g-good!" he said.

With so many canisters flatlining now, it was easy to find some of them, and he started loading them onto a handcart. But I knew we'd never find them all before they blew. I shoved the whole bin toward the air lock.

"What are you doing?!" Arthur yelled.

"There's no time. Open the air lock."

He hesitated. Now that we might have a chance to save the good Normanium, he knew there'd be a price to pay if we didn't.

"The guards will kill us," he said. "Like s-s-seriously kill us!"

"And if that bulkhead goes, the whole level could go!" I countered.

He gave that a second's thought, then sighed in resignation and hit the release for the interior door of the air lock. It slid open with a hiss, and I rolled the bin in. We heard the alarm tones reach a frenzied pitch just as he closed the interior door and opened the exterior door. The bin was sucked out into space a second before it detonated in a flurry of explosions, like a pile of fireworks.

We saw it and we felt it, but obviously there was nothing to hear through the void of space. We did hear something, though: a faint chorus of flatlining canisters. We looked at each other in disbelief, then over at another bin, some distance behind us.

I shook my head and groaned, "Son of a bitch!"

In the Scriptures, there would have been a massive starburst with the word KABOOM! The whole bin went up in a big ball of blue fire, followed by the one next to it, and the one next to that. The concussive force threw us across the chamber and on to the ground. As we landed, I felt a shower of debris rain down on us.

We lay there for a moment, attempting to regain our senses as level-wide alarms began blaring. I rolled onto my side and saw Arthur sitting up groggily. Apparently, we were alive.

Arthur reached out and picked up a strange red crystal from beside him, and I noticed that there were a few more of them in the debris lying on and around us. Some were the size of peas, others were the size of golf balls. Their roughly symmetrical star shape and bright red sheen made them stand out against the more prevalent irregular, chalky-white Normanium rocks. But there was something else that made them stand out to me.

"What in the w-w-world is this stuff?" Arthur asked.

I paused, struggling with the impossibility of what I was seeing, then answered, "It . . . it looks like Pentagramite. Like a lot like it."

"Penta w-w-what?"

"Pentagramite—it's like a superfuel, from Fate Force comics."

"Oh. Weird," he said.

"You don't understand," I responded. "Cateklysm mentioned it in his broadcast. And now it's . . . here? How is this possible?"

Suddenly, I was rethinking my dismissive attitude when it came to Fate Force comics. I was sure the mystery would grab anyone—even a non-Chowderhead like Arthur. But he just shrugged like he couldn't care less, and in my harried state of mind, I thought maybe I was making too much of it. He clambered to his feet and dusted himself off. I tried to do the same, but suddenly, I felt an intense bout of dizziness setting in. I'd hit my head when I'd fallen, and I suspected I'd earned myself yet another concussion. Everything started spinning, and I fell back to the ground as a fever came over me, like my veins had been filled with warm water. I had no idea what was happening, and I was starting to panic.

Then, it passed. As quickly as it had begun, it was over. Well, mostly. I still had a mild swollen sensation throughout my body. But comparatively, I felt fine.

"Sheesh," Arthur said, concern on his face. "You okay?"

"Um . . . yeah," I said. "Guess I hit my head harder than I thought."

Then suddenly, my episode dropped way down our list of concerns, as we heard a creaking noise. Looking up, we discovered the blast had done more damage than we thought. A hairline fracture had formed in the bulkhead—the only thing between us and the reactor—and it was buckling. Arthur looked down at me, terror in his eyes. We were sixty feet from the chamber exit. No way we'd make it out. There was no time to think, so I didn't. I leaped to my feet and slapped the air lock control pad, closing the exterior door and opening the interior door. Then, as a massive explosion unfurled toward us, I shoved Arthur into the air lock, where he was shielded from the direct impact of a torrent of flames and rubble that immediately engulfed me.

Pretty heroic, right? I mean I would have preferred for us both to make it into the air lock. But you win some, you lose some.

ISSUE 2 OF 4
ESCAPE FROM THE CHARON!

CHAPTER  07

ALL I REMEMBER AFTER THE EXPLOSION WAS A NIGHTMARE, in which I relived the worst day of my life. That day had started as the best day of my life. It was the day I'd solved 9 Down.

For more than a year, my parents had been stuck, without finding a single Conundrum answer. But they weren't alone. There were plenty of Chowderheads slowly being driven mad by the Conundrum. Mind you, it was almost certain that every answer had been found by someone somewhere, but very, very few people had compared notes. (Give away an answer, give away the world.) Moreover, with the pesky distraction of civilization imploding, the Chowderhead head count had dropped over the years. So the shortage of collaborative potential was shorter than ever. As such, the fact that we were three people working together should have given us a pretty substantial advantage. In theory, we were in a rare position to really divide and conquer the material. But my parents didn't quite trust me because I was unproven.

So for a long time, they had me focused exclusively on stuff outside the massive and intricately interconnected universes of the Big Two publishers (Marvel and DC), where collaboration mattered most. My world was the Conundrum's kiddie pool—less source material to reconcile and less overlap to miss. But I committed. I devoured every issue of *Shadowman, Painkiller Jane,* and X. I knew who knew what evil lurked in the hearts of men. I became the pinhead who preached cyborg Donatello wasn't Turtle-verse canon. I smelled fresh-roasted peanuts every time somebody said "Hellboy."

Eventually, my parents started bringing me fully into the fold. But even then, I would frequently find them reviewing issues for which I had been given responsibility. They were concerned that I might miss something. I understood it. But I hated it. I felt I had something to prove. And prove it I did, with issue #147 of *The Thunderbolts* (2010).

On the face of it, there was no reason to think the Thunderbolts would figure into the Conundrum. Featuring a ragtag team of pseudo-reformed villains, it was a second-string title by comparison to most of those that had come into play thus far. It had received a good deal of critical acclaim in its day, but it was no Avengers or X-Men. (That's probably why my parents had relegated it to my purview.) Regardless, I'd scoured each issue with a vengeance.

I saw a glimmer of my breakthrough as early as issue #145. Luke Cage, the Thunderbolt's leader/babysitter, had led the team to Oklahoma, where they were supposed to clean up a troll problem. Trolls in Oklahoma, you ask? Yup. During the culmination of Marvel's 2010 Siege storyline, some pretty bad shit went down in Thor town. Asgard, which at the time was hovering over Broxton, Oklahoma, was blown to crap by the Sentry on orders from Norman Osborn. (See? Told you Osborn was a heavy-duty douchebag.) This resulted in the Broxton area catching a hail of heavenly debris. Apparently, among said debris was a pack of savage Magzi Trolls. And among that pack of Magzi Trolls was a young girl of particular interest. Her father was a Magzi and her mother was an Asgardian, captured by her father's tribe back in the day. So the kid looked like a member of the Asgardian court, but she'd been brought up by a bunch of bloodthirsty beasts.

Anyway, she and a handful of her tribe were apprehended by Asgard's finest, and upon discovering what she was, they'd tried to tame her and assimilate her into polite Asgardian society. No dice. So it was back to the godly stockades for her until the sky fell and she touched down on the troll smorgasbord that is Earth. She and some pals were having a pretty good time until Luke and the gang found her chowing down on a hapless hunting party. Then, whammo! Tranq dart right in the ear, courtesy of Crossbones, and a stay on the Raft: a supermax lockup for super bad guys.

That's when things got interesting. You see, like every Chowderhead, I'd internalized every clue in the Conundrum, and as the pieces came together it was like Peter Parker's Spider-Sense going off. I felt a pounding in my head like a migraine when I learned the name given to the girl during her failed Asgardian assimilation, in honor of her mother: Gunna Sijurvald. And when a prisoner uprising on the Raft put Songbird in harm's way, and this little Asgardian troll girl tore through the bars of her cell to lend a hand, I nearly lost my mind—letting fly with a howl that scored somewhere above Black Canary but obviously below Black Bolt because it didn't destroy the Earth. My parents rushed over and shoved away the holo-pod, convinced I was having a seizure of some kind. I just stared at them with a dazed look on my face. Then I said, *"She'll protect birds, but she's GONNA eat people!"* It was the clue for 9 Down in the Conundrum.

After kicking off her superheroing career with her rescue of Songbird, Gunna would join the Thunderbolts and later the Young Avengers, using the alias "Troll." Five letters, fourth letter L, matching the L in Lor, the widely known answer to 10 Across. Cha-ching!

My parents were over the moon. Not only had I solved 9 Down, but my answer intersected and hinted at the elusive answers to both 8 Across and 9 Across. To celebrate, we headed to Golden Gate Park. My parents had told me that when they were younger, it had been a carefully manicured and maintained patch of paradise. That was hard for me to imagine. To me, it had always been wild and untamed, littered with dead trees and overgrown with weeds. Still, it was an extraordinary escape. It was the one place that made it easy to forget what was happening everywhere else in the world.

We must have spent three hours hiking around the park that day. Then we made the trek back downtown, stopping to gather water from the Hayes Creek (which had run beneath Seventh Street until it was surfaced by the devastation of the terrorist attack). Finally, we stopped by the government aid office to play the odds on rations. We scored big: enough bread for a decent meal. But that was where our luck ended. Because presumably, that's where he spotted us.

Most days we were careful to keep an eye out for folks following us back to our basement hideout for fear of landing ourselves new roommates, or worse. But today, we'd been distracted.

I'll never forget his face. It was somehow utterly empty and full of hatred at the same time. My parents both looked up in shock as he entered the basement, moving with ruthless purpose. He raised a handgun. My mother instinctively stepped in front of me, and my father instinctively stepped in front of her. Then, three shots rang out, echoing through the subterranean chamber, and sounding like ten. Both my parents slumped over and fell to their sides. I was still clinging to them sobbing when the bastard grabbed me and dragged me out of our home. I didn't understand why he'd done what he'd done, or why he'd spared me. Not until later.

You see, this was after the Labor Loaner program had been expanded to include orphans. So the more orphans the state inherited, the more Norman Corp cash it could claim. As a result, the state began incentivizing the public to escort any orphans encountered to an Orphan Care Station.

What did this have to do with the murder of my parents? The state didn't realize that their program, as messed up as it was, was breeding an even more heinous enterprise. Lowlifes known as Orphan Hunters were making a living by combing the streets for orphans, and some of those lowlifes were lazy psychopaths that decided it was easier to make orphans than find them.

My parents' murderer walked into an Orphan Care Station with me and walked out with a reward, as my hysterical accusations were met with incredulity and ambivalence. I don't know how many times he'd done this, but it was enough times to cultivate the seemingly sympathetic demeanor he used to paint me as a tragically confused kid—an act the greed-fueled Labor Loaner processing machine would never question as long as he never visited the same Orphan Care Station twice.

I vowed to find him one day. I promised myself that I would hunt him down and take from him what he'd taken from my parents. And if I could get my hands on the U.A.T., I'd make sure everyone like him got what was coming to them too.

✷

"He killed them! He killed them both!" I heard myself babbling as I awoke in the infirmary. Cassie was there, holding my hand. Relief covered her face, as if she hadn't registered my babbling, but only that I had awoken. She looked terrible, in a good way. Like she'd-been-worried-sick-about-me terrible. Like I-think-that's-when-I-fell-in-love-with-her-for-real terrible. She let go of my hand and took a moment to compose herself.

I realized Arthur and I had risked our butts for nothing. If I was alive, it meant the emergency systems had contained and controlled the fallout in the crating bay.

"How long have I been out?" I asked. It felt like a day at least.

"Two weeks," she answered.

"What?!" I gasped. "Are you telling me I've been . . . in a coma?"

She kissed me, hard. I didn't expect it, but kissing her back came easy.

"I'm sorry," she said, pulling away suddenly. "I shouldn't have done that."

"Um, apology accepted?" I said.

"It's just . . . I was so afraid I'd lost you. And I . . . I couldn't handle losing you."

I was still adjusting to the shock of waking from a two-week slumber, but I forced myself to shift gears. It seemed like she might be opening a door I'd been desperate to walk through for months—maybe years.

"Cassie, I feel the same way," I said.

"I know," she answered. "But there can't be any more kissing. Or . . . touching stuff. There definitely can't be any of that."

"Right. Definitely no touching stuff," I agreed. "But, um . . . why not?"

"Because it would make us feel . . . closer. And then we'd be tempted to team up on the Conundrum and the rest of the Challenge."

We couldn't have that. Give away an answer, give away the world. Except . . .

"Well my parents—" I started.

She looked away. "That's different."

"Not for me," I blurted. It hit me as it came out, like a haymaker from the Thing. I didn't know if the coma had made me delirious, but I let it ride.

"Cassie, I'd give you my Conundrum diary right now."

She went quiet. I could tell this was what she'd wanted to hear but didn't want me to say. Then, almost as if to herself, she said, "You're a Pun."

"What?" I said. "What does that have to do with anything?"

"Don't you get it?" she cried. "I have to win the U.A.T. So I can make up for everything my father did – so I can make a world without all the hate and violence that's in him. I can't risk losing focus or helping you because I'm . . . afraid of what you'd do if you won."

"You think I'm like your father?"

"No! No – but you're too close to the line. You're so angry, and you think violence will solve all the world's problems."

"Only when the problems are assholes who have it coming!"

She sighed. I'd proved her point. We'd argued the pros and cons of Pros and Puns many times over the years, so I knew there was no turning her. But I'd had no idea how much the discrepancy in our outlooks meant to her.

"So that's it?" I said. "We can't be together because you're a Pro and I'm a Pun?"

"Maybe when the Challenge is over –" she began.

"Unless I win it," I cut in. I didn't think her line of reasoning left room for me to win and us to be together. Of course, the chances against either of us winning were massive, but neither of us really accepted that.

"Clayton, I –" she started, but then the door opened and in walked Jerry. Jerry was half of a married couple that provided medical services on the Charon. He oversaw the infirmary on this level and the one below. His husband oversaw the two below that. He stopped short when he saw that I was awake.

"Well, welcome back!" he exclaimed.

"I should go," Cassie said, stepping toward the door.

"Wait," I pleaded. "Cassie, come on."

"I have to get to my shift," she responded, and stepped out of the room.

"Did I . . . interrupt something?" Jerry asked, approaching my bed.

I shrugged, not sure what to say about what had just happened.

"Well, buck up. You ought to be dead," he said.

"Good pep talk," I answered.

"I mean the bulkhead behind where you were standing was warped and melted. No one knows how you survived. As close to a miracle as I've ever seen."

"I don't feel all that miraculous."

In addition to the whirlwind of confusing emotions kicked off by my conversation with Cassie, I was finally starting to feel the ache from the partially healed cuts and bruises that covered my body.

"So, I've been out for two weeks?" I asked.

"Your friend was exaggerating wildly," Jerry answered. "It's only been thirteen days."

He smiled at me. Jerry was a good guy. He was in his late fifties and carried himself with a humble certainty. He'd seen me through a lot of scary times, but he'd never gotten too close. There were no paternal talks after my myriad beatings, no hugs upon my recoveries and departures. I assumed he'd learned that guys like me eventually ran out of luck, and an emotional investment was a bad investment. Still, you could see it took effort to keep his distance. He was a good guy.

He rifled through some files and pulled mine out. Then he came over, shined a light in each of my eyes, and asked, "How do you feel?"

"Beat up," I answered.

"But aside from the abrasions, nothing out of the ordinary?" he said as he disconnected me from my IV. I suddenly remembered the strange episode I'd had before the bulkhead went.

"How messed up was my head when they brought me in?"

"Cerebral edema, which explained the coma, but it's retreated predictably. Why do you ask?"

"I actually hit my head before the main explosion. I was really dizzy and felt kind of . . . bloated? It's hard to describe."

"Are you still feeling it?"

"Nah."

I wasn't sure if the feeling had really gone, or if I'd just gotten used to it. But I preferred to think it was the former.

"Well, you've taken a lot of radiation," Jerry said. "But virtually every test I've run has come back normal."

"What do you mean 'virtually'?"

"There was one that was inconclusive. Cellular structures were blurry. I'm sure it was a mis-scan. This equipment is awfully old. Anyway, now that you're off the IV, what you need is food. I'm going to grab you something from the mess. Back in twenty."

He walked out. I tried to distract myself from thinking about Cassie by gazing around the infirmary. It had been my second home for the last eight years, thanks to Malcolm and company. Carts of monitoring computers were parked here and there. Like Jerry had said, they were very old – so old that some of them actually had keyboards. Three of the walls were lined with beds, and the fourth was lined with drawers and cabinets, where medical supplies and implements were stored. The most advanced tech in the room was probably the biometric security measures controlling access to those storage areas, designed to prevent patients from taking home a souvenir scalpel. Those measures were far more necessary for the three lower levels. Many of the long-term guests down there would happily swipe anything they could to try their luck at perforating a guard. They had nothing to lose. However, for everyone on our level, there was a light at the end of the tunnel: age eighteen. It wasn't like winning the lottery, but we'd be given $4,700, two months of free lodging, and most importantly, our freedom. I thought about the fact that I was nearly there. Life beyond the Charon was about to begin.

Of course, as I thought about the future, my thoughts went right back to Cassie. I'd always pictured us together after the Charon, and now I finally knew with absolute certainty that she had feelings for me. But it didn't matter. The Challenge would be a wedge between us until it was over—and maybe after.

Looking back, her take on the situation was spot-on. My romantic invitation to join forces stemmed from a profound feat of denial. I'd realized that I was really and truly in love with her, but that didn't change how much I hated my parents' killer and all the miserable bottom-feeders like him. I know now that I was hiding from what I really wanted, which was for her to love me back enough to give up her own dreams and help me win the U.A.T., to use as I saw fit. It wasn't right, but the heart wants what the heart wants. And my heart was kind of an asshole.

When the infirmary door opened again, I expected it to be Jerry. It wasn't. It was Malcolm. I felt a sudden flush of anger as I remembered the smear of ink on the flatlining Normanium canister, before the explosions. It had clearly been an *F* that had been sloppily wiped off. I'd reasoned it wasn't the only one that had earned an F and been returned to circulation. Not by a long shot. There was no other explanation for so many canisters going critical. Idiotically, I hadn't checked the logs from the downtime before our shift. But I was pretty sure of what I would have found if I had: enough blown canisters to destabilize a lot more. There was only one suspect. Malcolm's bonus was based on the size of the haul, and obviously, not only had he put all reserve canisters into service, but he'd apparently pressured some poor Orph to redeploy God knows how many bad canisters. It hadn't occurred to him that the odds of a blown canister setting off others rose exponentially with every faulty one.

"You greedy piece of shit!" I spat, as I got to my feet and took a step toward him. It was stupid. I'd been hooked up to various electrostimulation equipment during my lengthy nap, but I was still very shaky and in no shape to mix it up with him. His hand went to his shock stick, but it just hovered there.

"Well I'm sure I dunno whatcha talkin' about, Clayborn."

There was something off about his tone. And I didn't understand why he hadn't gone at me with the shock stick. It wasn't like him to miss a chance to light me up. Then I realized he was playing it conservative—putting on a show for the person who stepped into the room behind him. At first I couldn't place the guy's face because it was so out of place. But that only lasted a second. He extended a hand in greeting.

"Mr. Clayborn. Nice to meet you. I'm Luthor Norman."

CHAPTER 08

I STARED AT NORMAN'S HAND, NOTICING A TATTOO ON HIS wrist that read "Excelsior!" which was Stan Lee's go-to closing in Marvel's Bullpen Bulletins. It's Latin for "ever upward," which I suppose suited a guy like Norman.

I didn't take his hand, and eventually he shrugged and retracted it. My eyes drifted up to his sandy blond hair and comically handsome face, then back down to his vintage Marvel T-shirt, which depicted Captain America leading Thor, Iron Man, and assorted other Marvel titans into battle. It was a screen-printed reproduction of the cover of *Avengers* #100, "the mightiest 100th issue of all."

He noticed me noticing it and said, "Pretty cool, huh? It's from 1972."

"I know," I mumbled.

"Right. Right—I hear you're a bit of a Chowderhead," he said like the condescending prick he was. "And something of a superhero in fact. Surviving that blast, after pushing your friend to safety? A double blessing that our amazing discovery came without casualties."

"Discovery?" I said. With the coma and all, I'd nearly forgotten about the Pentagramite-like crystals we'd found after the initial blast. But they came back to me now in a flash.

"Yes," he answered. "I wanted to ask if you could give me any details as to exactly what happened in the crating bay. Was it hot? Was it cold? How many canisters blew before the bulkhead went? Did they all go at once, or was it sequential? Anything you can tell me could be helpful."

I didn't know exactly what he wanted or why. All I knew was I didn't want to help him get it. I said, "Yeah. I think there was some kind of explosion."

He stared at me, trying to gauge whether I was being obstinate. I didn't want to leave him in suspense, so I added, "Then it started raining. Penguins. Pretty sure it was raining penguins. Or sandwiches. Definitely penguins or sandwiches. Maybe both. Is that helpful?"

In retrospect, I think I'd been emboldened by my near-death experience, allowing my disdain for Norman to hemorrhage. His congenial smile faded a bit and Malcolm drew his shock stick, taking a step toward me. But Norman put a hand on his shoulder, and he reluctantly retreated. Then Norman leaned in closer to me and said, "F.L.N., right?"

My face must have given away my surprise.

"Look, kid, I get it. You guys have it rough. And you think that's on me. But I don't make all the decisions. The company is run by dozens of managers working independently. I'm actually very focused on a pretty narrow area of the business. I don't weigh in on every little item."

Every little item, I thought. Yeah, he couldn't be expected to keep up to date on trivial matters like the fact that his business was run on the backs of tragically orphaned and routinely abused children.

He continued, "But the key to everything is in reach. And I can tell you this, Clayton: you help me here, and your hard times are over."

My common sense was taking a back seat to my emotions, and I blurted out, "And if I don't help you?"

"Hmph," he chuckled. "You people. You're all the same."

You people? Who did this cracker think he was? Did he mean Labor Loaners? Orphs? The poor?

His tempered demeanor was starting to waver as he continued, "You'll tell me what I want to know, and you'll tell me right now."

He stared me down, waiting for me to pony up whatever I knew. I thought about telling him to shove it up his ass, but he seemed like he was already on the verge of snapping, so that would be crazy.

"Shove it up your ass," I said. Oops.

He lunged at me and suddenly, the sheep's clothing fell away and I saw what was underneath. He smashed a fist into the side of my head, and I went down hard.

"You still think you can keep your secrets?" he snarled as he straddled me and hit me again and again. "When all that I've worked for is just . . . weeks . . . away!" He punctuated each of his final words with a punch.

"Eight or nine bins went up in a row!" I yelled. "Starting with the one closest to us!"

He stepped back, staring down at me. I made a show of balling up on the floor, covering my face and whimpering. He'd hurt me, but my reaction was mostly theater. I'd had worse beatings. I'd just finally come to my senses and realized that I needed to give the bastard the feeling that he'd won in every way. I needed to get the hell off his radar.

"There were dozens of faulty canisters!" I continued. "I don't remember whether it was hot or cold, but we saw some weird red rocks after the first explosion."

I didn't say why I thought the faulty canisters were in use because that didn't seem like it would help me at the moment. I also couldn't bring myself to share my observation that the rocks looked like Pentagramite. But he seemed convinced I'd spilled all I had to spill, and while I wasn't dumb enough to think he was going to arrange any special treatment for me, I hoped I'd avoided earning an extended stay on one of the lower levels. I was encouraged, as he seemed to lose interest in me. His eyes just fell away as he absorbed the information. Then he turned and walked out. Malcolm leered at me before following him.

I got up and looked in the mirror. Some swelling had already come up under my left eye. However, something else was bothering me much more than that. I felt like I'd seen everything Norman was during my brief run-in with the man, and it was plain ugly. I suppose I'd always thought maybe, just maybe, we'd all gotten him wrong. But we hadn't, and the question that I'd idly asked over the years took on more weight, the mystery of it deepening. Why would a person who cared so little about human beings dedicate his life to helping humanity? I felt like the answer was in the things he'd said. There was something there, looming below the surface. But my attention was turned to the door of the infirmary again, as it slid open and Arthur walked in with Darcy. It was good to see them—really good. I hadn't realized how much I needed a friendly face after the visit from Norman.

"Whazzup, Sleeping Beauty!" Darcy said, taking a seat at the foot of my bed. "Ran into Jerry on the way into the mess. Sounds like you gonna be back to hard labor hella quick. Congrats!" He gave me a wry grin.

Arthur peered at my face and asked, "What h-h-happened to your eye?"

"Luthor Norman," I answered.

"Why would the richest man in the world beat your ass?" Darcy asked.

I ignored the question and moved on to one of my own. "What the hell is he doing here anyway?"

"Was on his way to Mars but rerouted here a few days ago," Darcy answered. "Somethin' 'bout his F.L.N. drive."

"F.T.L. drive," Arthur corrected him.

"Whatever," Darcy said.

"What are you guys talking about?" I asked.

"Talkin' 'bout Richie Rich parking his fancy rides and his posse a' mad scientists on board, thanks to you," Darcy answered.

"What?"

"The explosion was the breakthrough of the m-m-millennia," Arthur explained. "It did something to some of the Normanium."

That put to rest any lingering doubts I'd had about the Pentagramite-like crystals being the reason for my interrogation.

"They're s-s-seeing exponential increases in output—it's a leap that dwarfs Enrico Fermi's experiments in 1934," he continued. "They're calling it Normanium Prime. Norman thinks it can power the Cunningham-Keyes d-d-drive, and preliminary diagnostics are all clear. But for a full test they need m-m-more, and they haven't been able to reproduce the conditions that yielded the existing supply."

"Why you talkin' all sciencey?" Darcy asked. "And how you know what's goin' on with Norman's nerd squad?"

Arthur looked a little uncomfortable and shrugged.

"I h-h-hear stuff. Nobody on this g-g-gosh darn ship can keep their mouth shut. You're exhibit A."

Darcy frowned but let it go, even though Arthur had ignored half his question, neglecting to explain why he was talking like a science book. I let it go too. I was more preoccupied with the bizarre revelation that Normanium Prime not only looked like Pentagramite, but apparently packed the same punch, putting Norman on the verge of breaking the F.T.L. barrier. I didn't know why, but Norman's words came back to me: "when all that I've worked for is just weeks away." The phrasing was bugging me, but I couldn't put my finger on why.

Arthur spoke up, pulling me out of my head.

"D-d-did Norman ask you a bunch of questions about the accident?"

"Yeah," I answered.

"Me too."

"Whad'you tell him?"

"I said it g-g-got really cold just before the explosion."

"I didn't notice that."

"That's . . . because it didn't happen."

He grinned modestly at his devious fabrication.

"Aww yeah!" Darcy said, as he raised a palm to Arthur. Arthur just stared at it.

"Up high, man," Darcy instructed him. Arthur flashed an embarrassed look and raised his hand. Darcy slapped him five, then sighed and shook his head at the clumsiness of the exchange.

High-fiving proficiency aside, I thought Arthur's response to Norman's interrogation was probably the smarter way to go, even if it lacked the fuck-you flare of a freak penguin-sandwich storm.

"Wait a minute," I said, reflecting on my earlier conversation with Cassie. "Why didn't Cassie mention anything about all this?"

"She couldn't care less," Darcy said. "Only thing that girl's given a shit about for weeks is holdin' hands with your nappin' ass. Skipped most of her meals."

Despite everything else, that thought felt like a warm blanket wrapping around me. The door opened and Jerry returned, setting a tray of lightly foomed sludge down in front of me. I couldn't believe it, but I was actually looking forward to eating it. Amazing what a week or two of intravenous meals will do to your culinary standards.

Jerry noticed Arthur and asked, "Ah, finally ready for me to take a look?"

"Oh, no. Just visiting Clayton," Arthur answered awkwardly.

"Take a look at what?" I asked, tucking into the sludge hungrily.

"It's nothing," Arthur deflected. "I'm fine. I have to g-g-go."

Without another word, he turned and walked out of the infirmary.

"What the hell was that about?" I asked.

"Your buddy took some shrapnel to the leg in the explosion," Jerry said. "I didn't get a close look at it because he walked out of here as soon as he came to. For all I know, the shrapnel's still in there."

"He's been acting whack ever since you guys got blown up," Darcy added. It was concerning, but I couldn't imagine the injury could be too serious. Arthur seemed fine.

Darcy stood up and said, "Anyway, next shift jumpin' off in three." He started for the door, then turned back and said, "Oh, almost forgot." He reached into his pocket and pulled out my holo-pod. He handed it to me and said, "Thought you might wanna nerd out while you're lying around in the lap of luxury." Then he waved and walked out.

I looked at Jerry and asked, "Speaking of lying around in the lap of luxury, how much longer is my stay scheduled for?"

"You're out tomorrow morning. I know you just woke up, but like I said, tests are clear. I have no authority to keep you off the roster."

He encoded and handed me an after-hours authorization pass that would let me out of the infirmary and into my quarters in the morning to prepare for my shift.

"I gotta head downstairs," he said.

I nodded and answered, "It's been fun."

He paused before making his exit.

"You're a good kid. I'd like to see less of you."

I slept through the afternoon. Then as evening rolled around, I tried to dig back into my research, but I couldn't concentrate. I was distracted by thoughts of Norman and his obsession with what seemed to be Pentagramite. Then, when I managed to put that out of my mind, what had happened with Cassie crept in and I found myself just staring at the door, wishing she'd walk through it. She didn't. But as second shift ended, Arthur did. And he brought along maybe the only news weird enough to get my full attention.

He sat down in the chair next to my bed, settling in as if he planned to skip dinner. At first, he just stared at the floor silently. I didn't know what to say, so I didn't say anything. After a while, he began.

"I never thanked you for s-s-saving my life."

"Well you don't have t–"

"You risked everything for m-m-me. And you should know the truth."

He looked up at me, tears welling in his eyes.

"Arthur, what's going on, man?"

"My d-d-dad risked everything for me too."

"Your dad? I thought you didn't remember–"

"It all came back."

"What? When?"

"When I s-s-saw this."

He put his foot up on my bed and pulled back his pant leg. As he did, I saw a nasty gash, with some twisted metal poking out.

"Jesus, dude. You've got to get that out of there."

"I can't."

"Why?"

"Because it's m-m-me."

"What?"

I looked closer and realized the metal wasn't impaled in his leg. It was his leg–under the skin, or whatever synthetic substance was serving as skin.

"You've got a prosthetic leg?"

"No."

"I don't understand."

"Neither d-d-did I, at first."

He looked down at his leg.

"But after this happened, I started to remember. S-s-some kind of emergency override in my programming, I g-g-guess."

I froze, convinced I must have misheard him. But as I stared down at his metal leg bone, I knew I hadn't. I leaned back away from him, in reflexive revulsion. He remained where he was, sitting very still. In an instant, the crazy rumors I'd heard about robots that could pass for human stopped being crazy and started being terrifying. I'd been conditioned like everyone else in my generation to believe that AI was to blame for all humanity's woes, and AI was clearly at the core of the thing sitting in front of me–the thing I had thought was my friend. As the deception of it struck me, my fear turned to anger.

"So you're ... you're a fucking robot?!"

"I think technically, I'm an android."

"Oh, well, that really softens the blow."

"Look, I—"

"How could you not know this?! It didn't strike you as odd that you pissed motor oil?"

"I d-d-don't! I was designed to pee and poop and eat and sleep, same as you!"

"Not same as me!"

I reached over and grabbed the massive folder containing my medical records and held it up.

"Pretty sure they would have noticed if my bones and organs had *made in Taiwan* stamped on them."

"I'm not m-m-made in Taiwan, you jerk. I—" He stopped short, and his eyes took on a faraway look for a moment.

"G-g-goldarnit!" he barked.

"What?" I said.

"I just ran a system check. Three of m-m-my components were made in Taiwan."

I stared at him blankly. Then...I laughed. I couldn't help it. It was all so insane. I kept on laughing, and after a moment, he cracked a smile. Then a dam broke, and he started half laughing and half sobbing. I could tell he'd been holding it off for a long time, and it went on for a while. Then he sniffled and looked at me.

"Clayton, please—I'm as s-s-scared of this as you are."

I looked back at him. *Him?* Was he still a *him?* Should I be thinking of him as an *it?* I didn't know how to digest it all, or how to see him now. At first my Chowderheadedness had kicked in for the worse. My mind had filled with images of Ultron, Amazo, Brainiac, Nimrod, Master Mold, Death's Head—the list of villainous murder bots served up by the Scriptures went on and on. But now, as I stared at my friend, his eyes still streaming with tears, the heroic counterpoints came to me. The Vision. Deathlok. Robotman. The Red Tornado. Not to mention Adam Aaronson, aka Machine Teen, who basically shared Arthur's exact backstory. I was picturing Adam's struggle to accept the truth about his robot origins as Arthur began pouring out his heart, or power source, or what have you.

"My d-d-dad was Dr. Sebastian Williams. He was doing illegal AI R&D, and after his son, Arthur, was killed d-d-during a riot, he made me in Arthur's image. So I've got most of Arthur's traits. Like the s-s-stupid s-s-stutter and even simulated asthma. I've got my own memories, but other than that, I'm a g-g-gosh darn knockoff."

I guessed the original Arthur hadn't been big on swearing. And I wondered if it had occurred to Arthur 2.0 that his simulated asthma was a blessing in disguise, as it had kept him away from Mars where he would have been messed up by the raw Normanium while we were refining it.

"Anyway, I'd only been around three m-m-months when they caught up to my dad," he continued. "Somebody must have s-s-seen something he was working on and reported him. Cops were in the building, and he wanted me to run–to g-g-get as far away as possible. But I couldn't just leave him. We argued, and h-h-he threatened to rewrite my memories–wipe himself out of them. I think he tried, but he must have run out of time. He m-m-must have had no choice but to drag me down the hall and leave me there, half rewritten–which I g-g-guess looks and feels like amnesia. Cops must have just ignored me–figured I was a junkie s-s-sleeping it off."

I could tell he was afraid that I'd never see him the same way–that I'd never trust him again. But as the initial shock wore off, I realized the way I felt about him was unchanged. I supposed I'd been unwittingly preparing for something like this my whole life. My obsession with a world of the fantastic, it seemed, made me uniquely open-minded about my friend turning out to be an android. It certainly didn't hurt that he was one of the more decent human beings I knew, even if he wasn't a human being.

"So do you know what happened to him?" I asked. My tone suggested I'd moved past the android elephant in the room, and this seemed to put him at ease.

"Not really. I've been digging around the web, but the records are a m-m-mess. He was arrested that day, taken for trial, but . . . I haven't been able to find anything after that yet."

I nodded sympathetically. But I'm ashamed to say my mind was beginning to wander, as I was overtaken by the bizarre sensation of surprise at my own rapid acceptance of the situation. And then the Chowderhead in me took over completely.

"So . . . can you do any cool roboty stuff?" I probed.

He rolled his eyes, and I thought he was going to tell me to go screw myself. Then one of the machines next to my bed beeped, and I looked over. On the monitor there was a message that read: "Does this count as cool roboty stuff?"

I looked back at Arthur, wide-eyed.

"I can interface with a lot of the ship's systems," he said.

My pulse quickened and I demanded, "What else?"

"Well, I'm s-s-smarter than I realized. A lot of stuff I've learned was cued to be overwritten in an idle d-d-directory–anything associated with memories of my d-d-dad and what I really am. But it's all back now."

That explained the science book-ese he'd spoken earlier.

"Also, I have near perfect recall, and m-m-my sensors pick up a ton. I can tell you the temperature in here is 61.6 degrees and—"

"Yeah, yeah, yeah," I cut him off dismissively. "What about heat vision?"

"I don't think I h-h-have that."

"Superstrength?"

"No."

"Flight! Can you fly?"

"No!"

"Right." I could see he was done with the topic, and I wanted to be sensitive to that.

"So, pyrokinesis?" I continued.

"No."

"Shape-shifting?"

"No. None of that! Only the things I s-s-said."

"Got it. Totally understand. But X-ray vision?"

"You already asked that!"

"I asked about heat vision. Completely different deal from X-ray vision, man. Get your head out of your ass."

He sighed, and I finally relented.

"Sorry," I said.

We sat quietly for a while as all of it sank in, but eventually, he broke the silence.

"I know my d-d-dad did his best to protect me. But even if he'd finished the rewrite, he was only putting off the inevitable. My s-s-synthetic skin can heal small lesions, but there's no way to repair damage like this," he said, looking at his leg. "I was bound to g-g-get a serious injury eventually, and now it's only a matter of time until somebody finds out I'm just a d-d-dumb old piece of illegal tech."

"We can hide the injury," I offered. "It's not like anybody wears shorts around here."

"Great. And w-w-when it comes time to test my biological age for release and they s-s-see I have no biological age because I'm not biological?"

"They're in no rush to run the test," I said. "You could avoid it."

"So I can have another g-g-glorious few years on the Charon before they notice I don't age?" he persisted. "I'm as g-g-good as dead."

As much as I wanted to keep arguing with him, I couldn't. The world was still pretty sore about what the AI revolution had wrought, and there was no question they would melt him down the second he was found out. He needed a solution I didn't have. So all I could do was try to think of a way to distract him from his woes – and then one came to me. I yanked out my holo-pod, powered it on, and pulled up the Conundrum site.

"Hey, any chance you can hack into this thing?" I said, rotating it toward him.

He shrugged, then he turned his attention to the screen. His eyes fluttered for a moment, and he stared off into the distance, as if he was seeing a whole lot of stuff I wasn't. Then, his body jerked and he looked back at me, like he was emerging from a trance.

"Well?" I asked.

"Nothing," he sighed. "I can't m-m-make any sense of it, and every time I try, I get . . . pushed away? It's hard to describe, but it's like a foreign language that d-d-doesn't want to be learned."

I'd been an idiot. I was lucky the site hadn't reacted by crashing my holo-pod, and Arthur seemed even more dejected now, as if the only upside of his condition was less upside than he'd thought.

"Oh well, no big," I said, forcibly burying my disappointment and rewinding to his dilemma. "Listen, we'll . . . we'll figure this out."

He just nodded mechanically. I felt awful, but it was lights out in a few minutes, and the last thing he needed was to be caught wandering the halls without authorization. So we said our goodbyes, and he headed out.

CHAPTER  09

AFTER ARTHUR LEFT, I WAS HIT BY A FEW AFTERSHOCKS OF what he'd told me. How could none of us have noticed? How could he himself not even suspect?

Marvel's perennial Avenger Hank Pym came to mind. When he created Ultron (*Avengers* #54, 1968), he thought he was heralding the dawn of a new age of technology to benefit all mankind. But he was actually unleashing a superpowered, indestructible machine that would brainwash him into forgetting he'd created it, then attempt to exterminate humanity. (You could say things kind of went sideways.)

Arthur was nothing like Ultron, but he was just like Pym. They were both examples of the fact that sometimes you can't see what's right in front of you, no matter who you are. I mean as far as smarts go, Pym's up there with Marvel's best brains. Some people put him in second place behind Reed Richards. Some push him into third behind Doctor Doom. Personally, I think he gets a raw deal in the rankings because of his little mystery-gas-induced schizophrenia problem. But I digress. My point is he's no dummy. And still, he was so blinded by his own idealism that he built one of the biggest robot assholes in the history of the Scriptures.

Of course, thinking about good intentions gone bad got me thinking about Norman again. Despite its many, many flaws, Norman's plan to "save the world, one shipment at a time" was arguably working out better than Hank Pym's Ultron plan. But then Norman's words echoed through my mind again: "when all that I've worked for is just weeks away." My problem with the phrasing finally began to crystalize. It seemed like Normanium Prime was the impetus for the statement—the thing he'd been striving for with the billions he'd spent on continued Normanium R&D. But from what I'd seen, his plans for Normanium Prime had nothing to do with a more expedient end to the energy crisis. He wasn't rushing into production on newfangled energy plants to harness the breakthrough for all mankind. He was paying people to pull all-nighters to outfit his ships for F.T.L. travel. How could that save the world, or help people at all? Building a civilization on a habitable planet in a neighboring solar system was a possible answer, but that wasn't "weeks away." More like years, or decades. It could be I was taking his statement too literally, but I didn't think so. I hadn't gotten a first-step-on-a-long-road vibe from him. I'd gotten a finish-line vibe. The fact was, from what I could tell, his crazy excitement had nothing to do with what he'd dedicated his life to. Unless the thing he'd dedicated his life to wasn't what everyone thought.

I recalled his shirt. And his tattoo. He'd literally been covered in the Scriptures, as he was in every picture I'd ever seen of him. Suddenly, that didn't feel like a nostalgic nod to his youth. All at once, I thought I knew who he'd meant when he'd said "you people."

My Spidey-Sense started tingling, like when I got close to a Conundrum clue, and more of his words came back to me: "the key to everything is in reach." His use of the word "key" was benign in and of itself, but seen as a part of the whole, it brought to mind a portion of Cateklysm's broadcast—the same portion that referenced Pentagramite.

The connections started forming in my mind, fast and furious, one explosive epiphany after another. I realized I was like Hank Pym and Arthur. The truth had been right there in front of me, but I hadn't seen it. Norman had perpetuated the spread of a new cancer, exploited innocent children, and created a drug that enhanced productivity at the expense of people's sanity—all apparently motivated by some desperate, uncompromising desire to reach a far-off planet as soon as possible. If you tuned out the noise generated by the PR snakes, the pieces didn't all fit a mission to save the world. But they did fit another mission. And they fit it perfectly.

"You're saying mother lovin' Luthor Norman is some kind of Chowderhead con man?" Darcy exclaimed.

After returning to my quarters, I'd started laying out my theory for him.

"Think about it," I said. "Everyone thought he quit Chowderheading and refocused his efforts on running his company. But what if he was really refocusing the company's efforts?"

"Huh?"

"When he first went MIA from the community, some Chowderheads were convinced he'd solved the Conundrum. I think they were right."

Darcy shook his head. "That doesn't make any sense. If he did that, he woulda won your lame game a long time ago."

"That's what everybody assumes. But I couldn't stop thinking about how excited he was about Normanium Prime. He said it was 'the key to everything.' And it hit me: in Cateklysm's broadcast, Cateklysm said the Conundrum would test our will, cunning, and valor, but the key was to take a shot of Pentagramite and just go for it!"

"Great," Darcy said. "Say more shit that means nothing."

"Will, key, valor, cunning? Bart Wilhelm Keyes and Valorie Cunningham! You know, the scientists who created the F.T.L. drive? The one that needed an incredibly powerful fuel—like Pentagramite!"

Darcy stared at me blankly.

"The stuff all the ships run on in Fate Force comics! And I still can't figure out how, but it looks just like Normanium Prime!"

"So?"

"So it's an Easter egg! I think Cateklysm was telling us that Normanium Prime will play into the Conundrum solution. We're going to need to be able to get somewhere that requires F.T.L. travel!"

I went on, my manic state growing as I spoke. "I think Norman solved the Conundrum and discovered he couldn't get to where it was pointing him. That's why he turned Norman Corp into an energy company. That's why he launched Project Javelin! And that's why he's so excited! Who knows when he figured out the Easter egg, but he did, and he knows it's telling him Normanium Prime is what he needs!"

"Yo, you sayin' he didn't give a shit about the energy crisis, he just wanted gas for his stupid-ass spaceships?"

"Is that crazier than the idea that all he cares about is helping the world, but he's doing it by giving people cancer and enslaving kids?"

Darcy paused at that. I could tell he was shifting from incredulity to skepticism.

"Well how'd your boy Cateklysm know somebody would discover Normanium Prime? Never mind what home girl and home boy's names would be? Can he see the future?"

"Maybe. Probably—I don't know. He can teleport and shit."

He looked at me, pondering everything I'd said. Then he snorted dismissively and decreed, "You're one crazy white boy." But I could tell his skepticism had taken a hit. He was a nonbeliever to be sure, and the fact that I'd come anywhere near selling him on my theory made it real in my own mind. I knew what I had to do.

CHAPTER  10

MY FIRST PRIORITY WAS TALKING TO ARTHUR AND CASSIE.
It was Tuesday, and I was in Group A for breakfast. They were both in Group B. Bad luck. But a meal was nowhere near enough time to work through everything I had to say anyway. So I needed to get the three of us some real time together.

I scarfed down my breakfast and ran to Arthur's room, then waited outside. The morning klaxon sounded for Group B, which meant Group A was now due at shift within five minutes. I would be cutting it close.

The second alarm sounded, and the door rattled open. Arthur walked out. Behind him, I could see Boyle, still buried under the covers, snoring like a narcoleptic on Ambien.

Arthur looked confused and asked, "What are you d-d-doing here?"

"I need a favor," I said.

After telling him what I needed, I ran to my first shift. I was replacing fuel cells again. I hardly noticed who I was sharing the shift with. I was too focused on the details of my plan—my whacko, almost-sure-to-fail plan. There were holes everywhere, and I was doing my best to fill some of them in before lunch. Then, as lunch approached, one of Malcolm's goons showed up to tell me my second shift had been switched. He was all too pleased to inform me that instead of reporting to mess hall maintenance, I would be on shit detail. He grinned and added, "Welcome back, dick wad." I gave him the dirty look he expected in return, rather than the satisfied smirk I was feeling. After all, he was following my orders. The updated work schedule that had pinged through to the holo-com on his wrist hadn't come from upper management. It had come from Arthur hacking central scheduling. Two other goons were probably alerting Arthur and Cassie about now that they had also been switched to shit detail, and the Orphs originally scheduled for it were getting the good news that they had all been switched to less unpleasant tasks. One of them would be thrilled because they'd be pulled out of their current shift for an early lunch with Group A in order to replace me in my mess hall maintenance shift.

I'd chosen to put us on shit detail because it required only three people, which would give us some privacy. Also, if Malcolm noticed the change, he'd be less suspicious of us. After all, who would go to the trouble to hack the schedule to give themselves the ship's most repulsive duty?

★

A theoretical perk of my schedule hijinks was the fact that I'd have a double lunch as I waited for my shift with Group B to come around. But I was too jittery to appreciate said perk. As Group A finished up and headed out, I watched Group B filter in. Cassie was in the middle of the pack. When she saw me, she was a little confused because I should have been gone, or at least on my way out. Then the confusion passed, replaced by a look of plain old discomfort, which I felt too. This being the first time we'd seen each other since our awkward parting the morning before, I don't think either of us knew what to say. She got her sludge and walked over.

"Shouldn't you be going?" she asked.

I could tell she hadn't meant for it to come out as forcefully as it had.

She continued, playing up a note of concern, "I mean Malcolm will probably come looking for you personally if he sees an alert that you're late to shift."

"He won't get an alert," I said. "Schedule change."

"Oh, really? Me too. Some schmuck put me on shit detail."

"Yeah. Sorry, I'm the schmuck."

"What?!" She looked confused. "How . . . Wait, is this about what happened in the infirmary, because I told you –"

"It's not about that. It's . . . complicated."

Neither of us had noticed Arthur enter, so we were both surprised to see him set a bowl of sludge down beside us and take a seat. He nodded nervously, then began wolfing down the sludge.

"It's weird that you eat," I said to him, in a hushed tone.

"Well technically, I d-d-don't need to," he responded in the same hushed tone. "M-m-microreceptors all over my body draw energy from any power source in the vicinity. But I still get 'hungry' because my d-d-dad wanted me to live 'as normal a life as possible.'"

"Gotcha," I said.

"What are you guys whispering about?" Cassie demanded.

"I guess you h-h-haven't told her," Arthur said.

"Told me what?" Cassie asked.

"It's complicated," Arthur answered.

Ten minutes later, we were beginning our shift. We may have been the only people ever assigned to shit detail to start a shift early, but I didn't want to talk with all the other Orphs around, and Cassie was in no mood to wait to hear what we had to say – even if she had to be cleaning up and patching sewage leaks while we said it.

First, we told her about Arthur. As expected, she thought we were joking. Then Arthur showed her his leg, and interfaced with the ship's systems to open and shut a few of the pneumatic doors in the hallway. At that, she got very freaked, taking several steps back from him. He averted his eyes in shame.

"I . . . how is this . . . I mean how could . . ." she trailed off.

She didn't need more answers, she just needed to come to terms with the ones she already had. But after standing in uncomfortable silence for another moment, she did something amazing. She stepped back toward Arthur, making earnest eye contact, and asked, "So . . . do you have heat vision?"

Arthur snorted and shook his head. She was something else. She'd acclimated to the fact that her friend was a robotic freak with even less shock and horror than I had. At first I thought it might be proof that she was more Chowderheaded than I was–more willing to embrace the fantastical. But that wasn't it. I knew she was able to quickly accept Arthur without prejudice because of the uncompromising compassion that often came with being a Pro. As I gazed at her reverently, I had to remind myself of which side of the scale I was on and why.

Anyway, after Arthur put to rest her subsequent deluge of questions about the superpowers he did not have, he turned to me and asked, "So what else are we talking about?"

"There's more?" Cassie asked incredulously.

"Clayton said there was s-s-some reason you needed to know about me," Arthur clarified.

"Oh," Cassie said. She seemed a little hurt that his news hadn't been an entirely voluntary disclosure. After all, she was as close with him as I was. He read her reaction and added, "Not that I was against it. I'm just saying, there's s-s-something else."

This seemed to mostly heal her hurt. She looked at me and said, "Well, let's hear it."

So I took them through my wild theory, start to finish. Arthur knew about the interrogation and beating Norman had given me, but the rest was as new to him as it was to Cassie.

When I was done talking, he asked, "W-w-why would you be the only one to ever put this together?"

He didn't seem particularly resistant to my conclusions, only curious why no one else had drawn them. It was arguably a vote of confidence.

"I don't know," I answered him. "I'm a Chowderhead and an Orph. I'm conditioned to see past Norman's bullshit."

"Cassie's a Chowderhead and an Orph," he rebutted.

"She wasn't there for his psychotic outburst."

"Hm. Fair point."

Cassie had remained silent. I was watching her, but couldn't read her. Finally, she spoke.

"It seriously looks just like Pentagramite?" she asked, as if that detail was the clencher. I nodded.

Then she sighed and said simply, "Okay. So what now?"

"You mean you buy my theory?" I asked.

This wasn't like the leap of compassion she'd made regarding Arthur's news. It wasn't simply about reacting to unexpected facts. It was about accepting my subjective interpretation of facts. And *subjective* may have been putting it mildly.

"It's flippin' meshuggeneh," she said. "But yes, I buy it. So what, though? What the hell can we do about it? And what does any of this have to do with Arthur's situation?"

"Yeah, I'm d-d-darn curious about that part too," Arthur said.

They both looked at me skeptically. I didn't blame them. Supposing I was right about Norman's secret, it wasn't like we could report him to the authorities. We were just Orphs. No one would listen to us, even if he was breaking the law, which he wasn't. And none of this seemed to relate to Arthur in the least. Until you considered one utterly preposterous possibility.

"I want to steal one of Norman's F.T.L. ships," I said.

"What?" Arthur and Cassie gasped in unison.

"We need to get Arthur off the Charon, and we need to get to some far-off planet. Two birds, one stone."

"You are bonkers!" Cassie said.

"This is Arthur's life we're talking about!" I cried. "And it's ours too! The U.A.T. is everything to us. And I know we've got different ideas of how its power should be used, but letting a guy like Norman get ahold of it? Imagine the damage he'd do. And all we have to do to get a shot at stopping him is steal one of those ships."

"That sounds great," Arthur said. "Except for the fact that the d-d-docking bay is on the bottom level of the Charon – maximum security, three times the g-g-guards."

"Which you might actually be thankful for when you consider the place is full of PDQ-addicted serial killers and rapists!" Cassie added.

"Not that w-w-we could even get down there," Arthur continued. "Don't forget the blast doors with a twenty-four seven w-w-watch between here and the lifts."

"It's not like I haven't thought this through, guys," I asserted. "Arthur, I was hoping maybe you could fake some orders to have us sent downstairs for some reason. A guard would escort us all the way down and—"

"They'd s-s-sniff that out in minutes," he cut me off. "Anyone receiving orders to move Loaners between levels has to confirm the orders in person. Extra security m-m-measure."

"How do you know that?" I asked.

"They m-m-move me and the other special circumstances cases around the ship a lot when the rest of you are on planet because they g-g-get shorthanded."

"Hm," I said. "I didn't know that."

"And you probably didn't know I can't g-g-get past the biometric locks to remove our ID anklets either."

I sighed. "No. I didn't."

"Great!" Cassie cried. "So even if we beat impossible odds to get downstairs, they'd know exactly where we were."

"Alright!" I exclaimed. "I didn't say I'd worked out every last detail."

She snorted. "Okay, well then let's talk big picture. Suppose we pull off this whole fakakta heist. We don't really know where to go because neither of us has solved the Conundrum!"

I said, "Well, I kind of thought you and I could work together on that, considering the situation."

She gasped, and a look of misguided realization dawned on her face. She became heated, accusatory.

"Oy gevalt! Did you just make all this up to get your hands on my Scripture notes?!"

I lost my cool. "Oh for God's sake. Yes! Yes, first I blew myself up, then I called my good buddy Luthor Norman to pop in for a visit, and then I built a perfect robot copy of Arthur here—all to see what you got for 9 Across!"

"When you say it like that, it sounds ridiculous!" she yelled.

"I know!" I yelled back.

We paused. Arthur looked at both of us and sighed.

"Look, the plan needs w-w-work. But if this is for real, I'm in."

We both frowned at him in surprise.

"I mean anything is better than w-w-what's in store for me as it s-s-stands."

"Seriously?" Cassie asked.

He nodded hesitantly. Cassie paused for a long moment. Then she pursed her lips pensively, and I could see it clearly. Like Arthur, after the initial shock of my proposal had passed, she'd just been playing devil's advocate. She knew

Norman claiming "the power to change the world" would be very bad news, and she wouldn't be able to forgive herself if she let it happen. But there was still another matter to consider. Namely, her pathological obsession with claiming the prize for herself.

"If we teamed up on the Conundrum, it wouldn't mean we were partners from there on out," she said.

"Of course not," I responded, as if parting ways later was fine by me, which it wasn't. When it came to the prize, I was no less pathological than she was. I was just still in denial. I still wanted us to be together and me to win the thing. I was still hankering to have my cake and eat it too.

She bit her lip and said, "Then I guess . . . I've got to be totally billy, but . . . I guess I'm in."

I smiled. I had my cake. I was halfway home.

"But wait," she said. "What about Normanium Prime? You said there wasn't enough to actually power the ships, and even Norman doesn't know how to make more."

"I might be able to h-h-help with that," Arthur interjected.

We both looked at him quizzically.

"I've been reviewing m-m-my record of the incident, and I think I know h-h-how to reproduce the reaction that creates Normanium Prime."

"Wow," I said. "Well, that's a start."

"Yeah," Cassie said. "That just leaves solving the Conundrum, getting past the blast doors, accessing the lifts, eluding dozens of guards and murdering psychopaths, getting to the ship, and figuring out how to fly it. All before our alarm-tripping, easy-to-pinpoint anklets get us nabbed."

"When you say it like that, it sounds ridiculous," I said.

Making our pact was a lot to process, and jumping right into perfecting the plan was daunting. But Arthur spoke up again.

"I could fly the ship right now."

"You're kidding," I said.

"No. I can access the s-s-specs and operational manuals through the Charon's network. And I suppose we could knock out a g-g-guard and use his fingerprints to remove our anklets. But as far as the trip d-d-downstairs, I don't know."

I sighed. I didn't know either. It seemed like any attempt to get through the blast doors and onto the lifts would inevitably get us caught or shot. However, as we talked, I'd been patching a particularly oozy leak in one of the main waste lines. Several other lines ran along the walls and terminated into this one. It was about thirty inches in diameter and angled into the floor at about forty-five degrees. I stared down at it, and I had a thought—a thought I instantly regretted because it wasn't the worst idea in the world, but it may have been the most disgusting.

"What if . . ." I shook my head, loath to continue. "What if we didn't go through the blast doors or use the lift?"

"There's no other way down," Cassie said, confused.

"Well . . . there might be," I said, looking at the sewage line. They both looked at it and then back at me.

"Oh, hell no!" Cassie said.

It was probably simply his desperation talking, but Arthur was less dismissive. "Gimme a sec," he said. His eyes fluttered and went distant. I'd seen that look a couple of times now, whenever he'd interfaced with the ship. He must have been accessing the specs and protocols for the waste disposal system because a moment later he said, "A big enough leak w-w-would shut the whole system down. Then the lines would be relatively clear until someone found and patched the leak. The diameter is inconsistent from section to section, but we m-m-may be able to fit thr—"

"What?!" Cassie cried. I thought steam was going to shoot out of her ears. "Look, Metallo, maybe you're immune to claustrophobia and maybe you can deactivate your olfactory simulators, but—"

"Dude, not cool!" I cut in.

She was immediately ashamed. Her overreaction was forgivable, given what we were talking about, but I knew she wouldn't think so.

"Oh my God, I'm sorry," she said, really meaning it.

"Who's M-m-metallo?" Arthur asked hesitantly.

"Cyborg murder machine," she said, wincing.

"But he's like super powerful," I added. "Especially after he sold his soul to this demon, Neron." In retrospect, that probably didn't help.

Arthur nodded dejectedly. Sensitivity to his synthetic status was going to take some practice for us, and unfortunately, that practice was going to happen while he himself was still very raw about the whole thing.

Cassie made a peace offering by humoring us. "Alright, so if we don't get stuck and spend our last minutes waiting to drown in sewage, what then?"

Arthur explained, "If we don't get stuck, I g-g-guess we'll probably be moving pretty fast, and we'll need to be careful to stop ourselves before we reach the purging chamber on the bottom level. Then we'll have to cut through the line from the inside to m-m-make an exit."

"Won't the purging chamber be sealed if the system is shut down?" I asked. The purging chamber was essentially an air lock that vented waste into space every few minutes.

"It continues functioning to clear blockages," Arthur answered. "And I don't have the access to s-s-stop it."

This was more and more an all-or-nothing gambit, and I wasn't loving our chances.

"Well I guess we would already be in the middle of the fourth level when we came out," Cassie said with surprising optimism.

Encouraged, Arthur said, "It'd take the g-g-guards some time to find us. With a little luck, we could make the hangar."

"But what about the prisoners?" Cassie asked, smothering the flames she'd fanned.

Arthur shrugged. "M-m-make that a lot of luck."

The klaxon sounded. Dinnertime.

"Look," I said. "We've just been spitballing here, right? This is an awful plan. Just awful. We'd be insane to try it. There's time to think while Norman is stumped on the Normanium Prime problem. Let's use it."

Cassie seemed relieved.

Then I said, "And speaking of Normanium Prime, Arthur, you should schedule us all for crating first shift tomorrow, to see if you can reproduce that reaction. If you can't, the rest of this may not matter."

"Right," he said.

If today was any indication, no one would notice us messing with the schedule. And if they did, we'd still be well outside of suspicion. Assigning ourselves to crating duty was right on par with assigning ourselves to shit detail.

"Who are you going to put in there with us?" Cassie asked Arthur. "They'll notice if our shift is short a person."

Arthur thought about it. "Well it probably d-d-doesn't matter who it is. If we skip breakfast, I think I can do what I need to before they g-g-get there."

"Still, we should pick somebody we trust," I said. "In case they see anything. Put Darcy in there with us."

Arthur rolled his eyes and said, "Darcy? The g-g-guy who told Norris I had a crush on him because he heard it from Schakter who heard it from D-d-duncan, who heard it from—who was it Duncan heard it from again?" He pretended to ponder.

"Darcy," I admitted. Arthur had let Norris down easy, but it had been uncomfortable for everyone.

"Imagine how excited he'd be to s-s-spread rumors he didn't hear from himself," Arthur said.

He had a point. I started to regret what I'd already told Darcy, but that was arguably a harmless theory that had nothing to do with our escape plans.

"I think Boyle," Arthur said. "He's late to every shift. That'll g-g-give us more time."

Cassie said, "So . . . it's a choice between a guy who'll give us a few extra minutes, or a yenta that'll probably land us a sentence on a lower level?" She made a show of weighing the options in either hand.

"Okay," I said. "Boyle it is."

Looking back, I would wish I'd pushed for Darcy, but hindsight is twenty-twenty.

As we sat down to dinner surrounded by the rest of Group B, we couldn't comfortably continue talking about our plans, so there was an awkward silence between us. Arthur tried to fill it.

"So," he said, "you g-g-guys ever try to shortcut your Conundrum research by watching movies based on comic books?"

"Nah," Cassie said. "I mean we watch the movies. But only to pass the time. If they were relevant to the Challenge, they would have made Cateklysm's list."

"Why do you think h-h-he excluded them?" Arthur asked.

"I think it's a translation problem," she said. "There's just something lost when you go from the printed page to the screen. Especially early on. They didn't even have color TV when they did the first Superman TV show in 1952. George Reeves just looked like a middle-aged guy in gray tights and a darker gray cape who jumped in through the window once in a while. But even with spot-on special effects, there's something missing."

"That's true," I agreed. "But the big issue is the lack of commitment to the source material – changing this or that to play to a broader audience. It's sacrilege."

This had always pissed me off. For at least half a century, comic book TV and movies had alienated their core audience in hopes of appealing to a larger audience. For example, the 1960s camp hit Batman TV show elevated the Dark Knight's popularity, but in the end, it made such a mockery of him it nearly did him in. Aside from a few faithful highlights, an egregious lack of purity plagued large- and small-screen comic book adaptations until the 90s and 2000s, when Hollywood adopted a more earnest attitude. Even then though, a good number of decisions were made that violated canon for reasons I'd never been able to fathom. In 2002's *Spider-Man*, the filmmakers decided Peter Parker's radioactive spider bite should allow him to spin webs organically. Not only did this strip him of the scientific nerd cred that came with inventing his ingenious web shooters, but it perverted him into a wrist-ejaculating freak that made diehards want to hurl. In 2015's *Age of Ultron*, Tony Stark and Bruce Banner are credited with the creation of Ultron. Hulk steal Hank Pym's thunder! And don't even get me started on 2017's *Wonder Woman*, in which all the Greek gods—essential to various canon storylines—are killed in the first few minutes of the movie. Hey, Olympians, thanks for creating the universe, but you're not resonating with our demographics, so we're murdering you in a throwaway flashback.

"Eh, you always kvetch about the canon problems," Cassie said dismissively. "But you overlook the fact that screen adaptations have actually added to canon. For instance, Firestar got her start on TV."

"We were talking about live action," I fired back. "But FYI, if we're talking animation, Harley Quinn is a way better example of your point. I mean if you wanted to make it convincingly."

"You're full of it!" Cassie squawked.

"I'm full of being right, because you know Harley Quinn has a way more legit rep than Firestar."

"You want to talk reps? Well gosh, who was that kangster[4] chick who clobbered Garthan Saal when he possessed the energy of the entire Nova Corps in *New Warriors* #41? Oh yeah! Firestar!"

"Whatever," I scoffed. "Harley came from Bruce Timm's acclaimed *Batman: The Animated Series*. Firestar came from the suck-fest that was *Spider-Man and His Amazing Friends*. Case closed!"

"Case so not closed! *Spider-Man and His Amazing Friends* was narrated by Stan Lee himself! It's Marvel gold."

I gasped in disgust. "I am genuinely embarrassed for you right now. I mean Spider-Man and his so-called amazing friends live with Aunt May to save on rent, but they've got the money to renovate one of the rooms so it transforms into a secret crime-fighting lab?"

"Are you brain-dead?" Cassie shrieked. "In Season 3, Episode 21, they reveal Tony Stark set them up with that tech as a reward for saving his life."

"Well he should have rewarded them with better writers—because Iron Man doesn't need teenagers to save his ass!" I shot back.

Weird as our version of flirting was, it felt good to be doing it again. But we noticed Arthur was shaking his head at us.

"S-s-sorry I asked," he said.

After eating, we headed out of the mess. Arthur's quarters were in the opposite direction from mine and Cassie's, so after he said his goodbyes, Cassie

---

4   *Chowderhead slang, meaning a boss, a badass. Origin: A mash-up of "Kang the Conqueror" and "gangster."*

and I walked together for a few minutes before reaching a forking hallway that would separate us. I suddenly realized we hadn't solidified a plan of attack for the Conundrum.

"So, I'll bring my Conundrum diary tomorrow morning," I ventured. "You gonna bring yours?" This felt like the moment of truth. Agreement would represent a more concrete commitment to the cause. But that wasn't all. It would be a crack in the wall that stood between us – a wall I was very intent on cracking. She paused for a long moment. Then she nodded. To my mind, the hesitance in her answer made it all the more meaningful. I told myself it meant she'd given the matter thorough consideration, so her answer would not be easily overturned.

Suddenly, I felt myself longing to pick up where we'd left off in the infirmary. Of course, it was absurd to imagine she'd take all we'd discussed today in stride and go right back to talking about what could happen between the two of us. It was even more absurd to think she'd reverse her position on the subject in the minute or so we had together. But I was seventeen, and absurd expectations were my jam. So I hoped, maybe even believed, something might happen before we parted ways in the corridor. Alas, she just gave me a nervous wave, turned, and headed off toward her quarters.

When I got back to my quarters, I asked Darcy to keep a lid on what we'd talked about earlier. I told him I was worried about both of us ending up on the wrong side of a shock stick if I'd guessed right and it got back to our glorious leader. That danger was real, but considering it was Darcy, I was still concerned about his self-control. So I was careful not to tempt him further by saying anything that would hint at my escape plans.

After we turned in, I lay in bed, gripped by a sense of dread. Sleep was a pipe dream. At the moment, I was just months from my release from the Loaner program, but I was planning a wild gamble that could backfire in a million different ways, landing me back in the program. And this time, I'd be part of the general population. Was I rushing headlong into certain doom, and bringing Arthur and Cassie along for the ride? What was driving me? Was I just nuts?

As I stared into the darkness, questioning my sanity, something compelled me to turn on my holo-pod and pull up the Cateklysm broadcast. I didn't really understand why I was doing it until I did it. But there it was – my call to action, sounding across the world eighteen years before, in Cateklysm's encomium to superheroes: "They exemplify the resolve to do right that should be your guiding light."

As much as I'd dreamed of winning the U.A.T., if it was a decent human being who was about to score the tech, I doubted I'd risk my hide to stop it. But Luthor Norman? Someone had to do something. It struck me that I had been programmed as surely as Arthur–only my programming had been delivered through thousands of stories in which the hero was faced with the easy choice and the right choice, never settling for the former. I thought of Superman giving his life to defeat Doomsday (*Superman* #75, 1992). Of course, Supes came back. Big-name heroes almost always come back, which is how Jean Grey has braved over a dozen deaths–close to two dozen if you count alternative-continuity bonus deaths like when she broke her brain by levitating a galleon for too long on Earth-313 (Marvel's *1602* #7, 2003).

But it's not some meta-awareness of imminent resurrection that fuels superhero heroism. Even heroes who aren't protected by star status are all in. Eric Masterson, the original Thunderstrike, fought the good fight right up until a psychic struggle with the Executioner's cursed axe made him split himself in two and beat himself to death (*Thunderstrike* #24, 1993). Sure, he'd pop in as a zombie in *Avengers* #3 (1998), but there would be no real comeback for Eric. No happily ever after.

It's not even their superpowers or amazing gadgets that make heroes do what they do. They aren't who they are because they're super. It's the opposite. When you look at most of their origin stories, you find their mettle preceded their might: from a bookish Bruce Banner pushing a teenager out of the way of a gamma blast, to a nine-year-old Matt Murdock pushing an old man out of the path of a truck full of toxic waste, to a ninety-pound Steve Rogers refusing to let a 4-F classification push him out of WWII.

The resolve to do right should be your guiding light. It was really the one and only message of the Scriptures. Norman was proof that not every reader had gotten that message. But I had. I'd gotten it loud and clear. What I was doing would almost certainly end badly for me. It was dangerous. It was stupid. But it was right.

CHAPTER  11

THE NEXT MORNING, I WAS THE FIRST TO ARRIVE AT THE crating bay. The canister alarms were much less prevalent than during my last visit, as most of the faulty canisters had blown, and those that hadn't had been jettisoned.

The reactor could be seen through a massive crack in the bulkhead, but it was cold and lifeless. The ship had been running on its solar cells, which would put us back on Earth a month later than scheduled. That, combined with the loss of three quarters of the Normanium in this bay, would usually have been a big problem for corporate. However, with the momentous discovery of Normanium Prime, it seemed all was forgiven.

Arthur and Cassie arrived at the same time. Arthur was holding a spray bottle, which he'd apparently pilfered from a supply closet.

"What's that for?" I asked.

"You'll s-s-see," he said.

I nodded, then excitedly noted the holo-pod tucked under Cassie's arm, which matched my own. But there was no time to talk yet. We needed to get to work. Arthur placed a canister in the middle of the chamber.

He said, "Push all the bins as far away as possible."

We did as he asked, then returned to watch him do his thing. I don't know what we were expecting, but it got a little bit weird. He knelt in front of the canister and held perfectly still, staring at the space around the canister for a while. Then, he raised the spray bottle, doused the area, and waited. And waited. And waited. It was easily a full minute. Then, something in his expression changed, and he bowed his head as he started working his mind-modem mojo. The temperature gauge on the canister started climbing fast. We heard the all-too-familiar beeping.

"You m-m-might want to step back," Arthur said, stepping away himself. "This is going to g-g-get a little explodey."

We stepped back, just as the canister went off with a flash. When the smoke cleared, we saw the twisted wreckage we expected. But amid that wreckage we saw an assortment of red crystals like those Arthur and I had found lying around us after the bins had gone up in the explosion two weeks earlier.

"I g-g-give you Normanium Prime," Arthur said. There was an unmistakable note of surprise in his voice. Clearly, he'd had his doubts that it could be this easy.

Cassie picked up one of the crystals.

"My God, it really does look just like Pentagramite," she exclaimed.

"I know," I said. We both took another moment to try to grasp how that was possible, then she turned her attention to Arthur and the more immediate mystery.

"How did you . . ." she started. "Didn't you say Norman's people have been working on this around the clock?"

"I d-d-don't think they've been lucky enough to have Schakter take a w-w-whiz on their test samples," Arthur answered. He looked at me and smiled.

"Schakter's piss is the secret ingredient in Normanium Prime?" I asked.

"Huh?" Cassie said, bewildered.

"Schakter pissed on the floor in here before the explosion," I clarified.

"Ick. That guy is so toynbee[5]. And the universe went and gave him magic pee?" she said.

"Never mind that, how the hell did you get more of it?!" I said, staring at the spray bottle Arthur was holding in horror.

"Relax," he explained. "It's only w-w-water. The crystals formed near where Schakter did his business. So I reviewed my record of the incident and found there was a brief elevation in h-h-humidity in that area when the bins blew. I think Norman's people are missing that humidity reading—there's no g-g-gauge for that in here."

"Unbelievable," I said.

Arthur started gathering up the crystals and shoving them into a canvas bag he'd apparently swiped along with the spray bottle.

"Wait," Cassie said. "What about the canister count?"

"Shit," I swore, realizing the danger. Norman Corp may have forgiven the Normanium lost in the explosion, but the remaining canisters were still Malcolm's bread and butter. His guys were keeping a closer count than ever, and any newly missing canisters would mean trouble.

Arthur didn't miss a beat. He stared into space for a moment or two, then looked over at us and said, "No w-w-worries. Filed a requisition entry in the s-s-system to make it look like this canister was transferred to Norman's makeshift workspace."

"Really?" I asked.

---

5   *Chowderhead slang, meaning gross, disgusting. Origin: The repulsive mucus-spewing Marvel mutant The Toad, aka Mortimer Toynbee. (The term is unrelated to Valiant's lesser known Natalie Toynbee.)*

"Really," he said.

This was a new Arthur. He was more focused, more self-assured. Androidism was starting to look good on him.

The klaxon indicating the start of shift sounded.

"Do we have time to make more?" Cassie asked.

"I think so," Arthur answered. "Boyle's probably just g-g-getting out of bed."

"Wait—do we even need to make more?" I asked. "Can't we use the Normanium onboard the Javelins, now that we know how to convert it?"

"That's been altered too much," Arthur said, picking up a new canister. "They d-d-do a lot of additional refinement to make w-w-what's in these canisters into standard-grade Normanium fuel."

He set up the canister, rebooting his ritual with the spray bottle and the far-off stare. Cassie and I watched as the temperature climbed on the canister's gauges. Then poof! Another batch of crystals, same as before. He repeated the process twice more and was well into a third round when things went to shit.

We'd become fairly engrossed in the project, and none of us had noticed how long it had been since the klaxon. I suppose we were a little lax because we thought the worst-case scenario was Boyle walking in on us. It wasn't. As the third canister's temperature neared the detonation point, the door burst open and a bloody and bruised Boyle tumbled in, propelled by a brutal shove from Malcolm, who wore a demonic grin. Boyle crashed to the ground next to the rapidly beeping canister.

"Next time I ain't gonna be so gentle!" Malcolm scoffed.

There was a half second for us to add it all up. Boyle had finally been really and truly late. Malcolm had intercepted him in the hallway outside, beaten the crap out of him, and now expected him to perform his duties. But that wasn't going to happen because Boyle was unconscious and about to get his face blown off by the now-critical canister he'd landed in front of.

Without hesitation, Arthur hurled himself on top of Boyle as the canister exploded, briefly bathing Arthur's back in flames and sending him rolling across the floor. He came to rest facedown near Malcolm. The explosion had wiped Malcolm's demented exuberance away, replacing it with shock. Now as that passed, he took in the scene: the smoldering ruins of our raw materials, the cluster of newly formed red crystals, and most of all, Arthur. Arthur's shirt was in tatters, and a good-size patch of skin had been burned away, revealing a section of his shiny metallic spine. Malcolm frowned, struggling to make sense of it. But after a moment, a dim understanding dawned on his face. Then I hit him in the back of the head with a Normanium canister.

CHAPTER  12

"I'M OKAY," ARTHUR SAID, AS HE CLIMBED TO HIS FEET. CASSIE and I stared at him in awe.

He shrugged. "No real structural d-d-damage – and my pain receptors shut down in extreme circumstances. Like with m-m-my leg."

"I'm starting to see a lot of perks to this android thing," I said, trying hard to normalize. Arthur ignored me, crossing to check on Boyle. Cassie and I followed. Boyle was hurt bad and only sort of awake.

"We have to get him to the infirmary," I said.

"Obviously," Cassie agreed. "But then what? This isn't going to blow over."

There were no two ways about that. Malcolm was out cold. But he wouldn't be for long. And if he'd done what he'd done to Boyle for sleeping in, what would he do to us? Arthur was doomed, and I probably wasn't far off. As for Cassie, we may or may not be able to convince the powers that be that she was simply on the wrong shift at the wrong time. But I knew she wouldn't be willing to let us take the fall on our own anyway. I started feeling out extreme possibilities.

"Arthur, can you access the tracking system for the guards' holo-coms?"

"No," he answered. "That s-s-stuff is locked down tighter than anything else. Why?"

"Doesn't matter."

Both he and Cassie seemed too strung out to follow my line of thinking back to making Malcolm disappear. But as I'd said, it didn't matter because we'd never get away with it. Malcolm's holo-com was always tracking and reporting his vitals and location – the records already indicated he'd lost consciousness. That wouldn't set off an alarm any more than a nap would, but if he turned up dead, there would be cause to review the data, and the fact that he'd been in a room with us when he went night night wouldn't look good. Ultimately, there was nothing we could do to stop him from coming to, and nothing we could do to stop what was going to happen when he did. The math was easy. The schedule for our escape had just moved from sometime soon to right fucking now.

"We have to go," I said. "We have to get off this ship."

"How?" Cassie exclaimed.

"The way we talked about," I answered with as much conviction as I could muster.

"But you s-s-said that was an awful plan," Arthur reminded me.

"Yeah," Cassie said. "What happened to 'we'd be insane to try it'?"

"We'd have to be more insane to wait around and see how this shit storm pans out," I answered.

"Unless . . ." Arthur started hesitantly. "Unless you have something to bargain with."

"What?" Cassie asked.

"Well there's . . . there's the secret to m-m-making Normanium Prime. You could trade it for your s-s-safety."

"What about you?" I asked.

I understood why he hadn't included himself in the bartering plan. There was no leverage in the world that was going to keep him safe, now that he'd been exposed.

"I could try to m-m-make it off the ship alone," he said.

His proposal was likely our best chance of survival. Only a crazy person wouldn't have considered it.

"Screw that," I said. "We're not going to abandon you. Plus, we turn ourselves in now, Norman gets the U.A.T. There's no way we'll get another chance to escape."

Arthur sighed in nervous relief. It was obvious he hadn't been wild about attempting the escape alone. He and I both looked at Cassie, awaiting her vote. We didn't have to wait long.

"Clayton's right," she said. "We gotta go."

We all took a beat as it sunk in that we were really moving forward with our nutso plan. Then Arthur spoke up.

"Okay. Well, I g-g-guess we'll need these."

He walked over to the pile of newly minted crystals and started gathering them up.

I focused on our anklets. They had to come off. Luckily, that wouldn't be a problem. I stooped down next to Malcolm, grabbed his thumb, and slid it into a small slot on the side of my anklet, where the biometric release was housed. There was a beep, and the anklet disengaged and fell to the floor. My signal had just gone dead, but there would be no alarms because the removal was authorized. I looked over at Cassie, who was still frozen in place, contemplating what we were about to attempt.

"Hey," I said. She looked at me, and I gestured to my now-bare ankle. "You're next."

She shook off her daze, walked over, and pulled up her pant leg. I removed her anklet. Then, as Arthur came over and I repeated the process, she stared down at Malcolm and said, "What are we going to do with him?"

I paused. Getting rid of Malcolm would only be a problem if we were around when he was reported missing and the records were reviewed. But now we were planning to be long gone by that time. I looked over at the air lock.

"No," Cassie said, reading my mind. "Absolutely not. We're not murderers."

"You want him coming after us when he wakes up?" I asked.

"We can . . . tie him up," she said. Searching the area, her eyes fell on some of the nylon tie-downs used to secure the Normanium canisters in the crates. She started toward them.

I followed her, raising my voice. "The things he's done. To me, to you, to every Orph on this ship. He doesn't get tied up for that!"

"Clayton," Arthur interrupted. "You can't d-d-do this."

"Why?" I yelled.

"Because!" Cassie jumped back in. "Because . . ."

As she struggled to continue, I saw what she was feeling. There was a sadness in her eyes that reflected her years of trauma, and I understood. Her soul wouldn't survive being party to cold-blooded murder—no matter the circumstances.

"Okay," I said. "I'm sorry." I grabbed a length of tie-down and yanked it free. Cassie didn't say anything. But as we worked to gather up the tie-down, she looked at me with a new kind of tenderness. It was a nice feeling, though I hoped she understood that things would have been different if she weren't there. After all, a Pun's a Pun.

None of us had ever tied anyone up before, but within a few minutes, we'd given it our best effort. We removed Malcolm's holo-com the same way we'd removed our anklets and chucked it across the room. Now the only way he could call for help would be to yell, and he'd have to get lucky to be heard in here. I leaned down and yanked his shock stick free of its holster. I knew we'd need it later.

The next priority was Boyle. I grabbed him under the arms, and Arthur grabbed his legs. We hoisted his body up, trying to avoid putting any extra strain on his obvious injuries. He was heavier than he looked, but the infirmary was only about fifty yards, and we were able to cover the distance in just a few minutes without encountering anyone else.

Jerry looked over in surprise as we opened the door and carried Boyle over to one of the beds. As we went, Arthur was careful to angle his back and exposed section of spine out of Jerry's field of vision. It was the wrong time to have the android conversation. The situation was irregular enough as it was—we were supposed to be working, and if Boyle needed medical attention, we should have summoned a guard to pick him up via the emergency pagers on our anklets.

"What the hell is going on here?" Jerry demanded.

"He's in bad shape," I said, as we set Boyle down and he gave a wheezing cough. We'd taken a risk by coming here, but I was sure Boyle had some busted ribs, and I knew from experience a punctured lung was a possibility. He needed Jerry's help. And he needed it now. Jerry looked down at him, then up at me. All I could offer was, "We don't have time to explain. We have to go."

He stared at me and noted Cassie and Arthur hovering anxiously near the door. I don't think he thought we were headed back to our shift, and neglecting to lock us down and report us immediately put his job at risk. As miserable as the gig was, I knew it hadn't been easy for him and his husband to land a station aboard the same ship. But apparently, he couldn't bring himself to sell us out.

"Good luck," he said. "With whatever this is."

He turned away from us to focus on Boyle, and we scrambled out into the hallway and headed for the east corridor, where the main sewage line passed through the floor to the lower levels. When we got there, Arthur covered one end of the hall and Cassie covered the other. They'd signal me if any of Malcolm's roving lieutenants or the Orphs assigned to shit detail were headed our way. I took a breath and stabbed the pronged end of the shock stick into the damaged line right above the coupling joint that sat at floor level. I yanked hard to the right. Raw sewage gushed out. The stench nearly bowled me over, but I steeled myself and worked the shock stick back and forth, creating an opening that stretched across the line's entire diameter. Then I gouged the shock stick in again two or three feet above the horizontal opening, and yanked up and down, creating a vertical opening. Thankfully, the line's preexisting damage made for relatively easy going and before long, the two openings met, creating an upside down T shape. Then I gave the line a kick where the two openings intersected, and it gave way. After a few more minutes of work, there was a triangular gap that we could fit through.

As I finished, a siren started blaring. I exchanged wide-eyed looks with Cassie and Arthur, fearing the worst. Had Jerry dropped a dime on us after all? No. We realized it was only an alarm sounding a full shutdown of the sewage lines, due to the dramatic drop in pressure detected. Good news, not bad. I motioned for the other two to join me.

Cassie gave voice to the sixty-four-thousand-dollar question: "Who's going first?"

"Well, it's my stupid idea," I answered.

"No," Arthur said. "It should be m-m-me." He took the shock stick from me, as whoever went first would need it to create our exit. "We're d-d-doing all this to save my life."

"That's not true," I rebutted. "We've all got our reasons for being here."

He seemed to have forgotten that the second Malcolm had walked into the crating bay, the septic Slip 'N Slide and the perils beyond had become the best option for all of us. But as he went on, I wondered how much of his opening argument had just been politeness.

"Clayton, there's m-m-more to it," he said. "You're the biggest of the three of us."

"So?"

"So if you go first and g-g-get stuck . . ."

I connected the dots, and finished, ". . . you guys wouldn't be able to try."

"That could happen no matter who goes first," Cassie argued. "We don't know if any of us will fit all the way down."

"Of course, but we h-h-have to play the odds," Arthur said.

"Well then I go first," Cassie concluded, gripping the shock stick. Arthur held on to it, looking sheepish.

"What? I *am* the smallest." Despite the grave circumstances, her voice was laced with offense at the suggestion that she wasn't as slim as she thought.

"You're s-s-skinnier, but not all over," Arthur said.

She looked confused.

"Boobs," I clarified.

"Oh," she said, blushing.

"Besides, if either of you goes first and g-g-gets stuck, you may not be able to access your holo-pod to send a m-m-message," Arthur said.

"Well you don't even have a holo-pod," Cassie countered.

Both our holo-pods beeped, and we pulled them from our pockets to see a message that read: "I don't need one."

Cassie rolled her eyes and gave a huff of resignation. Then she released her grip on the shock stick and said, "I guess you win, dude."

Glancing into the feces-stained cylinder, Arthur didn't seem that thrilled about his victory. Still he didn't hesitate for long. He dropped to all fours and started backing into the opening I'd made in the line.

I said, "Be sure to keep an eye out for the coupling joints – third one's the bottom level."

He nodded. I knew he knew what I was telling him, but saying it made me feel useful. As his legs disappeared into the line, he paused, resting on one elbow and reaching into the pocket of his jumpsuit to pull out the canvas bag full of Normanium Prime.

"You ought to hold on to this," he said. "If I don't m-m-make it, you guys might find another way down."

The naively optimistic notion that there was hope beyond our current Hail Mary seemed to bring him comfort, so I nodded and put the bag in my own jumpsuit pocket. He paused for a moment longer, and his eyes took on that far-off look again. A supply closet popped open behind us.

"You g-g-guys should wait in there, in case anybody comes by."

We hadn't considered how long we might be standing around in the hall. I was glad he had. He gripped the edges of the opening and lowered his mid-section into the darkness below. Then he clung on for a second and looked queasily up at us.

"FYI, I can't actually shut d-d-down my sense of smell at will. And I know I h-h-have to choose between this stench or being executed. But it's a close race."

He let go of the edge and slipped out of view at an alarming rate. We prayed he'd be able to brace himself against the sides of the cylinder enough to control his speed before he reached the disposal chamber. We also prayed he wouldn't hit a section that was too narrow and get stuck. And we prayed that if he made it, we'd make it too. There was a lot of praying going on. We retreated into the supply closet and sat on the floor with our holo-pods in front of us, staring at the blank space above them. At the moment, no news was good news because the only news we'd get this fast would be that Arthur was stuck and we were all screwed.

We both fell silent. It wasn't that we had nothing to talk about. It was that neither of us knew how to talk about it. But eventually, Cassie spoke up.

"Look, I meant what I said. This is just a short-term team up—and nothing has changed when it comes to . . . us."

"Got it, loud and clear," I said. "Nothing's going to happen between us."

"That's right," she said.

Then she kissed me. I went with it, and it went on for a while. Suddenly, the stench of sewage receded, and the many ways we might soon die drifted from my mind. I knew I should be focused on Arthur's success. I knew I should be sending him positive thoughts. But the moment had taken over. It was just Cassie and me, together. My imaginary visits from MJ suddenly lost their luster, and I knew that from here on out it would be Cassie I looked to in tough times. My daze was suddenly interrupted by the beeping of our holo-pods. We broke away from one another and waited with bated breath for something to happen.

A message popped up above both our units: "Good to go. Plenty of room all the way down." We gasped in relief. I think on some level, we'd all been feeling like there was no way our plan could work, but Arthur had come through.

Cassie gathered her courage and said, "Guess I'm next. I'm way skinnier than you . . ." She smirked and added, "Even with my boobs."

Then she tucked her holo-pod into her pocket and said, "By the way, what happened in here was a one-time thing. Don't get the wrong idea about it."

"Totally," I answered, pretending I hadn't pledged my soul to the wrong idea in question.

She turned and walked out into the hall. I followed as she climbed into the opening and paused at the point of no return, as Arthur had.

"Short-term team up," she reiterated firmly. "We're O'Neil and Adams's Green Lantern and Green Arrow. We go our separate ways after a limited run."

"We are one hundred percent on the same page," I lied.

Then she held her nose, took a breath, and let go of the edge of the opening, disappearing with a whoosh.

For a moment, I stood there, shell-shocked by the myriad of emotions swirling through my system. Then I returned to the supply closet. As I reflected on the last few minutes, I thought the fact that Cassie had done what she'd done with me made sense, even if she meant what she'd said about us being a limited run. She was afraid we wouldn't make it downstairs, and maybe more afraid of what would happen if we did. Why not do something impulsive? Or were her actions a sign that the wall between us was cracking—even crumbling? I was getting pretty twisted up, but then I pictured her flying toward the lower levels of the ship and the disposal chamber, and my obsessing was replaced by the worry I would have been feeling about Arthur during his descent, had Cassie and I not been lost in our steamy make-out session.

With nothing else to do, I simply sat there staring at my holo-pod. Unlike Arthur, Cassie wouldn't need time to create an exit. Still, less than a minute had passed, so I didn't expect anything to happen. But something did. The door of the supply closet swung open, and I saw Malcolm lean in and scan the area. Then his eyes fell on me.

It seemed Malcolm had gotten lucky yelling for help. Then he'd gone right into search-and-destroy mode. Now, the search part was done. He strode over and hit me with a brand-new shock stick. Once, twice, three times. Then he gouged the stick into my chest and gave me the voltage. But I realized that had just been the warm up, as three of his nastiest lieutenants crowded in behind him—Stavos, Andreas, and Rickie. All three joined in, swinging and stabbing with gusto, and I went fetal.

Things had definitely taken a turn for the worse. But then something strange happened. As the brutal onslaught rained down on me, I thought about the cover of *Superman* #32 (1945). It pictured Superman being bombarded by about half a dozen lightning bolts. A talk bubble hovered next to his serene face, reading simply, "It tickles." Why did I think of this? Well, as Malcolm and his guys continued to whale on me, it didn't tickle. But it didn't hurt as much as I would have expected. I supposed I'd simply gotten used to the sensation over the years. In any event, I was granted enough presence of mind to grab my holo-pod and plant my foot against the back wall of the supply closet. Then, marshaling every ounce of strength I had, I shoved off. I slid across the floor, through the forest of assailants surrounding me, then using my forward momentum, ambled to my feet and hurled myself out of the room. They would have been on me in a second, but that was a half second longer than it took for me to dive headlong into the triangular opening in the sewage line.

The world closed in around me as I flew down the cylinder at teeth-rattling velocity. The stench was overwhelming, and I started to gag but fought the impulse. Behind me I could hear Malcolm screaming at Rickie, the smallest and most vicious of his all-star squad, to follow me. Then I heard a metallic clunk as Rickie apparently complied. Now Malcolm would be contacting guards all over the ship, and an unwelcome welcome party would be on its way to wherever this line passed through each lower level. But I had to focus on one thing at a time. As I rocketed downward, my eyes adjusted to the darkness and I saw a coupling joint whip by. I had no idea if it was the first or second one I'd passed, and I realized I'd better try the brakes – I didn't know how far along Cassie was, and she didn't need me crashing into her. I strained to extend my elbows against the curved interior and felt a short swell of relief as I began to slow, followed immediately by a bigger swell of alarm as I realized I wasn't slowing very much. Another coupling joint blew by, and panic set in as I sensed the cylinder growing wider, making it more difficult to decelerate. I strained harder, awkwardly bracing one elbow and one palm against the sides as I went. It helped, but I was still moving awfully fast, despite the fact that I could feel the angle of the cylinder leveling out dramatically.

Then I saw it: a glimmer of light streaming in from an irregular opening to the right, up ahead. It was the makeshift exit Arthur had created.

As the passage continued to get wider, I brought my legs up under me and rose to my hands and knees, arching my back against the top of the cylinder with everything I had. To my astonishment, it worked. I muttered a heartfelt thanks to Odin as I came to a wobbly stop, like an old dog trying to stand on hardwood. I was only ten feet short of Arthur's exit. Great. Except now that I was stopped, I could hear the clatter of Rickie closing in on me. It didn't sound like he'd gotten the hang of braking.

A few feet beyond the exit, I saw the cylinder terminate into the inner workings of a massive valve, beyond which lay a black void. That had to be the disposal chamber. If I lost my balance and slid past the exit through that valve, I'd be dumped into a pool of sewage. That would be bad, but not as bad as when the chamber sealed, then vented into space. I had assumed Cassie must already have exited, and I'd been unable to hear the notification from Arthur on my holo-pod buried in my pocket. But as I peered through the valve, I was reminded that her absence could mean one of two things. I forced that thought to the back of my mind and started edging frantically forward, trying to move carefully enough to avoid losing control but fast enough to get clear of Rickie as he hurtled toward me. I failed on the second count. Rickie hit me – hard.

While I'd dived headfirst into the pipe, Rickie had gone feet first, and now, in this widened section, his feet slipped all the way up under my chest, and we lurched forward in a tangled mess. We were going way too fast, and one of my arms was pinned in place by one of Rickie's legs. I had the grim realization that there was no way I'd be able to stop us before we reached the disposal chamber. But I didn't have to. Suddenly, a hand latched on to the shoulder of my jumpsuit, and I felt myself being yanked partway out of the tube. Arthur had grabbed me as I slid past, but I wasn't clear yet. I felt a jolt of pain from my shoulder, as my clavicle was trapped across the jagged edge of the opening and ground against it by Rickie's weight. I thought I must have caught a break with the angle because when I glanced down I noticed that, amazingly, I wasn't bleeding.

I was relieved to see Cassie appear next to Arthur, but as she grabbed my arm, I realized they couldn't see Rickie. I needed to warn them.

"They found me!" I yelled.

They both looked confused – but not for long – because as they pulled me farther out, Rickie slid into view.

"Criminy!" Arthur cried.

Rickie's legs were past the opening, but his upper body was flush with it, allowing him to grab one of my ankles as I wriggled out. I kicked at him with the other foot, but he grabbed it and now I had no leverage at all. He started climbing hand over hand up my legs to free himself, like some deranged movie monster.

Arthur had handed the shock stick to Cassie when he was first trying to pull me out, and he didn't pause to recover it. He just charged forward and started smashing his fists into Rickie's arms and shoulders. In that moment, he may or may not have recognized that freeing me could send Rickie to his death. But Rickie did, and he needed to deal with the threat. He released my legs and grabbed Arthur's wrists. This allowed Cassie to yank me clear. Unfortunately, I fell on top of her, so neither of us was in a position to do anything about what came next. As Arthur tried to shake Rickie off, Rickie's weight shifted and he slid violently downward, disappearing back into the line and dragging one of Arthur's arms in up to the shoulder. There was a terrifying split second as Arthur turned to look at us. Then his feet lost purchase, and he was jerked wholly through the opening.

"Arthur!" I yelled. We heard him and Rickie grunt as they slid into the disposal chamber, and then there was a splash. We rushed over and looked through the opening in the line, but we couldn't see anything beyond the passage to the disposal chamber.

"Arthur!" I yelled again.

There was an eternity, and then we heard him. "I'm h-h-here. I think I can reach the −"

To our horror he was cut off by a shrill tone, and we saw a red light glow near the valve. A giant metallic disc slid into place, sealing the chamber. Then we heard Arthur and Rickie scream. After that, we heard nothing at all.

Cassie and I looked at each other, shock and demoralization washing over us. She fell to her knees with a choked sob. My insides felt like someone had taken an ice pick to them. But there was no time for what I felt because I looked up and saw two guards round the corner and spot us.

"Cassie," I said.

No response. She didn't hear me, or she didn't care what I had to say. But after losing Arthur, we couldn't give up. We couldn't just hand ourselves over. As much as it hurt, we had to move forward. Mourning Arthur right now would make his death meaningless.

"Cassie, we have to go now! Get up!" I grabbed her arm and dragged her forward, but her legs didn't start working until she saw the guards draw big, nasty pistols. No shock sticks. This was level one, and playtime was over.

We sprinted around a corner and down a corridor. Behind us we could hear one of the guards yelling into his holo-com, "Malcolm, we got your runaway brats down here!"

We took another turn to the left. We didn't know where we were going, and despite my resolve to push on, it was sinking in that without Arthur, our plan was shaky at best. I still had the Normanium Prime, but who was going to fly the ship? Forget that, who could even get us past the high-security door leading to the hangar? Of course, there were plenty of doors that we could get through, and I saw one as we rounded another corner. I made a snap decision, slapping the entry panel. The door hissed open, and we heaved ourselves through it. Two long seconds passed as we waited for it to hiss shut again. Then we crouched there, breathlessly hoping we'd had enough of a lead on the guards that they hadn't seen or heard the door opening and closing. Their heavy footsteps approached, then drifted past us. We both exhaled gratefully. They'd double back before long, searching every chamber along the corridor, but we had a little time to think. Unfortunately, there was a new problem. A big one.

We got to our feet and turned around to see four convicts staring at us, Normanium canisters in hand. We'd ended up in the level one crating bay. At first glance, the convicts were clichés: four men, heavily tattooed, with gnarled dispositions. But the longer I looked at them, the scarier they got. It was obvious that everything we'd heard about PDQ was true as I took in their bloodshot eyes, rapid breathing, and the frenetic mouth movements that accompany a fruitless search for saliva.

They were like starving hyenas—except for one of them: an intense, lupine Latino man who was all muscle and sinew. He seemed to be the alpha of the group, but that wasn't all that set him apart. It was his reaction to us. It wasn't merely surprise. It seemed more like elation. He stepped forward, and Cassie said a single word that made my jaw drop: "Dad?"

CHAPTER  13

"HELLO, PRINCESS," WILSON RAMIREZ SAID WITH A SMILE.
"This is impossible," Cassie replied. Her voice was brimming with confused dread. I knew the last time they'd seen one another was when she'd testified against him in court, shattering his warped image of her as his partner in crime once and for all. They'd dragged him out of the courtroom screaming, "I'll gut you like a fish!" So this wasn't exactly a storybook father-daughter reunion.

Cassie hadn't known or cared where he was serving his sentence, and it had never occurred to her that fate, in a nearly unthinkable twist of irony, could have landed him in the same place as her, albeit a few levels down. The chances of that, combined with us stumbling into his shift in the crating bay, were mind boggling. It was like Cassie had won the lottery on Bizarro's home world, Htrae.

Orphs were sequestered from lifers on the Charon and on Mars, so there was no way Wilson had seen this coming any more than Cassie had. But his manner was hard to read. So as Cassie backed toward the door, I hesitated. Despite everything Cassie had told me, and despite the damage wrought by the obvious PDQ addiction, I thought it was possible Wilson's incarceration had done some good. I thought maybe some small part of him would crave reconciliation with his daughter. But my optimism faded fast when he said, "I'm gonna kill you real ugly, you little bitch." He took off across the bay at us, full of hunger and hate, and his pack fell in behind him.

Cassie slapped the panel next to the door, and the door hissed open. We burst out of the chamber at a panicked pace, but it wasn't fast enough. Suddenly, Wilson was on Cassie. Within two seconds, he'd punched her in the face twice and started choking her. This was her father. The savagery of it was unnatural—unfathomable. I dived at him, landing clumsily on his back and sliding my forearm under his chin. I tightened my grip with an involuntary growl. He reared up, clawing at my forearm like a wild animal. But I had him in a solid hold—until I felt fists connecting with my kidneys. All three of the other guys were working me over. It was agony. My theory that I was becoming immune to pain due to my day-in, day-out beatings went out the window, and I started to lose my grip on Wilson. Then his whole body jerked violently, as if seizing. He flew back, hurling himself and me into the others, and we all spilled to the floor gracelessly. When I looked up, I saw Cassie was standing over her father, holding the still-sparking shock stick. I'd forgotten she had it. Her face was blank, and her hand was trembling. She was deep into shock.

I leaped up, grabbed the shock stick, and waved it menacingly at Wilson and his pack as they lumbered to their feet. Then I saw the bag of Normanium Prime crystals lying on the ground near them. Apparently, it had been knocked from my pocket during the scuffle. Wilson followed my gaze, and a Joker-like grin stretched across his face as he spotted the bag and leaned down to pick it up. I cursed under my breath.

"What have we here?" He peeked inside the bag. "Hm. Pretty."

He made eye contact with me, held up the bag, then tilted his head toward Cassie.

"Trade ya."

"You sick son of a bitch!" I growled.

Then he shrugged, pocketed the bag, and took a step toward me, testing my resolve. I lunged forward with the shock stick, and he backed off. But only half a step. All four of them shifted from foot to foot, as if weighing the risks and rewards of rushing us. The shock stick would hurt, but it wouldn't hold them all off. It was only a matter of time until they decided to overpower us. As I backed us down the corridor, that time ran out. They howled and charged toward us.

We turned and ran for it. Without the crystals, we were officially screwed, but I figured it didn't matter. Without Arthur, our chances of escape had been pretty near zero anyway. We were in pure survival mode. We rounded a corner, and then another and another, tormented by the echo of stampeding footsteps bearing down on us. We had nowhere to go. No plan to get there. No hope. It seemed like things couldn't possibly get any worse. But they could. And they did. As we barreled down the next corridor, the two guards that had pursued us earlier stepped into view, along with Malcolm and his two remaining henchmen. We frantically reversed direction, only to see Wilson and his pack rounding the corner from the other end of the corridor.

Everyone stopped. They'd registered they were all after the same thing: us. And both sides seemed hesitant to provoke a charge from the other by making the move to claim us. Apparently, everything we'd heard about the guards' precarious hold over the level-one lifers was true. The guards had the guns, but the prisoners had the PDQ addiction.

"Convicts!" one of the guards bellowed at Wilson and his hyenas. "Return to your duties." There was no response, and the pack stood their ground.

I finally noticed a door a few feet behind us and smashed my palm against the entry panel. It beeped but didn't open. I realized it was a high-security bay.

Then I knew where we were. We were standing outside the hangar. We'd reached our destination. Of course, we couldn't get in because we had no pass code, and now we were going to be killed or end up serving a sentence that would make us wish we had been.

"Convicts!" the guard repeated. "Stand down!" But Wilson took a step forward. The guards stepped closer now, too, the leader threatening, "Return to your duties! I won't ask again!"

I looked over at Cassie. We'd both been through a nightmare, but the trauma she was dealing with outweighed mine by a mile. Tears were running down her face, and she seemed almost catatonic. Seeing her like that might have been the worst part of it all. It made me feel like I'd been hit in the chest by the Rhino at a full sprint. I knew I'd done this. My stupid plan had led us here. Everything that had happened was my fault. I lunged at the entry panel again and hammered my fists against it in desperate frustration. Nothing.

And then . . . something. The door slid open and there, in front of us, was Arthur, covered in traces of ice.

"You knocked?" he said.

Wilson's gang rushed forward from one end of the corridor, and the guards rushed forward from the other as I shoved Arthur backward into the hangar, dragging Cassie with us.

"The door!" I yelled at Arthur. "Close the door!"

The door hissed shut as Arthur paused with that now-familiar far-off look. Then four red lights illuminated above the door, and a klaxon sounded in the hallway, drowning out the sounds of a short scuffle and several gunshots. I guessed the guards had subdued the inmates because only the guards would have the code we heard punched into the access panel on the other side of the door a moment later. Cassie and I braced ourselves for their entry, but the code was met with a sharp tone, and the door remained closed. We heard the code entered again with the same result. This continued.

"Hmph. G-g-good luck, blockheads," Arthur scoffed.

He turned to look at us. "They're quarantined. I flooded the system with fake s-s-sensor data indicating toxic contaminants in the corridor outside. They're not opening this door or any other door in that h-h-hallway. Not before the three-hour cooling-off period is up, anyway."

We didn't respond. We just stared at him, dumbstruck. Then Cassie threw her arms around him. I followed suit.

"How the hell—" I started.

"Well, I don't recommend going outside without a s-s-space suit. All the air tried to escape my body, and I bloated up to about twice m-m-my natural size. Then I started to freeze."

I cringed.

"But I didn't feel it because m-m-my pain receptors shut down, and I was able to g-g-grab hold of a loose cable running from an antennae array before I drifted too far from the ship. Then I clawed my way aft and g-g-got in here through one of the air locks."

"Took the easy way, huh?" I joked. Although I wasn't so sure I was joking, considering the hell we'd been through. I looked at Cassie. Discovering that Arthur was alive had triggered a rebound in her spirits, but the run-in with her father had left her shaken in a way that wouldn't fade fast. Arthur noted her troubled countenance and asked, "What exactly happened to you g-g-guys?"

"We had a rough go of it," I said. It was a gross understatement, but now wasn't the time to rehash it all. Arthur got the message.

"Well you're s-s-safe now," he said. "But our escape's not over yet." He walked toward the other end of the hangar, and I noticed them for the first time: the Javelins. There were two of them, occupying all but one of the docking ports. Portions of them were obscured by the hangar walls, but from the sections I could see, I was able to work out their basic form.

While presumably named for the Justice League's space jets, they didn't look much like them. Each one was roughly the length and width of a large city bus, contoured like an elongated bullet – with a bank of windows protruding from a front section through which a flight deck could be seen. About two-thirds of the way back, enormous doughnut-shaped structures wrapped around their hulls, anchored by six struts. And then there were the rear thrusters: triangular arrays of three sleek but gigantic disc-shaped drives, each at least eight feet in diameter.

Arthur tapped a panel beside one of the air locks, and it whirred open. "I've been interfacing with this ship since we h-h-hatched our plan," he said. "A lot of the science is beyond me, but I think I know my way around the controls w-w-well enough."

I looked over at Cassie, and her eyes fell, reminding me of what I'd forgotten in all the excitement.

"Shit!" I said.

"What is it?" Arthur asked.

"We lost the crystals," I answered cheerlessly.

"W-w-what?" He frowned in disbelief.

"We had to leave them behind. Cassie's father has them."

"What the—" he started. "How in the w-w-world could—"

"It's a long story."

"Goldarnit!" he exclaimed. "G-g-goldarnit!!"

He thought for a moment, then shrugged.

"Well I don't know about you guys, but I don't want to be s-s-standing here when they get that door open. And w-w-we've still got conventional propulsion." That was true, of course. We could still make it to Earth.

"Heck, maybe we can make it planetside and g-g-get ahold of some Normanium before Norman s-s-solves the Normanium Prime puzzle," Arthur ventured.

I felt a flutter of hope, but then I remembered Norman didn't need to solve the puzzle.

"Our crystals are bound to land in his hands long before we get back to Earth," I lamented. "No way the guards don't take them off Cassie's dad."

"Right," Arthur sighed. But he wasn't done trying to rally us. "Still, guys, escaping is s-s-something."

"Yeah," I agreed. "You're right." It wasn't everything we'd set out to accomplish, but it beat getting beat to death. I looked at Cassie, and I could tell she was feeling the same combination of resignation and consolation I was.

We followed Arthur through the air lock and onto the ship. The interior couldn't have been more like a sci-fi movie set. Soothing blue illumination emanated from sources unseen above us. Nearly every surface was polished black steel except the floor, which was lined with some sort of oversize industrial-grade Bubble Wrap that cushioned and cradled every footfall.

At the end of the hall to our left, there was a plexiglass panel, insulating a small chamber. The walls within were filled with dials, levers, and compartments of varying sizes. A holo-projection of the Javelin hovered centrally, with various parts of the vessel highlighted in green and data streams scrolling beside them. I knew the chamber must serve as the engine room because I'd seen a similar (though much more expansive) scene in the engine room of the Charon once while addressing a sewage line problem.

As we followed Arthur toward the front, we noted a small but well-stocked kitchen area and four habitation suites, running side by side. Glancing into one of the suites, I noticed a crate of explosives we'd often used to excavate large areas when we were working on Mars. They seemed somewhat out of place. This ship was a passenger vessel, not part of a mining fleet.

"What the hell are those for?" I asked.

"No idea," Arthur said.

It was strange, but the explosives were very stable stuff, and they posed no danger to us. So it wasn't a mystery that needed solving right now.

Arthur and Cassie continued up to the flight deck, but I hung back to poke around the hab suite a bit more. The accommodations were luxurious but superefficient, with a sink and shower module, wall-mounted holo-pod, and a very roomy, pseudo-amorphous orange chair.

I gazed out the window that occupied nearly an entire wall. The vastness of space peered back at me. Obviously, I'd seen it before, but right now it felt bigger, more endless than ever. I don't know how long I stood there, mesmerized, but I snapped out of it when I heard Arthur call out, "Here we g-g-go!"

I rushed up to the flight deck. There were two sets of two jump seats set against the walls to my left and right. Cassie was standing between them, and I could see Arthur seated beyond her in a fifth, more central command seat, behind a massive console arrayed with a mixture of physical controls and holo-readouts. Arthur tapped several buttons, and the ship's magnetic couplings disengaged from the air lock. Then he activated the lateral thrusters, and we drifted a few dozen yards from the Charon before he eased a slider forward, which I took to be the main throttle.

We sailed away from the Charon at a healthy clip. As I watched it slip into the distance behind us, I felt as if a weight was being lifted from my shoulders, and a swell of hope came over me. That hope grew as Arthur shared the next steps he'd been cooking up. He said he could easily create new identities for us, so if Norman Corp wanted us found, it would be an uphill battle. Plus, we'd never have to worry about money because he also had an idea of how he could digitally swipe all we'd ever need from Norman Corp's coffers. He called it "our retirement package."

We'd made it out, and it looked like we were going to be okay. It was hard to believe. But it would have been even harder to believe that we'd turn around and go right back.

CHAPTER  14

WE'D BEEN FLYING FOR AROUND AN HOUR, AND THE ADRENALINE of our escape was finally starting to wear off.

"I want to get a little farther out before I engage the autopilot," Arthur said. "But you guys can g-g-go get cleaned up if you want."

"You sure?" I asked.

"Yup."

The stench of sewage coming off the three of us had become hard to handle in the confined space of the flight deck. And I could tell Cassie needed to put more than physical distance between her and the episode with her father. A shower and a change of clothes might be a good start.

"Shall we?" I asked her.

She nodded, and we walked back toward the hab suites. As we reached the first one, I said, "You want to take this one?"

"No, you go ahead," she answered.

I didn't move. The fact that the cushy life ahead of us came at the cost of conceding the U.A.T. to Norman had felt bittersweet, but only now was the sweet part really sinking in. Without the Challenge, our philosophical differences were sort of immaterial. It seemed like we could be together. However, at the moment, she seemed further away than ever. Her recent trauma had set off a self-defense mechanism, and the wall between us had been fully restored, even fortified. I didn't know what to say or do to reverse that, but I made a feeble effort.

"Are you . . . okay?" I asked.

"Sure," she said.

It wasn't a convincing answer. Still, it felt like I should leave it alone—like what she needed was space. But as I reluctantly opened the door to the hab suite and entered, she put out a hand to stop the door from closing. For a second, I thought I'd read her body language all wrong and she was going to push her way in to initiate another face-sucking spree. I didn't know how I'd feel about that, considering her psychological state. But she didn't come in. She just held the door and peered up into my eyes. I could see she didn't know how to start.

"I'm . . . not okay," she finally stammered.

"Of course you're not okay," I said softly. "I can barely deal with what we went through. And for you, it was . . . I mean you'd told me some of the story—some of what he was like. But now with the PDQ, he's . . . he's an animal."

She looked away as tears began to run down her cheeks. I grasped her chin lightly and tilted it back up so her eyes met mine again.

"But you have to remember something," I said. "You ran fifty thousand volts through his ass. Maybe you're not okay, but you're not the frightened, helpless little girl he threatened in that court room anymore either."

Something flashed in her face. Pride or hope or a bit of both—not enough to light up the room, but a spark. Then she took my hand and kissed it. It felt like the first time I'd ever said anything that mattered. It was an amazing feeling. But three seconds later that feeling was replaced by pure, unadulterated agony.

It hit me hard and it hit me fast. It was like the episode I'd had in the crating bay after the Normanium canisters had blown, but the volume was turned up—way, way up. The world started spinning out of control, and I felt my body temperature spike through the roof as I fell to the floor, seizing violently.

I heard Cassie screaming for Arthur, and then I was dimly aware of both of them leaning over me, trying to hold me steady. But they started to fade away as the pain rose to an unbearable level. Then . . . it stopped. Just like in the crating bay, it ended as suddenly as it had begun, leaving only that strange swollen sensation throughout my body.

I opened my eyes to see Cassie and Arthur staring down at me, panicked and disoriented.

"I think I'm alright," I said shakily.

"What just happened?" Cassie cried. Her concern for my well-being seemed to have shunted aside her remaining gloom.

"I'm not sure," I said. "But it was worse than the last one."

"This has happened before?" she exclaimed.

"You m-m-mean after the explosion in the crating bay," Arthur recalled.

"Yeah," I confirmed. "I told Jerry about it. But he didn't seem that concerned."

"That g-g-guy couldn't even tell that I had metal bones," Arthur replied. "We're getting you a real doctor as s-s-soon as we get back to Earth."

I nodded. I'd been able to shrug off the first episode, but a second, more intense episode couldn't be ignored. There was something wrong with me, and it was getting worse. Arthur's misgivings about him aside, even Jerry had acknowledged that I'd taken a lot of radiation. That was hitting home now, and it was scaring me. From the looks on their faces, it was scaring Arthur and Cassie too. But I didn't see the point in letting them worry, so I did my best to quell my fears and get back to business as usual.

"I'm . . . gonna take that shower," I said.

As I got up, I could see they were trying to think of something to say or do to bring me comfort, so I added, "I'm okay, guys. Like Arthur said, I'll see a doctor when we get planetside. I'm sure it's no big deal."

The shower didn't wash my worry away. But it did get rid of the ungodly gunk that had been covering my body. I found several flight suits of different sizes hanging in a small closet beside the door. I put one on, then seated myself in the big orange chair. After pressing a few buttons on a control panel beside it, I found it was endlessly adjustable – the shape and density of its vinyl surface reconfiguring through the manipulation of some sort of gel filling. Within about a minute, I was out like a light. But even with the help of the wonder chair, I wasn't granted the peaceful siesta I'd hoped for. Instead I was treated to a message from my subconscious. And apparently, my subconscious was pissed.

I was once again transported into the pages of the Scriptures. This time, I was a passive observer in the latter half of the first issue of Marvel's limited series, *Infinity Gauntlet* (1991), in which the intergalactic supervillain Thanos uses the Infinity Gauntlet to harness the power of all six Infinity Stones, rendering him nigh omnipotent. I floated above the scene like a ghost, watching as Thanos and his sidekick, Mephisto, confabbed about Thanos's unrequited crush on Lady Death, whose insistence on giving him the cold shoulder was plunging him into madness. I heard Mephisto remind Thanos that all he needed to do to earn Lady Death's affection was fulfill his oath to her. What oath had he made? To wipe out half of all life in the universe. Because, you know, love makes a fool of us all.

I knew what came next. Thanos would turn away, raise his hand to the heavens, and snap his fingers, setting his diabolical plan in motion. Then, in one scene after another, I would see beloved residents of the Marvel universe fade from existence – a nice, palatable, PG genocide. But as Thanos's fingers snapped, that's not what I saw. I saw my parents' deaths. I saw cancer wards filled with victims of Normanium poisoning. I saw Cassie and Arthur and everyone else I cared about lying dead in a mass grave. Then, the scene cut back to Thanos, but as he turned to face me, I saw that it wasn't Thanos at all. It was Luthor Norman.

I awoke. Not just literally but figuratively. The hard knocks we'd taken during our escape had jarred my Scripture programming. My shortsighted self-preservation instincts had taken over. But the fog was clearing. The visceral power of my dream had triggered a primal fear of a future where Norman was allowed to attain the U.A.T.

On the surface, my seizure had made me ask, "What if I die?" But on a deeper level, it had made me ask, "What if I live?"

Now, more than ever, it felt like I had to measure up to my beliefs. And there was only one way to do that.

★

"We have to turn around," I said to Arthur and Cassie after assembling them in my hab suite.

"What?!" Arthur shrieked.

"We need more crystals, and the Charon is the only place to get the Normanium we need to make them before it's too late."

"Are you out of your m-m-mind?!" he shrieked louder. "What about getting you to a doctor?"

"It can wait awhile," I said.

"Clayton—" Cassie started. But I cut her off.

"We can't quit," I insisted. "We just can't. This is bigger than us. Look at what's happened with Norman as just a regular rich asshole—all the misery and death he's caused. How much worse does it get when he's in control of some otherworldly power? How bad will life on Earth be with a psychotic superemperor?"

"Yeah, we know, w-w-we know," Arthur said. "But what chance do we h-h-have of doing anything about it now?"

"Maybe the same chance Cap had against Thanos."

"What?" Arthur said. "What's that m-m-mean?"

"He's talking about Captain America standing up to an evil periwinkle space god," Cassie offered.

"How d-d-did it turn out?" Arthur asked.

"Cap got killed," she answered.

"Perfect!" he squawked.

"The point is, he stood by his principles," I said. "Plus his death was only implied. And Nebula reversed it."

"Well the stuff that's going to happen to us if we g-g-go traipsing back onto the Charon won't be implied or reversed!" Arthur responded. "And what if it's all for nothing? What if your g-g-guy Cateklysm is as big a fraud as everyone thinks?"

"He foresaw we'd discover Normanium Prime two decades ago," I countered. "How much of a fraud can he be?"

"Well, funny you should m-m-mention Normanium Prime because like you said, the batch we left behind is bound to make its way to Norman. He could already h-h-have it. He could have set sail already."

"Maybe," I said. "And maybe not."

"But there won't be any 'maybe' about it if we wait the six weeks it'll take us to get back to Earth," Cassie chimed in. I realized my revitalized conviction was quelling not only her resolve to get me to a doctor but any kindling fantasies she'd had about a Challenge-free future together. I knew I'd mourn the latter, but I had no choice.

"S-s-so you're in?" Arthur asked her, exasperated.

"Yes and no," she answered. Then she turned to me. "Why the Charon? Why not another mining ship? Or Mars, for that matter?"

"Schedule's the same as always," I said. "The only mining ship anywhere near us is the Christy."

"Which is on its w-w-way to Mars," Arthur interjected, finishing my thought. "The only Normanium onboard will be its fuel, w-w-which is as useless as the Javelin's."

"And as for Mars," I said, "Malcolm will have our bio-identifiers and mugs plastered all over the Norman Corp network by now."

"Which makes the single point of access at the worksites a deal breaker," Cassie conceded.

"So where d-d-does that leave us?" Arthur asked.

"You know where I stand," I answered.

Arthur looked at Cassie. "And h-h-how about you?"

She paused for a moment. She may have been game to re up for the Challenge, but knowing her father was on the Charon surely made the idea of going back more terrifying for her than us. Still, she steeled herself and said, "Never compromise. Not even in the face of Armageddon."

It was a quote from one of *Watchmen's* only pseudo-redeemable characters, Rorschach. And it left little room for interpretation.

Arthur shook his head and sighed.

"Arthur," I started. "Maybe we can leave you out of it. We could find a supply ship and –"

"Oh, shut up," he cut me off. "I was a g-g-goner before you guys put your lives on the line – for me and your Chowderhead crusade. So maybe you're too noble for your own g-g-good. Or maybe you're just crazy. But I'm not w-w-walking away until you do."

I smiled gratefully and patted him on the shoulder. Then he added, "But you w-w-will need to tell me how in the heck we're going to get on and off the Charon without g-g-getting our backsides handed to us."

"We'll think of something," I assured him. Though I had no idea what that something would be.

CHAPTER  15

ARTHUR WENT TO TURN THE SHIP AROUND, LEAVING CASSIE and me alone. She seemed nervous and restless. I wasn't sure what was bothering her, but there was a long list of suspects, from our yo-yo-ing feelings about the Challenge, to what she'd been through with her dad, to our plan to return to the Charon. I guessed the culprit was the last one.

"You sure you're sure about this?" I asked.

"If you hadn't turned us around, I eventually would have," she answered without hesitation. Apparently, I'd guessed wrong. She stood and walked out of the room. I didn't know if she was coming back. But she did, and she was holding her holo-pod.

"You show me yours, I'll show you mine," she said nervously. The source of her angst was clear now. If we were serious about all this – and we'd better be, considering what we were risking – we needed to start figuring out where we were really headed. And even though I'd said I was ready to share my Conundrum diary with her days before, I understood the jitters she was feeling because I'd just started feeling them too. Our Conundrum solutions were the product of thousands of hours of research, and revealing their contents to anyone else felt like handing over our firstborn. Still, the time had come.

I grabbed my holo-pod from the closet, then crossed to the wonder chair and tapped a few buttons on its control panel, configuring it into a giant bench. We both took a seat with our holo-pods in our laps. But as we powered them on and I prepared to enter my password, Cassie put her hand on mine and said, "In for a dime, in for a dollar."

She took my holo-pod and handed me hers, as if initiating some sort of trust pact. Then she said, "Hera give me strength."

I nodded because I was all for Hera giving her strength. But as she stared at me impatiently, I realized she'd just told me her password.

As I typed it in, I said, "No evil shall escape my sight." She didn't mistake this as a heroic proclamation. She just typed it in.

Our default feeds popped up. They were at miniature scale at the moment, so we weren't able to compare Conundrums yet. But even at miniature size, I recognized the M.U. homepage among her feeds. I also noticed a 3D model of Mjolnir. I tapped that feed, and it enlarged. The holographic hammer rotated slowly in front of us, with dozens of annotations noted in the air around it like a conspiracy theorist's mosaic. I looked over at her.

"2 Across is totally fakakta!" she growled in tight-lipped vexation.

I sighed and nodded. She was as clueless as I was about *The most worthy weapon*. I hoped we didn't have any more blanks in common. I tapped her Conundrum feed gingerly, and she tapped mine, both of us as nervous as if we were undressing one another for the first time. That metaphor fell apart pretty quickly, though, because when I saw the goods, I shouted, "What the shit?!" I was staring at her answer to 9 Across.

"You think *Green ring teacher* is 'Zreg?!'" I barked. "What the hell is a Zreg?! I've read every issue of Green Lantern ever. Ever! There is no Zreg."

"Aw. 'Green ring' made you think Green Lantern, huh?" she said. "Well, he's a Skrull."

"What?!" I yelled. "Did you just plug in some billy'd-up four-letter name that had r as the second letter?"

"Yeah. That's what I did, eye scream[6]," she retorted. As she continued, I saw her reinvigorated, her lingering anguish miraculously stripped away. "For your information, Z'Reg turned his back on his evil Skrull brethren to become Freedom Ring's mentor, starting in *Marvel Team-Up* #20, July 2006. And as I'm sure you recall, Skrulls are green—even if they're not good enough for your precious sludge scale."

I was flabbergasted. This was some next-level Chowderheading. I reflected in astonishment on the fact that she'd always been in it alone. Unlike me, she hadn't had anyone to give her a huge leg up.

"You're amazing," I stated matter-of-factly.

She blushed. Then her eyes went wide, and her mouth dropped open as she stared at my feed.

"Star Lord?" she exclaimed. "Star Lord?!"

She was staring at my answer to 7 Across, *The liberation he led proved the pen is mightier than the sword*.

"Oh come on," I said. "*Guardians of the Galaxy* #8, 2013? Star-Lord sneaks into the Peak space station to rescue Abigail Brand and blows the place up before Thanos can use it to attack Earth?"

"So?" she said.

"So the Peak is S.W.O.R.D. headquarters and Star-Lord is—"

"Peter QUILL," she muttered. "As in pen. I AM SUCH a schmegeggy!"

---

6   *Chowderhead slang, meaning a person who is lame beyond belief. Origin: The Marvel mutant Eye-Scream, whose claim to fame is the ability to turn himself into any flavor of ice cream.*

But our shame trading was just beginning. A tsunami of self-loathing crashed over me as I learned that the clue for 4 Across, *Without the gift he gave, the obelisk would have been transformed into trash*, referred to the sun god Ra, who granted DC's Metamorpho the powers of "transformation" he used to foil the Phantom of Washington's plans to topple the Washington Monument (*First Issue Special* #3, 1975). I hadn't read it, and I was still asking myself how I could be such a lazy, useless moron, when Cassie said, "The Shadow? No. No, that's wrong." She was referring to my answer to 5 Across, *The eagle who was trapped in Valhalla*, and her voice was shaking, as if she'd gotten the results of a medical test indicating a terminal condition.

"You're crazy," she asserted. "Did you read some crossover issue where the Shadow skips across the Bifrost to die a good death at the hands of a Frost Giant? No, you didn't, because there is no such issue! So there's no way the flippin' Shadow is getting into Valhalla, and no way you are not chock-full of horse shit!"

I gave her a moment to regain her composure, then reported the facts. "Actually, the Shadow's civilian identity is Kent Allard, famed French aviator in World War I, aka the Black Eagle or Dark Eagle, depending on your source. And in issue #90 (1948) of *The Shadow Comics*, the Shadow is trapped in the Valhalla Lodge by the evil Professor Sontalk."

Her face was a canvas of awe. She was speechless. To be fair, I'd been conditioned to see what most Chowderheads would miss by my early immersion in off-brand titles. But still, a few minutes later, I was surprised by Cassie's shocking ignorance regarding Valiant Comics. Not only was she a total tourist when it came to Valiant's raised-from-the-dead supersoldier Bloodshot, but she was wholly unaware of the fact that Valiant had been purchased by Acclaim Entertainment in 1994. This tidbit brought home the Bloodshot-based 7 Down, *Acclaimed undead's undercover underworld alias*, allowing me to score another point in our head-to-head Chowderhead duel with "Mortalli." (As in "Angelo Mortalli," the civilian identity Bloodshot assumed while infiltrating the mob.)

"I knew I shouldn't have back-burnered Valiant!" Cassie berated herself. "Oy vey! I'm such a dilettante!"

"Don't feel bad," I consoled her. "I only know this stuff because it's my specialty."

"Don't patronize me, nimrod. I'm not the one who's missing 1 Across."

I hadn't yet noticed her solution to 1 Across, *The Marvel with the greatest destiny*. There's a Marvel character named Destiny, which was the obvious and wrong answer. I'd tried other less obvious options like Destiny Ajaye, the teenage tactical savant heroine of Top Cow's Genius. And I'd tried plenty of long-shot options. But I'd never found a fit. Cassie had: Rick Jones.

She started rambling, "The dude's destiny was to be the ultimate Marvel kangster. He was host to Mar-Vell and Genis-Vell, he partnered up with Cap as Bucky, he was A-Bomb and the Whisperer. How many people have had that many hero identities? And even when he wasn't in tights, he was smack-dab in the middle of tons of major Marvel events, including Hulk's origin. Of course, if you want to get literal about it, there's the matter of being imbued with the Destiny Force and becoming so juiced he single-handedly took out the Kree's entire invading fleet in *Avengers* #97, 1972." She goaded me, "Remember that? Hm? Remember?"

I didn't remember. And hearing it now, the answer had actually been pretty damn obvious. I had no defense.

"Don't feel bad," she parroted my words from moments before. "I only know this stuff because I'm smarter than you."

"I won't argue with that," I said.

"Hm. Maybe you're smarter than I thought."

It was like we were suspended in a bubble, insulated from everything we'd been through and where we were headed. The fear of exposing our answers had metamorphosed into a thrilling intimacy, granting us a reprieve from our circumstances. We were our old selves again. But the magic of the moment began to slip away as we realized we'd run out of information to share, and we were still missing three answers.

"Shit," Cassie said. "What now?"

"I guess we could plug our new and improved set of key letters into the secret message grid," I answered.

It was a lackluster suggestion. Cassie's experience with inputting an incomplete solution set had been the same as mine, and the answers we had yet to find held a lot of key letters. But I figured it couldn't hurt to give it a whirl. I was wrong.

When we finished, the message read: C_ _ _ _ R _ REAARCRALEREL _ _ LRCL. We stared at it. Then we both said something like, "Goddamn it shit crap shit!"

It was worse than it had ever been before. The new key letters hadn't simply revealed a load of gibberish – they'd revealed the now-undeniable truth: we had to have a lot of wrong answers. That was hard to fathom when you took into account the overlaps between letters and the fact that we'd arrived at most of the answers separately, suggesting that they weren't crazy guesses.

"Maybe it's not as bad as it looks," I said, clinging to denial.

"Well that's a relief," Cassie answered. "Because it looks really bad. It looks like all we've got to go on is . . ." She squinted at our solution, sounding it out, "KREER-KRA-LEREL-LERKEL!"

Of course, I knew she was right. It did look really bad. We'd bet everything on the notion that we'd be able to fill in each other's blanks – that we'd come away with a complete or near complete Conundrum. Instead, we were staring at a dead end, and all our grand plans were going down in flames.

But I wasn't done. I refused to be done. My pigheadedness burrowed its way through the hopelessness and unfurled into an idea.

"This isn't over," I said.

"How do you figure?" Cassie demanded, as if I'd said up was down.

"We're going to get help."

"From who?"

"The M.U."

"What? No one there is going to help us. Give away an answer, give away the world. Sound familiar?"

"Sure, except Luthor Norman is about to get the world, and we're the only ones who can stop him."

"Says us," she scoffed. "Why would they take our word for it?"

"Well, for one thing, every Chowderhead is wired to believe Norman's the kind of underhanded, megalomaniac bastard who would do what he's done. And for another, we're going to give them all our answers."

She paused thoughtfully. Our case against Norman was mostly circumstantial. I knew, even to most Chowderheads, it could sound far-fetched. But ponying up sixteen solutions on an open channel was unheard of. Sure, we thought some of the answers had to be wrong, but plenty of them were right – and the bold gesture would prove we were legit. After all, if our story was bullshit, what would we have to gain by blindly leveling the playing field?

I waited for Cassie to respond. A half hour before, we'd barely been ready to share our answers with each other, so for me to propose sharing them with everyone on the M.U. was a dramatic shift. I'd rapidly moved through the emotions involved, but I wasn't sure she was with me.

"It could work," she said. "And I guess . . . I guess there's nothing to lose." Then, she looked at me and finished, "Let's do it."

With that, we started writing up our Chowderhead rally cry, channeling the pomp power of Stan Lee's mighty Marvel meter . . .

Attention, True Believers! We know your hatred of Luthor Norman burns hotter than the Human Torch! The Martian rocks he dug up are a cancer-causing calamity! The legislation he's launched makes a mockery of every child labor law on the books! Oh, and don't forget this frightful fiend has not one but TWO supervillain names!

Of course, some think his mission to save the world is his saving grace. But hold on to your hats, folks! 'Cause this nefarious nut job's not out to save anybody! That's all just PR puff! We believe he really did solve the Conundrum by coercing our ranks with bribes and even beatings. We also believe the solution pointed him to another solar system. Which is why he set out to build his fantastical faster-than-light ships and find an energy source to power them.

And now for the big, bad breaking news: he's just stumbled onto that energy source! The stuff's a dead ringer for Pentagramite, as foretold by Cateklysm himself! That's right, friends! Norman's got the goods to get to his goal! And we cannot let that happen. From Billy Kincaid to Kingpin to Red Skull to Ra's al Ghul to Brainiac to Brainiape, the Scriptures have spoken the truth: evil never rests! And the resolve to do right must be our guiding light!

Think we're all talk? Think again! We've stolen one of the F.T.L. ships in hopes of beating this dastardly do-badder to the booty. So it's us or him now. But we need your Conundrum answers to point the way. We know what we're asking, and we do not ask it lightly. That is why you will find every one of our own answers attached to this message. Some of them may be wrong. But helping us is right. Because the choice is simple: give away an answer or give the world to Luthor Norman!

We'd gone to the mat over various clauses and word choices, but reading it over one last time, we both agreed it was done. We posted it to the M.U. mass message board, setting it to resend every ten minutes, as we knew it would be gobbled up by a scrolling stream of babble on the channel. Then I turned on the wall-mounted holo-pod and brought up the site. This would allow us to accept audio chat requests.

I felt good about our chances. Despite the extreme measures we thought it had taken Norman to find all the answers, eleven years had passed. It was definitely possible, even probable, that others had since gotten it done the old-fashioned way—only to join Norman at the dead end of F.T.L. travel. If such people were indeed out there, they were both the most likely to buy our story and the most able to help us. I hoped our plea would inspire them to do exactly that.

A half hour later, we hadn't received a single response. Even though it was the middle of the night where most Chowderheads lived, this was discouraging. But our attention was redirected by Arthur when he popped his head in and said, "We're getting close. So now would be a g-g-good time to talk about the plan."

Both he and Cassie looked at me expectantly.

"Right," I said. In all the Conundrum excitement, I hadn't made much headway on how we'd accomplish the seemingly impossible feat of getting onto the Charon and back off with a boatload of Normanium.

But I was saved by the bell. There was a chime, and a green telephone icon began blinking on the M.U. interface, indicating an incoming chat request from R33D R1CHARD5. I'd never seen the handle before. I tapped the icon, accepting the request.

"Well I underestimated the shit out of you, kid. You've got balls. Big ones."

There was no mistaking the owner of the voice. Even before Arthur and I had had the pleasure of meeting Norman up close, we'd all heard enough Norman Corp PR broadcasts to recognize his syrupy intonation.

"The old M.U. boards," he mused. "I thought maybe I'd run across somebody who'd give me a clue as to how much you knew, but I didn't expect that somebody to be you."

Cassie hit mute and squeaked, "Holy shit!"

We'd known our misappropriation of the Javelin would ping on Norman's radar. But we hadn't thought it would rank high enough for him to come looking for us personally, never mind through the M.U. No one there had heard from him in years. It all added up to one conclusion.

"It's all true," Arthur said to me. "Everything you g-g-guessed."

"Yeah—and he knows we know!" Cassie added. "And now he's seen our post!"

"Hold on," I said, heading off the panic. "Let's not freak."

Jarring as it was, I realized Norman being wise to our M.U. post changed nothing.

"What's he gonna do, launch some smear campaign on the M.U. to attack our credibility?" I said. "He's using a handle no one's ever even seen before."

While Cassie was a bit of a cyberhermit, I had a standing that could easily weather flak from a newb.

"You're right," Cassie said, trying to calm her nerves. "And I guess it's our answers that are gonna make or break us. There's nothing he can do to put that genie back in the bottle."

Arthur didn't know what we were talking about, but he seemed relieved by our relief.

"Hello?" Norman prodded. "Anybody there?"

I unmuted him and said, "Fuck you and the horse you rode in on."

I figured we'd passed the point of no return, and polite word choices weren't going to save us if we were ever caught.

"Fair enough," he replied evenly. "Consider me and my horse fucked. But let me just say, you guys have blown my mind. I mean when Mr. Pincher told me three Orphs had somehow created a pile of Normanium Prime and swiped a Javelin – and that one of those Orphs was frickin' R2-D2?!?!"

"I'm an android," Arthur blurted. "Not a trash can on w-w-wheels."

I was surprised he'd caught Norman's reference, but apparently his dad had familiarized him with the classics.

"Right! My apologies," Norman chuckled. If he was curious why an AI had a stutter, he didn't let on. "Anyway, I am furious about all this, but the Chowderhead in me is doing jumping jacks of joy. I just—"

"Did you call for a reason?" Cassie cut him off.

It was clear that she and Arthur were now both feeling the same euphoric "point of no return" fearlessness I was.

"Ah. You must be Cassie," Norman said cordially.

"That's right. And like I said, did you call for a reason? We're busy."

"Gotcha," he said. "Straight to business then."

"We have no business with you," I said.

"Not yet, no. But I want to propose an alliance. I need fuel, you obviously need Conundrum answers. We should join forces."

Cassie muted him again. "He thinks we still have the crystals. Maybe the guards didn't find them on my dad."

"Maybe," I said. "But it won't be long."

Someone would say something to someone, and the guards would be onto the crystals soon enough. But now I understood why Norman was lowering himself to contacting us. He thought we had something he didn't. He thought it was a question of whether we'd figure out the Conundrum before he figured out Normanium Prime.

I unmuted him and said, "Alliance, huh? Sounds great. Give us the solution to the Conundrum, and we'll let you know how it goes."

"That's a negative, Ghost Rider," he answered as if he was expecting my response. "You're obviously smart kids. Downright reedy. But there's no telling what lies ahead. That means we throw all the experience, resources, and man power we can at it."

"You think I'm going to team up with a piece of shit who beat the crap out of me?" I said.

"Oh. Yeah," he answered. "I was afraid that might be a sticking point."

"You're goddamn right," I confirmed. "But that's just the tip of the iceberg, you evil, double-villain-name-having dick."

"Geez, Louise!" he said, mildly exasperated. "When are you people going to get it through your thick Chowderhead skulls that I didn't choose my name? And what's in a name anyway? Look at George Bernard Shaw—the guy popularized the term *Superman*, but he had three supervillain names if you count, say, George Tarleton, Bernard Venton, and Mark Shaw."

Some of his choices were pretty obscure, and I could tell he was trying to impress us. And then he laid it on even thicker.

"Granted, Venton's mucho mel[7]. Maybe substitute Bernard Hoyster or Bernard Bonner there. Or maybe Bernard the Poet! I know he's not a supervillain per se—but he's a beatnik, which is way worse."

"We don't need your help," Cassie said, cutting his detour short.

"Right," Norman said. "Because of your brilliant M.U. post. Speaking from experience, I wouldn't hold my breath for a bunch of Chowderheads to share their secrets."

"Yeah, well, we're not some power-mad spoiled brats trying to bully our way to the finish line," Cassie said.

I thought there was a chance this remark would trigger the rage I'd witnessed in the infirmary. But it didn't. Apparently, his temper tantrums were reserved for situations in which he held all the cards. He took a deep breath.

"I know what you think of me," he began with a somber tone. "But it's not as simple as that. I'm a Chowderhead, same as you guys."

Cassie snorted at that, but he let it pass.

"For me, it started as a refuge—a place to hide from my abusive dad and my drunk mother."

Cassie and I were taken aback at this. Seeking solace in the Scriptures was the story of our lives, and never in a million years would we have imagined Luthor Norman shared the same story.

"But the more I read, the more I realized I had a responsibility," he continued. "I looked around and saw that as miserable as my life was, it was literally as good as it got. The world was that shitty. And I believed the Scriptures were telling me to do something about it—even if it got ugly. I still believe that. I've done horrible things. The list is longer than you know."

He paused, as if weathering a storm of regret. Then he pushed on.

---

7 *Chowderhead slang, meaning insignificant. Origin: An acronym for Matter-Eater Lad, a member of the Legion of Super-Heroes, whose ability to ingest matter of all kinds fell well short of elevating him to star status.*

"But I've never doubted my purpose. I'm here to make a better world by any means necessary. Humanity is on its last legs, and all I've done so far is slow the bleeding here and there. There's so much more to do, and I have faith that the U.A.T. can help us do it."

We sat with his words hanging in the air for a long while. Now I admit, I was afraid we wouldn't solve the Conundrum—afraid that our best chance may be to leverage our knowledge of how to make Normanium Prime into an alliance before our missing crystals landed in Norman's hands. So it may have been just desperation, but right there, and right then, what he'd said didn't sound totally bonkers. I'd been sure his motives were diabolical. I'd had no doubt that he was simply a powerful jerk who craved what all powerful jerks crave: more power. But now, doubt crept in. Was it possible he was telling the truth? Could he be a decent human being underneath it all, driven to do terrible things by a noble purpose? In that moment, I thought *maybe*.

Then the moment passed and I said, "Not buying it, asshole."

I looked over at Arthur and inspiration struck. "And FYI, we figured out how to deactivate the safeguards that stop the Teen Machine here from going full Ultron. So we're coming in locked and loaded, and while my boy is ripping your guards limb from limb, I'm gonna track you down and get the answers we need while I'm punching your fucking face off!"

Then I disconnected from the session. Cassie and Arthur stared at me, slack-jawed.

"Don't worry," I said, "I've got a plan."

CHAPTER  16

ABOUT TWENTY MINUTES LATER, CASSIE AND I WERE SEATED around Arthur on the flight deck, watching the Charon lumber into view like a floating city, dwarfing our tiny vessel. Arthur banked and brought us around, lining us up parallel to the larger ship.

The crew of the Charon would know exactly where we were headed because we'd issued a request for docking permissions at the same air lock from which we'd departed. As we drifted within a few yards of the air lock, Arthur activated the magnetic contact plates surrounding the Javelin's docking port, which mated perfectly with those around the perimeter of the air lock, and we were pulled in with a soft clunk. Cassie and I left the flight deck and watched through the air lock window as Norman stormed into the hangar. While I'd been reasonably confident his pride would drive him to confront us personally, I was sure his common sense wouldn't allow him to show up solo, given my colorful claim about Arthur's "Ultron mode." I was right. He was flanked by a four-man security detail. Each of the men carried a gauss rifle, which could fire a round through a block of steel like it was Styrofoam at one hundred yards. The energy demands of the weapons had made them wildly impractical until the discovery of Normanium. Norman Corp: making murder faster and easier!

A moment after Norman's detail cleared the entrance, a steady stream of additional troops began filtering in. There had to be two dozen of them and counting. They weren't all carrying gauss rifles. Some were armed only with shock sticks. The fact that not everyone had broken out the heavy artillery suggested Norman was keeping his options open as to whether to capture or kill us. My guess was he was planning to send in the shock-stick brigade first, to see if he could take us alive, in order to beat the key to Normanium Prime out of us. But if Arthur really could tear them limb from limb as I'd claimed he could, I supposed Norman was confident the gauss gun firing squad could take any or all of us out as needed. Any losses would be acceptable losses, given his faulty operating assumption that we had plenty of the superfuel onboard our ship.

He led the mob over to our air lock and stared coldly at us as the transitional compartment between the Charon's interior and exterior doors began acclimating for passage. I was sure Malcolm was out there somewhere, but it was hard to spot him in the sea of identical uniforms, and my search was sidetracked when

I saw another guard running toward Norman. I recognized him as one of the bastards who had chased us to the hangar earlier, and as he reached Norman, he held something up, like an eager Labrador returning to his master with a dead duck. Unfortunately, the something wasn't a dead duck. It was the canvas sack Cassie's father had stolen from us. Sure, I'd expected him to be relieved of his treasure sooner or later, but I'd hoped for later.

"Shit," Cassie and I said in unison.

"What's g-g-going on back there?" Arthur asked.

We told him.

"Shoot," he said.

Judging from the unsuspecting look on Norman's face as he took the sack, the delivery boy hadn't called ahead. Maybe he thought making it a surprise would be more romantic. If so, he was right. Norman practically swooned when he saw what was inside. It was twenty times the amount of crystals he'd had to run his tests with. While he was a fan of the Scriptures, he'd clearly never put any stock in their intended meaning or Cateklysm's vision for humanity–but when it came to the power of the prize, he was as true a believer as any. And he now thought that prize was as good as his. He looked over at me smugly and activated the air lock intercom.

"Seems like that deal you didn't want is officially off the table. But there's still the matter of you 'punching my face off.'"

He stepped back, gesturing to his mob of stormtroopers.

"Well, bring it on, kid. My face is waiting."

Norman getting ahold of the crystals wasn't a welcome development, but given our master plan, it wasn't the end of the world either. I stared back at him with a forced calm that I hoped would mask my racing heart rate. Then, as a tone announced the completion of the air lock acclimation sequence, I called out, "Go ahead, Arthur!"

In the hangar, a klaxon sounded and four red status lights illuminated above the exit. A guard standing nearby looked up at the lights, befuddled. Then he tried entering the access code into the control panel beside the door and stared at it expectantly. Nothing happened. Norman glared at me, his arrogant facade cracking.

He stepped up and tried the air lock control panel. It beeped impotently. He tried several more times. Nada. Now he understood. The entire hangar had been quarantined. I waved and gave him a huge grin as the Javelin undocked and we drifted away from the air lock. We hung there for a moment to enjoy the growing discord. The guards tried the exit again. They tried the air locks to the other Javelin. They tried gesticulating angrily. All to no avail. They were trapped.

Norman looked like his head was going to explode. I didn't know if anyone had credited us with the faulty sensor readings behind the earlier quarantine. But even if they had, there was still no reason for them to expect this. On the face of it, it didn't make any sense. It seemed to amount to nothing more than a very elaborate, very risky prank – and it certainly wasn't going to get us the Conundrum answers Norman thought we'd come for. Of course, what we'd really come for was Normanium, and harebrained as it was, I had an idea of how to get onboard the Charon and get that Normanium without going through the hangar. We just needed room to operate. Now we had it.

My Ultron mode bluff had persuaded Norman to bring every last man he could find to take us down, leaving the rest of the ship running on a skeleton crew until the three-hour cooling off period had passed and manual diagnostics could be initiated to unseal the hangar. Yes, Norman's gang could try to free themselves with the welding torches lying around the hangar. But they'd find several of the adjacent areas were also quarantined. Plus, the torches weren't an option when it came to the air lock leading to the other Javelin due to the danger of uncontrolled decompression.

So while Norman now had our crystals, he couldn't use them any time soon, and once we had the raw Normanium we needed, we'd have a solid head start on him – assuming our M.U. gamble paid off. Things were going as planned. But there was some rain on the parade.

"Hey g-g-guys," Arthur said tensely. "I'm monitoring communications, and Norman just sent out a m-m-message to all security personnel." He paused and we heard him take a hit from his asthma inhaler. "H-h-he's offering a reward for killing us. A big one."

"Oy gevalt," Cassie muttered in shock.

I sighed heavily. There was now no question about what would happen to us if we were caught. But I tried to shrug that off and put on a brave face. "So what?" I said. "Most of security is locked up in the hangar, right?"

"I g-g-guess," Arthur answered half-heartedly.

As unsettling as it was that Norman had put a price on our heads, it wasn't surprising. Based on Arthur's energy consumption calculations, the son of a bitch now had enough Normanium Prime for a pretty long trip. And our deception had rubbed him the wrong way, so he wanted us dead more than he wanted help figuring out how to make more crystals.

Regardless, we needed to focus on the aforementioned harebrained idea I had to get onboard the Charon—which in and of itself had a decent chance of getting us killed.

✳

Arthur hit the vertical thrust, propelling us up the side of the Charon like a rising kite. We were headed for the fourth-level crating bay, where we knew we'd encounter Orphs rather than convicts on crating duty. Unlike our initial approach, it was a short trip—too short for any remaining guards to see where we were going and react before we got there and locked it down.

As the bay fell into view, one of the many reasons Norman wouldn't have anticipated our current course of action loomed before us. The crating bay air lock was huge because it was designed for gigantic hauling vessels. Its exterior door was easily half again as large as the corresponding door on the Javelin. Still, we thought there was a chance the air lock would achieve a vacuum. This wasn't totally loony because while the air lock's exterior door was much larger than the Javelin's docking port door, it wasn't larger than the docking port itself. So the connection would be like two elevators with mismatched doors opening on to one another, and the magnetic contact plates on the hulls of both ships would theoretically seal the area around those doors—assuming the plates themselves weren't too far out of alignment. Not totally loony, but pretty close.

Arthur initiated the docking sequence and we felt the Javelin jerk sideways, then collide with the hull of the Charon and vibrate violently. It was a far cry from the soft embrace of the hangar's air lock. After a moment, though, the ship settled and seemed relatively steady. The docking port pressure readings were jumping around, but the air lock's acclimation sequence activated, and it looked like the connection would serve its purpose for a short visit.

Of course, the fact that a jerry-rigged docking was pseudo-suicidal wasn't the last of the reasons for Norman to discard our plan as a threat. There was also the fact that he'd think we couldn't access any air lock aside from the one for which we'd been granted docking permissions—because he hadn't witnessed the close, personal relationship Arthur shared with every door on the ship.

Arthur did his thing, and the Javelin's exterior door and the air lock's exterior door creeped open in fits and starts, fighting past their poor synchronization. As we gazed into the air lock's transitional compartment, the ship suddenly lurched and wobbled, and our hearts stopped. Then, everything settled again, and I gathered my courage before stepping forward. Left foot. Right foot. Left foot. So far, so good. Arthur opened the air lock's interior door and I stepped through, with him and Cassie tiptoeing through on my heels.

As we cleared the air lock, we found four Orphs staring at us in dumbfounded shock: Atsumi, Duncan, Stibble, and . . . Decker. Ugh. The guy was like a bad penny. He shook off the shock and spoke.

"What the hell? I knew you were dumb as dirt, Clayborn, but to get away clean and then come back?"

"Pretend we're not here, moron," Cassie said. Suffice it to say, she shared my feelings about Decker.

"We only need a few minutes," I added, addressing the whole group.

"Screw that," Duncan said. "We don't want to be anywhere near you people."

He started for the exit, and the others followed him. News of our escape had traveled fast, and it wasn't a big leap to assume associating with us was bad for their health. However, apparently they hadn't registered the klaxon that had sounded in the hallway outside or the red lights glowing above the door. As they tried the control panel, it beeped irritably.

"S-s-sorry," Arthur said.

"Sorry? Sorry for what?" Duncan answered.

"Why does the door not work?" Atsumi asked nervously.

"The corridor outside is quarantined," Cassie said.

"What?!" Stibble broke character, speaking up aggressively for maybe the first time in his life. "Why?!"

"There's no danger," Cassie continued. "But you're going to be in here for a while."

"What about you?" Riley asked.

"We'll be gone as soon as we get what we came for," I answered.

"Not good enough. Not near good enough," Decker said. He stomped back over, red in the face. "You're gonna open up that damn door right now! And when the guards get here, you're gonna tell 'em that none of us"—he gestured to himself and the other three—"have any part in whatever bullshit you got goin' on!"

We ignored him and wheeled a Normanium bin over to the air lock. I wanted to put as little strain on the transitional chamber as possible. So I picked up a single canister and carried it gingerly through the passage. The chamber seemed stable, so Arthur and Cassie started passing me more canisters. They selected only the newest of the lot. We'd had our fill of chain-reaction explosions.

"Hello?" Decker said. "You sons o' bitches listening to a word I'm say—"

He stopped short, staring at Arthur's back. Arthur was no longer wearing his old charred and tattered jumpsuit because like me and Cassie, he'd changed into one of the flight suits hanging in his hab suite after showering. But I noticed now that the back collar of the flight suit was cut low enough to reveal a bit of his exposed metallic spine and shoulder blades.

"Shit fire!" Decker yelled, stumbling back several steps. "Are you . . . are you a goddamn robot?!"

Arthur shrugged and said, "I was as s-s-surprised as you are."

I saw the three Orphs near the door stiffen with disbelief and disgust. Their stunned expressions made it plain that whatever reports had spread about our escape had not included news of Arthur's androidism.

Decker retreated another few steps as we headed for a second bin of Normanium. We already had a whole lot, but we didn't know how much we'd need.

"You people are crazy as bullbats!" Decker yelled at Cassie and me. His resentment had boiled through his shock. "Harborin' an illegal AI? Stealin' Norman Corp property? And now you went and put us right in the middle of it! If you don't open that goddamn door right now—"

He was cut off by the hiss of a door opening. But it wasn't the crating bay door. We looked around, confused. Before we could make sense of what was happening, we heard the echo of hurried footsteps and saw a gauss pistol poke through the jagged tear in the wall between the crating bay and the reactor bay.

Malcolm started firing before his head had even cleared the opening. Cassie, Arthur, Decker, and I ducked behind the Normanium bin we'd been headed for as several rounds hit the wall behind us. It was an exterior wall, constructed of reinforced titanium. So as powerful as the gauss gun was, the rounds just bounced off and rained down on us as the manatee of a man clambered through the ruptured bulkhead and dropped clumsily to the floor below.

Evidently, the reason I hadn't been able to pick him out from the sea of guards in the hangar was that he hadn't been there. Maybe he was among the few guards assigned to other duties. Maybe he'd been late to the party and gotten locked out. I didn't know. All I knew was that we'd forgotten about the newly forged passage between the reactor bay and the crating bay, and we hadn't quarantined the separate corridor outside the reactor bay. That was the door we'd heard opening.

Like us, the three Orphs by the exit had taken refuge behind a Normanium bin, but Malcolm seemed to barely register them there as he advanced on us. It was obvious the beating he and his lackies had given me had fallen short of satisfying his need for payback. And given his lack of abandon, it seemed he hadn't been briefed about Arthur's alleged Ultron mode.

"Little piss ants are gonna get what's comin' to ya!" he yelled as he fired three more rounds. They all smacked into the wall four or five feet above our heads. At first, I thought he was just a crappy shot. Then I realized he was laying down suppressing fire to ensure that we'd stay put until he could get close enough to finish us off without hitting the Normanium canisters in the bin behind which we were hiding. Maybe he wanted to avoid another massive explosion, but more likely, the greedy bastard didn't want to waste any Normanium while he was wasting us.

I started to pull the bin toward the air lock in hopes of getting close enough to make a break for it. But as I pulled, I felt it pivot slightly, then pull back away from me. I looked down at the front right wheel – or where the front right wheel was supposed to be – and saw that it was busted clean off. I'd encountered the problem on many bins. So I knew this one wasn't going anywhere. And neither were we. In moments, Malcolm would be on us, and we would be done. But as he continued toward us, he put the other three Orphs well off his flank, and I spotted them dashing toward the crevice in the wall. From their position, it was a short distance and they scurried through like three panicked spider monkeys, clearing the passage at about five times the rate Malcolm had. Still, he spotted them out of the corner of his eye and fired two rounds after them. Maybe he thought they had helped us get on the ship somehow. Or maybe he was just drunk on the lethal authority he'd been granted by Norman. But luckily, both rounds missed, and his momentary lapse in focus gave me an opening.

I launched myself over the crating bin, driving my shoulder into his chest. We both went down with an ugly thud, and I grabbed his arm and tried to wrench the gun out of his hand. As I did, it went off again. This time the round smacked into the panel directly above the air lock door, sending a fountain of sparks showering down.

It seemed that this, combined with the questionable docking port coupling, had pushed the air lock's compensation systems to the limit because an alarm sounded, and red lights started blinking inside the transitional chamber.

Malcolm didn't even seem to notice. He just kept firing the gun wildly as I fought to prevent him from drawing a bead on me or the others. I was giving it everything I had, but his strength was overwhelming. A lifetime of carrying around 350 pounds has its benefits. I knew it was only a matter of time before he got the better of me, and by continuing to squeeze off rounds, he was making it impossible for Arthur or Cassie to get close enough to help. They were still pinned down with Decker.

Then I glimpsed Arthur's face and recognized his expression. It was that trademark far-off stare. I heard a beeping sound next to me as Cassie yelled, "Heads up, Clayton!"

I hurled myself clear as the pile of Normanium canisters beside Malcolm went up. Unfortunately, he wasn't quite close enough for them to take him out. Instead, the explosion just threw him across the chamber toward Cassie, Arthur, and Decker. He landed on the floor near them, gun still in hand.

With no better ideas, Arthur threw himself on top of Malcolm and picked up where I'd left off, wrestling for control of the gun. But he was even less effective than I was and suddenly, the gun was pointing straight at Cassie. Then Malcolm pulled the trigger.

Now, I knew Cassie would be okay, for the moment anyway. Because I'd just flung myself in front of her. There wasn't a lot of thought before I'd done it. It had been automatic. And in the split second I had to reflect on the choice, I didn't regret it one bit. Don't get me wrong. I was terrified. But even as my short life flickered before my eyes, I believed I'd done the right thing.

I felt the bullet impact. Dead in the chest. The weird thing was, it bounced off.

CHAPTER  17

EVERYONE STARED AT THE BULLET LYING AT MY FEET. THEN they stared at me, as if I could offer an explanation. I couldn't. I was as flabbergasted as anyone—maybe more so. Arthur scrambled up to get clear of Malcolm, who ignored him, aiming and firing again at me. The second round bounced off my shoulder. He grimaced and fired again, and again, with each round crumpling on impact and clattering to the floor in front of me like metallic hail.

Then the gun finally clicked empty. We were all in shock, both at the raw, unabashed spectacle of Malcolm trying to murder me and his inexplicable failure to do so. But there was no time for shock. Because the alarm that had been droning suddenly shifted to a higher, more urgent pitch. Then we found out exactly how much damage the gauss rounds had done to the air lock because as the door started to slide shut automatically, it derailed violently. There was a creak as the transitional chamber beyond began to buckle and collapse in on itself. We all knew what would come next, but Decker verbalized it.

"We're all gonna fuckin' die!"

Cassie, Arthur, and I didn't need to exchange words. There was only one place that was safe. We all made for the air lock. I was ten paces behind the other two, so I noticed that Decker hadn't gotten the hint. I grabbed him by the shirtfront and drove him backward like a linebacker tackling a quarterback. As we rounded the corner, I saw Cassie and Arthur ahead of us, ambling across the rapidly deteriorating transitional chamber and through the air lock's and Javelin's exterior doors, which were sealing automatically—slowed enough by their asynchronous mating that Decker and I just might be able clear them. I sensed Malcolm behind us, but he was a step too slow. As we stumbled through the passage and crashed to the floor inside the Javelin, the door clanked shut and we heard him yelling outside. Then the air lock gave way and the crating bay decompressed explosively, violently ejecting its contents into space. The Javelin heaved up and summersaulted outward, enveloped by flames and wreckage. We were tossed against the ceiling then back to the floor twice before the ballistic energy propelling us was finally spent.

Arthur rose and stumbled toward the cockpit. Cassie and I followed shakily. The space around the ship was littered with twisted metal: bits and pieces of girders, storage bins, and Normanium canisters. Some of the wreckage glanced off the cockpit window, but thankfully, the glass held. Then, suddenly, something hammered against the hull and floated into view. It was Malcolm's body. He was still alive but inflated like a blowfish and apparently trying to scream. Cassie jerked back and turned away. I didn't. Why? Because fuck him, that's why. I wasn't going to waste a second of compassion on the bastard.

A few seconds later, he was finally dead, and his body began drifting ever so slowly off into the big black nothingness. Arthur brought up a series of ho-lo displays depicting various system diagnostics. Even with his abilities, I knew he couldn't operate the ship without some physical interaction. But I didn't think he needed holo-displays to access diagnostic data, and I suspected he'd pulled up the displays as a distraction from the morbid scene outside. Regardless, after poring over them briefly, he nodded optimistically. I took that as a good sign. He was about to share the details when Decker stumbled in.

"You people have screwed me!" He gave me a shove to the shoulder. "You've screwed me!"

I'd dragged him to safety because, while he was a dick, I didn't think he'd done anything to merit the excruciating death Malcolm had experienced. But my position on that was wavering as he continued to bark at us.

"I had eight months left. Eight months! And now . . . now you assholes basically just killed a crew boss, and I'm ridin' shotgun in the getaway vehicle. There's no way I ain't implicated in this shit!"

"Calm down, Decker," I said.

"Fuck calm, and fuck you!"

He punched me in the face. And it hurt. I staggered back, putting a hand to my nose. The hand came away bloody. I studied it, confused. Everyone took a beat. Even Decker.

"How . . ." Cassie started. But she didn't know whether to ask how I'd been hurt by Decker's punch or how I hadn't been hurt by Malcolm's gauss gun. The adrenaline of the past couple of minutes had briefly supplanted the mystery of my inexplicably un-bullet-ridden body, but the non sequitur of my bloody nose was enough to put it center stage again. Setting aside the staggering coincidence of a comic book-obsessed kid developing a superpower, the superpower in question seemed to make no sense. Was I invulnerable but only sometimes? Were certain parts of my body less impervious to harm than others? I was thinking more scientific investigation was needed when Arthur hit me in the side of the head with a Normanium canister. I spun toward him, flashing rage, but he just nodded and said, "Hm. I get it." He was looking down at the canister, which had a dent in it. It occurred to me now that I'd felt no pain.

"H-h-had a hunch," he clarified.

"A hunch?" I exclaimed. "What if it had been wrong?!"

"Yeah, no, that w-w-would have been bad," he conceded. "But it wasn't wrong. I'm taking in a lot of data all the time – m-m-more than humidity readings. It's mostly irrelevant noise I have to tune out. But looking at it all right now, there's s-s-something going on in the area around you. Like a . . . an aura. It's really light over h-h-here," he said, gesturing to the space between Decker, Cassie, and me. "But it's really d-d-dense over here," he continued, gesturing to the space between the wall and me. "Seems like the density decreases with proximity to people, or s-s-something about people? Maybe just organic m-m-matter?"

"So you're saying . . ." Cassie trailed off.

"A mutation of s-s-some kind?" Arthur guessed.

I won't lie. As soon as I heard "mutation," I started picturing myself in an X-Men unitard, heading out to break a foot off in Apocalypse's ass. But then I remembered this wasn't the Scriptures. This was reality.

"Wait," Decker said. "So bullets bounce off him, but we can still bitch-slap him?"

"S-s-seems like," Arthur answered.

"Ha!" Decker snorted. "I vote you call yourself 'Irony Man.'"

"Shut up, you schmuck," Cassie said. I think she may have indulged in a short X-Men daydream herself, but like me, she was now struggling with a rapidly metastasizing fear of the unknown.

"How is this possible?" she said.

"I would think the obvious s-s-suspect is the exposure to Normanium Prime," Arthur answered.

"First the stuff looks exactly like Pentagramite, and now it's giving people superpowers?" I exclaimed.

"Is it?" Cassie asked. She held up her arm, which was scraped from one of the many tumbles she'd taken recently. "I'm not bulletproof, and I've been exposed. Come to think of it, so have lots of other people on the Charon."

Arthur shrugged. "The subject's physiology could impact w-w-whether they're affected and how. Who knows?" He turned to me. "But I'm s-s-surprised none of the tests they ran on you after the accident showed any abnormalities."

"Actually, Jerry did say that my cellular structures were 'blurry' in one of the scans," I recalled.

"Was it a brain scan?" Decker asked. "Seems to me you always been a mite blurry in that department."

I flipped him the finger. He flipped it back.

"If stuff's going on with your cells, wouldn't you feel it?" Cassie asked.

"I think h-h-he has felt it," Arthur interjected.

"Shit," I said. "The seizures."

Arthur nodded. I thought about the strange sense of expansion I'd felt after my first seizure and how I'd miraculously walked away from the reactor explosion with just bumps and bruises, and felt only muted pain during the shock-stick beating I'd taken from Malcolm's crew in the supply closet. Then I thought about the second seizure and how that sense of expansion had increased – apparently rendering me bulletproof.

"I have felt different after the seizures," I said. "Like I'm . . . changing."

"Into what?" Cassie said. "And how many more seizures can you take?"

She was right at pace with my downward spiraling inner dialogue. But a barrage of imagery from my Thanos/Norman dream came back to me – a reminder of what was at stake – and I realized I needed to get my focus off my condition.

"Alright," I said. "Nothing's changed. We stick to the plan."

"What? No! Everything has changed!" Cassie said. "Your cells are flipping mutating. We need to get you some help."

"Yeah," Arthur concurred. "I think seeing a doctor as soon as possible is –"

"No!" I said forcefully. "I'm the one whose cells are freaking out. So it's my call."

They both paused, then nodded reluctantly. They could see my mind was made up, and in the end, I guess they agreed it was my decision to make.

"Let's just get some distance from the Charon and figure out where the next stage is before the quarantine clocks out," I said.

Arthur shrugged off his qualms, tapped a few buttons, and said, "Autopilot's at the w-w-wheel. I'll start prepping the system to bring the Cunningham-Keyes drive onli –"

"Now wait a goddamn minute!" Decker broke in. He was just now realizing that we were leaving and taking him with us. "Are you people completely off your rockers?" he demanded. "You gotta take me back. You gotta make 'em understand I had no part in –"

"We're not going back – not now, not ever!" I snarled.

He took a step back as if my words were a gale-force wind. My emotions were spilling over from the previous topic, but my logic was undeniable. We'd used up our element of surprise, and any guards that were available were probably now stationed at the unexploded crating bays, to say nothing of the convicts that were certainly there. It wasn't fair to Decker, but there was no way we could take him back. Cassie stepped in to do some damage control.

"Look, there's an upside to all this," she said. "Arthur can set us up with new identities and all the cash we need for an easy life once we get back to Earth. You're going to come out ahead here. There's just . . . some things we need to do first."

Decker's sullen expression melted a little at the prospect of living the good life. For us, it had only ever represented a consolation prize, but she knew it would mean more to him.

"Besides, you said it yourself, there's no w-w-way you're not implicated in all this," Arthur added. "And there's probably nothing we could s-s-say to change that."

Decker sighed in resignation. I figured there would be a round two when he found out the Chowderheaded nature of the business we needed to attend to before heading back to Earth. But for the moment, he seemed to be accepting his fate, crankily changing the subject.

"How the hell you even possible?" he said as he watched Arthur open a panel and start toggling various switches to bring the F.T.L. drive online. "The AI R&D ban was on the books way before anyone was even close to building a thing like you." Aside from everything else, he was still trying to cope with the news that Arthur wasn't a real boy.

"So I'm a thing now?" Arthur replied. "Well, at least we've m-m-moved on from demon-powered Terminator. Baby steps."

He evaluated Decker for a moment, then apparently decided there might be some benefit to sharing his Teen Machine origin story. He opened another panel and started adjusting a series of knobs as he began, "My dad—or m-m-maker—wasn't a huge rule follower . . ."

As he continued, I made eye contact with Cassie and gestured to the hallway. She followed me out and I said, "Arthur's assuming we'll be able to tell him where we're going once he gets that drive online."

My implication was obvious. We needed to check my M.U. mailbox. Cassie nodded but said nothing. Everyone had been looking at me differently since the discovery of my superskin, but it was hard to talk about it without talking about the side effects. However, now that it was just Cassie and me, I thought I might be able to ease the tension by broaching the whole matter head-on. As we entered my hab suite, I said, "If only the Normanium Prime had made me smart enough to solve the Conundrum instead of making me an epileptic Luke Cage."

Her eyes met mine for a moment, and I had time to read the sadness and worry in them before she glanced away again. My tension-easing efforts had fallen flat as a pancake. I realized things might have been different if my situation wasn't just one item on a long list of messed up crap we'd endured in the last day.

But it was. And as much as we both ached to just sit and process everything, we needed to know if our M.U. gamble had paid off, and we needed to know now. Norman was less than three hours behind us.

As we sat down in front of the holo-pod in my hab suite, Cassie took my hand and gave it a hopeful squeeze. Processed or not, all the nerve-annihilating events of the last few hours receded to the background as our attention narrowed to the incoming message count in my mailbox. It was at ninety-six. No shortage of replies. That seemed like good news.

By sharing our own answers, we'd put it all on the line. Of course, our story could still be some kind of elaborate con – and the fact that some of our answers had to be wrong wasn't going to help build trust. But I believed the Chowderhead community would see and embrace the truth. I believed they would stand tall when it mattered most. I believed they would deliver. I opened the first message, and it read: "Go fuck a duck, scammer!"

Not a home run, per se. The message was from one Madame Xanadu, and unfortunately, it set the tone for the vast majority of what followed. A guy with the handle Krypto Knight asked if we had a bridge in Gotham to sell him. Snikt to 'Em invited us to "take a bumpy ride on a seatless bicycle." Shazama-la-ma-ding-dong recommended we perform unspeakable acts with Armless Tiger Man – a '40s-era Marvel villain that should never have been for so many reasons.

Even after we'd shared all our answers, apparently none of our respondents had solved the puzzle to discover the far-off destination of the second stage. Or they had and were still irrationally convinced we were trying to play them somehow. The few people who thanked us for the answers did so with sneering remarks that painted us as desperate, conniving swindlers. The outpouring of ill will was jarring and to our chagrin, it seemed our plea to the Chowderhead community was receiving exactly the reception Norman had predicted. That is, until we came across one enormous, mind-boggling exception.

My eighty-seventh message read: "Really? Dude, what kind of homo doesn't know Cap is Weapon I? Hello? *New X-Men*, #145, 2003?"

We stared at the message in disbelief. Was it possible we'd just been schooled by 1MP3R10US R3X? A wave of dread washed over us as we pulled up the Conundrum site and reviewed the issue to which he'd referred. Sure enough, the pieces clicked into place like the tumblers of a lock, and we knew the answer to 2 Across. *The most worthy weapon* wasn't a weapon in the literal sense. It was a man.

Evidently, both Cassie and I had forgotten that Project Rebirth – the experiment that had yielded Captain America – had evolved into the Weapon Plus program, which had created many more superpowered "human weapons," including most famously the tenth iteration, Weapon X, or Wolverine. Long story short, Captain America was technically Weapon I. With that, the solution was obvious because the flag-clad Avenger is also on a very short list of those who have been deemed "worthy" to wield Mjolnir, as witnessed in *The Mighty Thor* #398 (1988). Not to mention, he was often referred to simply as "Cap," which fit the Conundrum perfectly.

I looked at Cassie, and I could tell she was feeling it too: the unmitigated humiliation of being bested by the single biggest tool in the Chowderhead community—and maybe the world. The disgrace was palpable.

I slumped in my seat, realizing what must come next. Facing the horror, I said, "I guess we should . . . thank him?"

"Yeah," Cassie answered grimly. "And then commit hari-kiri."

I wasn't a hundred percent sure she was kidding about the last part. And I wouldn't have blamed her if she wasn't. Mired in shame, I fired off my best effort at a thank-you note. Then we scanned the last of the responses in my inbox. Nothing.

"Son of a bitch," I swore.

"What are we going to do?" Cassie asked, her voice brimming with apprehension.

We were still missing answers, and no light had been shed on which of our existing answers might be wrong. Had we had the chance to fully face the facts, we would surely have lost our shit. But just then, an audio chat request came through from C. B. Somehow, it hadn't even occurred to me that I hadn't seen a note from him or Dane in my inbox. I hurriedly accepted the request, and an audio channel came online.

"Finally—we saw you had audio access now, and we've been checking every half hour to catch you live!" He spoke in the English accent I knew he had but had never heard. "Are you alright, my boy?"

"Never better," I said.

He scoffed at my rehearsed response and pressed the point.

"It sounds like you've got yourself into real trouble."

"Really, C. B.," I assured him. "No need to worry."

"Oy!" I heard Dane call from somewhere in the background. "This better not be some sort of hoodwinking, you little scamp!"

"It's not," I said. We were desperate for any answers they could share, but I felt awful about the news my note had carried. Even though they weren't true fanatics, they'd invested a lot in the Challenge, and I'd shattered their hopes of taking home the prize.

"I'm sorry," I said. "I know how much time you guys have—"

"Pishposh," C. B. interrupted. "We've run the gamut from denial to acceptance since your message came through, but you know the two of us have already won." He was referring to the fact that the Challenge had brought them together. "We're just glad there's someone between that tosser and the U.A.T.—and glad that someone is you."

"Let's get to the point," Dane jumped back in. "You've stolen a bloody spaceship?!"

"There's a lot to tell," I answered. "But we can't tell it all right now."

"Who's 'we'?" C. B. asked.

"Um . . . me and Cassie," I responded, somewhat uncomfortable with where this could go—which is where it went.

"Are you two finally shagging then?" Dane shouted.

I was struck dumb with embarrassment. I'd shared way too much with them about my feelings for Cassie, but she didn't even know them, what with her antisocial tendencies when it came to the M.U. She jumped in and put me out of my misery.

"Um . . . hi, nice to meet you," she said. "We're still . . . figuring things out between us."

"Bollocks! Get to the shagging!" Dane retorted.

"Let them be," C. B. cut in.

"Hmph!" we heard Dane snort. "'Figuring things out.' You want something real to figure out, love? When I met this buffoon, he was married to a woman! Eck! Paging Dr. Toynbee! Can you imagine? A woman. With a vagina! Just disgusting."

He paused briefly, then added, "No offense."

"Um . . . some taken," Cassie said.

"Anyway, snap out of it, girl!" he continued as if he hadn't heard her. "You wouldn't be on this billy quest with our boy if you weren't planning to bed him."

That tore it. Cassie's face grew suddenly heated, and she fired back, "Look, I'll bed him when I'm good and ready! I just don't see what business it is of yours, you ebony-bladed schmo!"

"Oh! She's a fiery lass, this one. Well chosen, Thwppit!"

"Yeah. Uh...thanks," I said, my head spinning at the ramifications of Cassie's outburst. "But guys, we were actually hoping you might have some Conundrum answers we could—"

"Right! Yes," C. B.'s voice returned. "Afraid we don't have a lot for you, but we do have 8 Across, thanks to the brilliant and talented stark to whom I've given my heart."

"You sound like a right poof. You know that, don't you?" Dane exclaimed. We heard C. B. sigh. "I have sex with a woman, I'm disgusting. I say how I feel about you, I'm a poof. Is there no pleasing you?!"

"Guys?" I nudged.

"Right," C. B. said. "8 Across: *A nice little mountain home for bad guys.* For years, we assumed 'little' was modifying 'home.' But then with a stroke of genius, the light of my life here considered the possibility that it modified 'mountain,' i.e., little mountain, i.e., a hill, and the answer just fell into place: Pleasant Hill."

"Huh?" I said, as I glanced over at Cassie and saw that her expression reflected my own cluelessness.

"It's from the *Avengers: Standoff* miniseries in 2016," Dane elaborated. "Maria Hill used Kobic, the sentient cosmic cube, to warp reality and transform various supervillains into brainwashed Stepford people, residing in a bizarre American 1950s-esque gated community called Pleasant Hill. Fantastic stuff!"

"Dammit!" I cursed. I hadn't read the miniseries, and it seemed Cassie hadn't either.

"We can't all read everything, my boy," C. B. consoled me. "But here's the thing that's thrown us—while we got four answers from you all, every other answer you had, we had. Which was a bit of a disappointment because—"

"Because when you plugged the key letters in, you got a solution that was totally fakakta?" Cassie said.

"Exactly," he answered.

I sighed in frustration at the notion that we were all being mocked by the same punchline.

"Okay," I said, dispiritedly. "Thanks guys—we'll tell you everything that's happened soon, but right now we have to regroup."

"Good luck then," C. B. said.

"Hurry up and throw one into her, boy!" Dane added tastefully, just before I disconnected.

Thankfully, Cassie didn't seem to hear that. She was too pissed off as she struggled to accept that we'd now truly reached the end of the road.

"Shit!" she cried. "This is a fail. A big fat fail. We're done!"

At first I felt the same. And after what we'd been through to get more Normanium, the consolation prize of our new life on Earth offered no real consolation. A swell of regret came over me. I wished the Fate Force could swoop in aboard their time-traveling ship, the Eldridge, and launch some nutty scenario that would return us to the relative safety of our little hell on the Charon. I wanted to blink my eyes and open them in my quarters to hear Darcy regaling me with unfounded, outrageous rumors. But then, once again, something inside told me that this couldn't be the end. And the more I thought about it, the more my conviction grew. We couldn't be this far off.

"We've got to be missing something," I said.

"Yeah," Cassie replied. "The right answers!"

"No, I mean how could Cateklysm be sloppy enough for there to be tons of wrong answers that we all agree fit the clue? And for those wrong answers to fit the intersection of right answers and other plausible but wrong answers, over and over? It just can't seem this right if it's wrong."

"Seems like it can."

"I don't think so."

The coincidence of my errors matching Cassie's had been nagging at me all day, and the news from C. B. and Dane had been the tipping point. My Spidey-Sense was kicking in.

"Maybe we're wrong about being wrong," I said.

"So you're saying the big reveal really is gobbledygook?"

"No. Like I said, I think we're missing something."

It was just out of reach of my conscious mind. I could feel it, but I couldn't find it. Until I did.

"The Riddler!" I gasped.

"What about him?" Cassie said.

I quoted Cateklysm's broadcast, "It's a puzzle worthy of the Riddler."

"Ah. Okeydoke. You go get him. I'll wait here," she cracked cynically.

I rolled my eyes and pulled up our partially completed secret message grid. "Maybe the letters aren't supposed to spell anything. The repeating sets—don't they remind you of—"

"*Batman Eternal!*" she exclaimed. It was a series from 2014, in which the Riddler had taunted Batman with a cryptic message using an old cipher originally created by the German army in World War I. It was based on six letters that were easily differentiated over Morse code: A, D, F, G, V, and X. These six letters were used as the vertical and horizontal axis of a six-by-six coordinate system that housed the whole alphabet as well as the numbers zero to nine.

Secret messages could be encoded one character at a time using pairs of the six letters as coordinates that marked the grid location of each secret message character. A little confusing—but it got more confusing when the sender chose a "transportation" key word or phrase and plugged the letter pairs into columns below each letter of the key word or phrase, then scrambled them by putting them into alphabetical order and moving the columns along with each letter. The coded message would then be transmitted by Morse code, listing the vertical columns in groups. Which is all to say, to reverse engineer the whole perplexing process, the person on the other end would need both the coordinate system and the transportation key.

And that brings us back to *Batman Eternal* #15, in which Batman (the World's Greatest Detective) correctly deduced that the egomaniacal Riddler would use his own name as the transportation key: E. Nigma. I thought, what if Cateklysm had made the riddle his own?

"His name!" I cried. "The weird spelling!"

Cassie continued my riff. "He was avoiding repeating letters to make it a suitable key!"

My excitement was climbing off the charts. Then it crashed as I noticed the problem.

"Damn!" I said.

"What?" Cassie asked.

I went on, crestfallen. "Our solution set uses almost none of the letters from ADFGVX." I'd gotten so carried away with recalling a pattern of repeating letter sets that I hadn't thought about what the letters were.

"Oh, that," Cassie said. "Doesn't matter."

"How can that not matter?"

"Any six letters will do."

She pointed to our solution set, and I realized it only featured six unique characters: A, C, E, I, L, and R.

"Remember, the Riddler created a whole custom grid for his riddle, so the bat computer had to unscramble it?" she said. "I bet Cateklysm just changed the letters in the axis of the coordinate system instead, like a low-maintenance homage. I mean why make us do all that frequency analysis now? The jig is up."

She was right. About all of it.

I kissed her. It was the first time I'd made the first move, but I thought it was the right time.

She slapped me and cried, "Oy vey! What's a matter with you? We're about to solve the Conundrum here!"

Her words were more of a jolt than the slap. This was the moment I'd been imagining my entire life. The thousands of hours of research I'd done. The thousands more that had been passed down from my parents. It all led right here. I reigned in my hormones, and we got to work.

We laid out the coordinate system, using A, C, E, I, L, and R. Then we plugged in an alphabetized version of Cateklysm's name above the Conundrum's secret message grid and plugged our solution set into the grid itself. We used question marks for the two characters we were still missing due to our failure to solve 1 Down. With our recent breakthrough, we believed we'd be able to work around the two gaps.

At this step it became very clear why Cateklysm had included the grid in the Conundrum. Unlike with Morse code, the letter sets were not being provided to us in groups, so we wouldn't be able to determine the column breaks. The grid filled in this critical blank. We shifted the columns to spell Cateklysm's name correctly. Then we referred to our coordinate system to translate the pairs.

The result was: HBBI1?591?754. And that's when we knew two things. First, we knew we'd never use the phrase "dots and lines" the same way again because the Conundrum's much-debated digital imperfections were clearly decimal points and a demarcation line separating two GPS coordinates. Second, we knew where we needed to go. Well, mostly.

The HBB solar system was named for its discoverer, Henry Bingham Barnes, in 2024. There was a lot of hullabaloo about the discovery because the system was less than half a dozen light years away, and it had three planets in its habitable zone. Those planets were designated G, H, and I. We now knew Cateklysm had hidden something on planet I. And it was at latitude 1.?59 north and longitude 1?.754 east. It was great news, but Cassie called out the fly in the ointment.

"Without 1 Down, we're still a little screwed."

"Well, based on what we know, the first missing number has to be a 3 or a 9," I responded brightly.

"And the second one could be a 5, 6, 7, 8, 9, or 0," she countered. "That's a huge search area."

I nodded. "I guess we just have to hope we get lucky and/or have enough of a head start on Norman."

"Yeah, or you could just not be dumbasses."

We looked over and saw Decker standing in the doorway. We'd been so engrossed in our code breaking, we had no idea how long he'd been standing there.

"I mean if you people were ducks, you'd fly north for winter," he taunted. "What self-respecting Chowderhead doesn't know 1 Down?"

Cassie and I regarded him with a paradoxical blend of hope and contempt. Of course, I knew the situation called for finesse. He was clearly looking to be buttered up.

Cassie sighed and said, "Are you saying you know the answer, or are you just being a putz?" She'd come up a bit short of the gold standard for finesse, but to his credit, he didn't jerk us around. If I wasn't mistaken, there was something different about him. Something seemed to be awakening as he spoke.

"Good ole 1 Down: *69, 86, 92, 94. List the link.* Answer's 'Super Patriot.' The name was first used in 1969 by a villain in *Nick Fury, Agent a' S.H.I.E.L.D.* – fella called Patric List." He winked to emphasize List, then went on. "Then again in 1986 by a rival, and eventual replacement of, Captain America (*Captain America* #323), and again in 1992 by one of Erik Larsen's Image heroes (first appearance *Savage Dragon* #1), then yet again in 1994 by another Marvel villain (*Captain America* #425)."

Decker had just given us the missing coordinates. We were floored. Not so much because he knew the answer. As already stated, the guy's Chowderhead kung fu was strong. But why was he helping us? It didn't figure. He obviously saw the question in our eyes and decided to answer it.

"After Arthur got done fillin' me in on his sitch – still havin' a hard time with the whole robot thing by the way – he told me all about your billy theory."

I'd been sure that being roped into our Chowderhead treasure hunt would have pushed Decker over the brink, even with the promise of an easy life when we returned to Earth. So I'd thought keeping him in the dark for as long as possible was the smart play. But that wasn't the play Arthur had made.

"And it is billy – way billy," Decker went on. "It's plain ole ridiculous, no matter what the Conundrum solution says."

He paused, and for a moment, we thought he was done. He wasn't.

"But . . . there's an itty-bitty chance it's all true. Which means there's an itty-bitty chance that we're on course to seriously mess up Luthor Norman's program."

"And that's something you want?" I asked.

He looked me in the eye. Then he took off his shoe and picked it up.

"Last few years, there's only one thing pissed me off more than Chowderheads. And that's Luthor Norman."

He reached into his shoe, pulled something out, and tossed it onto the chair next to us. It was two spoons. As they clanked down, our jaws dropped open.

"No freakin' way," Cassie gasped. She'd drawn the same conclusion I had – the conclusion Decker had intended. He was the Spoon Bandit. The revelation was stunning. It was also infuriating because I thought the Spoon Bandit was kind of a kangster.

"The spoons are just a teeny 'screw you' to Norman. But it was worth it, 'cause I wasn't gonna get caught–most of 'em are hidden in the wall outside Schakter's quarters. That guy's a shithead."

Cassie and I both nodded at that.

"Anyway, point is, this thing you're doin' is riskier, to say the least. But on the off chance it pans out, it's a king-size 'screw you' to Norman, and I'm all in for that."

"So, what, you're a Chowderhead again?" I asked.

"No," he answered reflexively. Then, reevaluating, he added, "Maybe. I dunno."

His honesty was unexpected, and there was a strange exhilaration at the prospect of bringing a lost Chowderhead back into the fold. I thought I felt a warmth kindling between us.

"You're a goddamn hypocrite," I said.

"Fuck you," he responded.

Maybe warmth was the wrong word. Suddenly there was a small explosion from somewhere outside the hab suite. We rushed out and saw Arthur in the engine room, spray bottle in hand. At his feet was the smoking wreckage of a Normanium canister and a small pile of red crystals.

Decker stepped back, alarmed. He was the only one of us who had yet to be exposed to Normanium Prime and didn't seem eager for his turn. Arthur knocked on the plexiglass wall.

"No need to w-w-worry," he assured us. "This compartment is sealed."

Decker leaned back in, peering at the crystals.

"It really does look just like–"

"We know," Cassie and I said in unison, marveling anew at the crystals' resemblance to the Fate Force's star-shaped fuel.

Arthur scooped up the crystals, apparently unconcerned that they could affect him adversely. "You g-g-guys know where we're headed? Because the F.T.L. drive is g-g-good to go."

ISSUE 3 OF 4
ENTER THE
DANGER ROOM!

CHAPTER  18

"SO THEY'VE TESTED THIS, RIGHT?" DECKER SAID.
"M-m-more or less," Arthur answered.
"Well which is it, man? More or less?!"

Cassie, Decker, and I were buckled into the jump seats behind Arthur on the flight deck as he made final preparations to engage the F.T.L. drive. Decker's trepidation was understandable. We were about to become the first human beings to travel faster than the speed of light, in a craft powered by some nigh inexplicable energy source with a yield roughly equivalent to that of a small sun.

"Seriously, Arthur," Cassie said. "What kind of risks are we looking at?"

"Massive," he answered matter-of-factly. "But life's too short to w-w-worry about being disintegrated by stray hydrogen atoms."

"Seems like not worrying about that could make life a lot shorter," she retorted.

"Starting to regret all that dried fruit and jerky I put away just now," Decker said, referring to the truckload of snacks we'd all devoured in the kitchen. "You s'pose the 'wait ten minutes before swimming' rule applies here?"

"We're sure the diagnostics were clear after the crating bay explosion, right?" Cassie pressed.

Arthur leaned back from the control panel to take a beat. "Look, from inertial dampeners to w-w-warp trajectory plotting to about a million other things, this ship is an experiment, plain and simple. I've read all the d-d-documentation but I won't pretend I understand it all. I'm practically as much a passenger as you are, except for I'm the one who's s-s-supposed to press this button." He pointed to a holo-display in front of him with a prompt that read: *Initiate?* Apparently, he'd finished preparations. He continued, "S-s-so if we're not all all-in here, now is the time to cut and run. I won't lie, I liked the plan w-w-where we skipped to starting our new lives on Earth."

"Press the button, Arthur," I said.

There was no ambivalence in my voice. The others shifted nervously in their seats, but they didn't object. I think they secretly couldn't imagine turning back either—they were just trying to let their common sense have its say. All our other motivations aside, there's something undeniable about the human compulsion to plunge into the unknown. We were here on the precipice, and our natures weren't going to let us step away from the edge. We all knew we were going to jump.

Arthur didn't wait for more discussion. He just said, "H-h-here we go," and tapped the holo-display. The ship jerked once violently, and an explosion of light burst through the cockpit window. The world folded in on itself and stopped making sense, like we were watching reality rewinding and fast-forwarding at the same time. We were overcome with a sense of displacement for a few moments until we hit a sort of equilibrium.

We'd entered a warp field, which wasn't exactly what the movies had led us to expect. The stars didn't become elongated streaks of light hurtling by. There was no rainbow pinwheel swirling in front of us. There was just a centralized white glow outside, with a blindingly bright nucleus. And it was completely, deafeningly silent. Then the ship shuddered, and the view outside returned to a blanket of stars. That blanket rippled briefly as a swell of energy tumbled out in front of us, then dissipated.

"Are we . . . here? We make it?" Decker asked.

"S-s-seems like," Arthur answered. His face looked like he'd given us a fifty-fifty chance of surviving and maybe less of actually getting anywhere. In truth, I'd given us about the same chances. Suddenly, I thought of my parents and the nutty pride they would have felt at their son risking his existence to follow their Chowderhead obsession to another solar system.

"Oy gevalt!" Cassie said, pulling me back into the moment. She was staring out the window behind us and to our left. We all turned to look. The scene was awe-inspiring. We could make out two distinct nebulae comprised of stunningly vivid shades of green, purple, and burnt orange.

"We sure as shootin' ain't in Kansas no more," Decker said. Cassie leaned against the glass, struck speechless by the spectacle. It was like nothing we'd ever seen, outside of Scripture fodder featuring the Guardians of the Galaxy or Cyclops's star-faring, swashbuckling father, Corsair.

I began to adjust to the scene and noticed something was conspicuously absent. There were no planets in sight, which meant no HBBI.

"Where are we?" I asked Arthur.

"HBBI is about half a m-m-million miles behind us," he answered.

"Behind us?" I exclaimed.

"Warp fields pick up a lot of high-energy particles," he explained. "So when the field is d-d-disengaged, it releases an enormous shock wave."

I recalled the swell of energy rippling out from the ship when we'd arrived.

"It extends in all directions, but it's s-s-strongest directly in front of the field and weakest directly behind it. So in order to get as close to HBBI as possible without d-d-destroying it or any other substantial celestial bodies, the nav computer overshot it by this m-m-margin."

"I thought you didn't understand all the crap you read in the manuals," Decker said.

"I didn't," Arthur responded. "But I tried to pay special attention to the s-s-stuff about blowing up planets."

He fiddled briefly with various holo-displays, and answered our next question before anyone asked it. "At full burn with conventional propulsion, w-w-we should reach HBBI in just over two hours." Then he mumbled absentmindedly, "Should be just in time."

"Just in time for what?" Decker asked.

"It's . . . a figure of s-s-speech," Arthur answered awkwardly. Something was off about his manner, and one of us probably would have pressed him for further clarification, but we were all distracted by the interstellar vista on display outside as he brought the ship around to get us underway.

"So you guys really think there's technology more 'unimaginable' than this shit?" Decker asked, gesturing to the Javelin.

"What's that supposed to mean?" Cassie said. "You're off the Cateklysm bandwagon again?"

"Never said I was back on, officially. I'm still mostly about the cash and new identity you promised me. That mel, mel chance of dashin' Norman's hopes and dreams? Well, it's worth a look, but it's gonna take a whole lot to convince me the Conundrum's anything more than a wild-goose chase with a make-believe prize. And again, what prize could beat what this ship just did?"

It was a fair question. It may take time, but thanks to the Cunningham-Keyes drive and Normanium Prime, humanity was finally in a position to begin the process of colonizing resource-rich planets all over the universe. By now, we knew for sure that this hadn't been the motivation behind Norman's fiendish scheming. However, it was a profoundly serendipitous by-product – and to Decker's point, the idea that there could be something even more extraordinary at the end of the rainbow was hard to imagine, even for a dyed-in-the-wool Chowderhead like me. That is until Cassie launched her rebuttal.

"Bullshit," she said. "F.T.L. is amazing, but no more so than a guy who predicted who would invent it and what the fuel would look like back in 2036. And let's not forget he could open a sparkly, blue wormhole at will. You can bet your tuchus the U.A.T. will top everything we've seen so far."

The Decker I'd known would have kept at the debate for hours, but he just gave her a noncommittal shrug and said, "Guess we'll see what turns up at them coordinates."

There was a lull, and then Arthur asked, "H-h-how about aliens?"

"Whatcha mean?" Decker responded.

Arthur answered, "To any sensible person the question of whether they're out there has always been secondary to w-w-whether we'd ever be able to make contact with them. Now we can."

Cassie smirked at me. "Well when we meet them, I bet they won't look anything like Gamora."

"But a fella can hope," Decker said with a dreamy look in his eyes. To my dismay, he really was beginning to grow on me.

The subject of aliens petered out, and we all fell silent for another few minutes, gazing out at the uncharted miracle stretching endlessly before us. I could have stood there for hours, except I felt an overwhelming need to be alone with Cassie again.

"Cassie, can I talk to you?" I asked.

She raised a curious eyebrow, then nodded.

I led her back to my hab suite. Maybe my repressed fear of death by seizure was manifesting itself in the form of some evolutionary imperative, but I felt an urge to get closer to her. I needed to check in. I needed to connect. I needed to kiss her again without being slapped.

However, that was easier said than done. She'd obviously decided we needed to stick together as far as the second stage of the Challenge, considering neither of us had our own warp ship. But beyond that, I thought nothing was certain, despite her offhand remark to C. B. and Dane about her plans to "bed me."

With Norman lagging behind us, there was a bona fide chance of one of us winning the Challenge, so the divide between us was more real than ever. I imagined she felt every minute spent working with me might put a Pun closer to claiming the U.A.T. Sure, I could have argued that it might also put HER closer to claiming it, but that didn't even occur to me because I wasn't rooting for her. I was rooting for myself. I was still hiding from the selfish truth that I wanted her to do what I couldn't: to put us before her beliefs.

"What's up?" she asked.

"I guess I want to talk about . . . us," I began nervously.

"Oh," she said. "Clayton, you don't–"

"I know what you're going to say. We're O'Neil and Adams's *Green Lantern and Green Arrow*. A limited run, right?"

"Well–" she started to break in, but I barreled ahead.

"The thing is, that series was a major turning point. DC was billy to cancel it in '72–which is why they tried to recapture the magic sans Adams in '76."

There was no disputing my point. Denny O'Neil and Neal Adams's *Green Lantern/Green Arrow* series of the early 1970s had burst onto the scene, asking tough questions and tackling big issues to a degree that was virtually unheard of at the time. For instance, racism and drug addiction were both ruthlessly yanked from the closet. A black man called out Hal Jordan (aka Green Lantern) for flying around space helping "orange skins" and "purple skins," but never doing anything for the "black skins" back on Earth (*Green Lantern/Green Arrow* #76, 1970). And Oliver Queen (aka Green Arrow) was forced to confront the harsh reality of his sidekick Roy Harper's heroin problem (*Green Lantern/Green Arrow* #85, 1971).

Now, Hal was in no position to deny being 100 percent white-bread honky. A fact's a fact. However, he might have pointed out that he'd stopped alien invaders from destroying the entire Earth about a gazillion times, which helped out black folks just a little. And Oliver's approach to an intervention could have involved more reassuring his ward that he'd get the love and support he needed and less backhanding him in the face and screaming, "You're a lousy junkie!" But that's all neither here nor there. What's important is that the series started conversations that needed to be had by people who didn't want to have them. It was the power of the Scriptures taken to a new level.

Of course, there was an Achilles heel to likening our partnership to Green Lantern and Green Arrow's, and I was sure Cassie would pounce on it. So before she could get a word in, I cut her off.

"I know, I know," I said. "GL and GA are closer to each other on the Pro/Pun scale than we are. But there are plenty of great Pro/Pun partnerships. You've got Superman and Batman, Nightwing and the Huntress, Wolverine and pretty much any other X-Man, Spider-Man and . . . Venom."

She frowned. I knew I'd been stretching it with the last one. Venom tries to kill Spidey way too often for them to qualify as partners.

"Clayton," she started, but I pushed on.

"What about Apollo and the Midnighter? I mean I guess they're both kind of Puns, but the Midnighter is way more–"

"Clayton!" she repeated, more firmly this time.

"What?"

"You could go on all day listing team ups."

I was glad she thought so because I'd just now realized the list was actually pretty damn short. The vast majority of Pro/Pun partnerships flame out big time.

"But it doesn't matter," she added.

"How can you say that?" I exclaimed, frustrated. "You're keeping me at a distance because you're a Pro and I'm a Pun."

"Are you sure?"

"Well that's what you said."

"No, I mean ... I've been thinking about this a lot too. I've been thinking about you and how you live your life. Not the things you say, but the things you do."

It was my turn to frown as I started to suspect where she was going with this. But she forged ahead.

"The first time we met, you risked your life to keep Malcolm from hurting me. A couple weeks ago you ended up in a coma saving Arthur. You just jumped in front of a bullet to save me again. You even dragged Decker to safety, for Christ's sake! Protecting people is a reflex for you. And I know you think you were going to shove Malcolm out that air lock when he was knocked out, but I don't think you would have. You say you're a Pun, but your actions speak louder than your words."

The implication was everything I wanted. She was ready to let me in. The problem was the reason.

"Clayton, you're pure Pro," she finished.

She was looking at me like I'd sprouted a halo. But I hadn't. Sure, I'd done all the stuff she'd said. But I knew I would have finished Malcolm off if it hadn't been for her. After all, I sure hadn't shed a tear when I saw his bloated, soon-to-be-dead body slap against the cockpit window. I felt the same about Rickie. And if there were a magic button to press to send the rest of their gang on the same trip, I would have pressed it in a heartbeat. Not to mention Luthor Norman, who definitely needed to get dead. But that was all peripheral. It wasn't the core of my conviction. The reason I knew I was a Pun was a hunger – a hunger deep in my bones, to see the terror in the eyes of my parents' killer as I put him down. So Cassie was wrong about me – very wrong. And as much as I wanted to be with her, I needed her to know the truth.

I opened my mouth to speak, but then she unzipped her flight suit, and my judgment went out the window.

It was all very surprising. I mean, you hear about it. You see pictures and videos, but when it happens to you, it's a very different deal. Your whole life, you're walking around with these parts attached to you, and you think they're their own thing. Then suddenly they get around somebody else's parts, and you realize they're all puzzle pieces that fit together and add up to something astounding—something inconceivably right.

There wasn't any cognition going on. Once I felt Cassie's body against me—and by body, I mean boobs—my brain said, "I'm outta here." The rest of me had no problem with that, as it knew where to go and what to do, hardwired by millions of years of evolution.

We ended up on the wonder chair, reclined in the sleep setting. We weren't at it for very long. With our lack of experience, the finish line seemed like the reason for it all, but we discovered the real reason for it all afterward—as we lay there in each other's arms, feeling the comfort and confidence in the total acceptance of one another.

We both realized that this had truly been years in the making, with every moment of that time adding intensity to the consummation. I didn't see how I could pick up our conversation where we'd left off. She was happy. I was happy. Neither of us had experienced much of that, and it felt like it should be savored. I knew my conscience would make a comeback eventually, but until that time rolled around, I resolved to let it lie. And so we slept.

"So what about the Challenge?" I asked, after we'd awoken and begun getting dressed. It wasn't a direct line back to our earlier conversation, but it wasn't far off.

"What about it?" she replied.

"Are we a team now?"

"Um, I did what I just did with you, so . . ."

"Right. Well, what about Arthur and Decker?"

"There's no way I'm doing it with Decker, but Arthur's not out of the question." She gave me a playful smile.

"You know what I mean," I said. "Are we all partners? Will we share the U.A.T.? Is that even possible?"

My guilt about allowing her self-deception was clearly in overdrive because the idea of sharing the U.A.T. was almost unthinkable to me. My righteous plans for the thing notwithstanding, the closer we got to it, the more I felt a deranged greed coming over me, like Gollum chasing his precious.

"Right now, I don't know," Cassie said, turning serious. "The U.A.T. still matters as much as ever to me. But nothing is as cut and dry as it was. I mean, when you had that seizure, I just . . ."

Her words caught me off guard. I'd known what had happened between us had happened because she thought I was something I wasn't. But now I realized it had also happened because she was afraid I was dying. I knew the uncertainty about my condition was monkeying with my own emotions, but I stupidly hadn't considered that it could be monkeying with Cassie's as well. I felt like I'd taken advantage of her in more ways than one, and I needed to do what I could to make it right. I didn't know if I was dying or not, but I knew I was no Pro.

I was searching for the guts to say what needed to be said when the floor was yanked out from under us. We both hit the deck hard as the ship spun all the way around and tilted wildly upward, like a raft in rapids. The spinning continued for another few seconds, and then after a few more jolts, things settled down as the engines regained dominance.

"What in tarnation!?" we heard Decker yell from outside.

As we got to our feet and rushed out of my hab suite, we found him clambering up from the floor near the jump seats. Arthur took a hit off his inhaler and looked over his shoulder at us sheepishly.

"S-s-sorry. Looks like we caught the tail end of it," he said.

"Tail end of what?" I asked.

"I knew Norman's nav computer w-w-would plot the same arrival point as ours, to get him as close as possible to HBBI."

"So?" Decker said.

"So there was a s-s-small chance we'd be . . . inadvertently vaporized when his w-w-warp field vented," Arthur said, cringing.

"What?" Decker shrieked. "You didn't think that was something worth sharing?"

"I didn't see any point in w-w-worrying you," Arthur countered. "Like I s-s-said, I thought we'd get here just in time. And we did."

He gestured out the window, and what we saw there made us all forget our impromptu Tilt-A-Whirl ride and even the fact that we now knew Norman had made the warp jump successfully.

CHAPTER  19

"W-W-WELCOME TO HBBI," ARTHUR SAID. HE DROPPED US INTO orbit, and we stared down at the planet. It was a faded blue – nearly gray. From what we'd read, we knew it was considerably farther away from its sun than Earth was from its own. As such, it was most likely gripped by a perpetual winter.

"It looks like Jotunheim," Cassie said.

And it did. Jotunheim is the home world of Asgard's sworn enemies, the Frost Giants. It wasn't crazy to assume the planet's resemblance to a familiar Scripture locale had influenced Cateklysm's selection, but I hoped we wouldn't be dealing with any actual Frost Giants because, well, they're Frost Giants. Luckily, given his record so far, it seemed unlikely Cateklysm would take a tack that would be obvious from orbit.

As Arthur entered our destination into the navigational system, I noticed Decker was staring at Cassie and me.

"So, what exactly the two a' you been up to last couple hours?"

I think I actually blushed. Arthur smiled at the two of us and said, "About time."

Then a 3D model of the planet popped up on a holo-display in front of him, marking the route to the coordinates he'd entered, as well as our current position. He adjusted our thrust and reversed our orbit briefly, then took us in at a sharp angle. Intense orange-red light emanated through the cockpit windows as we broke atmosphere, but the effects of the searing heat were otherwise absorbed or deflected by the Javelin's thermal protection system.

As we tore through the thick cloud cover below, we discovered a seemingly endless expanse of dense, ice-covered rock terrain stretching out to our right. To our left, that terrain transitioned abruptly into an alien landscape, dominated by thousands of intersecting ice arches. In the distance beyond that, we could make out a coastline and a dark ocean.

"The Javelin's sensors aren't that comprehensive," Arthur said. "But from w-w-what they're picking up, there's no advanced life here. Some bacteria, but nothing exotic."

"Logical locale," Cassie reasoned. "After the work Cateklysm put in to getting people here, he wouldn't want them to get offed by alien apes or space microbes before they reached the main event."

After a couple of minutes, our marker on the holo-display converged on the marker for our destination. Arthur decreased our speed, engaged the low altitude maneuvering thrusters, and circled.

"Any idea w-w-what we're looking for?" he asked.

"Well, at the risk of soundin' cliché," Decker said, "I think *X* marks the spot."

He was looking out the left window with a stunned expression. We followed his gaze to the surface below and saw it. Standing out in stark relief from the otherwise bland landscape was an enormous black *X* sitting on a red background, contained in a circle with a thick yellow border. It was one of the more common color variants of the X-Men logo.

"Omigod," Cassie gasped.

I was speechless, but Decker sighed and said, "I guess now'd be as good a' time as any to announce I'm officially a Chowderhead again."

From the expression on his face, he was trying to avoid literally choking on his pride, but his air of defeat was already being replaced by one of excitement.

Arthur brought the ship around, then passed over the *X* again and veered to the right.

"Why aren't you landing?" I asked impatiently.

"I think I've m-m-managed to cloak our signature, so the ship will look like a blob of dense rock to the other Javelin's scans," Arthur answered, as he nosed the Javelin toward the forest of crisscrossing ice bridges. "But that won't do much for us if it's s-s-sitting out in the open when Norman gets here."

"If we're still 'round when Norman gets here, him spotting the ship won't be our only problem," Decker said.

"Still—doesn't hurt to remove one from the list," Cassie asserted. I nodded in agreement and thought for the millionth time how lost we'd be without Arthur. He dropped the ship into the middle of a tangled mess of icy tentacles and hovered laterally for several meters before extending the landing gear and setting us down beneath the intersection of two of the tentacles. The ship would be very hard to spot from the ground or air.

As the engines powered down, we heard the ice beneath the landing gear crack and felt a small jolt as the ship settled on the rocky surface below. Under any other circumstances, Decker, Cassie, and I probably would have peppered Arthur with questions about the stability of our landing spot. But right now, we wouldn't have cared if we were parked in Jell-O. This was it: the beginning of the second stage of the Challenge. Adrenaline coursed through me, forcing my need to come clean with Cassie and every other thought to the periphery, leaving only the here and now.

As soon as Arthur cut the engines, Cassie, Decker, and I headed toward the rear of the Javelin. He called after us, "Not that you people s-s-seem to care, but the atmosphere is breathable. Breathable and pretty d-d-darn near freezing, if you figure in windchill."

I gave him a "yeah, yeah, yeah" nod and hit the release for the outer door. A short ramp unfolded from beneath the Javelin and settled onto the snowy surface outside. As we stepped onto the ground, a chill took hold immediately. That's when Arthur's warning sank in. I hunched and hugged myself, rubbing my arms to fend off the cold. The others were doing the same, but they looked at me in surprise.

"You feel the cold too?" Cassie asked, with a puzzled look.

I shrugged. "'Irony Man' is starting to sound about right."

"We really need to find out m-m-more about that field around you," Arthur said, as he exited behind us.

"Can we do it when we don't have a trillionaire cizko on our tail?" Decker asked.

Arthur looked at him quizzically.

"Cizko means psychopath," Cassie clarified. "As in Edgar Cizko, Doctor Psycho."

Decker's use of Chowderhead slang had been on the rise as he'd made his way back from the dark side.

"Way I figure it, the cizko in question's only a couple hours behind us," he continued.

"And if that's not enough incentive to move our asses, there's always freezing to death," I added.

There were no EVA suits or even cold-weather gear onboard the Javelin, presumably because the discovery of Normanium Prime had taken Norman by surprise, and his ships hadn't been fully provisioned for interstellar travel.

"Maybe I should d-d-drop you guys off, circle back, and then come m-m-meet you," Arthur said. "The cold poses no real issue for me."

"That'll add a round trip," I said. "We gotta move."

So we set out at a walk-jog to keep warm and shorten the journey. Thankfully, after about fifteen minutes, we reached our destination. As we approached, we realized that the X we'd seen from the air was actually etched into the top of a large column, measuring roughly four yards in diameter and protruding from the surrounding landscape by about five feet. I wondered if a bad storm could deliver enough snowfall to cover it. But I doubted it. Following Cassie's same line of thinking about alien predators, it stood to reason Cateklysm hadn't gone to all this trouble to have the game derailed by bad weather.

We all examined the column, eager to find a clue of what to do next.

"Here," Decker said, from the far side of the column.

The rest of us joined him and saw he was standing in front of a panel housing a single large red button. He pressed it. At first, nothing happened, but then we heard the slow, mechanical groan of machinery left lonely for too long. The column split down the middle, and the two halves swung away from each other, falling against the ground to either side of a large opening. In the meantime, a steel platform rose from somewhere below to fill the opening–an ultraminimal lift. We all stared at it. This was a historic moment. We knew that. But thanks to the cold, we couldn't feel our faces. So we stowed the ceremony and stepped onto the lift.

It began to descend. As it did, the clamshell hatch swung closed above us, shielding us from the elements and leaving us to travel through relative darkness toward a dimly lit area below. About a minute later, we touched down with a gentle thud. I was the first to step off the lift, and when I did, the main lights came up, fully illuminating our surroundings. We were in an expansive chamber, about the size of a football field. The walls, ceiling, and floor were covered in square metallic panels that looked like blue steel. The pristine symmetry of the space was interrupted only by a few ventilation grids, as well as a room that protruded from one of the walls about fifteen feet up, with a large window overlooking the chamber. I noticed there was a door at our level that presumably led up, though it was easy to miss because it was lined with the same metallic panels as everything else.

Cassie, Decker, and I stared slack-jawed at the place. We knew damn well what it was supposed to be, even if there wasn't a lot of continuity to the visual references upon which it had been based.

"Sweet Christmas!" Decker muttered, à la Luke Cage.

"W-w-what?" Arthur asked. "What is it?"

"It's a replica of the Danger Room!" Cassie said.

The Danger Room was created by Charles Xavier to prepare the X-Men for any and all foes they may face. It used Shi'ar hard-light holographic technology to fabricate laser turret-laden obstacle courses, mutant-hunting Sentinels, Magneto's minions, and just about any other threat to life and limb one could imagine.

As we gawked at the living comic book backdrop before us, a beam shot out of the ceiling and scanned over each of us in turn. Then it narrowed its focus, rapidly etching something out of thin air on the floor in front of me. It was a belt, like those worn by the X-Men, complete with an X-Men emblem as the belt buckle. The beam rapidly swung over to the ground in front of Cassie, Decker, and Arthur, repeating the feat for each of them. Then it went dead.

I leaned down and touched the belt. It felt real. I'd heard of new technology that could give a hologram density through localized energy fields, but this was decades beyond that – at least.

The next step wasn't rocket science. I picked up the belt and put it on. Cassie did the same, followed by Decker and Arthur. As Arthur's buckle clicked into place, the laser overhead surged back to life, drawing a large circle in the center of the room. A series of glowing arrows then appeared on the ground in front of us, leading to the center of the circle.

Again, not rocket science. We followed the arrows to the circle and stepped inside. As soon as the last of us did so, the laser shot back out in a wide beam, drawing a glimmering, slightly opaque dome around us.

Arthur reached out to touch it, but his hand passed through. As it did so, a holographic warning shot out of the emblem on his belt and hovered in front of him. It was a countdown, starting from ten seconds. As the numbers began ticking by, we heard a synthesized voice sync up with the countdown: "Disqualification in seven, six, five . . ." Arthur yanked his hand back inside the dome. The countdown disappeared, and the voice went silent.

The laser overhead sprang back to life, moving at blinding speed across the terrain outside the dome. In a matter of seconds, a whole world began to take shape around us. The walls and ceiling depicted a detailed cityscape and sky fading into the distance, while the room was filled with physical manifestations of the scene, which was a slice of 1940s Manhattan. Our dome sat in an empty lot, facing a busy street filled with passing automobiles. The vehicles would segue from two dimensions to three dimensions and vice versa as they crossed out of and into the walls on either side. Nearly all of them had bulky front ends that seemed large enough to house three engines, and most of them were black or white, save a few yellow and green pastels that stood out from the herd. Pedestrians also milled by, the women in A-line skirts falling below the knee and the men in double-breasted suits with wide lapels and padded shoulders.

Across the street, a large art deco building stretched thirty-three stories above us. At its base, its terra-cotta tiling shone emerald but transitioned to blue as the building climbed skyward and crossed into two dimensions on the ceiling of the chamber. The green metal windows trimmed with vermillion signaled a full commitment to the architect's vision, which had been received with mixed reviews. I knew all of this because I'd seen this place in pictures and read all about it. The tenth floor of the building before us was home to the pulp fiction company Timely Publications, which would become Marvel Comics. This was the birthplace of Captain America, the original Human Torch, and Namor the Sub-Mariner, among others.

But the building was not what demanded our attention. What stood out most in this extraordinary historical re-creation was the freakish assembly in front of the building: a group of slightly robotic holo-protestors, marching back and forth with signs that read "Down with the Jew Deal" and "Protect pure Americanism" while chanting "Hear Hitler now!" in time with a bullhorn-toting ring leader. Of course, the signs and the chanting weren't the only thing we noticed about them.

"Holy shit, they're all Cateklysm!" Decker gasped.

Indeed, while their attire was varied and period-appropriate from the neck down, they all shared the same face – a blue domino mask-clad face no one had seen since ComicCon, eighteen years before. That fact definitely bumped up their creepiness factor, which was hard to do, considering who they were supposed to be: the German American Bund. Previously known as the Friends of New Germany, the German American Bund was one of the more extreme groups of Nazi sympathizers that had sprung up in the US in the late 1930s and early 40s before the country entered World War II. Most Chowderheads knew about such groups because some of them had made death threats toward Jack Kirby and Joe Simon after the two artists produced the first issue of *Captain America*, featuring Cap socking Hitler on the cover.

Kirby and Simon were Chowderhead icons – two Jewish kids who had used their artistic talent to create a superhero who would stand up for American values, even before America was willing to do so. And make no mistake, they didn't hide behind their creation. At one point, Kirby got a call from three guys in the lobby of the building, promising to show him "what real Nazis would do to Captain America" if he came downstairs. A distinguished street brawler, he told them, "I'll be right down." But by the time he got there, sleeves rolled up and ready to rumble, the cowards had cleared out.

Incidentally, both Kirby and Simon would find out all about real Nazis when they answered the call to serve in World War II. Then they would return to comics, with Kirby in particular going on to revolutionize the industry, earning him the title Jack "King" Kirby.

"What is g-g-going on here guys?" Arthur asked.

"We're outside the Timely Publications office in the 1940s," Cassie answered.

"Okay," Arthur said. "And w-w-what's with the Cateklysm-faced Nazis?"

"No idea," she responded.

But Arthur got his answer a moment later when one of the Cateklysms turned and seemed to notice us. A nasty sneer spread across his face, and he stepped out into the street, crossing toward us. He reached the sidewalk and pushed through the passersby – empty-headed holo-sprites, who seemed not to see us at all. I felt a sense of unease as he paused at the outer wall of the dome. Then his sneer hardened, and he stepped through. As he did, the laser shot down from above and washed over him, transforming him before our eyes. While his blue domino mask was untouched, the face beneath it darkened to a bloody crimson as the flesh was drawn taut against the bone. His clothes transmuted from a utilitarian jacket and slacks to a rich black military uniform – his right lapel adorned with a metal emblem of an eagle perched on a swastika. His left arm had a red band wrapped around it, stamped with the Iron Cross. He still looked like Cateklysm, especially with the blue domino mask. But unlike the other Cateklysms, he was now channeling a second, more bone-chilling presence.

"Guys?" Arthur whispered, once again bewildered. "W-w-what am I looking at here?"

"It's. . . a Red Skull Cateklysm," I whispered back, now wildly unnerved. There had been many Red Skulls, but I was sure the one the Cateklysm before us was channeling was the only one that mattered: Third Reich MVP Johann Schmidt. He'd been the bane of Steve Rogers's existence since *Captain America* #7 (1941), but he'd also gone toe to toe with the Invaders, the Avengers, and scores of other superhero teams. And now, this cosplaying Cateklysm clone was bringing him to life. In an effort to stave off a bout of hyperventilation, I told myself that none of this was real. Still, it wasn't just a fancy light show, either, any more than the belts strapped around our waists were. The number twenty-five appeared in glowing green numerals over the skullified Cateklysm's head, as his gaze passed from one of us to the next until finally settling on me. Decker took a big step away from me, and I gave him a look that said "What the hell?"

He shrugged and said, "Just a precaution. I'm sure you gonna be fine."

As a counterpoint, the Red Skull Cateklysm proclaimed, "Und now you vill die, Americane schweinhund!" in a cartoonish German version of Cateklysm's voice.

Nobody likes being called a pig dog, but I was more concerned with the "now you will die" part. The list of things I was vulnerable to was growing, and there was no telling if the Danger Room replica's version of Shi'ar hard light was on that list.

The Red Skull Cateklysm strode purposefully toward me, and as he drew nearer, a message was projected from the X-Men logo on my belt. It read:

Who created the superserum responsible for Captain America's powers?
a) Dr. Hugo Strange
b) Dr. Curtis Connors
c) Dr. Abraham Erskine

A super-Nazi impersonator was about to murder me, and my belt was administering a pop quiz. Luckily it wasn't a hard one. I swiped a hand through the air where "c) Dr. Abraham Erskine" hovered. Then suddenly, the laser shot down from above and a second later, I was holding Captain America's shield. I knew what to do. As the Red Skull Cateklysm broke into a run and craned back his fist to deliver a crushing blow, I hurled the shield. It whirred through the air and smashed into his chest. He staggered back as the shield ricocheted off toward the side of the dome, then faded out of existence. It had been a terrible throw, but it seemed like the system running this little game had guided it. That was fair. The point wasn't my throwing expertise. In fact, as with the Conundrum, the point wasn't even the answer to the question per se – the point was that I had done my reading.

I noticed the number above the Red Skull Cateklysm change to twenty-four, as he returned to his starting position, leaving me be.

"See," Decker said. "You're fine. Ol' Skull-head probably can't really hurt any of us." Then we saw a question projected in front of Arthur, as "Ol' Skullhead" drew a luger pistol and started stomping toward him. From where Decker, Cassie, and I were standing, the question was backward, so we couldn't make it out. Arthur's total lack of Scripture knowledge had just become a problem. He panicked and swiped frantically at the air in front of him. But his random choice was clearly wrong because we all heard *ehhhhhh!* as a buzzer sounded and the Red Skull Cateklysm fired the pistol. The round smacked into Arthur's chest, and he toppled over backward.

"Shit fire!" Decker yelled.

Arthur landed half in and half out of the dome but dragged himself back inside almost immediately, stopping the countdown that had begun again. We all ran to his side as he got to his feet, holding his chest tenderly.

"I'm g-g-going to have to disagree about whether he can hurt us!" he growled.

I couldn't understand why being shot hadn't triggered the emergency shutdown of Arthur's pain receptors. But as it turned out, he hadn't been shot. There was no sign of an entry wound. The ghost bullet had stung, but so far, it seemed the simulation wasn't really trying to kill us. Moreover, our adversary was behaving more like an old-fashioned video game NPC than a supervillain genius. He turned and strode back to his starting position to take another pause, giving us a moment to collect ourselves.

But that was all cold comfort because he'd be at us again—and while he may have been calibrated to deal out something short of lethal force, we now knew he could deliver some nasty bruises, and maybe worse. No doubt about it, the bar had been raised in a big way. This was a whole new level of proving our Chowderhead prowess.

Apparently, Arthur had been identified as the weak link because the Red Skull Cateklysm drew a bead on him and charged again. As he did, Cassie jumped between them. She'd guessed that her belt would dispense a question if she put herself in harm's way. She'd guessed right. As the question popped up, she processed it so fast, I only registered the answer she was swiping her hand through: "Professor Phineas Horton." Suddenly, her body was consumed by flames, like a blow torch igniting. She was a raging inferno in the form of a person.

"Oh my G-g-god!" Arthur shouted. He was no doubt expecting her to stop, drop, and roll. Instead, she extended a hand and a torrent of flames shot out toward the Red Skull Cateklysm, who reeled back, fire dancing across his face, chest, and arms. Then the flames engulfing Cassie vanished as the number above the Red Skull Cateklysm's head fell to twenty-three. I was sure I knew what that number was now: a hit counter. Our job was to get it to zero. Another parallel to old-fashioned video games.

"What just h-h-happened?" Arthur demanded.

"Freakin' Human Torch just happened!" Decker yelled.

As the Red Skull Cateklysm flailed around, violently pawing at his upper body, the flames died down. But as he lowered his arms, we saw much of his clothing had been burned away, along with most of his face. I felt a knot in the pit of my stomach as I saw what was underneath. A glowing red sensor shined out at us from where his face was supposed to be, and inset into a metallic torso, now visible through the tatters of his uniform, was a digital display projecting a furious skeletal visage, sporting Cateklysm's trademark domino mask. The Cateklysm clone wasn't channeling the regular Red Skull. He was channeling the Red Skull in the robot body loaned to the Skull by Arnim Zola, starting in *Captain America* #42 (2008). He was faster, stronger, Nazi-er.

I glanced over at Arthur. As I'd suspected, he was more unsettled by the unveiling of a killer android than any of us. I felt for him. But those feelings were ill-timed because they divided my attention, and I was slow to notice a question flashing up in front of me. I'd barely had time to skim it and glean that it was something to do with the Winter Soldier when the Red Skull Cateklysm lunged and hammered a fist into my chest.

I felt almost nothing from the impact. Evidently, whatever he was made of couldn't penetrate the field around me after all. However, the blow did knock me out of the dome and smash me into the ground – which was also no match for my protective coating. The concrete exploded around me like Styrofoam, the broken chunks flickering to reveal cracked blue paneling shining through sections where the hard hologram illusion was failing.

The shot would have killed anyone else. I thought the system must have picked up on my mutation when it scanned me, and it was hitting me hard enough to make things interesting. But being that I was feeling no pain, as the countdown began, it occurred to me that maybe the others should stay safely out here, and I should go it alone with them yelling any answers I didn't know. Unfortunately, that scheme went out the window as I noted that from out here, I could neither see nor hear anything that was happening within the dome. There was no way for anyone outside to help anyone inside. However, as I rushed back in to beat the countdown and watched the Red Skull Cateklysm march back toward his starting position, I realized my invulnerability presented another possibility. Maybe I could just kick this Nazi dickhead's ass! The notion untethered something inside – some sort of berserker fury lying dormant. I bared my teeth like a feral beast and launched myself at the skull-faced creep, bellowing "It's clobberin' time, bitch!"

Then I bounced off him like a beach ball and hit the ground with a thud. Not the clobberin' I'd hoped for. In retrospect, my miscalculation was obvious. When I'd been hurled into the ground with superstrength, the ground had shattered. But the strength with which I could hurl myself was decidedly unsuper. Just because I was indestructible didn't mean I could destroy stuff – especially not stuff like a super robot.

Cassie, Arthur, and Decker watched me pitifully amble to my feet as the Red Skull Cateklysm reached his starting position, turned, and surveyed our ranks. I looked over at the others. It was one thing for Cassie and Decker to take the punishment promised by this contest, but Arthur was different. With none of the answers on tap, the punishment he'd be taking wouldn't help anyone.

"Arthur," I said, "Maybe you should bow out."

"I don't know, man," Decker interjected. "We may need all the cannon fodder we can get." Despite the indelicate phrasing, he was right. We didn't know what would happen if we blew it. I was reasonably sure we'd be allowed to try again, but there was a chance there would be a cooling-off period. And with Norman arriving soon, that wasn't a chance we could take.

I think Arthur had come to the same conclusion because he sighed and said, "Let's d-d-do this."

I nodded respectfully, humbled by his mettle.

"We need to keep me between you guys and him," I said, turning my attention back to our robot Nazi guest. I half expected Cassie to take issue with using me as a human shield, but even she yielded to the wisdom in it. We formed a triangle with her and Decker flanking Arthur and me out front.

A grimace spread across the Red Skull Cateklysm's chest-mounted CGI face, as if our new configuration was some kind of challenge.

"Insolent velps!" He yelled. "No von opposes zee vill of zee Red Skull!"

Then, it was on. As he rushed forward, our belts started throwing up quiz questions, and we started knocking them down. Who was the original Human Torch's sidekick? Toro! What was the Whizzer's civilian identity? Bob Frank! Who gave the Red Skull his initial training? Hitler!

Every question related to a title that had had something to do with the Red Skull over the decades, and every answer yielded a single-use weapon or endowed us with a single-use superpower that appeared in those titles. But annoyingly, with every blow we landed, the questions were getting harder. Meanwhile, our sparring partner was growing in ferocity, recovering more quickly and lunging more aggressively. But his attacks weren't just designed to leave bruises. They seemed more focused on knocking us out of the dome—and each successful attack knocked us farther and farther out. On occasion, we'd step out intentionally to avoid an attack, but he'd be on us as soon as we were forced back in by the countdown.

It was an uphill battle, but we were bringing our A game and slowly but surely, the hit counter tumbled to twenty, then fifteen, then ten, driven by a barrage of flying shields, fireballs, exploding arrows, and Widow's Bites.

Then, as the counter fell to five, the Red Skull Cateklysm went into a frenzy, leaping into our midst and swinging wild. We scattered left and right but miraculously kept our wits, maintaining the hail of projectiles. Before we even knew it was happening, the counter hit zero, and he fell to his knees, fading out of existence.

I stared around at the others and saw the same expression on their faces I felt on my own: the shell-shocked look of a tornado survivor.

"That was pretty hairy," Decker said. "But not near as bad as the matum meal[8] I was expecting." In an uncharacteristic bout of optimism, he seemed to think we were done.

"Level two, commencing in thirty seconds," the synthesized voice echoed through the room.

"Happy now?" I said to Decker.

"Not even a little."

Short as the intermission was, it did give me a chance to marvel at what we'd walked into. I looked across the street at the mob of Cateklysms masquerading as Bundsmen. Technically, the German American Bund had never gathered en masse to demonstrate outside the Timely office. They'd just lurked in small, semi-anonymous groups like robbers casing a bank or jackals testing the perimeter of a village. But historical accuracy be damned. Through his dramatization, Cateklysm had used the mask of the Red Skull to make real-world evil more recognizable – just as Kirby and Simon had done more than a century before. It was the embodiment of all we believed, distilled into a single moment in history. The starred-and-striped shield I'd thrown was weaponized creativity – powerful positive propaganda that denounced the racism and fascism hiding in the shadows. The game was brilliant indeed. But it wasn't over.

The timer hit zero, and we noticed one of the other Cateklysms breaking away from the group and crossing the street. He stepped through the outer wall of the dome, and the laser scanned over him. As it did, he grew in height, and his skin and clothing tore away like a candy-bar wrapper, revealing a giant praying mantis-like beast. Of course, Cateklysm didn't want us to forget who was testing us for a moment, so the thing still had his face, despite the red insectoid eyes glowing out from behind his blue mask and the bony pinchers protruding from where his ears should have been.

"Gimme a break!" Arthur groaned. "What the h-h-heck is this thing supposed to be?"

It was a so-so rendition, but again, the intent was clear.

"Violator Cateklysm," I mumbled, shakily.

Violator is one of the many minions of hell haunting the pages of *Spawn*. The title was born long after the 1940s, but it made sense that the Cateklysm clones would borrow from every epoch's vanguard of villainy. The World War II-era setup epitomized comic book creators rallying their readers to stand up for what was right, but that was just the beginning of the movement.

---

8   *Chowderhead slang, meaning a total clusterfuck. Origin: Shorthand for "Ultimatum Meal," a reference to the moment where the mayhem of Marvel's Ultimate Comics miniseries Ultimatum crescendos with a bizarre two-course meal, involving the Blob eating the Wasp, before having his own head bitten off by a giant-size Hank Pym.*

A number thirty appeared above the Violator Cateklysm's head as he addressed us, the system infusing his voice with a raspy demon-esque quality. "Prepare to feel the flesh stripped from your bones!"

"I'm not prepared for that," Arthur said. "W-w-what if I'm not prepared?"

"I expect he'll go on ahead with the flesh-strippin' either way," Decker answered.

I told myself the gruesome threat was hyperbole, but it was hard to be sure. The monster stalked toward us and we crowded together in our little phalanx.

The Violator Cateklysm didn't go down easy. But he went down, and level two became level three, which became level four and so on. There were fifteen Cateklysm Bundsmen in total, and one by one they crossed the street for a showdown. With hit counts ranging from thirty-two to sixty, the batting order for the next twelve rounds included an Atrocitus Cateklysm, a Green Goblin Cateklysm, a Master Darque Cateklysm, a Redeemer Cateklysm, an Amazo Cateklysm, a Doctor Doldrums Cateklysm, a Kingpin Cateklysm, a Mandarin Cateklysm, a Circe Cateklysm, a Joker Cateklysm, a Gorilla Grodd Cateklysm, and a Lex Luthor Cateklysm. All the choices made sense, as they were blue-chip bad guys balanced across the top publishers. The only exception was Doctor Doldrums. He was a joke, whose only appearances were in the short-lived Strain Comics' *Helix* 38 series, (2028–2029). Every one of those appearances had ended in a humiliating defeat at the hands of the Helix 38 team. I was convinced Cateklysm was making a point with the obscure inclusion. That point? Evil should always be taken seriously, even if it seems impotent. Attila the Hun, Pol Pot, and Ivan the Terrible were all relatively harmless before they made the big time.

Alas, the moments for such insights were scarce. As we slugged our way through the conga line of Cateklysms, the questions got harder, the attacks came quicker, and the concern for our safety seemed to edge ever closer to the line.

Still we were holding our own. Cassie was performing as brilliantly as I'd expected, and I wasn't too shabby–but Decker was a revelation, reclaiming his Chowderhead roots with a vengeance. In one highlight, he identified Aunt May's rest home suitor, Nathan Lubensky, to earn a pair of web shooters with which he yanked the Green Goblin Cateklysm from his soaring glider, sending the cackling nutzoid plummeting to his demise as his hit count fell to zero.

Like every Chowderhead, Decker, Cassie, and I knew activating Spidey's web shooters required not a single tap to the palm, but a quick double tap. (Otherwise Spidey would be shooting webs all over the place every time he went to climb a wall.) But none of us had imagined our grasp of superhero weapons and powers would ever have such a practical application. We threw Thor's hammer, Batman's Batarangs, and yes, Wonder Woman's tiara. We fired Iron Man's pulse blasters, Green Arrow's bow, and Punisher's trusty Colt M1911. We unleashed Banshee's sonic scream and wielded Spawn's shape-shifting cape and chains. And every now and then, we'd get up close and personal with Ninjak's collapsible steel blades or Danny Rand's Shou-Lao infused Iron Fist.

With Cassie and Decker flanking Arthur and taking turns answering his questions between their own, even he was doing his share of ass-whooping. But don't get me wrong. We missed questions. Plenty of them. I idiotically chose the *Daily Planet* when asked where Clark Kent went to work when he got to Metropolis, when any nitwit knows the Planet was originally known as the *Daily Star* (*Action Comics* #1, 1938). When asked who joined the Avengers first, Cassie embarrassingly answered Iron Man over Captain America and Kraven the Hunter because she'd boneheadedly forgotten *New Avengers* #10 (2011), where it's revealed that Kraven was a member of Nick Fury's Avengers way back in the 1950s.

Errors like these took their toll, no matter how hard I tried to put myself between the bad guys and the others. After all, the system was simulating all the powers of the supervillains channeled by the Cateklysms, enabling them to go around or over me a lot of the time. So Cassie, Decker, and Arthur were all battered, bruised, and even a little burned. But none of the three of them seemed to feel it. For the most part, the only thing they seemed to be feeling was the same thing I was: exhilaration.

Lost in this daze, we barely noticed when the supply of Cateklysms dwindled to just one. All that remained was the shithead who had been leading the chanting.

A cloud seemed to roll in, displacing our earlier euphoria. The worst would undoubtedly have been saved for last–and as close as we were to the finish line, we suddenly felt our confidence waver dramatically. Decker decided to try to overpower the feeling.

"Well come on and turn into Galactus, asshole!" he yelled at the last Cateklysm.

"Don't give him any ideas, you schmo!" Cassie replied. She turned to me, anxiety building. "There's no way to fit Galactus in here, is there?"

I shrugged helplessly as I pictured the world-eating entity that was Galactus. Trying to avoid being stomped by a foot the size of a building didn't sound that great. But as the Cateklysm across the street dropped his bullhorn and started toward us, I decided Galactus was a long shot. Aside from the practical issue that it would be very hard for the room to accommodate a being his size, I just didn't think he'd make the cut. I mean not only have his efforts to gobble up Earth always been repelled handily, but his motivations simply aren't that sinister. He's not such a bad guy, he's just hungry. Plus there were plenty of other all-star contenders for the big finish. A list of names scrolled through my mind: Doomsday, Apocalypse, Ultron, Doctor Doom, Thanos, Malekith, Magneto, Shadow King, Satan. Hell, given the prominence of *Fate Force* in the Challenge so far, even General Genocide from the series's seminal issue #100 (2020) was a candidate.

But as the last of the Cateklysms stepped into the dome and the laser passed over him, I realized there had really only been one possibility. Beneath the ever-present domino mask, the Cateklysm's complexion faded to gray, and his body took on the form of the nine-foot, blue singlet-clad, two-thousand-pound "God of Evil." There, standing before us, was a Darkseid Cateklysm.

The fact that Darkseid was created by Jack Kirby offered some symmetry to Cateklysm's game. But that isn't what made him the obvious choice. Darkseid is the ultimate supervillain: a cold, calculating embodiment of darkness who lives to conquer and control all life, everywhere. Debates have raged over whether he is in fact more powerful than Superman. But both sides of those debates would agree you wouldn't want to meet the guy in a dark alley. We were in deep shit, and we found out just how deep when the number appeared above the Darkseid Cateklysm's head.

"One hundred?!" Decker yelled. "Fuck me!"

That about summed it up. We were about to do battle with a Cateklysm lookalike channeling the father of all badasses, and to top it off, our window of time was nearly shut. Based on Arthur's estimate, Norman would be landing above us in about twenty-five minutes. But I was reminded that Norman was our second problem as our first problem spoke up, the system endowing his voice with the resonance of tectonic plates shifting against one another.

"So you have bested the rank and file offered up so far? You should be commended."

Despite myself, I felt a tinge of pride. Darkseid was evil, but he was kind of a big deal in the Scriptures. And with Cateklysm's face, his praise was a double scoop of validation. But the second part of his speech left me less warm and fuzzy.

"Of course, your time is now at an end," he rumbled. "But you can take solace in the knowledge that it is the almighty Darkseid who shall crush the life from your bodies."

He advanced on us with booming footsteps that actually shook the ground.

As he did, messages appeared in front of each of us. Mine read:

In what title was Darkseid introduced?

That was it. There were no options to choose from. I didn't know what to do. But I did know the answer because it had always stuck with me as further evidence of what a stand-up guy Jack Kirby was. He'd created Darkseid during a run at DC, where he'd insisted on working on a lesser-known title that had no assigned talent in order to avoid putting any artists out of a job. For lack of a better idea, I just shouted the name of the title: *"Superman's Pal Jimmy Olsen!"*

Suddenly I was seeing red. Literally. My range of vision was actually flooded with a red haze. Then two beams burst from my eyes and bashed into the Darkseid Cateklysm's chest. His hit count fell to ninety-nine, and I reveled in the fact that I'd just borrowed Superman's heat vision. On the downside, the blast had barely faded before the brute resumed his relentless march toward us. Not only had the quiz questions graduated to a much more challenging format, but this last Cateklysm wasn't starting the bout by retreating to the center of the dome after each attack, as all the others had.

I heard Decker yell, "Thomas Oscar!" as two swirling blasts of air shot from his hands, à la the Red Tornado. The blasts crashed into the Darkseid Cateklysm's midsection.

"Tom Kalmaku!" Cassie cried, summoning a twenty-foot tall hard light sledgehammer projected from a green power ring that had materialized on her finger. The hammer slammed down on the Darkseid Cateklysm's head.

I didn't know exactly what questions they'd been answering, but the results were impressive. Sadly, they weren't impressive enough. Aside from losing a couple of ticks off his hit counter, our terrifying playmate just shrugged off the blows and kept coming. We huddled together in our phalanx again and rotated around the dome, battering him with everything we had. But this was a new game in so many ways. Questions hung in front of us for around a minute or until someone shouted the right answer, and in the meantime, we were constantly dodging attacks or getting hit. It still seemed that the system was calibrated to avoid doing long-term damage, but the Darkseid Cateklysm was cutting it a lot closer than any adversary before him. Cassie later likened his blows to being hit by a rolled-up bed mattress swung by a bear. Not fatal, but not a ride that attracts a very long line.

As soon as his hit counter fell below seventy-five, he picked up his already-frenzied pace, throwing haymakers so fast it felt like we were being hunted by helicopter blades. It wasn't long before he sent both Decker and Cassie careening out of the dome with a single blow. They'd just barely made it back in before their countdowns hit zero. Of course, we got pretty used to those close calls when the system started simulating Darkseid's telekinesis to grab cars from the street and hurl them at us. Fortunately, the others managed to keep clear of those because I'm sure they would have hurt more than a rolled-up mattress.

Suffice it to say, it was no picnic. But Cassie and I had essentially been waiting our whole lives for this—and you'd think the other two had, too, based on their grit. We scraped, we clawed, we gave everything we had to keep our heads in the game and our bodies in the dome. When the Darkseid Cateklysm's hit counter fell to fifty, we thought we might just be able to come out on top. When it fell to twenty-five, we became sure of it.

But that didn't last. Because when the counter fell to ten, his eyes began glowing red. Now, in the Scriptures, when Darkseid's eyes turn red, people's pants turn brown—because it means he's about to unleash his Omega Beams. They're kind of like Superman's heat vision, except they're arguably more deadly, and they can chase you down like heat-seeking missiles capable of right-angle turns. As he started blasting away, we knew it wouldn't be long before somebody's luck ran out. That somebody turned out to be Decker. The hit counter had just fallen to three when one of the beams nailed Decker and sent him flying. He bounced a couple of times, then tumbled across the concrete of the vacant lot before coming to a stop far outside the dome. It had to hurt, but he rolled to his feet and sprinted toward us, racing against the countdown. It was a race he couldn't win. As he reached the wall, he bounced off. He'd been disqualified and barred from entry. Worse still, his loss proved enough of a distraction for the Darkseid Cateklysm to get ahold of Arthur by the leg and start swinging him at me and Cassie like a giant pair of nunchucks.

I couldn't imagine there wasn't some real danger here—either to Cassie if Arthur hit her, or Arthur if he hit me (assuming my superskin would bust his synthetic body). It was beginning to look like the system's safety measures had taken a powder all together, and it wasn't a great time to be racking my brain for "the supervillain identity of John Monroe." But that was what my dumb belt was asking for. So I dug deep and there it was.

"Weasel!" I yelled. A split second later, I was firing a Firestorm fusion blast and knocking the Darkseid Cateklysm back. Unfortunately, that really seemed to piss him off, and he started swinging Arthur around more violently. As Arthur was whipped back and forth, we heard him yell, "This g-g-guy . . . is just . . . the worst!"

I was so busy diving and rolling out of the way now, I barely had the composure to register the question flashing in front of me, never mind read or answer it. However, as long as the Darkseid Cateklysm was coming after me, Cassie had a second to focus. And she used it to answer the question before her.

"Jackie Reynolds!" she yelled, naming a racketeer and coconspirator of the Ultra-Humanite.

I didn't know what she was swinging when she appeared behind the Darkseid Cateklysm, but I recognized it when it collided with his shoulder. It was Hawkgirl's Nth metal mace. The impact sent out a shockwave, and the titanic gray bruiser actually stumbled and fell to one knee, dropping Arthur, who scrambled clear of him.

This was it. The hit counter was at one, and the Darkseid Cateklysm's attention had turned to Cassie. I glanced down at the question in front of me:

Who was Supergirl's first boyfriend?

I yelled "Rich—" on my way to saying "Richard Malverne," but I didn't finish because Cassie's body flew through the air and bashed into me, knocking us both out of the dome. Her melee attack had been epic, but the follow-through of her swing had left her open to an equally epic forehand from the Darkseid Cateklysm. As we toppled out of the dome, part of me thought it was lucky people could penetrate the field around me, so Cassie wouldn't feel like she was hitting a brick wall. But a bigger part of me thought, *Shiiiiiit!!!*

The countdown started the second we breeched the dome, then we hit the ground and rolled across it like Decker had—but we rolled farther. We ended up in a pile about twenty feet away. Decker hurried over to help us up, but it was no use. As we clambered frantically toward the dome, we heard the synthesized voice calmly sealing our doom. "Three, two, one . . ." We reached the outer wall to find it now solid and impassable.

I pounded a fist against it and screamed. Cassie and Decker stood speechless and motionless on either side of me. We couldn't see or hear anything through the opaque, soundproof dome, so there was no way to know what was happening inside. But we had a pretty good idea. With no Scripture knowledge whatsoever, Arthur was at the Darkseid Cateklysm's mercy. He would be ejected from the dome any second now.

All the years we'd spent preparing for this, all the risks we'd taken over the last couple of days—none of it would count for squat. Norman would be here in minutes. If we weren't gone by then, we'd be dead. I had no doubt he'd be traveling with enough muscle to make sure of that. Of course, it was more than likely that he'd fail to beat all the Cateklysms on his first pass, but sooner or later he'd finish the job. Then he would know where to go next. And that would be that. We could come back to the Danger Room after he left and try again, but it would be pointless. He'd post guards at the entrance to the final stage until it was all over.

I pounded on the dome once more, then I fell against it and slid down it, exhaustion and demoralization dragging me to the floor like an anvil chained around my neck. There was nothing I could do but sit there waiting for the inevitable in grim, defeated silence.

But then . . . providence kicked the inevitable right in the teeth. Instead of seeing Arthur ejected from the dome, we saw the dome begin to dissolve, revealing an impossible scene inside. The Darkseid Cateklysm was in a crumpled heap on the ground, and Arthur was standing over him, reskinned from shoulders to shoes as the heroic half-man, half-machine Cyborg—his hand cannon blasting away, tearing the almighty God of Evil wannabe apart.

The hit counter hit zero, and the last of the Cateklysms faded away as the floor tile in the middle of the space slid aside and a pedestal rose from beneath it, bearing a small black box. Arthur turned to us, his face illuminated with a huge smile, and as our belts and the scenery slowly decomposed into nothingness, his Cyborg body overlay went with them.

"How did you . . ." I trailed off, too stunned to finish the question.

Arthur shrugged and said, "Neron, m-m-man. Neron!"

CHAPTER  20

FOR MOST OF THE LAST LEVEL, ARTHUR HAD BEEN STRUGGLING past his stutter to call out his questions, hoping one of us could spare enough attention to shout an answer. But with the cars being chucked around, and the Omega Beams, we'd gotten a little distracted. So he'd just started ignoring the questions. After all, he didn't know anything about the Scriptures. Well, except one thing. Thanks to me, he knew being called Metallo was kind of a compliment because, robo-jerk or not, Metallo was a total kangster after he got upgraded by Neron. You can imagine Arthur's surprise when he glanced down in desperation at the question before him, after Cassie and I were thrown from the dome:

What was the name of the demon who granted Metallo new powers?

After gathering around him for hugs and high fives, our eyes fell to the pedestal that had risen from the floor and the box sitting atop it. The box was glossy onyx and about half the size of a brick. Cassie stepped forward and picked it up. She turned it over in her hands, examining it. It seemed to be a solid block with no seams or hinges, but after a moment, one of its faces illuminated. Cassie looked down at the glowing face, sighed, and rolled her eyes. She handed me the box, and the rest of us looked at it. A virtual keyboard had appeared below a message that read simply:

To plot your next stop, name the thing that put him on a path with possibilities.

"Tee-riffic," Decker exclaimed in mock glee. "A new riddle!"

We all nodded at the sentiment. To say it had been a very long day was the understatement of the millennium, and none of us had the energy to think about what the cryptic missive could mean. But it would've had to wait even if we did. Because at that moment, there was a metallic groan as the lift began to rise toward the surface. We were all jarred back into the reality of our situation. We looked up to see a plume of snow cascade down toward us as the clamshell hatch forty feet above cracked open. Our time was up. Norman and his crew were on their way down. I stuffed the black box down the front of my pocketless flight suit as we all scanned our surroundings in a panic. Then we spotted our salvation.

★

As Norman and his men descended into the chamber, the look on his face was a combination of glee and awe. We could see it clearly as the lift fell past the master control room, where we were crouching out of sight. The door below had indeed led up, but the control consoles we'd discovered there were all just props, dashing our hopes of unleashing an army of Sentinels on Norman. The room was embellishment, nothing more.

As the lift continued its descent, I noticed the five men with Norman didn't share his enthusiastic expression. Expressions of disinterest wouldn't have surprised me. After all, they weren't Chowderheads. But they didn't wear expressions of disinterest. Instead, they wore no expressions at all.

"What in Sam Hill's up with his bodyguards?" Decker said.

I wasn't imagining things. There was definitely something off about the dudes, but I didn't have the first clue what it could be.

The lift reached the floor, and the whole party stepped off. As they did, the system sprang to life, and a laser swept over them. They all wore holsters, and when the laser hit those, the gauss guns within crumbled to dust that scattered across the floor. I guessed firearms would somehow disrupt the dynamics of the upcoming game. Norman stared down in mild surprise at the fine powder his firepower had become, but his attention was rapidly redirected as a belt magically appeared on the ground in front of each man. Norman was visibly giddy as he picked his up and put it on, the guards following suit. I wondered if the system would adjust to account for their greater numbers, increasing the difficulty of each level. If so, it would put Norman at a disadvantage, given his crew knew even less about the Scriptures than Arthur. On the other hand, I supposed they could just form a human shield around him, absorbing all the punishment that came his way. Bad day to be one of Norman's minions – though from the looks on their faces, they didn't seem like they'd feel one way or the other about it.

As the arrows glowed into view on the floor in front of them, Norman led the way into the circle, and the dome shot up around them. That was our cue. We bolted down the short flight of stairs, burst through the doorway, and leaped onto the lift. There was a moment of panic as we failed to locate a control panel. But we were relieved when the lift came to life, presumably activated by some pressure-sensitive mechanism. It shuddered, then pulled free of its cradle and began to rise. As it did, Norman and his men lunged out of the dome and ran toward us, seemingly oblivious to the dazzling re-creation of 1940s New York unfolding around them. Norman reached for the gun in his holster only to remember it wasn't there. But that wasn't the only ace up our sleeve. Norman and his guys froze as countdowns were projected from their belts and the synthesized voice boomed through the chamber, issuing its familiar warning: "Disqualification in seven, six, five ..."

I stared down at Norman defiantly, convinced he'd be unhinged by being outplayed by us again. But he didn't seem particularly peeved. He just turned and ran back toward the dome with his men, shouting over his shoulder, "See you soon, kid!"

I wrote it off as his usual arrogance, and as he disappeared within the dome, we heard the hydraulic drone of the clamshell hatch opening above us and felt the frigid air waft in, convincing us we were home free. But as we breeched the surface, we got a rude awakening. Two men were there waiting for us, gauss pistols at the ready. Norman had left them back to keep watch. Their faces bore the same blank look we'd seen on his other five men, despite the freezing cold they were enduring. But their expressions were far from the most unsettling thing about them. They both opened their mouths and spoke, as if wired to one brain.

"I told you I'd see you soon," they said.

"What in blazes?" Decker exclaimed.

Then several things happened in rapid succession. Both men aimed their gauss pistols and started firing. I leaped off the lift toward the barrage of bullets, shielding Arthur, Decker, and Cassie, who leaped off the lift in the other direction. Relieved of our weight, the lift began its return trip, and the clamshell hatch began to close. But as bullets ricocheted off me, several slammed into the mechanism beneath the hatch door on the right side, throwing off sparks and shrapnel. There was a grating, mechanical wail as the doors jammed, convulsing between the open and closed position as the lift continued to descend into the chamber below.

The two men stopped firing for a moment as they noted my lack of deadness. Weirdly, they didn't seem shocked or confused. It was more like someone had hit pause.

"Hm. Goddamn crystals are full of surprises," they said in their synchronized zombie chorus. "But I like my thing more than your thing."

Then it clicked. Norman was like me. Well, sort of. He'd been exposed to the crystals, and it had changed him – but in his case, he'd gained some kind of mind control powers. It was all too much to take in as the two men started advancing and firing around me at Arthur, Cassie, and Decker. The only blessing was that the men moved with the lumbering gait of Solomon Grundy. I had a few seconds to act, though it didn't seem like anything I could do would make a difference. I grabbed the gun arm of the guy nearest me and tried to wrestle his pistol away from him. We stumbled into the path of the second guy, delaying his advance toward the others, but it was a short-lived win. As the guy I'd been wrestling yanked his hand across his body to free his pistol, his fist smacked me in the face, splitting my lip. I started bleeding profusely. He stared at the blood, then quickly over at his fist. He was putting two and two together—or rather Norman was.

"Oh, I definitely like my thing better!" the two guys said.

My dance partner started hammering at my head with his free hand, opening a cut over my left eye, and I fell to one knee. That gave the second gunman a clear shot at Arthur, Cassie, and Decker, who were attempting to take cover behind the right half of the malfunctioning hatch. But the gauss rounds punched right through it. They might as well have been hiding behind a silk curtain.

I heard a grunt and looked over to see Decker fall out from behind the hatch, blood pouring from his chest. Arthur and Cassie both lunged out to grab him, but the gunman fired again, and a round grazed the side of Arthur's neck. Sparks shot out, but Arthur didn't miss a beat. As more rounds flew their way, he tackled Cassie, propelling both of them back behind the hatch, where they'd at least be out of the gunmen's line of sight.

Even if the two of them were willing to leave Decker and me behind, there was nothing but open ground surrounding us, and they wouldn't get far. Tears of frustration filled my eyes. All my friends were about to be shot dead, and then I'd be beaten to death—all because my so-called superpower didn't give me the ability to take these zombie bastards out. But as the first guy rained punches down on my head and shoulders, and the second guy rained bullets down on Cassie and Arthur, I realized my power may not be able to get the job done, but gravity could. I didn't wait to weigh pros or cons. I just lunged at the second guy, grabbing his shirtfront while keeping hold of the first guy's arm. Then, I planted a foot against the half-open hatch door and shoved off hard. We all tumbled to the icy ground and half rolled, half slid toward the open hatchway behind me. And then . . . we were plummeting into the abyss.

As we fell, I heard the two men screaming. Suddenly, there was nothing emotionless about them. Whatever connection they'd had with Norman was severed, and they were just two guys plunging to their deaths. We bounced off a wall and continued falling. It seemed to take an eternity, and I had ample time to think how comfortable I'd gotten with being impervious to most hazards and wonder if it might be different this time. It wasn't. I hit the floor like a mortar round, punching through the Danger Room's simulated concrete floor, leaving a crater of malfunctioning blue steel tiles. It felt like I'd fallen into a plastic ball pit at a children's play center.

"Clayton!" I heard Cassie screaming from above. I looked up and saw her leaning over the opening. I waved to indicate I was alright. Then as I got to my feet, the "welcome wagon" laser swept over me and to the right, where it disintegrated the gauss guns still clutched in the hands of the two gunmen who were lying broken and lifeless beside me. It was hard to look at them, but I warded off my guilt, telling myself they'd gotten what they deserved for throwing in with a maniacal dickhead like Norman.

I noticed something sharp was poking me in the ribs. A wave of nausea washed over me as I realized what it was. I reached into my suit, pulling out the black box, which had shared my express trip from the surface. It was smashed—a crumpled pile of circuits and wires. It wasn't going to be helping anyone "plot their next stop."

Just then I heard the synthesized voice begin its countdown, and I looked up to see Norman had stepped out of the dome. He stood there, staring at me. It was plain to see that there was no way he could get to me before I could get to the lift. But as his eyes went to the ruined box in my hands, it seemed to me that he had an inkling of what it was and what its destruction meant because a faint smile spread across his lips. He turned and rushed back into the dome as the countdown hit two. Whether he'd guessed what the box was or not, he'd know once he completed the gauntlet. I thought about the fact that we'd been celebrating our victory fifteen minutes earlier, and felt like a fool.

I saw the crowd across the street from the dome was down two members and knew the Violator Cateklysm was inside the dome, doing his best to strip the flesh from Norman and company's bones. Then I realized Norman had been fighting Red Skull Cateklysm while remote-controlling the gunmen who were trying to kill us. I didn't know if that talent for multitasking was one he'd always had or one he'd gained with his power. But I didn't care. I needed to find out how Decker was doing. I stuffed what was left of the black box back into my flight suit and walked over to the lift, which now sat on the edge of the vacant city lot, an incongruous five-by-five chunk of technology out of time. I stepped onto it, and it activated.

As I reached the surface, I knew the prognosis was grim. It was written all over Cassie's and Arthur's faces. The bullet had left a hole the size of a lemon just below Decker's right clavicle, and blood was gushing out. His face had gone ghostly white, and it was clear he knew where things were headed.

He gestured weakly to me, and I crouched down next to him.

"X," he said hoarsely.

"What?" I answered. I thought he might be delirious, babbling. But he repeated it, more insistent.

"*X!*"

I looked confused.

"Element X, dumbass," he coughed. I realized it was the answer to the black box's riddle. He'd figured out "the thing that put him on a path with possibilities."

"Don't you get it? Put HIM-ON a path?" Decker went on. "Himon! And the reference to possibilities?"

It had seemed that the riddle had given us virtually nothing to go on. But now it was so obvious. Another creation of Jack Kirby, Himon was an Apokoliptian revolutionary, renowned for various things – including the invention of the Mother Box, a sentient supercomputer capable of teleporting people wherever they wanted to go. (The packaging of the clue as a box was itself a clue.) And Himon's breakthroughs all started with his discovery of a substance dubbed "the metal of pure possibility," aka Element X. It was an elegant, unexpected way for Cateklysm to get a little more mileage out of the X theme that had been a mainstay since our arrival here.

I grimaced, unable to bring myself to tell Decker what had happened to the box. I had no idea how he'd managed to focus on the brain teaser, considering his circumstances, and I wasn't going to take the win away from him. He blanched from the pain, and I could see he was fading.

"Y'all are gonna be so screwed without me," he said, smiling faintly. Then his eyes went wide, and his head lulled to one side. He was gone. That was it. Only hours after I'd decided he wasn't the biggest jerk I'd ever met, he was dead.

I didn't move. I just stayed crouched there by his side as a sob burst forth from Cassie. Arthur put an arm around her.

At some point a snowstorm had begun to roll in, and the temperature was dropping at a scary rate. I noticed now that I was starting to feel numb all over.

"Well put it in," Cassie said, choking back another sob.

I looked at her, confused.

"Put the answer into the box!" she clarified. "He died for it."

I could see she desperately wanted to honor Decker's death, and I dropped my eyes, anguish welling within them. I reached into my flight suit and pulled out the wreckage of the box. The other two looked down at it, then up at me.

"Criminy!" Arthur cried out.

Cassie just stared in stunned silence. Then, after a moment, she grabbed the crushed box from my hand and shook it at me.

"So it was all for nothing?" she said, a new level of shock setting in. "Decker died for nothing?!" She hurled the ruined box to the ground.

I knew how she felt. I felt the same way. But I tried to stay calm. I tried to find solace by focusing on what we needed to do as the temperature continued to plummet.

"We have to get to shelter," I said.

Arthur followed my lead.

"You're right," he said. "You guys will be h-h-hypothermic soon."

"What about Decker?" Cassie said. She was trying hard to stave off her instinct for self-preservation, but I noticed her teeth were chattering and she was shivering. The same thing was happening to me. Arthur hesitated, then responded, his voice filled with guilt and regret.

"W-w-we can't carry him through this," he said, gesturing to the worsening storm. "We have to leave him." Even though he'd gotten it out without a stutter, the last part wasn't easy for him to say. It looked like a thousand pounds had just been dropped on his shoulders.

"Leave him?" Cassie gasped. "For how long?"

Arthur didn't know how to answer. He clearly hadn't been planning a return trip. But I decided I was, and soon.

"Just a few hours," I said.

The other two looked at me.

"We're coming back for Decker. And we're coming back to get what we came for in the first place," I said firmly.

"You mean you w-w-want to go back down there?" Arthur asked. "D-d-do it all again?"

"Why bother?" Cassie piled on. "Maybe we earn a second box. Maybe we get to the final stage. But Norman will already be there with bouncers at the door." She was echoing the feelings I'd had earlier. But I realized now that the insurmountable deficit I'd feared wasn't so insurmountable because there was an unexpected obstacle between stage two and stage three: the black box's riddle. However, it wasn't an obstacle for us, thanks to Decker.

"Nobody else in the world could solve that riddle that fast," I answered Cassie. "Not me. Not you. And definitely not some third-rate wannabe Chowderhead who stole most of his Conundrum answers. It could take Norman weeks. It could take him forever. We can beat him to the finish line."

Cassie absorbed my revelation and brightened a little.

"You're right," she said. "Of course. You're totally right."

"Okay," Arthur said, mirroring the slight uptick in Cassie's spirits. "S-s-so we retreat until Norman and his men leave and then—"

"We take another shot," Cassie finished with solemn conviction.

I nodded. Then I looked down at Decker. We were going to do everything in our power to make sure he hadn't died for nothing. But painfully, that began with leaving him behind.

Arthur helped me shift his body so the jammed hatch doors would keep him out of sight of Norman's crew as they exited. Then we struck out for the Javelin.

While the trek to the Danger Room entrance had taken fifteen minutes, the worsening storm made the trip back a whole different story. It was easily forty-five minutes and felt like hours. Before long, Arthur's emergency pain-receptor override had kicked in, so he was mostly unaffected by the conditions. That was less and less true of Cassie and me every minute.

For a time, we held out hope that we'd come upon Norman's ship sitting in plain sight and trade ours in for his. But in the storm, there was no plain sight. It was as though we were being buried alive as we walked, and Cassie and I were depending almost entirely on Arthur's flawless sense of direction. After twenty minutes or so, we were shaking uncontrollably and struggling to keep track of where he was—especially as we ventured into the labyrinthine field of ice arches. A heavy fog settled over our minds, and our bodies began to fail as hypothermia took hold. Arthur had to drag each of us back to our feet more than once. We realized there was a real chance we weren't going to make it, but then, finally, the hull of the Javelin came into view.

I awoke with my arms and legs tangled up with Cassie's, lying on the wonder chair in my hab suite. I vaguely remembered Arthur helping us into the Javelin, out of our icy clothing, and onto the chair, then activating a heating feature. I guessed we'd made it inside before permanent damage was done because I felt okay.

Cassie was still out. I just lay there, watching her sleep and trying not to think about Decker, or the busted black box, or any of it. It wasn't easy.

Eventually, Cassie's eyes popped open, and she blinked herself into consciousness. I could see recent events were coming back to her, too, because a wave of sorrow broke over her features. She was fighting to hold back tears.

"Are you okay?" I asked. I was reminded of asking her the same dumb question after our narrow escape from the Charon. In retrospect, it seemed like an even dumber question now.

"Okay?" she growled back. "Okay?! In the last twelve hours, I've nearly been killed by Norman Corp goons, my father, Norman Corp goons again, a bunch of supervillain Cateklysms, and then, you guessed it, more Norman Corp goons. And none of that even gets the top score because after all that, I watched a guy who I'd begun to think of as a friend bleed to death in the snow, where I had to leave him to save myself. So, no! No, I am not okay."

"I get it," I said. "I'm sorry."

"You're sorry? Really?!" She seemed enraged by my apology, but her rage wasn't directed at me. She leaned up on one elbow.

"What in the hell are you sorry for? Don't you dare be sorry! The only one who should be sorry—the only one who carries any of the blame for any of this—is that bastard Norman who, if I've got this right, has now become flippin' Purple Man!?"

Purple Man, aka Zebediah Killgrave, is a Marvel supervillain. Due to an accident at a chemical refinery, he gained the ability to control those around him through the power of suggestion, fueled by enhanced pheromones. Also, he turned purple.

But the analogy was off base. Norman wasn't giving suggestions, he was actually controlling people in real time. What was happening with him seemed more like psychic possession, à la the X-Man Blindfold. Of course I knew it would be petty to point out Cassie's blunder under the circumstances.

"When did you turn stupid?" I asked, leaning up on my elbow to mirror her. "What we're dealing with here is obviously more of a Blindfold situation. You're embarrassing yourself. Get your shit together, woman."

Her face went blank, and she stared at me. Then, she laughed. My gamble had paid off. The tension fell away. She leaned her forehead against mine, letting her eruption of fury subside.

"Fate Force'll fix it," she said.

"Hope so," I answered.

She pulled away as a thought occurred to her.

"So, why do you think Norman didn't use his Blindfold shit on us?"

"I had that s-s-same question," Arthur said, as he entered from the direction of the flight deck. He looked tired and grief-stricken, maybe even more so than us.

"Hey," I said. "Where have you been?"

"Up front," he answered. Then he glanced away and added, "I didn't want to sit in h-h-here and creepily watch you two sleeping in your underwear."

We sat up, suddenly self-conscious of our state of undress. We saw he'd draped two fresh flight suits over the back of the wonder chair, and we started putting them on.

"Anyway," he continued, "it kind of makes sense Norman's thing wouldn't w-w-work on me, but you'd definitely expect him to use it on you guys. I thought maybe it had limited range, but he was controlling the guys w-w-way up on the surface. So maybe he needs to establish an initial connection through close proximity. M-m-maybe even physical contact?"

He'd clearly been using the mystery to distract himself from the anguish we were all feeling.

"So once we catch up with him, we'll be fine as long as we keep him at a distance?" Cassie asked.

"M-m-maybe?" Arthur said, without any real conviction.

There were a lot of other unanswered questions. Were Norman's powers increasing with a series of painful seizures? If so, would he survive them? And what would he ultimately become if he did? The lack of information was maddening, but we'd have to deal with that later. Right now, we had to focus on getting back into the Danger Room and back into the ring with the Cateklysm crew.

"How long have we been out?" I asked.

"Close to seven hours," Arthur said.

With Norman controlling all his guys, they'd be more than just human shields, and seven hours was a long time.

"Norman has got to be done and gone by now," I said.

"Not yet," Arthur countered. "I've been s-s-scanning for the other Javelin every few minutes. It's still here."

"Pretty lame," Cassie scoffed. "He must have failed a ton of times. It really will take him forever to solve the riddle on the black box."

She'd barely finished the sentence before she went quiet. We couldn't think about the solution to the black box riddle without thinking about Decker. In his last act, he'd proven once and for all that his Chowderhead kung fu was full-on Shaolin grade.

As we paused, scrounging for a change of topic, Arthur absentmindedly dabbed at the bullet wound in his neck with a rag. It seemed he'd cleared away most of the mess, but the bullet had carved a deep trench, and beneath all the very convincing synthetic flesh and sinew, there was a hint of charred wiring and circuitry.

Cassie cringed sympathetically. "Are you gonna be alright?"

He shrugged. "I guess. What about you guys? H-h-how are you feeling?"

"Alive," Cassie said. "Thanks to you."

He looked away and answered, "Well it's kind of thanks to me that we're in this m-m-mess in the first place, right?"

I frowned and said, "What?"

"If I weren't what I am, maybe you guys would still be s-s-safe on the Charon."

When he'd claimed responsibility for the danger we were in during our escape from the Charon, I'd thought it was mostly a smoke screen to talk me out of being the first into the sewage line. I knew now it wasn't. He really thought he was to blame for everything that had happened.

"Dude, are you joking?" I exclaimed. "I can't say for sure that we would have tried to escape without you. But if we had, we'd be dead three or four times over by now."

"And w-w-what if you hadn't?" he asked.

"Uh, maybe you've forgotten," Cassie cut in. "But we just fought a flock of superpowered Cateklysms in a magic room on an alien planet. That means the U.A.T. is real, and if we were still on the Charon, there would be nobody to stop Norman from getting it. And somebody needs to stop him."

Arthur's face brightened a little, and I probably could have left it there, but I didn't.

"Cassie's right," I said, putting a hand on his shoulder. "Thanks to you, we have a shot at beating Norman to the U.A.T. And at ending the evil bastard for everything he's done."

Cassie gave me a hard look and asserted, "That's not what I said."

My words had shaken her. I'd convinced myself she'd become a little less Pro and a little more Pun after her rabid rant about Norman being the only one to blame for Decker's death and the rest of it—but now I knew that had just been wishful thinking. For the third time today, I was at a crossroads. I had to tell her I'd never let Norman keep breathing if I had the chance to stop it. I couldn't let it lie for another second. I loved her, and I was desperate for her to love me back, but to do that—to really do it—she needed to know what I was and accept it.

"Cassie," I started. But my attempt to set the record straight was thwarted yet again as we heard a thunderous boom, and a violent tremor rocked the ship. We all looked at each other in alarm. Another boom. And another. We heard and felt chunks of the surrounding ice arches crashing against the side of the ship, which bucked furiously as the ground beneath us shifted.

"Are we under fire?" I asked. I was sure that was it. I thought how naive we'd been, assuming Norman would just pack up and go when he was done in the Danger Room. But Arthur dismissed my theory.

"W-w-we're invisible to their scans!" he yelled. "And the Javelins have no w-w-weapons systems!"

"So is it an earthquake or something?" Cassie asked, her voice cracking with panic as more ice crashed against the hull.

"I don't know," Arthur said. "But we need to g-g-get airborne!"

He hurried out of the hab suite and toward the flight deck. We followed him, and as we did, we passed the pallet of explosives set against the wall. I hadn't given any thought to it since I'd first noticed it. But now my heart fell as I began to suspect what had happened. I hoped I was wrong. I prayed I was wrong.

Arthur powered up the Javelin and engaged the vertical thrust. The ship lifted off shakily, and he forced the nose down, pitching us forward. We swooped out from under the intersection of ice arches above us just as several neighboring arches collapsed to either side of us. Cassie and I nearly fell out of our seats as Arthur banked sharply to avoid more falling debris, then put us into a steep climb, carrying us free and clear of the chaos.

As we leveled off, I noted the storm had mostly cleared during the last few hours, but visibility still wasn't great. Arthur brought us around and began circling. He'd known we needed to get off the ground, but he had no destination in mind.

"Take us to the Danger Room entrance," I said.

Arthur adjusted our course as Cassie objected, "Wait – shouldn't we check for the other Javelin? Norman could still be there!"

"I hope he is," I said. "Because that would mean we won't find what I'm afraid we'll find."

"Which is?" Cassie asked, frowning. But the answer was appearing right in front of us as we cleared the lingering storm clouds and looked down on what had been the site of the Danger Room.

"Oh no," Cassie gasped.

Arthur brought us to a hover over an enormous chasm, running the length of the chamber that had contained the Danger Room. But there was no sign of the blue steel-paneled interior. Aside from roiling smoke and myriad outcroppings of flames, there was just rubble. The chamber had been torn open, and thousands of tons of ice, rock, and earth had rushed into the void from either side – the product of two dueling avalanches.

"Holy m-m-moly," Arthur muttered. "What happened?"

"Norman," I answered grimly.

The explosives we were carrying, and that I'd reasoned every Javelin had been carrying, were designed to break up the surface of Mars for excavation. They'd done their job here.

I thought back to my last glance of Norman, or more accurately, his last glance of me – and our busted black box. After attaining a black box of his own it was certain he understood what I'd been holding. I didn't think his conceit would leave room for the chance that we'd solved the riddle in the short time we'd had before our box's demise, even though Decker had come damn close. So Norman was confident we'd have to start again, and he'd made sure we couldn't. Then again, it wasn't personal. The fact that the explosives had been onboard in the first place suggested that this had been his plan from the start. Whatever he found on HBBI, he'd intended to destroy so no one else could find it. We'd been even more naive than I thought, and the advantage Norman now held was impossible to overcome.

"I just checked," Arthur said. "The other Javelin's g-g-gone."

Neither Cassie nor I responded. But things on the surface had settled, so he added, "I guess I'll . . . s-s-set us down." It was somewhere between a statement and a question, and this time Cassie and I both managed to nod numbly. We all knew there was nothing to find, but we needed to look.

As we touched down and exited the Javelin, we noticed the temperature had risen drastically since the storm's retreat. But that wasn't a mercy. It only afforded us more time to pace back and forth along the edge of the chasm, fruitlessly straining to spot some sign of the chamber or Decker's body. The sense of loss was crushing.

Cassie just sat down in the snow, despondent.

"It's alright," I started, lost in denial. "We can still . . . we can . . ."

"We can what?!" Cassie barked. "There's nothing left, Clayton. Decker, the Challenge, it's all gone and there's no getting it back!"

"No!" I said. Then I started grasping at straws. "Arthur, can you . . . can you detect whether there's anything left of the system that was running everything?"

He shook his head dolefully. "I'm not picking up any sign of it. And even if I could . . . I w-w-wouldn't be able to do anything with it. I tried to access the system during the Danger Room fight—the language it was all running on was the s-s-same as that website you wanted me to hack. It . . . pushed back, hard."

Cassie stood and stared down at the chasm one more time before turning and walking toward the Javelin.

"Cassie!" I called. But she kept walking. It was just as well. I didn't know what was left to say.

CHAPTER  21

WE CAME OUT OF WARP ABOUT THREE DAYS FROM EARTH. Not ideal, but according to the Javelin's navigation system, if we'd come out any closer, there was a good chance we'd destroy the planet. I supposed that would have made us feel worse than we already did, but not by much. While we knew it would take a good long while for Norman to solve the black box riddle, he would. Then he would complete the final stage and claim the U.A.T. After that, there was no telling exactly what he would do. But we didn't need specifics to warrant the deep-seated foreboding we felt.

We'd considered not returning to Earth. We'd considered floating from uncharted system to uncharted system in search of intelligent life. There was a chance we'd find some advanced race of aliens that could set things right on Earth, or at least offer the three of us a new start. But in an infinite universe with limited communications, the chances were greater we'd search a hundred systems without finding anything that could walk or talk and end up stranded in space with no fuel or food. Besides, when all was said and done, I think we all felt it was our duty to face the consequences of our failure with the rest of humanity. So we'd decided to return home.

Arthur and I spent most of the trip on the flight deck, trying to keep each other's minds off all the emotional wreckage that was gnawing at us, not the least of which was a heap of survivor's guilt. Among other distractions, we wiled away most of a day poking and prodding my superskin. We found nothing new. As it stood, the field around me seemed to render me invulnerable to everything except living matter and extremely low temperatures.

Cassie spent nearly all her time holed up in her hab suite. Unlike the first time the Challenge was removed from the equation, neither of us seemed able to contemplate a happy future together. Still, I'd tried to talk to her. I'd tried to comfort her. But she was unreceptive. I didn't blame her. We were all trying to cope in our own ways, and hers was isolation.

That said, she did emerge briefly when Arthur had the idea to track Norman's communications through the Norman Corp network. We knew we wouldn't be able to trace the communications to their physical origin for the same reason no one could trace our own communications back to us: the complexity of the mess of satellites involved in transmitting messages through space. But we thought maybe Norman would reveal his destination to some confidant if and when he ever solved the black box riddle, pointing the way for us to stage three. Then maybe we could beat him there, and maybe it wouldn't matter that we didn't actually have a black box in hand. Too many maybes, but we were desperate.

Surfing the aforementioned mess of satellites, Arthur dug around for quite some time. Finally, he found not a communication from Norman but a record of a Javelin – which had to be Norman's – being granted docking permissions by the Charon about half a day earlier.

"Why the hell would he go there?" I asked.

Arthur paused as he mentally scanned through more records, then answered, "Logs show the people he assigned to figuring out how to m-m-make Normanium Prime had a deadline, which they hit."

"Shit," I said. "Wait, why would he care about that? He has the fuel he got from us."

"The trip to and from HBBI w-w-would nearly have exhausted it," Arthur answered. "Guess he decided to fuel up w-w-while he's trying to solve the black box rid –"

He paused suddenly.

"What?" I said.

"A bunch of records are being purged."

His gaze seemed to shift as he took a detour through the records.

"Anything to do with Norman?" I asked.

"No," he answered, as he dug. "Looks like an inmate on the first level . . . killed five other inmates and two g-g-guards? That's all I could g-g-get."

"My God," Cassie spoke up for the first time.

But I was less moved. The inmates were likely murderers, and the guards weren't much better. Plus, whatever secrets the purged records held, they were gone. We needed to keep our eye on the ball.

"What about Norman?" I pushed. "Is he still on the Charon?"

Arthur's gaze shifted again as he aborted the detour and dug around for another moment.

"No. H-h-he left about three hours ago."

"Any word where to?" All our hopes hung on that question, so Arthur's answer was an arrow to the heart.

"No," he said, slumping in his seat. "Nothing."

I urged Arthur to keep looking, but it was clear Norman had gone dark. After his departure from the Charon, there were no communications to or from him – or between any other parties discussing his whereabouts. We didn't think the radio silence was a coincidence. He had obviously anticipated that we might try to track him, and he didn't want loose ends popping up unexpectedly. If he was communicating with anyone at all, he was using proxies. I wondered briefly why he hadn't saved himself some trouble by sticking around on HBBI to eliminate us. Then I remembered Arthur had cloaked our ship, so as far as Norman knew, we'd left before him.

In any event, while we'd known the plan to eavesdrop our way to stage three had been a long shot, when it struck out, it still felt like the straw that broke all our backs. Cassie fell into an even deeper depression and returned to her hab suite without a word. An hour or so later, Arthur and I ran out of distractions, and I found myself following Cassie's example.

I sat in my wonder chair, staring out at space for the better part of an hour. My faith had been shaken like never before. I'd been working hard to overlook the massive shadow of doubt cast by a Chowderhead breaking bad and becoming an egomaniacal murderer, intent on conquering the world. But now, on top of that, I had to contend with the fact that we'd given all we had to stop the fucker and failed. This seemed to fly in the face of everything the Scriptures had taught me. Spider-Man always found a way to swing in and save the day. The Green Lantern's will always won out. Atticus Slade and his fellow Fate Forcers never fell short.

Or had I only been seeing what I wanted to see? I thought of the death of Mar-Vell. Considered by many discriminating Chowderheads to be the one true Captain Marvel, Mar-Vell was a Kree warrior who renounced his own people to protect Earth and its inhabitants from a potpourri of apocalyptic threats, including an attempted Kree invasion (*Avengers* #90–91, 1971). He was a Marvel comics mainstay for decades until he died of lung cancer of all things – nothing alien or exotic, just a dose of mundane but merciless real life (*The Death of Captain Marvel*, 1982). Despite his star status, Mar-Vell did not come back in any of the comics on Cateklysm's list (aside from that little zombie dustup in *Avengers* #3 in 1998). So maybe the Scriptures had warned me after all: eventually, the cruel and unjust reality beyond comics comes for us all.

Of course, at least Mar-Vell had been able to do some good before being undone. I hadn't – and I felt cheated. I thought about all the horrible things I'd witnessed. I thought about the fact that I'd never been able to stop any of those things, or even see any of the people responsible punished. But as that last thought passed through my mind, I suddenly remembered. I remembered a promise I'd made to myself – a promise I could still keep. I'd been robbed of just about everything in life, but for the time being, I was still breathing. And I had unfinished business.

"Arthur, you think you can hack some hard-to-hack government records?" I said, as I stormed back onto the flight deck.

"Um ... s-s-sure," he said. There was a forlorn look in his eyes, and I could tell he'd been preoccupied, but I was too focused on my own stuff to pay it any mind.

"Okay. I need the intake logs for 2045, from the Orphan Care Station at 42 Sixth Street in San Francisco."

I could see him pushing his preoccupation aside as he worked to connect the dots.

"Are you s-s-sure about this?" he asked.

It didn't take the World's Greatest Detective to figure out what I was after. Anyone who brought an orphan to an Orphan Care Station was processed through fingerprinting and other measures. That way, if parents reported a kid had been abducted and fraudulently turned in for a reward, the cops might eventually find the perp. Or, hypothetically, if the perp killed the kid's parents to avoid this possibility, the kid could serve eight years plus on a Norman Corp shipping freighter, then escape in an experimental warp ship, steal the perp's file from the Orphan Care Station's records, and personally hunt the murdering scumbag down. Hypothetically.

"Yes, I'm sure," I answered Arthur.

He nodded, and his eyes went distant. I had never come close to accessing the records myself, no matter how many hours of hacking I'd put in. But after just a few moments, my holo-pod chimed, and Arthur said, "There you g-g-go."

"Seriously?" I heard Cassie cry out from behind me. I didn't know how long she'd been there, but it had obviously been long enough. She knew who I was looking for, and my demeanor didn't suggest due process was part of the plan.

"So that's what you're going to do? Go looking for someone to ... to what? Execute?"

She looked as though her last thread of hope was giving out. If I'd been paying attention to my heart, I would have felt it breaking. But I wasn't.

"I made a promise to myself," I said simply. All the speeches I'd rehearsed in my head for this moment were irrelevant. It was plain to her what I intended to do and what I really was.

"A promise? What promise? To kill somebody in cold blood?"

"You don't understand—" I started, but she cut me off.

"I understand perfectly. It's more important to end someone else's life than to save your own."

"What?" I said, confused.

"Your seizures! Or have you forgotten all about those?"

"They've stopped. I feel fine," I said dismissively. I still had no idea whether another seizure would come around to finish me off, but amid all the mayhem, it had been easy to put that nagging fear out of my mind, and I didn't want to let it back in now.

"You're full of shit!" Cassie yelled. "You need to get to a doctor. That's what you should be thinking about. Because fulfilling this . . . this blood oath won't change what happened to your parents."

Her words triggered something in me, and I lost all restraint. "What the hell do you know about it?!" I yelled. "You think you know what I've been through? You think you're a victim of what your father did? You're not a victim. His victims are the victims. Their families are the victims." I pointed a finger at myself. "Their CHILDREN are the victims! And you'll never know what that feels like!"

She didn't yell back. Her face just went ice cold. Then, still glaring at me, she said, "What about you, Arthur? Do you really want to be part of this?" She looked over at him and continued, "Think about your father. Shouldn't you be trying to find him?"

Arthur flinched slightly. Then after a moment he said, "He's . . . d-d-dead."

Cassie clamped a hand over her mouth, stifling a gasp.

"I finally tracked the records d-d-down about a half hour ago," Arthur continued. "He d-d-died last year of pneumonia, in prison. He wasn't fit enough for s-s-service as a Loaner."

Cassie thawed immediately, overcome by compassion. She rushed forward and put her arms around Arthur. I just sat there, unsure of what to say or do, and ashamed of how I'd barged in and demanded Arthur's help without paying more attention to what was going on with him.

"I'm so sorry," she said. "I'm so, so sorry."

Arthur shook his head, fighting back tears. "I know he wasn't really my d-d-dad. Still, he made me – and he made me to feel everything everyone else d-d-does. So I'm angry that they took him from me." He paused, swallowing a sob. "But there's no one to blame. Everyone thought his work was d-d-dangerous. The people who locked him up were public servants, not evil m-m-men."

He grabbed Cassie's shoulders softly and put some distance between them.

"But it's different for Clayton. So I can't judge w-w-what's right for him And neither can you."

He'd taken her side when it came to not killing Malcolm, but this was another story. He wiped the tears from his eyes, and the shakiness in his manner vanished. "This is his d-d-decision. And I'm with him either way."

His name was Richard Bollard. A bolt of nausea shot through me when I saw his picture in the Orphan Care Station records. Searching various other city and state records, Arthur learned that he was fifty-four years old, and despite murdering my parents, he had managed to avoid racking up a criminal record of any kind. This was no surprise really, given the feeble state of law enforcement. Likewise, the feeble state of government record keeping meant that the last known address we'd dug up was a shaky bet. Still, it was a place to start. It was a repurposed dormitory room on the campus of what had been San Francisco State University. The school had been closed in the mid-'30s, like all other state-run schools, in favor of far more cost-effective online alternatives. Then the city had put the campus to use as best they could, leveraging some extremely relaxed Section 8 housing regulations.

After establishing where we were headed, I just sat there, fantasizing about what I would do to Bollard when I got my hands on him. The fantasies were borrowed mostly from gore-splattered panels from the *Lobo's Back* series (1992), in which the Main Man rampages through Heaven, forcing the head honchos to undo his death by maiming every poor bastich[9] that crosses his path and kicking one holier-than-thou heavenly bureaucrat in the nuts so hard, the guy's spine flies out of his body.

They were childish daydreams, but I couldn't help indulging them—until we arrived in a shallow orbit around Earth. As I took in its details, it struck me that the damage we'd done to the environment hadn't marred its blue green beauty one bit. In fact, I thought, we hadn't really damaged the planet at all. For all the time we spent talking about "saving the world," we were really talking about saving ourselves. The earth couldn't give a shit how much CO_2 was floating around for a millennium here or there.

We breached the atmosphere, and I thought about how often I'd imagined this moment. I'd seen Earth many times since the beginning of my tour of duty on the Charon. But our Normanium shipments were picked up by shuttles in orbit, so I had never returned to the surface. I'd never been home. I was staggered by the feelings that awoke within me as we emerged from the clouds and caught sight of the ocean and coastline below. This was where almost everything good in my life had come from—and where it was taken away. Tears welled in

---

9 Common slang, originating in Lobo comics: a combination of "bastard" and "bitch," applying to both sexes.

my eyes, but I was jolted back into the moment as Cassie entered the flight deck. She'd returned to her hab suite after the emotional exchange two hours earlier, so she hadn't been present as we'd pored over the Orphan Care Station records to figure out our destination. I expected her to be angry as she entered. But instead, she seemed strangely mournful.

She glanced at the location highlighted on the holo-map and said, "San Francisco?"

"Yeah," Arthur answered. "We found a m-m-most recent address for ..." He trailed off, seeing from her face that she wasn't interested in the details.

She was quiet for a short while, and then she looked at me and said, "The way you talked about Golden Gate Park, I've always wanted to see it."

I think my description of the park had become an oasis in her mind, what with how dramatically it contrasted the most urban area of Detroit, where she'd spent her hellish childhood.

"Drop me off near the lake you told me about," she continued. "I'll figure the rest out from there."

Her words knocked the wind out of me. I hadn't expected her to change her mind about the mission we were on. But I'd figured she'd just sit it out aboard the Javelin. Instead, she was leaving – and from the look in her eyes, it was for good.

"Cassie," I said. "I didn't ... I didn't mean what I said."

"Yes. You did," she responded softly. "And you were right. So was Arthur. I can't really know what you feel. But I know what it's done to you, and I can't let it do the same to me. I lost the Challenge. I can't lose myself."

I didn't know what to say to that, and an uncomfortable silence set in.

Arthur broke it by focusing on some logistics.

"Um ... I managed to exploit some w-w-weak points in Norman Corp's financials and redirect funds from a couple dozen subsidiaries," he said. "Auditors w-w-won't notice because individually, the missing amounts look like rounding errors. But we each have an account with about forty m-m-million dollars, mapped to our new identities through our biometrics."

"We have new identities already?" Cassie asked, as if she hadn't heard the rest. "So I'm not Cassie Greenbaum anymore?"

"Umm ... no," Arthur answered.

Setting up our new names and records was one of the tasks Arthur and I had used to keep ourselves busy at the beginning of the trip. But we hadn't gotten around to telling Cassie about it.

"So who am I?" she asked.

"Joanna Shuster," he answered, looking over at me. Her eyes followed his, and she gazed at me wistfully. I'd proposed the name because it would not only preserve the coveted Jewish heritage that made her feel closer to the early greats, but give her an upgrade. If she so chose, she could now go by "Jo Shuster," à la Superman cocreator Joe Shuster.

"I can change it to anything you w-w-want," Arthur said. "I just—"

"No. It's good," she said quietly, still looking at me. "It's perfect."

I'd traded in my own identity for Henry Heywood, and Arthur had kept his first name, but taken the last name Tobor, which was a hilarious inside joke because it's robot spelled backward.

We set down in a clearing in Golden Gate Park at around 5:00 a.m. There was literally no one around, and we were all grateful for the privacy in light of the circumstances. Cassie walked back to her hab suite to get her holo-pod. Arthur and I followed drearily. This wasn't what any of us wanted, but in that moment, I don't think any of us thought we had a choice.

Her holo-pod in hand, Cassie stepped back into the hallway and hit the release for the outer door. It squealed open, and the ramp below unfolded and touched down on the grassy earth. She stepped onto the ramp, then stopped, turned, and hugged Arthur tight before gently placing her hands on either side of my face and kissing me softly on the lips. Then she walked off the ship without a word. It was agonizing, and I began to doubt everything I was doing. I began to think that maybe I'd lost sight of what really mattered. But as I watched her disappear into the early dawn haze, I remembered the last time I'd been in Golden Gate Park. I'd been here celebrating solving 9 Down. I'd been here the day my parents were murdered. I felt a surge of emotional alchemy as my heartache turned to fury and my doubts were demolished. My hand shot out automatically, palming the control panel beside the door. The ramp contracted, and the door slid shut with a clank.

ISSUE 4 OF 4
Enter the Batcave!

CHAPTER 22

THE SEARCH FOR BOLLARD WENT BADLY. AS I'D FEARED, THE dormitory address Arthur had dug up was a red herring. The place had been condemned after a roof collapse, and the people we found squatting in the ruins had never heard of Bollard. Over the next few days, we canvased the neighboring dormitories and surrounding area doggedly. I must have jammed my holo-pod into the faces of 150 people, hoping one of them would recognize Bollard's image. None of them did, and we were getting nowhere.

The lack of closure had been jarring. I'd been counting on that closure to offset my regrets about Cassie's departure and my fears about Norman's return, not to mention the weight of all the other horrible shit that had happened. I was in awful shape.

Arthur couldn't have been doing much better, but he was still thinking more clearly than me, and by the fourth day, he convinced me that we needed to take time to deal with the Javelin. Spanking new identities or no, our faces were probably on display in various law enforcement databases. And while that didn't pose a huge threat with the widespread shortage of cops, it was still a really bad idea to be living in the flashy high-profile ship Norman Corp had no doubt reported stolen. We could have just scuttled it in the Bay, but you never know when an interstellar spacecraft can come in handy. So Arthur rented a private jet hangar at the San Francisco International Airport. Such hangars had cropped up all over SFO and other airports after public air travel had dropped off to nothing. Mind you, private air travel hadn't exactly seen a massive bump in volume, but the margins were better because AI Broker Barons and other super rich folks didn't balk at paying ungodly sums for a place to keep their toys.

We made the trip in the middle of the night, and access to the hangars was automated, so we dealt only with keypads and retinal scanners. We didn't think we'd been seen by a soul. There was certainly security footage, but it was unlikely that anyone would be reviewing it unless some incident prompted them to do so.

It wasn't easy maneuvering the ship into its parking space without taking the roof off the place, but Arthur managed it. Then we returned to the city in an auto-cab. All my adventures in space aside, that was a little surreal. I'd never dreamed I'd ride in an auto-cab, with its in-seat masseuse, holo-entertainment, and fully-stocked snack and beverage bar. There were certainly cheaper ways to travel, but we had Norman Corp cash to burn. Speaking of which, we burned some more on some ridiculously pricey street clothes. And with the Javelin tucked away miles outside the city, we needed a new place to sleep, so we rented a unit in one of two apartment buildings still being maintained by what had once been a sprawling Lake Merced rental development a few blocks from the condemned dormitory.

Over the next two weeks, our search for Bollard continued as we settled into a new life of sorts. The unit we'd rented was palatial by comparison to the quarters I'd shared with Darcy: two bedrooms and two bathrooms. The decor called to mind the most modern depictions of the Fantastic Four's famous home in the Baxter Building. The immaculate matte white of the carpets, walls, and modular furniture was lightly contrasted by the mostly glass finish of the appliances, fixtures, and cabinetry. The unit's AI system learned our habits, and after just a few days, the place was adjusting lighting, shower temperature, news feeds, and everything else to suit our preferences, with little or no input from us. None of that was exactly miraculous, considering my best friend was an AI that could pass as human, but it was convenient just the same.

San Francisco had always been jam-packed with close-quarter juxtapositions of poverty and prosperity, and the implosion of the economy in the late '30s had pushed that quirk into truly absurd territory. Hence the contrast between our perfectly maintained, amenity-equipped accommodations and the squalor just a block beyond our walls. Our building's dining level alone made me feel like a member of some royal court of assholes. The vast, three-a-day buffet spreads offered everything but a vomitorium.

Thanks to the magical energy osmosis his father had invented, Arthur's energy cells pulled their charge from the sun and/or the city's power grid, but he'd still been compelled to belly up to the buffet by his programming. That is, until he'd set his mind to overriding that programming. He said he didn't want to waste the food, but I think he wanted to feel a little less human – to dull the pain that had come with that condition lately. I think it was to that same end that he'd vanquished his asthma attacks. I wondered if his stutter would be next to go, but it seemed he was unwilling or unable to part with that particular mark of his father's design.

In any event, where he tried to starve his demons away, I took the opposite tack, gobbling up course after course, hoping to blot out my woes with decadent overindulgence. It was impossible to imagine a more welcome change from the freeze-dried what-have-yous and powdered rations on which we'd subsisted aboard the Javelin, never mind the sludge we'd been forcing down aboard the

Charon. But neither the food nor any of the other creature comforts of our new home helped fend off the bleak future I felt closing in.

The only thing that did help was focusing on my obsession. More and more, finding Bollard crystallized as my reason for being, even though I was making little or no progress. Arthur had thought to locate Bollard through his financial transactions, but they were tangled up in a rat's nest of records scattered across dozens of payment systems. Day after day, he chased down dead end after dead end online, while I filled my time scouring the city in ever increasing search radiuses around the dormitory and anywhere Arthur found a record of Bollard making a purchase. Such purchases were spotty, and their timing didn't even prove for certain Bollard was still in the area. But I didn't let myself think about that.

Sometimes, I'd stay out for days at a time, sleeping wherever I happened to be when I got too tired to keep at it. I was often slow to respond to Arthur's text communications during these long hauls, so he'd bought me a new holo-pod, sans AV transmission inhibitor, through which he could shout at me until I answered. But through it all, he never questioned my fixation. He didn't bring up Cassie or even push me to find a doctor that might be able to help with my seizures. I thought maybe he figured I was beyond common sense, but if so, he could have just left me to my own devices. Helping me identify Bollard was one thing. Following me down the rabbit hole was another. This errand had turned into way more than he'd signed up for, and even in my mania, I wondered if his loyalty was misplaced. However, when I'd raised the point with him, he'd said simply, "I'm not w-w-walking away until you do."

Well, I wasn't walking away. I pushed on, ferociously committed to my search. I was so absorbed that I hardly noticed when I entered my childhood stomping grounds a little after 2:00 a.m. one morning. I only realized where I was when I saw the bent and broken street sign in front of me. I stopped cold. I was standing at the corner of Market and Powell, where the Flood Building had once been. I was standing directly above the basement in which my family had found shelter and made a home, before being torn apart by Richard Bollard.

I was Bruce Wayne at the mouth of Crime Alley. I was J'onn J'onzz returning to a post-holocaust Mars. I was Kal-El floating in the empty space where Krypton had once been.

I'd been hiding from the impulse to return here, forcing it out of my mind each time it tried to claw its way to the surface. I'd been too afraid to face the emotions it would awaken. But now, whether by accident or some trick of my subconscious, here I was.

I didn't think. I just headed for the collapsed section of sidewalk I knew was half a block down and wound my way back through the sewers to the hidden entrance of the building's basement, my holo-pod lighting the way. I was on autopilot, divorced from my body. It was as if someone else was feeling the profound sense of dread that settled on me as I entered the concrete chamber, unsure of what would be left of my home, and my parents.

But aside from a few crates we'd used for furniture, I found nothing. The entire basement was six inches deep in sewage that was running freely through the space and back out to God knows where. Every trace of my parents had been washed away in a flood of shit. They were utterly gone.

As fearful as I'd been of seeing what was left of them, this was worse – much, much worse. I came off autopilot, and the full power of the moment hit me. Tears broke over my cheeks, and I felt my long-buried sorrow well up within me. I leaned against the wall and sobbed. Then, as always, the sorrow turned to anger. But it was a new magnitude of anger now – a white-hot rage I'd been stockpiling for nine years, amplified by all the pain and heartbreak I'd endured in the last few weeks. As I struggled to contain it all, my hands began trembling, and my holo-pod fell to the ground and shattered, leaving me in darkness. There was no hiding from the truth. I was no closer to finding Bollard, no closer to eking out a single measure of justice. I felt like a nuke with no target.

"Clayton?" It was Arthur, pinging me through what was left of my holo-pod. "Clayton," he repeated. Then just as warbling distortion overtook the signal and the unit went dead, I was able to make out five words that changed everything. "I think I found h-h-him."

CHAPTER  23

THE WALK HOME WAS LONG AND FELT LONGER. I SPENT THE whole journey vacillating between wild optimism and mindful skepticism. I needed to quell the hysteria that had nearly overwhelmed me, but I couldn't afford to be taken in by false hope. I was still riding an emotional rollercoaster when I walked through the front door of our apartment.

"I've been trying to reach you," Arthur said.

"I know," I said.

"Well why didn't yo—"

"Where is he?" I cut him off.

He forgave me my impatience like the saint he was and said, "Bolinas. I think h-h-he's in Bolinas."

"Why?" I asked, anxious to anchor my now-prevailing optimism in facts.

"I finally got enough data to do some real analysis," he answered. "About a year ago he s-s-started making bulk transactions at a grocery store in Stinson Beach."

"Stinson Beach?" I asked. "But you said he was in—"

"Once I knew w-w-what time frame and general area to focus on, I d-d-dug some more and found it—a cabin rental in Bolinas. Payments are irregular, but there is a recent one."

I felt my breath catch. This was it. I knew it. We really had found him.

Arthur stared at me, waiting for me to say something. I said the only thing there was to say.

"How are we getting there?"

Bolinas was about twenty miles northwest of San Francisco, but it was in a remote, rural area, lacking the repair stations required to qualify for auto-cab service. Of course, remote, rural areas were one of the safer places to land a stolen spaceship. And it being 3:30 a.m., we didn't think we'd be seen lifting off from SFO.

It took us around an hour to get an auto-cab and get to the airport, and we were in the air twenty minutes after that. As we headed back over the city and across the bay, signs of sunrise teased the horizon. In an effort to keep the Javelin on the DL, we maintained enough altitude to take advantage of cloud cover. Still, through a brief break in that cover, I caught a glimpse of the crumbling Golden Gate Bridge below. The bridge had fallen into disrepair long ago after a partial collapse, and what little traffic there was had been rerouted to the Bay Bridge. I remembered there being talk of repairs when I was a kid, but it was clear they'd never happened. World-famous landmark or no, it seemed the bridge was a luxury the city could not afford.

I caught a glimpse of the Marin Headlands next, shrouded in a cloak of mist that even global warming had failed to eradicate. But as visibility dropped off again, I was acutely aware of the silence on the flight deck. Neither Arthur nor I had said a word since departing the airport. So I was rattled when he spoke.

"This is crazy," he said.

For a moment, I was sure he'd finally woken up to where we were headed and what I was going to do when we got there. I'd known that epiphany was a possibility, and it scared the crap out of me because it could mean I'd lose him, just like I'd lost Cassie.

"I m-m-mean if you're serious about this, we need to get you a g-g-gun or something," he continued.

I felt the knot in my stomach dissipate. He'd said "I'm not walking away until you do," and he'd meant it. Relief settling on me, I answered him, "I've actually given that some thought."

"And?"

"I'm going to use his. I'm going to turn his own gun on him."

Arthur furrowed his brow. "Poetic. But w-w-what if he doesn't pull a gun? What if he doesn't even have one?"

I shrugged. "Kitchen knife, screwdriver, hammer, whatever's around, I guess."

"Could get m-m-messy."

"I'm okay with messy."

The truth was, I was more than okay with messy. I was hoping for it. I wanted to get my hands dirty. I wanted it to be personal. I thought that was the only way to free myself of all the anger and hatred I'd been carrying around for so long. And while my superpower wasn't perfect, it did ensure that if there was a weapon of any kind on hand, the fight would be heavily weighted in my favor. The only danger was collateral damage, and I needed to make sure Arthur understood the ground rules.

"Just so we're clear, I'm going into his house by myself," I said.

Arthur shrugged and replied, "I'll try not to feel left out."

We set down in a forested area, about twenty yards from the west shore of the Bolinas Lagoon. Bollard's address was less than a hundred yards south. Arthur walked with me back to the Javelin's exit ramp, and I extended it.

"If I'm not back at the ship within half an hour, you go, okay?" I said. "Just take off and don't look back."

He answered with a noncommittal nod.

"I mean it," I insisted. "If something goes wrong, it's on me. You don't owe me anything."

"S-s-sure," he agreed.

I lingered for a moment, not knowing how to end the exchange. He seemed to be in the same boat until he patted me on the back awkwardly and said, "G-g-good luck."

I nodded, turned, and headed off. It only took me a couple of minutes to cover the distance to the house. At some point it had been green, but the paint was so chipped and faded, it was now mostly the color of raw wood. It was a ramshackle single-story structure, with two windows set on either side of a crooked front door like eyes and a nose. The cracked and warped porch stretching beneath these features added a mouth, making it seem even more like I was staring at the cast-off head of a decapitated wooden giant. The homestead was surrounded by forest on three sides, with the fourth side opening onto a dirt road that led out to a stretch of cracked pavement tracing the perimeter of the lagoon.

As I approached, I couldn't see anyone through any of the windows, but that didn't mean there was no one there. It was dark inside, and reflections obscured my view. I tried to keep my gait casual. If Bollard was in there watching, I didn't want to look like I was trying to sneak up on him. If he wasn't, my approach would be undetected whether I was in stealth mode or not.

There was a dilapidated rocking chair sitting on the porch to the left of the door, with an old blanket lying across the seat. Ironically, looking at the blanket gave me the chills. I pictured it draped over Bollard, resting cozily on his porch, while my parents' bones lay rotting somewhere in a cold, dark sewer twenty miles away.

As I set foot on the first stair, it creaked forebodingly. I moved up the other two swiftly, cutting their protests short. Then I was at the front door. The chills I'd had passed in a hurry as I felt a flush of warmth on my face and a pounding in my ears. After all these years, I thought I really could be just moments away from avenging my parents.

I considered knocking but thought better of it. It didn't seem like the place got many visitors, so if Bollard was in fact home and knew I was out here, chances were he would have met me at the door. At this point I had to assume he wasn't home or he hadn't seen me yet, and if there was a chance at the element of surprise, I didn't want to lose it.

I tried the doorknob. It turned easily, and the door swung inward, reveal ing the interior of the cabin. I didn't see anyone. I stepped cautiously in, and the smell of rot wafted over me. Directly ahead, there was a small kitchenette, the sink piled high with filthy dishes. A cockroach scuttled across the floor and disappeared beneath the cabinetry. Directly to my right there was a small bathroom and beside that an ancient, broken-down couch and dusty side table piled high with romance novels of all things. I heard a swell of music playing very faintly and looked over to see a closed door to my left, beneath which I glanced shadows shifting. I stopped for a moment, unsure what my next move should be. Then I heard a muffled scream. Without thinking, I lunged forward and kicked open the door to see a man tied spread eagle to the bed. His filthy undershirt and boxers were caked with dried blood, and there were half-ass duct tape bandages over his left eye and various other spots. He squealed in desperate panic as Bollard leaned over him and wedged a pair of pliers into his mouth.

I'd thought I'd known what Bollard was capable of, but the grotesqueness of the scene went beyond my darkest imaginings. Lining the windowsill beside the bed were jars filled with severed body parts. I recognized a toe, a finger, and an eyeball. They were all arranged in plain sight of Bollard's victim – a ghoulish and constant reminder of what he'd lost by Bollard's hand.

I had a few seconds to register all this because, as if the horror movie decor and DIY dental surgery weren't macabre enough, Bollard was wearing an enormous pair of headphones and swaying gleefully back and forth to some disturbingly happy-go-lucky tune being piped into his ears so loud I could now hear it plainly. I supposed this was intended to spare him from the unpleasant wailing of his victim, but it had left him deaf to my dramatic arrival. He didn't turn around or even pause his gruesome work. And I wasn't going to wait for my luck to change.

I hit him like a freight train, tackling him with such force, we tore the footboard off the bed as we collided with it on the way to the ground. I landed on his back and decided what had worked with Cassie's father would work here. I slipped a forearm under his chin and craned back, tightening my grip as he gasped for air. My senses were dulled by adrenaline, and his pleas for mercy were a distant jumble of sounds with no meaning. The back of his head was pressed hard against my cheekbone as I closed my grip still tighter under his jaw and wrenched his body from left to right. The years of pain came flooding back. All the anger, all the loss, all the longing for one more day with my parents. This was the vengeance I'd vowed I would take.

Or was it? I finally registered the gurgling, rasping whisper coming from the person beneath me. It didn't make any sense – until I looked over at the man in the bed. The bandages on his face and head had thrown me before, but now I saw it. The hairline. The nose. The set of his jaw. My eyes went wide, and my arms went slack. The person beneath me slumped forward, gulping air desperately and repeating her words more clearly now: "He killed my parents!"

★

She went by Alexa, but her name was Alexandra—Alexandra Sandoval. A close-cropped haircut and heavy jacket had made it possible for me to peg her for Bollard from behind, before recognizing him in the bed. As she sat on the moth-eaten old couch and told me her story, it was hauntingly familiar: Bollard killing her parents, then dragging her to an Orphan Care Station where she'd be drafted into service as an Orph and spend several years fantasizing about finding Bollard and taking her elaborate, mutilation-based revenge.

At first it had all seemed like an inconceivably improbable coincidence, us arriving here at the same time. But we hadn't arrived at the same time.

"I've been here since late December, I guess," she said. "I take a piece of him every few days. Just little pieces mostly."

I had no idea how she'd tracked Bollard down, but that was the least of my questions.

"I feed him a bit—to keep him alive as long as possible," she said. Then she pulled a pistol from the couch cushions and held it up. "Only time I let him up is when me and Betsy here take him to use the bathroom, so he doesn't stink as much." She put the pistol back and gestured to the romance novels. "Other than that, I spend my time reading my stories."

This girl was definitely several fries short of a Happy Meal. She'd been doing this for more than a month and planning the details for nearly a decade. She'd come stocked with medical supplies and armed with online medical training to fend off sepsis and other things that might cause Bollard to die "too soon." She talked about it all in the unguarded manner of someone who was relating the humdrum details of how they'd spent their weekend. She didn't even know she was talking to a fellow victim. She just seemed to believe anyone would agree that what she was doing was empirically justified.

As she spoke, a shiver ran down my spine, and I knew. Everything had changed. But I didn't want to accept it. I walked to the bedroom doorway and looked in at Bollard.

"Don't get too close to him," Alexa said. At first, I thought she was concerned for my safety, but then I realized her manner was more that of a lioness protecting her kill from interlopers.

Bollard turned his head to look back at me, straining against the binds that held him to the bed, which was sitting at an awkward angle now that the footboard had been knocked loose. There was no way of telling if he was still in the killing and kidnapping business, but he looked too old for it, especially after the month he'd had. Beneath the duct tape bandages on his face, I knew he was missing an eye and an ear. I didn't know the extent of what was missing under the bandages on his hands, feet, and abdomen. She'd gagged him, but he was making a muffled attempt to communicate. I'd wanted it to get messy. It didn't get any messier than this.

I just stared at him, trying to focus on my loss and my anger—trying to hold on to what I'd thought I needed. I took a step closer and said quietly, "You know you had this coming."

His good eye went wide and he began babbling more urgently now in a pathetic, pleading tone. This was the intended effect, but my small act of cruelty didn't bring me the satisfaction I'd hoped for. Not even close.

I thought of the Justice Lords. They'd made their first appearance in "A Better World," a two-part episode of Bruce Timm's *Justice League* animated TV series (2003), and they'd made the jump to canon when Grant Morrison mentioned them as residents of Earth-50 in his *Multiversity Guidebook* (2015). They'd protected their version of Earth as perfect parallels of the Justice League until Lex Luthor killed their version of the Flash. Then they'd snapped, adopting a zero-tolerance totalitarian philosophy. Their brutal regime began with Superman murdering Lex Luthor, then going on to hand out heat vision lobotomies like parking tickets.

In the episode, the Justice League and the Justice Lords switched places for a time, and all hell broke loose. However, it was the aftermath of the episode that came to mind now. After learning of the existence of their lawless, merciless doppelgangers, the Justice Leaguers constantly questioned whether they themselves may be just one bad day away from becoming monsters. As I looked over at Alexa, I realized I was asking myself that same question. I didn't like the answer. I didn't like it one bit.

If it had turned out to be Bollard I'd been strangling, would I have finished the job? I thought about the satisfaction I'd felt at Malcolm's accidental death, and how I'd callously dismissed the deaths of the two men I'd had to kill in self-defense in the Danger Room. I finally saw it all for what it was. It was the beginning of a road I did not want to travel because Alexa had given me a glimpse of where it led.

I knew now just how deluded my Lobo-esque daydreams had been. For nine years I'd believed I'd do anything to see Bollard like this. I'd believed it would fill a void deep inside. But while I still had a powerful hatred for the man, there was no catharsis in witnessing his torture — just revulsion. Was doing bad things to bad people closer to right than wrong? Maybe. But now I knew, for me, it wasn't close enough. After all my Pun posturing, I reeled with the inescapable truth: Cassie had been right about me. I was a Pro and always had been.

"I said don't get too close," Alexa called over my shoulder. It was more forceful this time, and I looked over to see she'd gotten to her feet, Betsy firmly in hand.

I stepped out of the bedroom, closed the door, and walked back toward her. Then I did something I'd never have imagined possible. I said, "You have to stop this."

"What?!" she shrieked, as if I were the crazy one. "You have no idea what he took from me!"

"I know exactly what he took from you!" I yelled, losing control for a moment. "Because he took it from me too."

That shut her up. Oddly, it had never occurred to her to ask what I was doing here, and only now did I see her start to put it together.

"I thought I wanted him dead," I said. "Hell, I thought I'd want to do what you're doing until I got here and saw it happening."

The situation was ludicrous. I was trying to convince someone to spare Bollard's life.

"This isn't the answer," I went on. "I don't know what is. I'm not sure where to go from here. But you just . . . you have to stop. You're letting what he did turn you into him."

She stared at me, speechless. I knew how she'd suffered. I knew her rage and her loss. What I didn't know is if she could come back from where she was now. Every piece of Bollard she'd cut off had left less of her, and it was hard to tell if there was enough remaining for her to hear me. As it turned out, there wasn't. She raised the pistol and aimed it at my face. Maybe she was going to try to kill me. Maybe she was just going to try to run me off. But before she could do anything, we heard the sound of cracking wood in the bedroom, followed by hurried movement and shattering glass. She ran toward the door with the gun still pointed my way. As she passed me, I took a step back toward the room myself.

"Stay where you are!" she yelled, shaking the gun at me. Then she pushed the bedroom door open to reveal Bollard disappearing out a shattered window. I saw the bed was now in pieces and realized, in the privacy afforded him by the closed door, he'd finished the job I'd inadvertently started when I'd tackled Alexa.

As he regained his feet outside, he set out at a limping gallop toward a nearby outcropping of trees. Alexa aimed the pistol and squeezed off several shots.

They all missed. Apparently, she hadn't been able to practice her marksmanship during her years of revenge prep.

She howled in frustration and hurled herself out the window after Bollard. With his injuries, his top speed was no match for hers, and she tackled him before he reached the trees. Decrepit as he was, he grabbed her gun arm and tried to wrench the weapon away from her.

I started toward the window, but there was no time for me to act. As they rolled across the ground screaming and clawing and biting, there was another shot, and Bollard went limp. I could see blood gushing from an exit wound in the back of his head.

Alexa looked down at him in shock. Judging from her reaction, the kill shot had been accidental.

"No! No, no, no!" she bellowed. "Not yet!"

I heard footsteps behind me and turned to see Arthur come running in.

"What are you doing here?" I said.

"I heard g-g-gunshots," he answered, as if that was something everyone ran toward rather than away from. He looked around the room, taking in the bottled body parts, the bloodied bed sheets strewn across the broken bed frame. Then his gaze fell to Alexa on the ground outside, staring catatonically down at the gory mess that had been Bollard's head.

"What the h-h-heck happened?!" he cried.

"It's . . . complicated," I said.

I didn't know where to start and how to explain that after years of fantasizing about Bollard's death, I was basically disappointed in myself for failing to stop it. God. Bollard was really dead. It was going to take awhile for that to sink in, never mind everything else that had happened here. But I was reminded that what had happened here was still happening, as we heard a bone-chilling scream from Alexa. We looked out at her and she looked back, her eyes burning with the fury of the Dark Phoenix.

"You ruined it!" she howled. "You ruined it all!"

She ambled to her feet and sprinted back toward us, raising the gun and firing several rounds as she went. This time she got lucky. Arthur didn't. A round tore through his shoulder, and he crashed to the floor.

"D-d-dagnabbit!" he yelled.

As I ran to his side, Alexa reached the window and vaulted back through it with shocking athleticism. She fired several more rounds in our direction, but I shielded Arthur, and the few rounds that were aimed true hit me and bounced off. She paused only momentarily to puzzle at that, then fired again, only to find the gun empty. Then, insanely, she threw it aside and launched herself at me, dragging me to the ground. We rolled away from Arthur, and she ended up above me, hammering at my face with both fists. She was an animal gone rabid, and it was all I could do to fend off her blows. Finally, I heard a crash, and shards of glass showered down around me as her eyes went blank. She slouched to the floor beside me, out for the count. I looked up to see Arthur standing over her with the remains of a large lamp in his hands. I thought the bullet had probably done enough damage to trigger the shutdown of his pain receptors, but he still looked very much the worse for wear.

"W-w-what . . ."—he paused to catch his breath—"is g-g-going on?!"

I started to explain, but then things got really crazy.

CHAPTER  24

THERE WAS A SOUND LIKE CRYSTAL RENDING—A HIGH-PITCHED, unrelenting screech. Then a dazzling light came pouring in from outside. I got to my feet and we both rushed to the window, peering out at the sky above. What we saw was like nothing we'd ever seen in our lives. It looked like the sky had torn open, and it was hemorrhaging blue-green energy like a busted water main. It began closing back up, but before it finished, a sleek, otherworldly spacecraft burst through it and swooped over the cabin. We ran out the front door in time to see the ship bash into the ground fifty yards down the dirt path leading away from us. It toppled end over end, snapping a series of eucalyptus trees like matchsticks and carving a deep gash in the landscape. Finally, it barreled into the shallow lagoon at the end of the road, digging into the silty, sandy bottom and coming to rest twenty yards offshore.

Fires raging all over the hull were slowly being extinguished as the water that had been displaced returned. It was an utterly astonishing spectacle, made even more so by one shocking fact: I'd seen the ship before. In *Fate Force* comics.

For a moment, we just stared slack-jawed at the path of destruction leading away from the cabin. Then we looked at each other.

"What in the w-w-world was that?" Arthur said.

"I can tell you what it looked like," I answered. "But it can't be that."

"W-w-why?"

"Because . . . it can't."

I started toward the lagoon and he followed, silently agreeing that the details of what had happened with Alexa and Bollard—no matter how crazy they were—would have to wait. As we reached the water's edge, we saw that most of the ship was now a few inches under water. However, there was still a small section of the hull exposed, and we heard an explosive hiss as a hatch burst open in the middle of that section. Three people clambered out. The first was a tall, grizzled Caucasian man in his mid-forties with a predatory scowl that seemed like a permanent fixture. He had a ghastly scar running down the left side of his face, directly through the socket that had once held an eye but now held a robotic implant. (I thought idly how bizarre it was that I'd encountered two one-eyed men in a single hour.) To his right was a short, rotund Indian man in his thirties. To his left was a stunningly beautiful Eurasian woman in her very early twenties. All three of them were covered from the neck down by metallic gold body armor—which, like the ship and the people themselves, was unsettlingly familiar to me. The tall, scary guy surveyed the area briefly until he noticed us. Then he turned to the others and gestured in our direction. All three of them paused, staring intently. Then metallic hockey mask-like helmets formed as if from nowhere around their heads and faces, and blue jet streams shot from their hands and heels, carrying them into the air directly toward us.

Arthur looked over at me and said, "Should w-w-we be running away?"

I opened my mouth to answer, then did something midway between shaking my head and nodding.

The three people touched down in front of us, and their helmets folded back into the collar of their suits like metal origami. The tall guy took a step toward me and looked me up and down. His face suggested he wasn't impressed. Then his non-robotic eye glazed over, not unlike Arthur's eyes when he was doing android stuff. But in this case, I could see a series of rapidly changing reflections in the guy's eye as it darted around. Then the reflections vanished, and he looked at me and growled, "That's you, right?"

"What do you mean?" I said.

The woman nudged the tall guy. "He's not receiving," she said, with a slight British accent. "It's 2054. No neural implants."

"Shit," he responded. "Still? Fuckin' dark ages."

The woman rolled her eyes at him, then opened one of several compartments built into the utility belt hanging around her waist. She removed a small, metallic disc. It beeped softly, then projected a holographic screen in front of us. It was an excerpt from a news site dated March 22, 2054, which was more than a month away. The headline read: "Clayton Clayborn, aka Henry Heywood, cleared of murder charges but sentenced for theft of Norman Corp property." There were photos of the Javelin, Bollard's maimed and lifeless body, and . . . me.

"Is that . . . Clayton, is that you?" Arthur gasped. "What's g-g-going on here?"

I didn't respond. I didn't know how to.

"They nab you a few weeks out," the tall guy said. "Apparently a psycho by the name a' Alexandra Sandoval did the deed, then went to the cops and tried to frame you as payback for messin' up some kinda . . . torture marathon. Lucky thing too—without all the coverage in the feeds we never woulda found you here. Then we'd all be shrucked."

I still said nothing. I was dumbstruck. And not just because of the article, or what I'd just been told.

"W-w-what is happening here?!" Arthur cried.

"You must be the robot," the tall guy said.

"What?" Arthur replied. "H-h-how could you—"

But he didn't finish the question because the tall guy cut him off with the words I'd been waiting for—the words I feared would be the end of my sanity.

"Gentlemen, I'm Commander Atticus Slade."

"Nope," I croaked, shaking my head resolutely.

"What the hell you mean 'nope'?" he growled.

"I mean, nope, you're not Atticus Slade. Because he's made up."

I pointed to the other two. "And so are Meylene Lee and Rachit Sadana. So don't say you're them."

They looked startled.

"How do you know—" the woman started, but the Indian man interrupted. "Ah, yes," he said, also with a slight British accent. "The comic books."

"Of course!" the woman said.

Arthur frowned and cocked his head. "Is anyone g-g-going to explain any of this?!"

The Indian man replied, "Well, Seymour—the principal on this project—used some of our previous scenarios and our likenesses to generate the Fate Force comics. The system embellished a bit of course, but—"

"What are you talking about?" Arthur cried.

"Well as I understand it, the higher-ups thought the materials Seymour was working with didn't hit some of the key points as plainly as they'd like."

"What? W-w-what materials?" Arthur demanded.

"Comic books, dumb shit," the tall guy answered. "So old Seymour had the system whip up the Fate Force series with plot lines to appease the brass, set up a dummy publisher, and voilà, the Cateklysm Scenario was a go."

"Oh my God," I whispered. *The Cateklysm Scenario*? My mind was racing to grasp the implications. "Are you telling me . . ." I dropped off, gulping in skeptical wonderment before beginning again, "Are you telling me that the Fate Force is real, and Cateklysm is . . . a dude named Seymour?"

"You catch on quick, kid," the tall guy answered.

"Though technically, we're the B.H.C.—the Bureau of Historical Corrections," said the woman. "Seymour just needed a catchier name for the comics."

"Of course, it seems the creativity ran dry in other regards," said the Indian man. "Could have changed our names at a minimum, even if we are ghosts."

As much as Cassie and I had debated when and how the Fate Force could theoretically intervene and change our stars, I was in no way prepared to hear what I was hearing. Recent events had shaken my faith, but this? This was dismembering my faith and stitching it back together like Frankenstein's monster. These people were telling me that the being to whom I'd pledged fealty wasn't an all-knowing, interdimensional titan – he was just a guy, like me. They were saying the Challenge was nothing more than an elaborate bit of theater. The bedrock of my existence was turning to cotton candy, and I felt a bout of vertigo setting in.

"You expect me to believe the thing that's defined my whole life …"– I paused, numbly –"is just one of your fucking time-tweaking scenarios?!"

"Roger that," answered the guy who was supposedly Atticus Slade.

"W-w-wait," Arthur said, frowning at me. "Time tweaking? Bureau of Historical Corrections? So these guys are supposed to be w-w-what, some kind of time repairmen?"

I nodded.

"That's ridiculous." He turned back to them. "If you can m-m-make wrong stuff right, why is history so full of terrible stuff?"

I knew what was coming. It was the cop-out I'd hated in the comics.

"We've done the best we can up to this point," answered the guy who was supposedly Rachit Sadana. "Many events find a way to occur no matter what."

"Like the last twenty years?" Arthur asked skeptically. "You're telling m-m-me there was nothing you could improve there?"

"No. There wasn't."

"Okay …" I said, still willing my way through my own disbelief. "So … what was 'Seymour' doing in 2036 then?"

"He was laying the groundwork for a scenario targeting next year," explained the woman who was supposedly Meylene Lee.

The idea that these people were in fact the Fate Force, or B.H.C., or what have you, was nonsensical. It was utterly outside the realm of possibility. But suddenly, just like that, I decided I believed it all. The reason was simple.

"So … Fate Force really is going to fix it," I said. As insane as this turn of events was, it translated to salvation from the awful future Norman was poised to bring about. "You guys are here to patch the scenario, right?"

"What's that m-m-mean?" Arthur asked.

"In the comics, if a scenario doesn't go as planned, they make small adjustments down the line," I said.

"What? Well how the h-h-heck are we involved?"

"Well," Meylene said, "there's quite a lot to tell. So we'd rather wait until you're all together."

"What do you m-m-mean?" Arthur asked.

"Cassie," I guessed.

"Yes," Meylene confirmed. "Assuming she's somewhere nearby, our data suggests she could be very helpful."

"We're also gonna need transpo," Slade added, glancing at their wrecked ship. "That stolen Norman Corp ride around here somewhere?"

I nodded. Then I remembered.

"Wait. What about Alexa?" I said. "And Bollard's body . . ." I started toward the cabin.

"No time," Slade said.

"But—"

"Spoiler alert," he interrupted. "She takes off, and you decide to clean up the scene, bury the body and them jars a' eyes and fingers, all in a misguided effort to spare poor, mixed-up Alexandra the consequences of her actions. 'Course in the process, you leave enough of your own bio evidence on everything to make her story about you kidnapping her and Bollard stick—at least for long enough to blow up your fake identities. Then bada boom, bada bing, back to the Labor Loaner program for you and off to the junkyard crusher for the robot here."

"Jiminy Christmas!" Arthur yelped.

"But none of that's gonna happen now," Slade continued. "'Cause you're with us, and we don't give a shit about the mess in that cabin."

As Slade paused to let the speech sink in, Arthur looked over at me.

"D-d-do you really buy all this?" he asked.

I paused and looked back at him, weighing everything one last time. Then I nodded and said simply, "Let's go get Cassie."

CHAPTER 25

*"IF YOU'RE FROM THOUSANDS OF YEARS IN THE FUTURE, W-W-*why do you talk like us?"* Arthur asked Meylene as we walked back toward the Javelin. "In fact, why do you even s-s-speak English?"

"We all speak several languages," Meylene answered. "Plus, our neural implants are somewhat versed in the vernacular of every era and geography. Granted, some of us have more linguistic experience in your general temporal neighborhood than others."

She glanced over at Slade, who clarified, "Yeah. Some of us were lucky enough to get stranded in goddamn 'Nam for three tours due to 'technical difficulties.'"

Arthur had asked me a few questions to fill in the blanks on what had happened in the cabin, but he'd spent most of the walk interrogating our new friends. Out of curiosity, I'd inquired about the Pentagramite Easter egg and learned that the Fate Force fuel was depicted to look like its soon-to-be-discovered real-life equivalent as a mysterious hint to drive intrigue and indoctrination. But unlike Arthur, I didn't need any more convincing that the B.H.C.'s story was on the level. Believing they were a cadre of tech wizards from the future made the future a lot brighter. Plus, nothing they'd said was really any crazier than what I'd believed about Cateklysm my whole life.

"This thing is going to stick out like a sore thumb," Meylene said, as we reached the Javelin. "We need a lower profile if we're going to avoid attracting unwanted attention from any law enforcement straying into our path."

"S-s-speaking of ships attracting attention, don't you think the one you left back in the lagoon will arouse some curiosity?" Arthur asked.

"It's a secondary concern," Rachit said. "There's no danger. Power core's shot—it's dead in the water, so to speak."

Meylene seemed deaf to the discussion. Her eyes had glazed over with sparkling reflections, and she was mumbling, "No, no, too small, no . . ." Finally, she said, "Ah, there we go."

She extracted another small metal disc from her utility belt, walked over, and slapped it on the side of the Javelin, where it adhered through some magnetic means. Her eyes glazed over for another moment. Suddenly, a massive hologram blinked into existence around the Javelin, and it stopped being the Javelin. Now it looked like a dual-engine Chinook helicopter. It sounded like one, too, as the props spooled up to their pre-takeoff RPMs. Boeing had manufactured a limited number of this particular model as "sky yachts" for the superluxury market in the 2030s. These days they were a pretty common buy for broker barons. We'd still attract attention, but it would be a less problematic kind of attention.

"Holy mackerel," Arthur gasped as he examined our newly disguised ride. He extended a hand to touch it, but his hand passed right through to the hull of the Javelin beneath. This was more conventional hologram technology than what we'd encountered in the Danger Room, which made sense considering it was being projected from a device that fit in the palm of your hand. The lack of debris being kicked up by the downdraft of the props took away from the effect somewhat, but that would be mostly remedied as soon as the vertical takeoff thrusters were engaged, and once we were twenty or thirty feet up, no one would be able to see past the illusion. Of course, questions would be raised if anyone saw us doing ten or twenty times the top speed of a Chinook, but that would be at altitudes where there weren't any eyes around. Judging from the look on Arthur's face, Meylene's display of techno-magic had edged him ever closer to believing the story the B.H.C. was selling.

As we lifted off, Slade and Rachit took a seat around the table in the kitchen area, but Meylene joined Arthur and me on the flight deck. I noticed she was staring at Arthur while he adjusted our course. She seemed to be transfixed. He peered over at her, uncomfortably, and tried to cut the awkwardness with conversation.

"Aren't you a little young to be a time-traveling commando?"

Her age hadn't surprised me because I'd assumed her real-life backstory tracked against the comics, which would make her a child prodigy who'd joined the team when she was just fifteen. But she seemed too fascinated with Arthur to get into all that.

"What a miraculous creation you are," she remarked to him.

"Huh," he responded. "That's an upgrade on w-w-what people usually call me."

"Well, they're philistines. Your design is twenty years ahead of its time, at a minimum. Dr. Williams was a genius. More than a genius. He was an artist."

"You knew Arthur's father?" I said.

"Only by his legacy. His work is the building block for every breakthrough for a century."

Arthur shook his head. "Yeah. Too bad nobody recognized his genius w-w-while he was alive."

"Yes," Meylene said, wincing. "Bloody shame."

I thought I read a note of guilt and supposed she regretted bringing up Arthur's recently deceased father.

"But how the heck will his w-w-work even be discovered?" Arthur continued. "I'm the only piece of junk left—and I doubt I'll be around by the time AI comes back into s-s-style. Not at the rate I'm going."

He gestured to the damaged areas on his neck and shoulder, left by the bullets he'd caught. Meylene ignored his question about the future, seizing on his ailing self-image.

"You are not junk," she said firmly. I could see him warm to the words, though he didn't turn away from the Javelin's controls.

"And I wouldn't worry about that," she added, pointing to his injuries. She rooted around in one of the pouches on her belt and pulled out something that looked like a small black plastic screwdriver. Then she took a step toward him.

"Hey!" I said, grabbing her hand as she extended the thing toward Arthur's neck. "What have you got in mind here, lady?"

"It's okay," Arthur said. He was looking at her now with a glint in his eyes. I took my hand away.

Meylene smiled and placed the gizmo close to Arthur's neck. She squeezed the handle and waved the thing back and forth. There was a gentle hum and suddenly, the frayed circuits and charred synthetic skin began to reconstitute themselves. With each pass of the device, the area looked more and more like new, until there was no sign of the damage. Then she repeated the process for the hole in his shoulder.

Arthur ran a hand over both areas and stared at her. "Are you an angel?" he asked. He seemed at least half serious.

She chuckled and held up the gizmo. "It's called a temporal reversion scanner. It can sort of roll back time for machinery in a limited radius." I could see from Arthur's face that any remaining doubts he had about Meylene and the other two being time-traveling adventurers were vanishing as swiftly as his wounds had.

She took a step back. "Anything else I can help with?"

Arthur didn't say a thing. He just enabled the autopilot, stood, and started taking off his shirt.

"Whoa," Meylene said. "I meant in a professional capacity."

Arthur paused, naked to the waist and embarrassed. "Oh, I w-w-wasn't . . . I didn't—"

"I'm kidding," she said. Then she touched him lightly on the back, examining his burns and exposed spine. "We'll get you all patched up in two shakes."

She smiled at him . . . again. He smiled back, and I got the distinct feeling that three had just become a crowd. But to my relief, a tone sounded a moment later, indicating we'd reached our destination, and she hurried to finish up.

We'd located Cassie the same way we'd located Bollard. However, having structured all her financials, Arthur had known exactly where to look, so it had been a vastly easier process. It seemed that only a few hours after we'd parted ways, she'd checked into the Stanyan Park Hotel, and she had yet to check out.

The hotel wasn't far from the park clearing where we'd dropped her off, so we set down in the same place. Even disguised as a sky yacht, the Javelin caught the interest of a few park dwellers, and I wanted to be taking off again before it actually drew a crowd. So I headed out to collect Cassie at a brisk pace. I went on my own because I knew there were some things I'd need to say that would be easier to say without an audience. Of course, I wasn't sure exactly what those things would be, and I still hadn't figured it out as I emerged from the wild tangle of weeds forming a border between the park and Stanyan Street.

I saw the hotel about half a block down. Its construction was thoroughly modern – a polished cobalt exterior bulged with convex windows, and a well-manicured jungle of gravity-defying vegetation clung to all sides, in compliance with the city's new climate-mending ordinances. Meanwhile, structures on the verge of collapse stretched off to the left and right, as far as the eye could see.

I was about to cross the street when I heard a voice call out, "Clayton?"

I turned to find Cassie standing behind me and froze up. I wasn't ready for this. I still had no idea what I was going to say.

"What are you doing here?" she asked.

It was hard to understand her because she was speaking around a mouthful of chocolate bar. I saw she was holding one in each hand. She glanced down at them and looked embarrassed, but I understood. I thought back to the endurance eating I'd done on the dining level of our apartment building. Like me, she was trying to wash away the taste of eight years of foomed-out sludge with everything her eight-year-old self missed most.

I smiled and took a step toward her, but she took a step back, her manner hardening.

"You should leave."

"Cassie, we need to talk."

"I thought you understood. What you've done. It's a line that I can't–"

"I didn't kill him," I blurted out.

"What?" she said, relieved and confused.

"I mean he's dead," I added. "But I didn't kill him. In fact, I tried to stop it. It was a total matum meal. There was this girl—this crazy girl torturing him at his place for weeks and . . ."

So much had happened, and I wasn't sure what details mattered right now. But as I struggled to decide, Cassie took my hand and looked into my eyes. Then I knew what I'd come to say, more than anything else.

"Look, I'm not who you think I am. But . . . I'm beginning to believe that I could be."

It was about as corny a line as anyone had ever uttered. But it was true.

A look of sublime contentment spread across her face, warming the space between us like a fireplace in winter. Then she kissed me. It was a long, chocolatey kiss.

"So," she said as she leaned back, "any other news?"

"Um . . . yeah, actually."

CHAPTER  26

FOR A MOMENT, CASSIE JUST STARED AT SLADE AND THE GANG, dumbstruck. They stared back from where they were seated in the kitchen. I'd done my best to prepare her for the meeting, but that was a tall order. After a moment, she looked at me and said, "I win."

"What?" I responded.

"I win!" she said again. "Every argument we've ever had about the Fate Force. I win!"

I rolled my eyes and nodded.

She took a step toward Slade and peered at him, like he was a museum exhibit. "He's even more gnarled and menacing in real life!"

"Nice to meet you too," Slade said.

"Sorry, I just . . . I mean . . . holy shit, you guys exist!"

She glanced briefly at Rachit and Meylene, but her eyes kept coming back to Slade. I could understand why. I imagined he was the reason this particular team had been chosen as the model for Fate Force. Per Cassie's observation, his general demeanor, coupled with his grizzly scar and cyborgian peeper made him a hundred-proof cliché of battle-hardened grit, primed and ready for the comics.

"Wait a minute," Cassie said. "So we're Sub Rosa?!"

"We're what?" Arthur asked.

"Sub Rosa!" Cassie explained. "The select group of civilians chosen to help execute scenarios!"

"Yeah, sure," Slade said. "You're all kinds of Sub Rosa. Let's get this show on the road."

He gestured for Cassie and me to join them at the table. While the other two had removed their cybersuits, he still wore his. It was difficult to imagine him ever taking it off, though I thought he probably did when he showered. Probably.

Cassie shook hands with everyone as we seated ourselves. She was doing her level best to set aside her lingering shock and awe, and I think she decided the best way to do that was to dive right in.

"Okay, okay," she said. "Fangirl mode off. This situation needs a patch more than the Teen Chimeras Gone Wild Scenario. So what's the deal?"

"It's a long story," Rachit answered.

And then he began to tell that story. He started with the B.H.C. basics. The supernatural beasts and impossible feats lining the pages of Fate Force comics were born of a mixture of exaggeration and fabrication. But just like the Fate Force, the Bureau of Historical Corrections had been formed in a war-torn world by a scientist named Moira McCaffrey, who had discovered time travel and decided it was her moral duty to improve history wherever possible. And just like in the comics, she believed that if her agency operated in the open, people would become overly reliant on it. Every misstep prevented by a B.H.C. warning would make the populace less wary of consequences and more reckless, and soon even the B.H.C. wouldn't be able to head off all the disasters. So just like in the comics, her teams concocted sometimes outlandish scenarios to alter history indirectly—like when they orchestrated the release of a Christian missionary from North Korean custody by manipulating Kim Jong Un into becoming besties with pro basketball weirdo Dennis Rodman.

Anyway, several generations of agents in, the bureau was still working through history's problem points. So, what was the problem the Cateklysm Scenario was intended to fix? Well, just like in our current timeline, around 2055, people began developing extraordinary mutations caused by exposure to Normanium Prime. (This trait wasn't attributed to Fate Force's Pentagramite because the point of the Easter egg was only to foreshadow Normanium Prime's role as F.T.L. fuel.)

Interestingly, in pre-Cateklysm Scenario history, Normanium was discovered by NASA, not Norman, and it was called Polemoside. In that history, the discovery of the material's true potential had come much earlier, as had the breakthrough of F.T.L. travel. However, more care was taken with the material, so mutations still didn't appear until 2055.

Regardless, of the people who experienced mutations, some survived the subsequent series of seizures and some didn't. Not great news for me, as the data the B.H.C. had on me at the moment extended only a month or so into the future, and my fate after that was unknown. Even more concerning was the fact that in our sibling timeline, even those who survived the mutations were unlucky. Why? Well, just like in our timeline, biases based on race, gender, sexual preference, and the other usual suspects had been somewhat dulled by the efforts of civil rights groups and the passage of time. But the lessons learned there were not great enough to prepare people for the emergence of superhumans. In fact, this new group of minorities inspired a unifying prejudice—a fear-based hatred every "normal" human being could agree on. So mutation survivors were labeled a danger to society, rounded up, put in prison camps—yada, yada, yada. It was all very déjà vu for anyone who had ever cracked open an issue of the X-Men

Only in this case, there was no Charles Xavier to temper the tempers of those with powers. So the powered people in question went full-on Magneto, forming a militia, seizing military complexes and WMDs. Boom: worldwide war, over two million dead. Not good.

According to projections, the only way to prevent the mutations was to prevent the discovery of Polemoside, but that would lead to an end-of-days-esque energy crisis and/or climate catastrophe. Enter B.H.C. Agent Seymour Lawrence, who proposed the Cateklysm Scenario to condition humans to accept and embrace superhumans, and superhumans to serve a superior code of ethics. Now I understood. It wasn't a coincidence a kid obsessed with comics had developed superpowers. Like every Cateklysm follower, my obsession was engineered to prepare me for the possibility of those powers in myself or others.

Fun fact: after dozens of pitches, this was the very first time Seymour had ever gotten a scenario approved. Even for the B.H.C., the scenario was pretty out there, and there were definitely those who questioned it. Slade, for instance, thought it was "crazier than a bag a' cats in a bathtub." But the probabilistic outcomes projected by the B.H.C.'s system looked just good enough. So the scenario was green lit in a close vote.

As overwhelming as all this was, the story wasn't over. Not even close. Because when Seymour was setting up the scenario, he'd been traveling via "Translocator." Cassie and I knew this device as the "Skipper," which is a handheld unit that allows Fate Force agents to "skip" through time and space without the aid of any craft. In the comics, it's pictured as a clunky box, operated through relatively primitive holo-menus. And it turns out that's pretty accurate because its real-life counterpart never made it past prototyping. Early tests indicated a small but real chance that the Translocator would not deliver agents to their destination with all their parts in the right place. So needless to say, they preferred to stick with the Eldridge and other vessels in the B.H.C.'s small fleet. That is, except for Seymour. He'd elected to use the Translocator because he thought it "really sold his Cateklysm performance." It was increasingly evident that the guy was a total nutter. However, the problem wasn't him using the Translocator. The problem was someone from our era somehow getting ahold of it. One guess who that someone was.

It took Luthor Norman just twenty minutes to lay siege to the B.H.C. HQ. From the B.H.C.'s perspective, the changes they had just made to the past became instant history. So they hadn't had time to dig into the data and decode the results before one of those results showed up and started raising hell. They had no idea what hit them. Norman swept through the compound, taking control of every agent along the way, which, as Arthur had more or less hypothesized, required nothing but a single touch. Worse, through the voice prints and biometric signatures of his hijacked hosts, he gained control of the compound's AI and all of its knowledge. Who knows if he ever recognized the place or the people from Fate Force comics, but if he did, it didn't give him pause. Slade, Rachit, and Meylene were the only ones to escape, taking heavy fire as they went, which explained the clumsy landing Arthur and I had witnessed.

At this point in the story, Rachit paused, letting it all sink in. It was a lot. For one thing, Cassie and I had just learned that our entire belief system was the product of a wackadoo B.H.C. agent's first at bat, barely approved by his superiors. I could see a cloud had formed over Cassie. I took her hand in mine and felt her squeeze, drawing strength from our connection. Then she pressed on.

"So as bad as we thought Norman winning the Challenge would be, it's worse?" she said. "If you don't stop him from reaching the compound, he'll . . . take control of all history?"

"Bingo," Slade answered. "That'll teach us to go on vacation."

"What?" I asked.

"The three of us—we were out on vacation throughout the scenario prep and execution," Rachit answered. "We returned about ten minutes before Norman arrived."

Cassie shook her head, no doubt picturing her favorite superheroes stumbling into their base, mai tais in hand, as a supervillain took over the joint. Then she refocused and asked, "So wait, why hasn't he already traveled back to before you escaped and killed you?"

"We fired an E.M.P. charge as we cleared the compound's space time," Slade said. "Standard protocol for a breach. All their systems'll be down for ten hours while we make the changes needed."

That protocol was news to Cassie and me. The comics had never covered the possibility of a compound breach.

"Okay," Arthur said. "So what the h-h-heck are you doing here? With us?"

Rachit explained, "Well, time travel is a bit like old-world sea travel—there are currents that determine where you can go. Though in the case of time travel, those currents change minute to minute. So typically, our AI analyzes the changes we need to make, assesses relevant jump points, then jumps us to the best option when the window opens."

"'Course," Slade cut in impatiently, "sometimes a madman severs your connection to the mainframe before that window opens and tries to blow you to shit with surface-to-air fire. Then you gotta jump to whatever point is on the menu at the moment."

"Cripes!" Arthur gasped. "Are you saying you're ... shipwrecked with no idea how to stop Armageddon?"

"We wouldn't put it that way," Rachit said. "While we weren't there for the scenario debrief, we were able to upload a good deal of data to our neural implants before the connection was severed."

"Which is w-w-why you knew who we were and where to find us," Arthur said. "So don't you know where Norman is?"

"Unfortunately, not exactly," Meylene answered. "There's no historical data indicating his whereabouts at the moment, and our scans aren't turning up any communications or other records that can help."

"Yeah, he's laying low," Arthur said. "Very low. But you s-s-said you didn't know 'exactly' where he was. So you have an idea?"

"Well not of where he is," Rachit answered. "But we all know where he WILL BE: the final stage of the Challenge. And that's the only place where he would have crossed paths with Seymour—at some sort of awards ceremony Seymour has planned. So we just need to get there before that occurs, in about ... three hours."

"Three hours?!" Cassie cried. "Why aren't you already there?"

"Well, as I said, we were able to download a good deal of information before losing our connection to the mainframe, but there are ... blind spots."

"Oh my God," I gasped. "You don't know where the final stage is!"

He nodded. "That's why we need you. Our data shows you finished the second stage, which directed you to the third, yes?"

Cassie, Arthur, and I looked at each other in wide-eyed mortification.

"Actually, in truth, even if we did know where it was, we'd likely need your help," Meylene added. "We don't have the tech to hack our way through Seymour's game to catch up to Norman if it comes to that. So your expertise could be invaluable."

We all stared at them, dumbstruck by the absurd irony of the situation. Meylene misread us.

"Look, it's obvious you've given up," she said. "And fair enough. You expect to find Norman at the final stage, and he's a very dangerous man who will most likely try to kill you. But that's why we told you the whole story. We needed you to know how much was at stake. And now that we're here to protect you—"

"You don't understand," Cassie interrupted.

"Then enlighten us, goddamn it," Slade growled.

It was all too much for me, and I snapped.

"We didn't give up!" I yelled. "We have no idea where the final stage is!"

"What the hell you talkin' about?" Slade demanded. "'Course you do! The data says—"

"Your data missed some details!" I responded hysterically. Then my voice dropped in volume, as the hopelessness of the situation really began to settle on me.

"We were awarded this black box thing," I said. "It had a riddle we had to answer to find the last stage. But it was destroyed by the time we had the answer."

"Holy mother of Keee-riste!" Slade moaned.

"There's got to be something we can do," Cassie said.

"Like w-w-what?" Arthur asked woefully.

"Where's the box now?" Meylene asked. "Or what's left of it?"

"HBBI," Cassie sighed.

"Even if it can be fixed with your m-m-magic wand, it'd take us more than three hours just to g-g-get there," Arthur lamented. "And who knows how long to get to wherever we're supposed to g-g-go after that."

Everyone sagged visibly in distress, and I thought things were as bleak as they could get. As usual, I was wrong.

We heard a tone coming from my hab suite. At first I didn't recognize it, then I realized it was an audio chat request coming through from the M.U. on the wall-mounted holo-pod. I walked in to see that C. B. was hailing me and swiped a hand through the vibrating telephone icon on the holo-screen, accepting the call. I don't know why. I guess I thought a friendly voice would be a welcome distraction. But the voice wasn't friendly. It was frantic.

"Thwppit!" he cried. "God in Heaven, I don't know what to do. They've taken Loyd!"

CHAPTER  27

"WHO'S LOYD?" I SAID TO C. B.
"Loyd – my Loyd – Dane Whitman!" He was utterly distraught.
"C. B., try to calm down," I said, struggling to get my brain around what he was saying. "You said they took him. Who's 'they'?"
"Norman's bloody stormtroopers!" he moaned. "I was at work, and when I got home, the neighbors . . ."– he stifled a sob –"the neighbors said they saw him being shoved into a Norman Corp van this morning."
"What the hell?" Cassie said.
"And he's obviously not the only one," C. B. went on. "It's all over the M.U. They've been snatching Chowderheads from across the globe."
One glance at the M.U. home page confirmed what he was saying. The mass message board was scrolling steadily as the rumors and panic spread about Chowderheads gone missing. With Norman Corp's resources, locating the targets would be easy, as would repressing the abduction reports no doubt flooding into area police departments. A theory came to me in a flash.
"It's the Conundrum all over again," I said. "Norman can't solve the black box riddle, and they're bringing him Chowderheads so he can put the screws to them."
"You think he's having people shipped to him in space?" Cassie exclaimed.
"Or he's here on Earth. He doesn't have anywhere better to be until he cracks the riddle."
"What are you people talking about?!" C. B. demanded.
"Norman is close to completing the Challenge," I explained. "But he needs Scripture knowledge he doesn't have, and I think he's kidnapping Chowderheads to get it."
While most of the community had been dicks to us when we'd asked for their help, they didn't deserve what Norman would do to them to get what he wanted. But at least we knew they were probably alive. Cassie had the same thought.
"If Clayton's right, Loyd is okay," she said, trying to comfort C. B. "They need him."
"Damn it," C. B. said shakily. "Bloody fool's always telling the world he's 'minutes from solving the Conundrum' and look what it's got him."

It suddenly occurred to me that helping C. B. could help us – finding Loyd could mean finding Norman. And that would be easy if . . .

"C. B., does Loyd have a holo-pod with him?" I asked.

"No," he answered. "I found it in the hallway, guts ripped out."

The wind went out of my sails, but as the B.H.C. agents entered the room, Meylene pointed out the paper-thin silver lining.

"Holo-pods can only be tracked on planet. And confiscating it suggests the kind of security they'd reserve for Norman. You're right about him being on Earth."

"Great," Slade said sarcastically. "Search radius is the whole goddamn planet. We gonna start goin' door to door?"

I didn't know if C. B. had heard them, but if so, he wasn't interested in introductions.

"Thwppit, please . . ." he said. "Tell me there's something you can do."

"I'm sorry," I answered, feeling sick to my stomach. "The only thing that could help was smashed to bits in another solar system."

My sense of helplessness was growing by the second. Then I heard Arthur say under his breath, "It W-W-WAS smashed to bits."

Cassie and I looked over at him, bewildered by his mumbling. He'd been standing in the doorway silently taking in the painful exchange with C. B. Now, he turned, opened my closet, and rummaged through it. He came up with a crumpled and stained flight suit. I recognized it as the one I'd been wearing back on HBBI, before he'd stripped it off me to treat my hypothermia. He unzipped it and stuck his hand inside. His arm disappeared as he probed the length of one of the legs. He frowned and retracted his arm. His conviction seemed to ebb, but he dived back in, fishing around in the other leg. Suddenly, his expression changed. His hunch had paid off. He pulled his hand out to reveal a fragment of glossy onyx fiberglass, peppered with copper circuitry. It had been left behind in my flight suit, where the box had been during my fall into the Danger Room. He turned to Meylene and held it up.

"Is it enough?" he asked.

She paused, deducing what he must be holding and what he meant for her to do with it. Then she said, "Let's find out."

"Thwppit? What's happening? Who's there with you?" C. B. called plaintively, finally noticing the unfamiliar voices in the room.

"Give us a minute, C. B.," I said.

We stepped back out into the kitchen area as Meylene produced the temporal reversion scanner. We all crowded around her as she placed the hunk of black box on the table and passed the scanner over it slowly. Nothing happened. She repeated the procedure. Still nothing.

"Shit on a shish kabab!" Slade cursed.

But then, suddenly, a glimmer of new surface area appeared beside the fragment. Then another. And another. As Meylene continued to pass the scanner back and forth, the fragment began to grow in every direction, rising to accommodate the volume materializing below it.

"Sweet Baby Jesus, we're back in business!" Slade cheered.

The energy in the room was electric as we all stared reverently at the miracle in progress.

"Thwppit? Thwppit, what's going on?" I heard C. B. call out as the box appeared in its entirety. The screen lit up, displaying the riddle and virtual keyboard.

"C. B.," I called back. "I think we can help."

I filled C. B. in as much as I could, and he took solace in the fact that heading Norman off at the final stage would allow us to find out where the abductees were being kept, among other things. I told him we'd contact him as soon as we had any news, disconnected, and walked back over to where the others were standing, staring down at the black box's virtual keyboard.

"Here goes nothing," Cassie said.

Decker had intended for his final words to carry us to the final stage, and we were about to find out if he'd gotten his wish as Cassie keyed in "Element X." A moment passed, the combined anticipation of the group settling around us like humidity. Then there was a pleasant tone, and everyone breathed a sigh of relief as a new message began to appear one letter at a time. We all stared intently at the screen, hoping whatever planet we were headed to would be closer than HBBI. And it was. A lot closer. When the message was complete, it read: 3530 Central Ave, Cleveland, Ohio.

"Are you kidding?!" Arthur gasped. "To reach s-s-stage two we had to rewrite the laws of physics and travel five and a h-h-half light-years to an alien planet. But stage three is . . . in Cleveland?!"

"Of course," Cassie said.

"We should have known," I added.

"W-w-why?" Arthur asked, exasperated.

"Because that's where it all started," I answered.

Conventional wisdom says superhero comics are the product of a gradual evolution of the pulp publications of the late nineteenth and early twentieth centuries. But that's only half the story. Because the notion of a superpowered symbol of virtue and valor colorfully clad in cape and tights truly began with Superman, whose conception was not fueled by a slow and steady genesis, but a violent bolt of lightning that struck in the early 1930s.

Yes, Superman was a gestalt of centuries of accumulated pop culture – a mash-up of Hercules, Samson, and other heroes of myth, infused with shades of science fiction and dressed up by Jerry Siegel and Joe Shuster in the garb of the wrestlers and circus strongmen idolized by boys of their era. But these are attributes and window dressing. Most Chowderheads believed the heart of the hero was born on June 2, 1932. That night, Jerry Siegel's father, Mitchell, died during a robbery of the men's haberdashery he owned and operated. Reports vary as to whether Mitchell was shot or simply suffered a fatal heart attack during the incident. But one thing is for sure: he would have lived, if he'd been a bulletproof superhuman. So that's what burst forth from his grief-stricken son's imagination just months later.

Admittedly, Jerry Siegel himself never confirmed this connection, but Chowderheads didn't need him to. As his friend Joe helped him flesh out Superman's character and backstory, a new archetype was born that would echo through the ages. Superman's powers would be borrowed and built upon by thousands of artists. The notion of his mild-mannered alter ego and his commitment to "truth, justice, and the American way" would become fundamental tenets of superherodom. But the most poignant aspect of Superman's profile to be ripped off time and time again was the tragic loss of his parents. Siegel's heartbreaking embodiment of art imitating life became the original origin story.

Needless to say, the fact that losing a parent or parents was central to super-hero DNA and the birth of the Scriptures was never, ever lost on me or Cassie. So we weren't a bit surprised that the final stage of the Challenge would take place at the site of Jerry Siegel's father's death – the address where the family's haberdashery once stood: 3530 Central Avenue in Cleveland, Ohio.

"W-w-wow," Arthur said, after we'd explained the significance of the address. "You guys really should have known."

Arthur engaged the Javelin's vertical thrusters, and we lifted off. The trip to Ohio would take around half an hour thanks to our course, which would carry us up and out of Earth's atmosphere for most of the journey. We traveled in silence for a time, with everyone seemingly lost in their own thoughts. Then Arthur turned to Rachit and said, as if they were in the middle of a conversation, "W-w-what about the paradox problem?"

"Hm?" Rachit responded.

Arthur elaborated, "If you stop Norman, he'll never g-g-go to your compound. But if he doesn't go to your compound, you won't come back to s-s-stop him. And then doesn't the universe explode or something?"

"Ah. No, there's no paradox," Rachit said. "Time isn't always linear. Now that we've traveled back, the future in which Norman infiltrates the compound will become part of a loop that took place in the past. We'll just be the only ones to remember it."

"H-h-how?" Arthur asked, clearly strained by the exotic science. "Wouldn't the changes you m-m-made affect you too? How do you even stay you? Spill a cup of coffee in 1920 and bam, one butterfly effect later, the three of you are beat cops . . . or d-d-dog nannies."

Slade grimaced at that thought and grunted, "Ain't gonna happen."

"W-w-why not?" Arthur asked.

"Ripple Resistance," Cassie jumped in, to show off. Rachit gave her the nod of approval she was after.

Arthur frowned. "Huh?"

"Think of time as a pond," Rachit said. "Every change is a stone dropped in that pond, with ripples traveling outward. To your point, the ripples can have profound and unexpected effects. But there is a natural phenomenon that shields time travelers from the ripples they cause."

"Sounds like sci-fi h-h-hogwash," Arthur said.

"Yes," Meylene said. "But it's not. We've actually been able to manipulate the phenomenon to create a field that surrounds our compound at all times – protecting it and everyone within from the changes made by any agent. Though it isn't perfect. It erodes pretty dramatically when someone starts making changes within a week or so of our present."

"Which is actually working in our favor at the moment," Rachit said.

"Because Norman just g-g-got to the compound," Arthur postulated.

"Precisely," Meylene confirmed. "There's nothing to stop us from changing what happened."

I thought Arthur probably had a lot more questions. How did the B.H.C. gather data from throughout history? If our future was their past, was their future someone else's past? How were they protecting alien civilizations from the changes they were making? But before he could get to any of that, Cassie cut in and asked, "So what exactly is the U.A.T.?"

We'd had a lot to process over the last few hours, but I was still amazed it had taken this long for one of us to bring this up.

"The what?" Rachit asked.

"You know, the prize Catekly–" She caught herself. "The prize Seymour promised in his broadcast. The 'unimaginably advanced technology.'"

"Oh. Yes, of course," Rachit said. He looked over at Meylene. I thought I saw a hint of shared consternation. Rachit answered, "It's terraforming tech."

"You're kidding!" Cassie cried.

If there was something in the glance between the two agents, she was too excited to notice it.

"Like in the comics?" she continued. "The machines that produce fresh air and water, regulate atmospheric hazards, and transform barren deserts into lush, crop-friendly paradises?!"

"Yes," Meylene answered. "It'd accelerate things by a century or so, but scenario projections suggest that in the right hands, the tech could stabilize the future – securing unity through the common goal of healing the Earth and colonizing other worlds."

"The power to change the world," Seymour had hinted in his broadcast. And apparently, he'd meant it literally. If I'd still planned on using the U.A.T. to rain hellfire down on evildoers, I would have been sorely disappointed. But as it was, I could share Cassie's elation. The U.A.T. had turned out to be exactly what she would have wished for.

"Hold on," she said. Her excitement was palpable. "So if we pull this off – if we stop Norman – the scenario will play out with us winning the tech, right?"

Us? I thought. Apparently, to her it was now a foregone conclusion that we would somehow share the prize. The only thing more surprising than that was the fact that I felt the exact same way. But was it really going to happen? Was our faith in the Scriptures about to pay off? Would we be the ones to usher in a brighter future?

"Fuck no," Slade answered Cassie. "This here's a lost cause."

Rachit and Meylene cringed.

"What?" Cassie said, in shock. "What do you mean?"

"Damn it, Slade," Meylene said. I'd read her and Rachit right earlier. They'd definitely been uncomfortable with this topic, and this was why.

Slade shrugged, belying a hint of remorse that he tried to extinguish with a splash of self-righteousness by barking, "Well, how long you wanna keep 'em in the dark?"

We weren't fooled. It was clear he'd slipped up and would have put the cat back in the bag if he could. But he couldn't.

"I'm sorry," Meylene said, her voice thick with contrition. "Our assessment of the data—even the incomplete data—indicates the Cateklysm scenario . . . isn't viable."

"Which m-m-means?" Arthur prompted.

"We're gonna reset it, dipshit," Slade blurted.

It's never directly addressed in the series, but over the years, Fate Force fans had speculated that some scenarios must have turned out too badly to patch, compelling the team to revert the timeline to its previous state and try a new scenario. Based on what Slade had just said, the fans had speculated right.

"No," Cassie gasped. She looked like she'd just taken a shot to the head from the Wrecker's crowbar. "No, that's not fair. We're gonna stop Norman!"

"Yup. That's step one," Slade said. "Then the compound'll wake up to a world without that rat-jacker, check the data, and finish the job."

"S-s-sorry," Arthur piped in anxiously. "Are you people saying w-w-what I think you're saying? We're just gonna be . . . erased?"

"At least in your current incarnation, I'm afraid so," Meylene answered gingerly. "It's truly not up to us."

"Even if we found some way to insulate you, protocol would dictate sending someone back to stop it," Rachit added. "Aside from the founders, everyone enjoying the B.H.C.'s temporal protections has been raised in the compound—groomed from birth for our purpose."

"That's bunkum!" Arthur yelled.

"Wait," I said, struggling to make sense of it. "There has to be more."

"W-w-what?" Arthur said.

"If stopping Norman won't save the scenario," I clarified, "there has to be more wrong with it."

"You're right," Cassie said. "There has to be a lot more. It has to be totally fercockt!"

"Well, the indoctrination rate was less than five percent of projections," Rachit offered. Now that he said it, it was obvious that there weren't anywhere near enough Chowderheads to affect the change intended by the scenario. But I knew that was only half the truth.

"No," I said. "If the indoctrination numbers were the problem, you'd just patch the scenario. It has to be bigger than that for you to revert it."

He fell quiet. I looked at Meylene, and I knew.

"The reckless AI expansion," I said. "The economic collapse, the climate and energy crisis . . . all of it?"

She nodded solemnly. Arthur looked over at Rachit.

"You said there was nothing you could d-d-do to improve the last two decades!" he yelled.

"And there WAS nothing we could do!" Rachit answered defensively. "I mean, before the Cateklysm Scenario, it was a very positive period. No improvements needed." He obviously knew hiding behind a semantic loophole was a dick move. Then again, I understood why they'd done it. Telling us they'd created our living hell and they were going to delete us wasn't exactly a great incentive to secure our help.

"We have no idea what happened," Meylene said. "It's unprecedented. Our system clearly missed something—some chain reaction that—"

"You assholes!" Cassie cried, like a steam kettle blowing. "All that suffering! All that death! It's all your fault!"

There were tears in her eyes, and I understood her outrage—but for some reason, I didn't feel it. And then I realized why. I put a hand on her shoulder and said, "It's okay."

"W-w-what?!" Arthur exclaimed. "What exactly about any of this is okay?"

I looked at Cassie and saw the epiphany dawning as I went on.

"They could all live," I said. "Decker, my parents . . ."

"Every person my father killed," Cassie continued.

Arthur's face metamorphosed, and he looked over at Meylene.

"My d-d-dad. His life was s-s-supposed to turn out differently, wasn't it?"

She smiled sadly and nodded.

"And you can fix it," he continued. "W-w-we can fix it."

"Yes," she said. "I'm sorry it comes at such a price."

He nodded. The price was high, but not too high. Not for him. Not for Cassie. And not for me.

CHAPTER  28

CASSIE, ARTHUR, AND I SPENT AWHILE QUIETLY TAKING IN the ramifications of what we were about to do. There was a lot of loss to come to terms with. The future I'd envisioned with Cassie was moot – as was any future any of us had envisioned for ourselves. Of course, if there'd been another way, we would have leaped at it. But I don't think a single one of us wavered in our conviction. After all, giving your lost loved ones and millions of others a chance at a better life while thwarting a supervillain's plans for world domination is a pretty good way to go out.

In any event, we were shaken from our thoughts as we dropped back into Earth's atmosphere and began our precipitous descent. Lake Erie came into view, littered with the enormous green algal blooms spawned by climate change. Arthur engaged the maneuvering thrusters and cut the main engines, leveling us off at a couple hundred feet and dramatically reducing our speed to a clip that jibed with our holographic helicopter disguise. I scanned the cityscape for the landmarks appearing on the holo-display on the flight deck as we skirted the edge of the lake and entered the Cleveland area.

We sailed past the ruins of what had been the Greater Cleveland Aquarium on a plot of land tucked into the U-shaped bend formed by the meeting of the Old River and Cuyahoga River. Then we drifted over the dilapidated Cleveland Indians stadium and cleared a series of collapsing, crisscrossing freeways before finally meeting Central Avenue.

There was no trace of the commercial presence of Mitchell Siegel's day. The neighborhood was now purely a residential area, comprised mostly of crumbling single-level prefab housing, separated from a deteriorating sidewalk by long-dead lawns reincarnated as patches of dirt and weeds.

I was starting to wonder what we were going to say to the current residents of 3530 Central. I didn't think we'd get far with "What a lovely home you have! Now leave so we can toss the joint to find a time traveler's magic doodad before it falls into the wrong hands."

However, Meylene ran a check and found what she apparently expected. There was no record of any residents, and the house was owned by a holding company called CC Consolidated. *CC*, as in Cateklysm Catholicon. So our opening spiel wasn't going to be a problem. What was going to be a problem was what we saw as we drew within half a dozen blocks of our destination.

There was a crowd of uniformed people milling around the streets, as well as a few people in hazmat suits. Official vehicles of various sorts were parked haphazardly in a manner suggesting no traffic was expected. A checkpoint adorned with yellow caution tape and warning signage indicated a hefty perimeter being maintained on all sides.

As we dropped to a hundred feet and hovered within a block of the house, we were able to make out familiar logos on the trucks, but we didn't need to see them to know who was behind this.

"The hell's going on?" Slade asked.

"Norman Corp quarantines areas all over the w-w-world to clean up toxic contaminants in the soil," Arthur answered. "Officially the s-s-sources are unknown, and Norman Corp's just being a civic-minded corporate citizen. Unofficially, they're the s-s-source, and they're covering their behinds."

"There's nothing to clean up here," I said grimly. I was sure Norman had already arrived, and in his Chowderhead paranoia, he'd cooked up a cover story to evacuate the entire area and keep it clear while he trotted across the finish line.

"Oy gevalt!" Cassie exclaimed, no doubt thinking along the same lines. "We're screwed."

Based on Loyd's abduction, we knew Norman had still been collecting Chowderheads as recently as last night, US time. But since then, one of the abductees had obviously solved the riddle, and he now had the head start Cassie and I had feared back on HBBI.

"Okay," Arthur said. "So he beat us h-h-here. So what? We're still more than two hours from when he's supposed to g-g-get ahold of the Translocator. And we've got the Fate Force on our side."

Slade frowned at the fanciful misnomer. But Arthur was right. It had obviously taken Norman several tries to get through the second stage, and the final stage was bound to be harder. With the B.H.C.'s help, there was a chance we could get to him before the fat lady sang. All was not yet lost. I looked at Cassie and could see she was feeling the same sense of relief I was. But that relief was reversed as we heard a booming voice from below.

"You are in restricted airspace!" We looked down to see a man holding a bullhorn. "Clear the area immediately!"

"Crap," I said. "What should we do?"

"Set it down," Slade said. "Right outside the house. Frontal assault."

"I'm not sure that's the best course," Rachit cautioned.

"Yes," Meylene agreed. "We ought to assess the numbers before—"

"Um, are those guys doing what I think they're doing?" Cassie said, pointing to a small group of Norman Corp personnel that had gathered near the front of the house. One of them was hoisting a large metal tube up onto his shoulder. It took me a moment to register what we were looking at, but it became awfully clear when a burst of fire and smoke shot out the back of the thing and a conical projectile rocketed toward us.

"Shit!" Slade yelled. "Take evasive action!"

Arthur did what he could, but we'd been hovering at a standstill, and as we swung clumsily to the left, the missile adjusted course, presumably following our heat signature. A teeth-rattling explosion sent a shockwave through the ship, and we whirled across the sky like a damaged chopper, adding credibility to our disguise. I heard a deafening howl and felt the temperature drop suddenly. Looking back, I saw there was now a gaping eight-foot hole in the bottom of the ship, directly in front of my hab suite. The bottom half of the suite's steel door was warped and stained by the scorching heat of the blast. I watched as every one of the Normanium canisters stacked near the engine room tipped over and rattled across the floor, pouring out of the rupture. Fortunately, we were all able to brace ourselves quickly enough to avoid the same fate, and the ship started to level off thanks to Arthur's frantic efforts at the controls.

"We need to put some distance between us and that rocket launcher!" Rachit yelled.

"W-w-working on it!" Arthur yelled back. He reengaged the main thrusters, and the ship jerked violently as we began to climb up and away. Unfortunately, we could see the smoking contrail of a second surface-to-air missile barreling toward us outside the window.

"Christ!" Meylene yelled. "Here comes another one!"

Arthur veered away from it, but we could still see it giving chase as he brought up the rearview holo-display. The use of the rocket launcher seemed like an insanely overt act of aggression, but Norman had clearly empowered his people to do whatever was necessary to discourage visitors, even if he likely hadn't told them why they were really here. Compared to some of the company's other indiscretions, the cover-up would be child's play. The PR snakes were probably already drafting a press release about a tragic helicopter crash involving a misguided flock of birds.

"If it hits the rear thrusters, we'll g-g-go up like a firecracker," Arthur reported grimly.

"Can we outrun it?" Rachit asked.

"I don't think so," Arthur answered him. "That breach in the hull is creating a lot of d-d-drag, and one of the engines is pulling against the others – I think it w-w-was knocked out of alignment."

"Can we jump to F.T.L.?" Cassie asked.

"We'd h-h-have to break atmosphere," Arthur answered.

It was obvious we wouldn't make it that far, hobbled as we were. Granted, we were still easily doubling the speed of any known helicopter, which blew our cover as a regular old sky yacht, but that was the least of our worries as we watched the missile gaining slowly but surely in the rearview holo-display. We had a couple of minutes at most. If we tried to land or even ditch into Lake Erie, the missile would catch up in a hurry and impact the ship before we could get clear.

"This heap got any countermeasures?" Slade growled.

"Any w-w-what?" Arthur answered.

"Chaff, decoy flares, anything to throw the missile off our tail," Rachit clarified.

"No," Arthur answered. "Nothing. The ship's not m-m-meant for this kind of –"

"Wait," Cassie said. "What about the demolition explosives in Clayton's hab suite?" But as she glanced down the hall, she deflated, noting the gaping chasm in front of my suite and the warping around the bottom half of its door, suggesting it wouldn't be easily opened.

"Crap," she said.

Slade rushed down the hall and leaned across the hole to try the door. Even with the enhanced strength his suit provided, it didn't budge.

"Shit in a thimble!" he cursed.

"Don't you have a micro-torch in one of your gauntlets?" Rachit asked him.

"'Course, but it'll take more time than we got to cut through this bastard."

"Come on!" I said. "You guys must have an arsenal of future tech to solve a problem like this!"

"We were cut off from the armory during our escape," Meylene answered. "We're lucky our suits are stored onboard the Eldridge, or we wouldn't even have those."

"Speaking of which – get 'em on, goddamn it!" Slade said. His voice was full of reproach at the fact that the other two weren't already suited up.

"Why?" Meylene asked. "What good will our suits do?"

Slade gestured to Cassie, Arthur, and me and said, "We'll each take one of them and bail out of this tinderbox!" There was no uncertainty in his manner, and for all his foibles, I now saw why people wanted him calling the shots when the shit hit the fan.

"Oh. Right," Meylene responded. "Yes, that could work."

Then her face fell, and she added, "There's just one problem." Her eyes went to my damaged hab suite door. She didn't have to elaborate. They'd obviously stored their suits in the suite.

"Sonofabitch!" Slade moaned.

For a moment, I thought Arthur could repurpose a Normanium canister into a bomb that would attract the missile. Then I remembered all the canisters had been lost through the breach in the hull. We were running out of time, and our options were running dry. We needed to think outside the box. So I did.

"So your suit can only carry one more person?" I asked Slade.

"Affirmative," he answered.

"Take me," I said.

"What?" He cocked his head in shock along with everyone else. "Goddamn, kid! Chivalry really is dead."

"Get me outside and throw me at the missile," I clarified.

"Hm," he grunted, seemingly impressed. "I retract my previous remark."

"Wait, what?" Cassie yelled.

"The heat signature of Slade's suit will attract it, then he can use me to deflect the impact," I explained.

"Absolutely not!" Meylene cried.

Slade peered at the rearview display. The missile was closer than ever and gaining steadily.

"Works for me," he said.

I saw the sparkle in his eye that indicated he was interfacing with his neural implant. Then his helmet slid up and out of his collar, unfolding and forming around his head as it went. We'd given him, Meylene, and Rachit the rundown on my powers, and apparently, he was sold on my plan. The others, not so much.

Rachit shook his head. "This is insane."

"Certifiably," Meylene agreed.

"There's g-g-gotta be another option," Arthur piped in, looking away from the controls for a split second.

"You can throw something else at it!" Cassie exclaimed, with a note of desperation. She started shuffling around the flight deck looking for something big enough to stand in for me, but there was nothing.

"It'll be fine," I said to assure them and myself.

"No!" Cassie called out. "Clayton, I know you think you're indestructible, but ... think about Civil War II!"

"What the hell's she goin' on about?" Slade growled.

Cassie was implying that I might not be as unbreakable as I believed by citing a ludicrous moment in the first issue of Marvel's *Civil War II* (2016), in which the nigh invulnerable She-Hulk had taken a stray War Machine missile to the chest and lapsed into a coma.

Blech. Even though it WAS a super jacked anti-Thanos missile, and even though it DID hit her right in the milk makers, she's a hulk for Christ's sake! So, you know – missile, schmissle. It shouldn't have made a scratch. But it had put her out for the count. Fans had been furious.

"They retconned that in *A-Force* #8," I said, because they'd later explained the whole thing away with a shoe-horned flashback that revealed She-Hulk had actually been clobbered by Thanos under cover of the debris storm kicked up by the otherwise benign missile impact.

"I know they retconned it!" Cassie exclaimed. "I just thought you might not."

"Gimme some credit!" I responded.

"Chop-chop, people!" Slade yelled, eyeing the rearview holo-display.

I ignored him, continuing condescendingly, "Also, a way better example would be issue #4 of *The Dark Knight Returns*, when Superman got nuked."

"It only took two pages for Supes to bounce back from that!" Cassie balked.

"Hmph!" I scoffed. "Two pages in which a superhero god shriveled up like a thousand-year-old mu–"

Mummy. I was going to say mummy. But I didn't get the chance because Slade yelled, "Geronimo!" and tackled me out the hole in the bottom of the ship. As we went, his boot jets kicked on, and we closed on the smoking red-tipped rocket at blinding speed. He arched his back, and we climbed to a few dozen feet above the altitude of the missile. It took the bait, changing course to intercept us.

I could barely hear Slade's voice over the blasting air all around us as he shouted, "Having any second thoughts?"

Then he dropped me. Apparently, it was a rhetorical question. But as it happened, I did have second thoughts. Cassie had planted a seed of doubt, and while I'd accepted that one way or another I wasn't long for this world, I wasn't ready to check out just yet. Obviously, my known vulnerabilities weren't an issue because missiles aren't flesh and blood, and they don't get particularly chilly when they detonate. But if I had two weaknesses, why not three? Aside from the amateur experiments Arthur and I had conducted, my experience with extreme heat was limited. So as I collided with the twenty-two pounds of rocket-propelled explosives at three hundred miles an hour, I thought my survival was a bit of a coin toss.

★

I won the coin toss. By that I mean the explosion didn't do me any real harm. But it did launch me skyward, significantly increasing my altitude, and as I began my vertiginous plunge to earth, I got a firsthand glimpse into life as Nova the Human Rocket. I wondered what sort of destruction my velocity plus my powers would reap—but I didn't wonder for long. I touched down on an abandoned blacktop playground like an angry meteor. Just as it had during my lesser fall into the Danger Room, the force field around me shielded me and cushioned my impact at the expense of everything I hit. I bounced across the concrete, punching a hole through a chain-link fence and decimating a jungle gym before colliding with the east wall of the Marion-Sterling apartment building with enough force to shatter a dozen windows.

I just laid there for a moment as an alarm of some sort began wailing, and people began pouring out of the exits.

"Hell's bells, kid," I heard Slade say from somewhere above me. I rolled over and looked up to see him hovering overhead. Then he dropped down beside me, retracted his helmet and said, "Hope you ain't expecting me to go halfsies on the property damage bill."

He reached down and offered me a hand. I thought he was smiling, but his face seemed so unaccustomed to the act that it looked more like he was baring his teeth menacingly. I took his hand, and he hoisted me to my feet. Looking around, I marveled at the fact that I'd ended up only a few blocks from the Norman Corp quarantine zone. The missile chase had involved a number of sharp turns that had evidently taken us in a circle.

The apartment building's residents were milling around in search of the cause of the incident. We did our best to blend in with them, but our best wasn't all that good, what with Slade's X-O Manowar getup and my tattered clothing that made me look like I'd just reverted from the Hulk to Bruce Banner. Suffice to say, we were definitely arousing some curiosity, which was only heightened a few moments later when the giant Chinook appeared in the sky above us, pirouetted in a half circle, and touched down a dozen yards away. The Javelin's exit ramp sliced through the holographic helicopter exterior and Cassie sprinted out, threw her arms around me, and kissed me like no one was watching. Then she pulled away a few inches and whispered ardently, "You freakin' shmendrick."

The others were only a few steps behind her, and as Arthur reached me, he patted me on the back and said, "I may be a robot, but you're the one w-w-with a screw loose."

"'Nuff chitchat," Slade interrupted. He raised his right gauntlet, and a small torch popped out of a compartment in the back of his hand. Then he looked at Meylene and Rachit.

"What do we know about where we're headed after I cut that hab suite door open and get you two suited up?"

Rachit thought for a moment, then ventured, "Well, Seymour wouldn't have risked the final stage being discovered by passersby or squatters. I think we can safely assume that what we're after is concealed below ground, with an entrance located somewhere in the house."

Meylene nodded. "And I think it's even safer to assume some esoteric knowledge of comic book lore will be required to find and/or access that entrance – and navigate whatever's beyond."

"Then it's settled," Slade said, as he looked at Cassie, Arthur, and me. "Rachit, Meylene, and I will hold off Norman's people while you three find the entrance and nerd it open."

"Okay," I said. "But how are we going to get into the house?"

I didn't love the answer.

CHAPTER  29

TWENTY MINUTES LATER, SLADE DROPPED ME THROUGH THE roof of 3530 Central Avenue from about seventy-five feet up. He seemed to have decided that throwing me at stuff was the solution to every problem. As I crashed through the ceiling and struck the weathered laminate flooring, it splintered, revealing the concrete below. Roof shingles were still showering down around me when the three Norman Corp guards stationed in the house converged on me, guns blazing. The fact that the bullets they fired pinged off me like popcorn popping didn't seem to deter them from firing more. A second later, Slade came down feet first on one of them and pointed his fists at the other two as a cartridge emerged from each of his armored forearms. A fusillade of microdarts flew out, each one carrying a payload of fast-acting sedative. The remaining guards dropped in their tracks as Rachit and Meylene touched down beside us, carrying Cassie and Arthur.

As soon as we'd drawn within range of the blockade, Rachit had jammed all transmissions, and Meylene had tossed down several discs from her utility belt, which had manifested a staggeringly realistic squadron of holographic commandos. As we'd hoped, these measures triggered panic among the Norman Corp ranks and proved enough of a distraction for us to fly all the way to the house before the dude with the rocket launcher could spot us and knock us out of the sky like clay pigeons.

This was a relief because I'd been worried about Cassie and Arthur's safety. While our streamlined mode of transit made us harder to spot, it also made us easier to kill. So I'd tried to talk the two of them out of coming, but Cassie had set me straight.

"The future of humanity is on the line here," she'd said with steely resolve. "We already signed on to get erased from existence, so if you think we're gonna sit out the main event just because we might get a rocket up our tuchus while jet-packing over enemy lines, you're billy bigly."

After depositing her and Arthur with Slade and me in the living room, Meylene and Rachit began a sweep of the house. Predictably, the place had been ravaged by time. The front door hung half on and half off the hinges. Most of the windows were cracked or broken, and the gable roof was pockmarked with cave-ins even before I'd dropped in. Aside from the piles of garbage, tattered blankets, and broken-down shopping carts left behind by various squatters, the house was barren. Seymour hadn't seen fit to furnish it, possibly because he wanted to save people the trouble of digging through a bunch of rat-eaten furniture just to make sure the U.A.T. wasn't tucked away in the seat cushions of a La-Z-Boy.

"All clear!" I heard Rachit call out, once they'd reached the back of the house.

"That means Norman's definitely already found and gone through the entrance," Cassie lamented. "He really is into the final stage."

"So we're playin' catch-up!" Slade barked. "Ain't exactly a news flash! Get your asses in gear!"

Gruff as he was, he was right. The guys outside wouldn't be fooled by Meylene's holographic commandos for long. Their lack of casualties hadn't given them away because they were keeping to cover pretty convincingly, but eventually someone would notice the rounds they were firing weren't impacting anywhere. We needed to find the entrance fast.

"Anything on the box?" I asked Cassie.

She'd brought along the black box, assuming it would indeed come into play. But as she held it up, we all saw it was still simply displaying the address.

I shrugged and said to her and Arthur, "You guys should search the back rooms. I'll take the living room and kitchen."

They didn't argue. They recognized the front of the house would likely become a war zone in a minute or two, and gung ho as they were to do their part, they didn't need to risk their non-bulletproof necks unnecessarily. I watched them head to the back of the house and began my search of the living room. But I noticed Slade collecting the sidearms of two of the unconscious guards.

"What are you doing?" I asked.

"Suits weren't fully rigged," he answered. "Darts are our only built-in ordnance. And non-lethals are too good for these shit heels." He looked out the window as half a dozen guards broke away from the defensive line formed to deal with Meylene's holo-commandos and headed for the house.

We were now in a position of relative strength, defending limited entry points, and from the way Slade had handled the first three guards, I knew that while we were outmanned, we weren't really outgunned.

"These guys are dickheads," I said. "But they're no real threat to you. And they could have families – kids, maybe."

"Kids that're about to be wiped from history," he scoffed as he raised both pistols, taking aim at the front door. He was right, of course. Everyone in our timeline was done for, regardless of who prevailed here. Just the same, I stepped in front of the pistol barrels, recalling that moment in Bollard's cabin when everything had changed – when I'd realized that there was always a price to be paid for taking a life. It always mattered.

"There's no reason to kill them," I said. "And that's reason enough not to."

Slade frowned. Then in one smooth motion, he tossed both guns to the ground, redeployed his forearm canons, and fired a flurry of microdarts over my shoulders, dropping two guards as they reached the door.

He shook his head. "You are a pain in my ass, kid."

It felt good to stand up for what I believed in, under pressure. It felt super-hero-y. But as Meylene and Rachit rushed back to the front of the house and I stood there watching the three B.H.C. agents take down several more guards who'd breached the front door, I was reminded that I was less superhero and more superzero. I was all defense and no offense – and in hand-to-hand battle, I was as helpless as Arthur and Cassie. Without Slade, Meylene, and Rachit, the future had no chance at all. So I was gladder than ever that they were here because evidently the army outside had finally figured out they'd been had, and they were turning their full attention to us.

Most of the mob rushed toward the front lawn. However, a few guys peeled off to circle around the back of the house, and a few more hung back to take potshots at us, seeking cover behind a large van parked on the lawn. The van looked like an armored prisoner transport of some kind, with the front cab divided from a roomy but windowless passenger compartment.

I could only think of one group of people Norman would be carting around in a prison transport. After all, if squeezing his Chowderhead captives had gotten him to the final stage, why not squeeze them a little more to complete it? If I was right, Loyd and the others weren't in the van now. They'd be wherever Norman was. Still, there was something about the van that held my attention. It was the back doors. They were badly dented. I was trying to sort out why that bothered me, but my focus was redirected abruptly as Norman's troops burst into the house in full force, knocking the front door wholly off its feeble hinges.

I fell back from the front lines to continue searching the living room and kitchen for some sign of a hidden entrance to a basement level as Slade, Rachit, and Meylene deployed their helmets and rushed deeper into the fray. Bullets flew. Bodies fell. And suddenly, to my eyes, the B.H.C. agents were gone, replaced by the unstoppable badasses of the Fate Force. They moved around the room like circus acrobats, spinning and rolling, firing salvo after salvo of microdarts and landing cybersuit-enhanced punches and kicks that sent Norman's forces careening through the air like rag dolls. The snipers outside barely got off a shot between the makeshift sonic pulse grenades Meylene was chucking out the windows and front door. (Apparently, there was a long list of feats her amazing discs could be configured to perform.)

None of Norman's people seemed to be under his psychic control. Even so, very few of them fled. I guessed they were extremely well paid – or just idiots – because their assault seemed doomed to failure. Until the rocket-launcher guy showed up again.

Rachit and Meylene had withdrawn to the back of the house to repel a detachment of guards coming in through the bedroom windows, and Slade was finishing off the stragglers from the head-on assault. Consequently, I was the only one to notice when Bazooka Joe strode in and took aim at Slade, seemingly unconcerned about hitting his own people. The cybersuits were mostly bulletproof, but I figured they must have their limits as Slade had agreed to let me take rocket-catching duty earlier. I needed to do something, but there was no way I could contain the blast in such close quarters. So I tackled the guy before he could get off the shot.

It was a solid hit, and it made me feel like maybe I wasn't such a superzero after all. Unfortunately, as he whirled around on his way to the floor, his finger depressed the launcher's trigger. A rocket streaked out of the cylinder and went tearing out the front door, colliding with the side of the van on the lawn. It detonated with a blinding blast, and the van was pitched five or six feet into the air, crumpling and igniting with flames as it went. As it crashed back down, the surrounding Norman Corp personnel froze, a look of unease on their faces. Then they scattered like panicked animals fleeing a forest fire. It seemed like an overreaction. These guys were battle-tested mercs. What were they running from? The explosion was over. The danger had passed. Or had it?

"He's coming out!" I heard one of them scream. "Fall back! He's coming out!"

Slade retracted his helmet and looked over at me. I could tell he was as unnerved as I was. He reached over and grabbed one of the guards he'd pummeled. The guy was trying to drag himself out the window farthest from the front door, with a wild-eyed look of fear.

Slade shook the guy forcibly and yelled, "What the hell's goin' on out there?"

The guy tried desperately to pry Slade's hands off him, but Slade punched him in the face and snarled, "Talk!" through clenched teeth.

"He had a seizure or something, and the mind control drugs or whatever Norman gave him started to wear off," the guy babbled. "We barely got him into the van. He's unstoppable."

Then I remembered the dents in the back doors of the van, and I knew what had bothered me about them. They weren't inward facing, as if the van had been rear-ended. They were outward facing, as if someone had taken a battering ram to the doors from within. But from the look in the eyes of the man Slade was interrogating, there was no battering ram. Slade relaxed his grip, and the guy finally managed to break loose and scramble out the window, making for the hills.

Then Slade looked out at the front lawn, redeployed his helmet and said, "Find that entrance, kid."

But I didn't move. I couldn't. I had to see it for myself.

Outside, something lurched from the smoldering wreckage of the van and grabbed one of Norman's men as he ran by. We heard the man's screams intermingled with the crunch of bone and tearing of flesh, then nothing. As the last of the smoke cleared, I couldn't make sense of what was crouched over the man's body. It paused for a moment, tilting its head back and sniffing at the air, ignoring the last of Norman's troops as they fled from its line of sight. Then, it growled a single word that filled me with a mixture of abject terror and déjà vu.

"Princess?"

"Oh, come on!" I gasped, unable to believe my eyes and ears.

"Princess, zat you?!" Cassie's father shouted in a mixture of berserker fervor and incredulity. He was staring directly past us, nose twitching, as if he'd pinpointed Cassie's location by some unconsciously cataloged scent. He hardly resembled the man I'd encountered aboard the Charon. He was bulkier by at least thirty pounds. His jaw protruded abnormally, and fur-like hair had cropped up all over his body. Most uncannily, the gruesome burns and cuts he'd sustained from the blast he'd just endured were healing like time-lapse medical footage. I wondered for a moment how he'd become what he now was, but then I recalled the bag of Normanium Prime he'd stolen from us before the guards had relieved him of it.

"What is that thing?!" Slade asked.

"That's ... Cassie's father," I said. "He's totally insane. And he's been exposed to the crystals."

Slade sighed dispiritedly and said, "Sounds about right."

I thought about the purged records Arthur had found in the Charon's database: the details of seven murders on the lower level—almost certainly Wilson's handiwork. But who had purged the records, and what was Wilson doing here? The answer was obvious. The timing of the purging coincided perfectly with Norman's visit to the Charon after leaving HBBI. I imagined Norman's glee at acquiring an off-the-books killing machine he could remote-control with his newfound powers.

Of course, Wilson Ramirez wasn't one for being controlled, and his seizures were making him more of what he was. From what the guard Slade had interrogated had said, Norman must have gotten Wilson into the van just before the last of the puppet strings snapped. His regenerative powers explained why they'd locked him up instead of killing him. They probably didn't know how to kill him.

"You can't hide from me, Princess!" Wilson bellowed.

The others rushed out of the bedrooms behind us. Cassie pushed to the front, desperately hoping what she thought was happening wasn't. But it was. The unbelievable run of bad luck that had put her on the same ship as Wilson and reunited them during our escape had just reached its apex. Her nightmare had come to life.

"Princess!" Wilson roared again as he stalked across the decaying lawn toward the front door.

Slade aimed both microdart canons and loosed a barrage of tranquilizers. But they didn't slow Wilson down. If anything, he sped up.

"Find that entrance!" Slade repeated at the top of his lungs as he, Rachit, and Meylene picked up various pistols and rifles dropped by their fallen adversaries and began firing.

Needless to say, I didn't question the use of lethal force at this point—especially because the bullets weren't as lethal as they were supposed to be. The wounds they left seemed to close almost as quickly as they opened as Wilson crossed the threshold and broke into a run.

He barreled into Slade, and the two of them flew through the air, then hit the floor growling and grappling savagely. It was as if Wilson didn't even feel the rounds Rachit and Meylene were still firing into his chest and back. I thought in vain how excited I'd be to see a real live Wolverine if only he hadn't been trying to murder us all.

Wilson's grip closed around Slade's throat, warping the cybersuit shell. The shell was tough but apparently less so than the prison transport door that had contained Wilson. No surprise. It was a hundredth of the thickness. Plus, it was engineered to bend, expand, and contract with the body of the wearer, which involved design trade-offs that were definitely working against Slade at the moment.

I saw Arthur trying to drag Cassie clear of the scuffle, but she was slapping him away in a defiant trance of denial. Then Wilson looked up and saw her, and his eyes went crazier than ever. He lunged for her, but I dove into her, knocking her clear of him. She and I crashed into Arthur and the three of us went sprawling through the adjacent doorway into the kitchen. On the way, my shoulder brushed a grandfather clock, partially inset into the wall. It shattered, and shards of lacquered wood and metallic gears clattered down around us as we hit the floor.

When we regained our senses, we heard a high-pitched beeping coming from the black box still clenched in Cassie's hands. We glanced down at it, but after a moment it stopped, and it was the last thing we could focus on as Wilson burst through the doorway. He would have been on us if Slade, still on the floor, hadn't grabbed his ankle and yanked him back. Wilson clawed and growled like a coyote caught in a steel-jaw trap. Then Rachit stepped close to him and fired three shots to the side of his head. The impact of the shots sent Wilson reeling to the right, and he smacked against the wall, sliding down it.

None of us thought three bullets to the brain could fail to do their job. That's why Slade relaxed his grip on Wilson's ankle. It's also why everyone was slow to react when Wilson caught himself halfway to the floor, spun around, and grabbed Rachit by the neck, then slammed him headfirst into the exposed concrete foundation beneath the splintered laminate where I'd touched down. There was a sickening pop as Rachit's helmet cracked and blood gushed out of the opening. There was no question. He was dead. Cassie screamed, but I barely heard it because I was well and truly in shock at that point.

"Motherfucker!" Slade yelled, as he bounced up and threw a boot jet-assisted roundhouse kick to Wilson's midsection.

An audible crunch signaled that many of Wilson's ribs had cracked or broken. But the murderous rage in his eyes didn't waver, and clinging on to Slade's leg, he looped one arm over the thigh and one under the calf. Then he shoved the calf up and the thigh down, breaking the leg and leaving it bent the wrong way at nearly a right angle. Slade gave a howl of agony as Wilson released him and he fell to the floor.

Then Wilson turned and started toward Cassie, Arthur, and me again. There was no way past him, but that didn't matter. None of us had even gotten to our feet. We were completely shut down. Even after all we'd seen, Wilson's savagery had blind-sided us, surfacing a fact we'd begun to forget: we were still just kids.

Our freeze-up would have been fatal, but as Wilson reached down for us, we saw Meylene soar through the air over his shoulder. As she went, she cocked both fists back over her head, winding up for a massive double-hammer fist strike.

It was an impressive maneuver, but it seemed futile considering the punishment Wilson had withstood thus far. He spun and grabbed her by the throat.

He moved so fast, it was like watching a movie that was skipping frames. He squeezed hard, and we heard her neck snap just as her clenched fists came down on both his shoulders. But as her fists connected, they sprang open, and I understood that her maneuver hadn't been simple desperation. It had been calculated self-sacrifice. The two discs she'd apparently been holding exploded into a white foam that surrounded Wilson's torso and upper legs as it hardened into what looked like an ill-fitting polyethylene body cast. He dropped her body and fell back, landing awkwardly on his side.

But as he strained spastically against the spray-on straitjacket, the foam surface began to crack, and it seemed Meylene's sacrifice had been for nothing. He managed to get to his knees, still blocking our only way out, and locked eyes with Cassie.

"I'm comin' for you, Princess!" he snarled. "This shit can't hold me for long!"

And then we heard Slade grunt, "Wasn't supposed to."

A rocket flew across the room and hit Wilson. It exploded in a flash of roiling fire, launching him into a backflip and taking out a huge chunk of the wall behind him. As his body bounced off what remained of the wall and flopped down in the middle of the room, we saw half of his head was missing, along with his left arm and most of his left shoulder. He didn't move.

For a moment, Arthur, Cassie, and I just stared. The trauma of the conflict had put our senses on pause, and as they rebooted, we were lost. We didn't know what to say or do.

"Hell's bells," we heard Slade say weakly. I ambled into the living room and found him propped against the wall, clutching the rocket launcher Bazooka Joe had left behind when he'd fled. Conveniently, Joe had also left behind the bag containing his single remaining rocket, which Slade had put to good use.

Unfortunately, a large chunk of shrapnel had pierced the armor over the B.H.C. agent's chest. He'd fired on Wilson from less than ten feet, and while Cassie and Arthur had been shielded from the concussive force, flames, and flying debris by me and the wall between the kitchen and living room, he'd had no such protection. I was dumbfounded by the fact that he was still breathing. Blood was everywhere, and there was a faint whistling when he exhaled.

He retracted his helmet, looked over at Wilson's remains and grunted, "Our data definitely missed some details."

Then his body tensed violently as something inside stopped working, but he fought past it and asked, "Find the goddamn entrance yet?"

"No," I answered almost inaudibly. I crouched next to him and put a hand on his shoulder helplessly.

"Well, get to it," he said. "Soon as Norman's men regroup with all the re-inforcements they got littered across the quarantine zone, they'll be back for him. Clock's ticking."

"What about you?" I asked.

He glanced down at his injuries, silently confirming my fears.

"It ain't about me," he said.

Then, looking at his fallen comrades he added, "Or them."

I thought he was done, but he went on, "'Course, you finish the job, we'll never be here to get wasted by your girl's dad."

He coughed violently. "And not for nothin', but you get this done on your own, it'd be a first–kinda thing that merits an audience with the B.H.C. big wigs to talk about who gets to sit out the reset at the compound."

He coughed once more. "The me you meet probably won't agree . . ."

His body tensed again, more dramatically this time. ". . . but he's an asshole."

Then he let out one long breath and went perfectly still.

I started to break down immediately. Tears streamed down my face–for Rachit and Meylene–but most of all for Slade. Aside from my anemic interactions with Jerry aboard the Charon, I hadn't had a father figure since the death of my parents. It might be hard to understand how I could feel that connection with Slade after just a handful of hours in his company–but those hours had been made into months by the intensity of the experiences they held.

I felt Arthur's hand on my shoulder and looked up to see him standing behind me. Tears were running down his face, same as mine. Cassie was next to him in worse shape than either of us.

"W-w-we have to keep it together," Arthur said. "W-w-we can fix this."

He glanced over at Meylene's body, and I saw fresh tears pool in his eyes and start to overflow. I could tell he was trying to stave off a full breakdown by clutching at the straw Slade had just offered us. But the forced optimism was lost on me. Sure, theoretically, we could overtake Norman, win the Challenge, and intercept Seymour before Norman could get the Translocator from him. In so doing, we'd prevent Slade, Rachit, and Meylene's deaths, stop the Cateklysm Scenario from derailing history, and apparently possibly compel Seymour and company to allow us to opt out of the reset. But the hope all that might have kindled was smothered by the facts. We weren't prepared to deal with Norman's superpower and the heavies he'd surely have on hand. And even if we were, our chances of catching up with him were nil–like Slade had said, the Norman Corp army would be back any minute, and we had no idea where the entrance to the basement was.

Arthur's failed pep talk faded, and a dead silence fell over the house. As we waited for the end, I thought I could hear the clock Slade had said was ticking. But then, suddenly, my Spidey-Sense started tingling because I realized I really could hear a clock ticking. Tick. Tick. Tick.

I looked back at the grandfather clock I'd inadvertently destroyed as I dived into the kitchen. The bits and pieces that had been scattered on the floor were gone. It was no longer in ruins. It had been perfectly restored.

I rose and walked tentatively over to it. As I did, the other two looked over.

"Wasn't that–" Arthur started, but I cut him off by kicking the front panel of the clock.

The wood cracked. I waited. Nothing happened. Not what I'd anticipated. Cassie and Arthur stood and started toward me.

"It's g-g-got to be a hard hologram, right?" Arthur asked.

He got his answer as they came near and we heard the same beeping sound we'd heard earlier, coming from the black box Cassie was still holding absent-mindedly. Above our heads, a laser shot out from a hidden fold in the molding where the wall met the ceiling. The laser danced over the clock, repairing the damage as it had obviously done before while we were distracted by all the mayhem. It was certain now that we would have been screwed without a black box because the box was clearly the key to the clock's secrets. I looked over at Cassie, and I knew there was only one question.

"Forty-seven or forty-eight?" I asked her.

While the clock's modern, minimalist design had allowed it to hide in plain sight among the other decor, now that it had our attention, its significance was glaring. You see, one of the entrances to the Batcave in Wayne Manor sat behind a grandfather clock, with access being granted when the clock was set to the exact minute Bruce Wayne's parents were killed. But it's tough to say if that was 10:47 or 10:48 because there are discrepancies in the Scriptures. For instance, in *Batman: Legends of the Dark Knight* #16 (1991), the clock is clearly shown to be set to 10:47, but in *Batman and Robin* Volume 2, #1 (2011), Bruce tells his son, Damian, the clock needs to be set to 10:48.

As with the second stage of the Challenge, I was concerned about a cooling-off period between attempts if we blew it on the first try. And we had less time to lose than ever. Regrettably, in my mind, the choice we had to make was a toss-up, and I desperately hoped Cassie could tip the scales. Alas, her silence and the emotionally depleted look in her eyes didn't give me a lot of confidence. I understood how she was feeling, but the clock was ticking.

"Well? Do you guys know what to d-d-do?" Arthur asked anxiously.

"What do you think?" I asked Cassie softly.

She still didn't answer. Instead, she simply stepped forward and turned the hands of the clock to 10:47. The black box beeped again and the clock sprang toward us, swinging from hinges along its right side.

"Seymour kidnapped Morrison just to get him to read a few sentences from his book," Cassie said quietly. Her voice was hoarse from the ten minutes she'd spent screaming in terror.

I nodded, awed by her flawless deduction. Seymour was clearly a fan of Grant Morrison, who had done a stint on *Batman and Robin* Volume 1 in 2009, including issue #14, in which the clock is definitely set to 10:47. If Seymour had to side with somebody on the 47/48 debate, it would be Morrison.

We looked through the opening behind the clock. We could make out a staircase winding down into all but total darkness. It was a steep descent—steep enough to dip below floor level without leaving a lot of space unaccounted for between the kitchen and the bedroom that bordered it.

Given the nature of the entrance, Cassie and I had a strong sense of where the staircase led and what pitfalls may lay ahead, in addition to the danger posed by Norman. This concern was heightened by a single framed comic book panel affixed to the back of the clock. I recognized the panel from issue #1 of *The Web* (2009). A villain wearing robotic armor was threatening John Raymond, aka the Web, via a talk bubble that read, "Don't expect me to take it easy on you this time."

It was a forgettable sequence, but in the current context, it made a statement, due to the villain's name: Deadly Force. Had Seymour decided that anyone worthy of the U.A.T. should be ready to risk their life to secure it? That was the obvious implication. Even so, it didn't matter. Maybe we were still just kids. But we were the only ones left. Cassie summed up this sentiment with two words.

"Let's go."

She took a step into the stairwell and paused, blinking vigorously and willing her eyes to adjust to the darkness. Then she took another step, but as she did, there was a clicking sound and suddenly, the clock swung shut violently. It barely missed my face as it smacked Arthur in the back, shoving him all the way into the stairwell.

As the thing shuddered back into place and the minute and hour hands spun wildly around, I just stood there, frozen in stunned disbelief. The clicking sound we'd heard when Cassie had put her weight on the second step had been a trigger. Of course there was an automatic locking mechanism. Seymour wouldn't want the door left open for passersby, and I was sure no one on Earth could force their way through the hard hologram tech without a black box. But thankfully, when I turned the minute and hour hands back to 10:47, I heard the beeping sound from the box Cassie was holding within the stairwell, and the clock sprang open again.

Cassie and Arthur peered out at me in relief, and I gave them a little "no worries" wave. Then I stepped slowly onto the first step as they proceeded around the bend. As I went to place my weight on the second step, I braced myself for the entrance sealing. But before my foot fell, I was jerked back as if my shirt had caught on the fender of a speeding truck headed the opposite direction. Something spun me around, and suddenly I was staring at Wilson, or what was left of him, backlit to provide an ironic halo effect. He grabbed me by the throat and shook me like a helpless toddler. Then he spoke, shakily at first, as if he was remembering how to do it as he went.

"Wh . . . wh . . . wheeeeere's the rest of my fffffucking face!?"

The right side of his head was a nauseating collage of blood, brain, sinew, and skull. It was actively regenerating, but it had a ways to go.

"And whazzis?!"

He held up what had been his other arm but was now a skinny, veiny stub on its way to full regrowth.

The others were concealed in the darkness around the turn of the staircase, and I hoped they wouldn't be foolish enough to think there was anything they could do for me.

I cursed myself for being surprised at this turn of events. I mean at this point, how could I not expect my girlfriend's psychotic, drug-addicted serial-killer father to grow back half his body after it got blown off by a rocket-propelled grenade? My only solace was that based on his apparent disorientation, losing a sizeable chunk of his brain seemed to have taken a toll on his memory. I thought maybe he wouldn't recall that Cassie was in the vicinity. Hell, I thought maybe he'd have forgotten his obsession with killing her altogether. But no.

"Priiiinzess!" he screamed down the staircase. "Princess!!"

He squeezed my throat and hoisted me into the air. I remembered how Meylene had gone out and wondered why I wasn't dead already. After all, my neck wasn't protected by a cybersuit shell. Then I realized Wilson had no idea where the staircase led or how much distance it would allow Cassie to put between them. He was using me as bait to lure her back. Thankfully, either she was restraining herself or Arthur was holding her back.

"Run!" I yelled to them. "Run!!"

Slade's parting words had given me a few minutes to half hope that I might have a future, but all I wanted now was to survive long enough to help my friends get clear and take their shot at whatever was waiting downstairs. I needed to try to free myself and preoccupy Wilson for as long as possible.

I kicked my legs viciously and dug my nails into his forearm, refusing to succumb to the fear that had paralyzed me moments before. Then, as he squeezed my throat harder, weighing whether I was worth the trouble, my flailing left foot caught the edge of the wall and he lost his balance, falling forward. He tried to grab the doorway with his free hand, but his eyes went wide as he remembered he didn't have that hand. He staggered down the stairs, attempting to steady himself. Then his lead foot hit the second step and I knew it was all over. There was a click, and the clock face slammed shut, crashing into his back. We both toppled down the stairs.

Unlike on HBBI, yanking my assailant into the abyss was not at all my intent. Instead of giving Arthur and Cassie a chance to get clear, I was dragging Wilson toward them at top speed. I felt the collision with them about halfway through our violent, blind descent down the twisting, turning stone steps. Moments later, all four of us spilled out onto a dimly lit platform, and I knew Wilson would kill us all.

But instead, a T-Rex ate me.

CHAPTER 30

WELL, THE T-REX DIDN'T EAT ME IMMEDIATELY. IT ACTUALLY paused after stomping out from its post on the platform, and we heard a voice echoing forth from what sounded like a megaphone embedded somewhere in its giant head.

"If you would, please name one of the items used to destroy this monstrous behemoth."

The words were spoken with a painfully proper English accent that made the scene all the more ridiculous, as if the twenty-foot lizard would be inviting us to sit down for tea and crumpets next. Of course, we recognized the voice underneath the stuffy, put-on accent – and we now knew it belonged to B.H.C. Agent Seymour Lawrence, or yet another artificial manifestation of him anyway, this time in the role of Alfred Pennyworth: Bruce Wayne's butler, the keeper of the Batcave, and on more than one occasion, the operator of the cave's robotic dinosaur sentry.

Per his request, I guessed calling out an object that had been used to destroy the T-Rex would shut it down. That job fell to me because Arthur was clueless and Cassie was still lying on the floor, dazed and possibly concussed after her tumble down the stairs. The T-Rex roared a warning in its own terrifying voice. I knew I had only a few seconds to think before it attacked. But as Wilson ambled to his feet, it occurred to me that I was rushing to stop a giant robot dinosaur from killing us so a crazed mutant manimal could kill us. Then I knew what to do.

The T-Rex had been destroyed on various occasions with various items. It had been beheaded by the giant Lincoln penny of Batcave fame in *Batman* #48 (1948). It had taken a stalactite to the head in *The Brave and The Bold* #182 (1982). It had been shot to pieces by Hush in *Detective Comics* #850 (2009). It had even been blasted with an RPG by Alfred in *Justice League* #8 (2016). However, the T-Rex had definitely never been destroyed by a pancake. So that's what I yelled: "Pancake!" Then I leaped at Wilson, wrapping both arms and legs around him tightly.

Being that he had recently become nature's newest apex predator, Wilson didn't see my koala hug coming, so he paused for a beat in disbelief. And that's when the T-Rex ate me – along with Wilson.

The thing's massive jaws opened nearly ninety degrees as they hammered down in front of us and behind us, knocking us to the floor. Wilson clawed to get clear. However, his regenerating arm was still more of a flipper, and the lack of leverage was negating his superstrength as I clung to him with everything I had, praying Seymour's warning about deadly force had been genuine.

My prayers were answered. The eighteen-inch teeth descending from above hit me and screeched in metallic agony as they bent and curled harmlessly around me. The teeth ascending from below did the same, but only after punching through Wilson's body in eight or nine places. He wailed and thrashed around like a dissected frog that had woken mid-science class.

I felt the inertia of being swung into the air as the robotic beast reared back up. Then I heard a grinding noise, and the motors in its jaws shivered violently as my unsquashable body prevented them from reaching their intended closed position. Ironically the bent teeth that had punctured Wilson's body were protecting me by forming a barrier of inorganic material between us. Without them, his body would have penetrated the field around me, and I would have been crushed against him. Smoke began to pour out around us, and the grinding of gears got louder. Then the whole machine gave several explosive jerks before falling chin first to the floor.

In the process, I was thrown free, ejected from the metal jaws like a marble popping out from under the tines of a fork. I heard Cassie yell, "Stalactite!" as she and Arthur rushed over to me. I supposed Arthur had filled her in on what she'd missed while she was out, and she was covering all the bases – naming an item that had actually taken out the sentry to make sure it would stay down. Sure enough, I heard the fading whir of the whole machine powering off as she and Arthur helped me to my feet.

Wilson was now perfectly still, but we all watched him tensely. Shish-ke-babbed as he was, we still fully expected him to wake at any moment. Then .. . he did. We all gave a start, prepared to run for our lives. But then he passed out again. Until he woke up again. And passed out again. Again and again, he came to and lost consciousness. With each waking, we glimpsed a look of sheer terror in his eyes.

Turning the dino against him had been a Hail Mary. I'd expected it to slow him down at best, but I'd gotten lucky. I took a hesitant step forward and saw one of the T-Rex's teeth had clearly gone through his heart. From the looks of it, as long as the tooth was there, his heart couldn't fully regenerate, and thanks to its run-in with my body, the tooth had been bent at a sharp angle after exiting Wilson's chest. Now, in his weakened state, he wouldn't be unbending it or the other half dozen on which he was impaled. He was trapped in a living death. I was horrified, but mostly I was relieved. I saw that same relief on Arthur's face, but what I saw on Cassie's face was indescribable. Arthur and I had been running scared from Wilson for less than a half hour. In a sense, Cassie had been doing it her whole life. I couldn't imagine what she was feeling now as she stared down at her father's body pinned and seizing between the jaws of a mechanical giant. However, whatever she was feeling vanished in a flood of worry as a thought occurred to her.

"Isn't this thing a hard hologram?" she asked.

"M-m-must be," Arthur answered.

"What if it resets to its starting position?"

The answer was obvious: Wilson would be free and more pissed off and crazy than ever.

A voice from behind us interrupted our growing apprehension.

"Fortunately, it only resets when someone enters the stairwell, and everyone who can do that is already down here."

We turned to see Norman, grinning smugly at us. The apprehension we'd been feeling went through the roof as he continued, "I'm so pleased you could join us."

We weren't surprised Norman had detected our arrival. Our approach hadn't been the stealthy affair we'd planned. On the upside, Norman had no reason to lie about the T-Rex resetting only when someone entered the stairwell upstairs. So being that a black box was needed to do that, and the only ones in existence were with us, we were indeed in the clear where Wilson was concerned—for the foreseeable future.

Norman paused, as about twenty people filtered up a set of stairs behind him, to join us on the platform. Some of them were armed guards, but most were civilians. They all had that blank look on their faces. His ability to control so many people at once may or may not have been something new, but all his subjects were definitely moving more smoothly than the guys back in the Danger Room. His powers were evolving, no doubt through seizures like my own. I knew those seizures may kill him, just as they may kill me. But according to the current forecast, he'd take the B.H.C. compound before that happened—unless we did something about it.

I started toward him, ready to throw down. Then I came to my senses. I had no chance of doing any real damage before his mind-melded horde took me out and/or he got his hooks into my brain. As I backed off, he noted my change in course and smirked.

"And once again, my face goes unpunched-off," he taunted.

The zombie guards approached us, brandishing handcuffs. All three of us backed away instinctively. But then I stopped and offered them my wrists. Cassie and Arthur hesitated a moment, then did the same. None of us knew why Norman had opted not to add us to his horde yet, but we all knew it would be easy enough for him to do so if we put up a fight. Whatever his plans for us, our best chance was to play along – buy time and search for an opportunity to gain the upper hand.

The guards cuffed Cassie's left wrist to my right, and my left wrist to Arthur's right. I didn't give this much thought. I figured maybe they only had two pairs of handcuffs. When they were done, they shoved us over to join Norman, who had stepped to the edge of the platform. From that vantage point, we could see the lower platforms as they curved along the wall out from under us. The Batcave had been through many iterations during its evolution from a nameless underground garage to the world's most renowned superhero haven. But the version Seymour had replicated here made perfect sense. It was the Batcave reborn out of the wreckage of a massive earthquake occurring in a story line called – drumroll, please – "Cataclysm." As you'd expect, the series had been picked through by Chowderheads for years. But it had never provided an epiphany of any sort.

We could easily make out the details of the seventh level below us. But a semi-opaque blue-tinted force field stretched horizontally across the cave, partitioning that level from the six below it. As a result, our view of those levels was muddied. But what did suddenly stand out in chilling intensity were the Batman corpses. Yes, plural. Strewn across the sixth level were three cowl-clad bodies, chests emblazoned with the bat symbol. However, as I looked closer, past the molded neoprene and Kevlar body armor, I saw that they were not all the Batman I knew. In fact, none of them were. Two of them had beards grayed with age, and one was a woman.

A moment later, a second woman decked out in Bat garb stumbled into view. She was bleeding profusely from her nose and mouth and limping badly on an ankle that looked to be broken. As she yelled at someone behind her, her words were muted by the distance between us, the force field, or both.

"I don't know!" she shouted plaintively to some unseen inquisitor. "I don't know the answers! I don't even know how I got here!" She looked around, lost and confused. "All I remember is . . . Luthor Norm –" Two beams of glowing red light burst from the darkness and punched clean through her chest. She tried to cry out, but the wound robbed her of her voice as she fell backward off the platform. Her body hit a second force field separating the sixth level from the fifth and combusted, burning into nothingness in seconds. Then, impossibly, Superman stepped into view, his eyes still flickering with red energy as he stared after her. But as the glow faded from the killer's eyes, his features came into focus, along with a familiar blue domino mask. It wasn't Superman. It was a Seymour holo-clone, wearing Superman from the neck down.

A moment later the force fields faded away, he disappeared, and to my horror, the costumes dissolved from the bodies of the deceased, revealing them to be regular people in civilian attire. I'd wanted to hold out hope that they were just holograms like Super-Seymour, but there was no denying the stench of burning flesh as it wafted up from the site of the instant cremation we'd witnessed. The intensity was only partially depleted by the lengthy journey.

"Christ," Cassie whispered, as a series of lasers shot down from overhead and incinerated the remaining bodies one after the other. We couldn't believe what we were watching, even in light of the "Deadly Force" warning. It was totally out of line with the character of the Challenge so far. It was barbaric.

"Ouch! Am I right?" Norman said. "Questions are harder than on HBBI, but I felt like I was doing okay in that last lady for a while."

At first, I couldn't make sense of what he was saying. Then I understood. There was no way he'd risk anyone but himself being first to the finish line – but that didn't mean he had to use his own body.

"You were controlling her," I said.

"Her and the rest of them," he confirmed. "Until you people distracted me. After that, they really didn't have a snowball's chance. But don't feel guilty about getting them killed." He gestured to the mob behind him. "I've got more."

Even in light of everything we knew about him, it was impossible not to be shaken by his cavalier tone.

"All these people," Cassie said, her voice dripping with irrepressible loathing. "They're the Chowderheads you abducted."

"Some of them," Norman answered pleasantly, as if her tone had been congenial. "But most of them are neighborhood folks I grabbed from upstairs to use as crash test dummies." He looked down at the sixth level. "I'd never waste my Chowderheads in there. I need their reedy brains. I let them off the leash to give me advice every time I send in a new batch of dummies."

Cassie, Arthur, and I exchanged stunned looks. How many "batches" had gone in? How many massacres had Norman been responsible for?

"I think your brethren appreciate the special treatment. They've been very cooperative," he continued. "I barely had to kill any of them to motivate the rest." He jerked his head toward the stairs behind him, and for the first time I noticed two men's bodies – bullet wounds visible in their foreheads.

The sight was mortifying, but it was made worse by the fact that one of them was wearing a T-shirt with a red bird in a red circle screen printed across the chest. It was the symbol worn by the Black Knight. I knew I was looking at the body of C. B.'s beloved Loyd. A pang of anguish shot through me. I'd come to accept that a reunion between the two of them wasn't our priority. I knew whether we succeeded or failed in our mission, they would likely both cease to be who they now were. But that didn't make Loyd's murder any less heartbreaking.

"Unfortunately, even with all the help, I have to admit, I am just stuck as hell," Norman went on. "But I'm very optimistic about what you bring to the party."

We weren't sure exactly what he meant by that, but we knew he didn't really need us. Our visitors from the future had proved that his current ruthless strategy would work, and quite soon if we didn't find a way to stop him.

"Nevertheless, I'd be lying if I said I wasn't curious about how you got past my people upstairs," he said. Then he gestured to the black box Cassie had dropped as she rolled onto the landing. "Not to mention how you got ahold of another one of those."

The fact that he had no idea what had happened upstairs confirmed his communications were every bit as jammed as we'd hoped. But we said nothing to relieve his curiosity on that count or the matter of our black box. He moved toward the T-Rex and peered down at Wilson's impaled body.

He gave a short whistle and said, "Must have been a real matum meal when this bastard got loose. But very nicely handled." Then he winked and added, "Thank God for #48, huh? Doubt an herbivore could have gotten the job done."

He knew the robotic dinosaur had been introduced as a brontosaurus in *Batman* #35 (1946), but been retconned into a T-Rex in issue #48 two years later. And he wanted us to know he knew. After all this time, I thought he was still starved for Chowderhead validation. Then I realized that wasn't quite right. He didn't just want Chowderhead validation; he wanted OUR validation. That was why he hadn't assimilated us into the horde yet. We were the only ones who had been through the journey he had, and he wanted worthy witnesses to affirm the magnitude of what he was about to accomplish. He'd devolved into a clichéd, monologuing supervillain, and the narcissism of it was sickening. But I knew it was our only hope of turning the tables. If and when he got around to taking control of our bodies, all would be lost.

"Anyway, let's get to the tour," he said.

He turned and began descending the steps toward another platform. His captive entourage followed automatically, and we were shoved along with them. For the time being, there was nothing to do but take in our surroundings in greater detail. And Seymour had gotten every one of those details right. The spectacle before us made the Danger Room look like the low-fidelity set of a B movie. A vast subterranean estate stretched in every direction, contained by limestone walls that seemed to reach down into endless darkness. But I knew there was a bottom, and a river ran through it. The cave's eight levels of walkways were affixed to various walls, and between the monolithic stalagmites and stalactites that intersected the space, I could see a laboratory, library, several training areas, and a garage/hangar where the Batmobile, Batwing, and other vehicles sat, poised for deployment. I also spotted the giant Joker playing card, a number of freestanding display cases containing various versions of Batman's and Robin's costumes and a wall-mounted display case containing several of the Penguin's umbrellas, as well as Deathstroke's sword. I scanned the area for the giant penny, but then remembered that at this point in the continuity, it was still lodged in a crevice in the cave's floor.

As we reached the bottom of the stairs, we were steered roughly away from the next flight, which led down to the sixth level on which the hard hologram Super-Seymour had committed mass murder moments earlier. Despite our fear of being added to the body count, we knew that level was where we ultimately needed to be, and I thought if we were able to get down there unchaperoned, the force field would likely activate, locking out Norman and his horde. But chained together as we were, there was no doubt our captors would be all over us before we got that far. A series of glowing arrows like the ones we'd seen in the Danger Room appeared on the ground, directing us toward the central island, which was perched at the peak of an extension that branched off from the seventh-level walkway at a right angle. It had been occupied by the Batmobile in one of the cave's previous incarnations, but now it held Batman's command center. Nestled behind an array of Kevlar shields stood seven linked Cray T932 mainframes, a series of retractable glass maps, and a hologram projector.

As we reached it, the projector activated, and a flickering 3D depiction of a balding, black-suited Seymour appeared – a dead ringer for Alfred Pennyworth, aside from the ubiquitous domino mask.

"Congratulations are indeed in order," he began in his over-the-top British Butler speak. "You should be proud to have reached this juncture. However, I have been charged with informing you that your trials have only just begun. Our mechanical watchdog was merely a warm-up. Few will have the knowledge and insight to survive this final test, and if you should choose to continue, you'll most likely wind up dead. Of course, it shall be a hero's death, but a hero's death renders you no less dead than any other sort."

He paused, as if awaiting our departure. I assumed there was a lever or something somewhere that would open the clock and let us out if we wanted to go. But we were all staying.

"Still determined to see it through?" he started again. "Very well then. The rules are simple: what you seek is located in a vault on the sixth level, but it will be accessible only after you've proven yourself worthy. So, there you have it. Lasciate ogni speranza, voi ch'entrate."

He dematerialized, and I thought about his parting words. They were Italian, and they were inscribed above the gates of Hell in Dante's *Divine Comedy*. I knew them because they'd been borrowed by many comic book writers over the years. They translated to "Abandon all hope, ye who enter here." Subtle.

"Alright then," Norman said, glancing over at me, then at the platform below. "Hopefully I'll have more luck down there with your bulletproof hide."

This clarified what he'd meant when he'd said he was "optimistic about what we brought to the party," and as much as I was feeding his ego as an audience member, it was obvious my time in that role had come to an end.

"How's it work anyway – anything but a punch just bounces off?" he asked.

"Go to Hell," I answered.

"Gotcha." He shrugged. "Guess I'll find out soon enough."

He stepped toward me, clearly preparing to jump into my head. If I was going to do something, now was the time. But what could I do? We were farther than ever from the stairs, and the angle of the extension leading to the island on which we stood made leaping to the lower platform impossible. I glanced over the edge of the island and finally understood why we'd been handcuffed together. While I could survive the fall to the bottom of the cave, Cassie and Arthur couldn't, and Norman didn't think I'd trade their lives for the slim chance I'd have to thwart him from down there. In the end, he was right, even though he didn't have all the facts I did.

Yes, first and foremost, we were here to prevent him from warping history and to help the B.H.C. fix it. But now there was a possibility that Cassie, Arthur, and I might win an appeal to be spared from the B.H.C.'s repair plans – an appeal we could only make if we survived. If any of us bought the farm, unlike Slade, Meylene, and Rachit, our resurrection would not be a causal corollary of the others stopping Norman.

Our flip-flopping destiny was enough to give us whiplash, but we'd landed right where we'd started, and I couldn't bear the consequences of letting my friends die. I tried to rationalize doing nothing. I told myself my powers wouldn't help Norman's cause. The system would see what I was, just like the system on

HBBI, but it wouldn't hold back as that system had. It would find a way to do me in as soon as Norman blew a few answers, and my sacrifice would give Cassie and Arthur time to hatch a plan.

Sure, deep down I knew my rationale wasn't rational. I knew there was no viable plan to be hatched. I knew my escape, whatever the cost, was likely our best option. But I couldn't bring myself to act. And then, as Norman reached out for me, I heard Cassie's voice.

"Arthur, hold us for as long as you can."

I felt her hand close around mine and squeeze tightly. Then I was tugged out into space as she launched herself backward.

I heard a chorus of Norman's remote-controlled voices yell, "No!" But there was nothing he could do. We tumbled off the island as Arthur dived in the opposite direction, grabbing hold of the base of a nearby control panel with his free hand. As we fell, he was jerked down to his stomach, and I felt the cuffs tighten on both my wrists as my arms were pulled taut and Cassie and I swung violently back toward the island. All I could see above me was Arthur's arm hanging over the edge, and I was sure Norman's horde would be reeling us up momentarily.

Then, suddenly, the force field partitioning the sixth level from the seventh activated. It sliced across space, severing Arthur's arm just above the wrist, the stump snapping back toward him like a broken rubber band. Then Cassie and I were falling, flipping end over end but still tethered together. I pulled her toward me, and her eyes met mine. There was no fear in them. No panic. Just a note of sadness. And then I glimpsed a glimmer of blue energy behind her, and she hit the force field between the sixth and fifth level, her body incinerating on impact in a flash of brilliant blue flames.

A primal scream was on its way to my lips as I hit a split second later and bounced and rolled to my hands and knees. Arthur's severed wrist and hand burned away along with the parts of my clothing and shoes that had made contact with the force field. But I was unharmed, as Cassie had known I would be.

"Hold us for as long as you can," she'd said to Arthur. And he'd understood. She'd gambled that the force fields containing the sixth level would be triggered by any prolonged presence on that level—even in the space beside the platform. She'd gambled, knowing winning would mean losing her life.

A haze of tears clouded my vision as I stared over at the place where her body had been. The deaths of Slade, Rachit, and Meylene were still fresh in my mind, but in that moment, they were swept away like bread crumbs. This was something different, and it was beyond what I could bear. I realized I was sobbing as I looked up at the island and saw Arthur looking down at me. Even through the distortion of the force field, I could read the devastation and guilt on his face. Beside him, Norman peered over, furious. He yelled something, but I couldn't make it out, and I didn't care what it was. I was done. I couldn't go on. Without Cassie, everything else was meaningless. I didn't get up. I didn't move, aside from the gentle spasms of my sobs.

Then I heard Arthur calling desperately from above, as Norman's horde dragged him back from the edge.

"M-m-make it count, Clayton! Make it count!"

I wasn't magically invigorated by the words. I didn't spring to my feet with a battle cry. But I heard him. I heard him and knew that I'd been here before. When I thought I'd lost him. When I really did lose Decker. I had to act, as I had then. What I was feeling—despite its truly crushing weight—did not matter. What mattered was what Cassie had sacrificed. What mattered was making sure that sacrifice wasn't in vain. And I was the only person in the world who could do it.

I got to my feet unsteadily. I could barely feel my heart thundering in my chest as a numbness came over me. I felt disconnected from time and space. But I forced myself to take a step. Then another. And another. I reached the platform and looked over at the stairs up to the seventh level and down to the fifth level. I could see the telltale shimmer of the force field blocking the way up and down. There was no way in or out. I noted Norman on the other side of the field, glaring at me psychotically as his horde dragged a one-armed Arthur down behind him. In my haze, they all seemed a million miles away.

A laser shot down and swept over me, and I knew the system was scanning me as the system on HBBI had. Then I heard a gritty, intense version of Seymour's voice coming through a com device that had apparently materialized in my ear.

"Clark, can you hear me?"

CHAPTER  31

"CLARK, IT'S THE QUESTION. YOU THERE?"

I looked down at my body. The laser hadn't just been scanning me. It had given me a skin-deep makeover, like the contestants before me. However, I was cast in the role of Superman, not Batman. I had no idea why. But that made me Clark – Clark Kent. And the voice in my ear was Seymour's take on the Question, aka Vic Sage: the fearless, faceless, shit-disturbing, conspiracy-obsessed truth seeker created by Steve Ditko in *Blue Beetle* #1 (1967), during Ditko's stint at Charlton Comics, where he was given the creative freedom to indulge his black-and-white Ayn Rand-inspired values.

"Clark?" the voice called again.

"What am I doing here?" I demanded, with no patience for niceties.

"You're here to answer the big question."

This explained why Seymour had chosen the voice he had for my com, though the wordplay was a little heavy-handed.

"Okay," I said tersely. "So what's the big question?"

"Who wins in a fight? Batman or Superman?"

"What?" I asked, genuinely shocked. I knew I was walking into a gladiatorial contest, but I'd expected far more substance in the setup. While there was some poetry in ending the Challenge where the Scriptures had truly begun – with Superman and Batman – this unmotivated grudge match felt like a trivial, pedestrian effort by comparison to the elegant, inspired subtext of the second stage. I'd given so much to get here. Others had given everything for me to get here. And this was what was waiting? I felt a flush of disdain for Seymour. After everything he'd put us through, he'd just gotten lazy and phoned in the finale.

I was jolted out of my ruminations as another laser shot down and began etching a figure out of thin air. In seconds, I was staring at a holo-Seymour, dressed as the Dark Knight. It was a fair likeness, even with the Cateklysm mask wedged incongruously beneath the mask built into the cowl. The number thirty-six glowed into existence above his head – the same hit counter I'd seen so many times in the Danger Room. I knew, even though the setup was a hack job, the next few minutes would be the most important of my life. I needed to force the feeling that I couldn't go on out of my mind.

There was no preamble. Bat-Seymour went for his utility belt as the Question-esque voice in my ear asked, "Who killed Larry Bodine?"

It was a trick question about an X-Men story line, and it nearly caught me out. But not quite.

"He did. He killed himself," I answered, beating Bat-Seymour to the draw. My vision went red, and I knew from experience that a blast of heat vision was pouring out of my eyes. It grazed Bat-Seymour's shoulder as he twisted out of the way and dived behind a stalagmite.

To the uninitiated, it may seem like Batman would have no chance against Superman. But that's just not so. The tally of their skirmishes—and surprisingly, there have been many—is actually pretty even. Batman can always resort to Kryptonite. Or a red sun ray. Or something else that basically turns Superman into a regular guy. And you don't want to be a regular guy in a fight with Batman.

That brings us to the battle in which I now found myself. The abilities I was borrowing from Superman were only available in bursts, accessed by my knowledge of the Scriptures. And my hunch that the system would find a way around my own unique physiology was about to be confirmed as the voice in my ear demanded, "Who rescued the New Men when they were cornered by the Brotherhood of Man in Seattle's sewers?"

I had no clue. Not even a guess. Bat-Seymour rolled out from the other side of the pillar and hurled a Batarang that exploded into what seemed to be a localized snowstorm. The temperature in the air around me fell to below zero—way below zero. I doubled over, instantly overcome by the cold. The system definitely had me figured out, and ultimately I was only as super as I was smart.

I wondered briefly why the system hadn't somehow accounted for Norman's mutation as it had mine. But I supposed the deadline for the Challenge suggested Seymour expected the scenario to accomplish its purpose before mutants started appearing en masse. So it was likely the anti-mutation measures were a half-baked afterthought—and they were handicapping the wrong guy.

In any event, the Batarang-borne frost storm was short lived, but it gave Bat-Seymour time to collect himself and seal his shoulder wound with a foam of some kind, applied with what looked like an EpiPen. As he returned the device to his utility belt, he removed a black canister and lunged at me. I didn't know what the canister held, and I wasn't sure I'd survive finding out.

The voice in my ear barked, "We live in each blow you strike for infinite justice, always in the hope of what?"

It was a reference to *Amazing Spider-Man* #36 (2001), and I knew it cold.

As Bat-Seymour reached me and raised the canister, I yelled, "Infinite wisdom!"

Then I flew off the ground, levitated by an anti-gravitation field of some kind, and bashed into Bat-Seymour like a cannonball. He dropped the canister as he was launched backward, wriggling through the air. But as he smacked into the wall behind him and slid down to the floor, I got the really bad news. I hadn't noticed before, but the counter over his head hadn't changed. It wasn't at thirty-four, as it should have been after I'd given two right answers. It wasn't even at thirty-five. It was still at thirty-six. I recalled Norman saying "I'm just stuck as hell" and felt a knot in my stomach. Was it a glitch? That seemed impossible. I thought this technology must be beyond glitches. But the alternative was that I was playing a game that didn't make any sense. And it was a deadly game.

Bat-Seymour was back on his feet and running at me when the voice in my ear piped up with, "What planet was the Evolution Kid from?"

"Plowdar!" I yelled, but regretted it immediately. I couldn't recall the answer, but I knew mine wasn't quite right. Bat-Seymour reached me and leaped into the air, rising over my head in an astonishing feat of acrobatics. He flipped and contorted his body while flinging another Batarang down at me. This one was trailing a thin cord, and before I knew what was happening, the Batarang had encircled my wrist, tangling it in the cord. Bat-Seymour landed behind me and yanked the other end of the cord, hard. My hand smashed into my face, breaking and bloodying my nose. The only organic thing in the area with which to hit me, was me. So the system had figured out how to do it. The fact that I'd just been punched with my own fist might have been funny under other circumstances, and I half expected Bat-Seymour to start chanting "stop hitting yourself!" But that would be more Deadpool's style, and the stoic silence of my adversary showed he was fully committed to his role.

As I frantically worked to untangle my hand from the cord, the voice in my ear asked, "Where did Mikhail Rasputin train Gene Nation?"

I knew it was some weird dimension. There'd been a whole explanation in *Uncanny X-Men* #373, (1999). Reflexively, I thought, *Cassie would know this*, and the thought sent a fresh wave of heartache crashing down on me, breaking my concentration. Bat-Seymour lunged to the left and yanked the cord again. My hand thundered into my jaw, knocking two teeth clean out. As they arced through the air and clattered across the floor, I watched in confused disgust as the counterfeit caped crusader dashed by and snatched them up. Then, as he disappeared into the shadows, the voice in my ear asked, "Name an Indian subsidiary of Harada Global Conglomerates."

It was a Harbinger reference. I knew that. But I was having a lot of trouble thinking, what with the throbbing face pain left by my busted nose and missing teeth. Alas, I was distracted from that soon enough when I felt a searing pain slash across my right shoulder blade and blood began gushing down my back. I whirled to see Bat-Seymour crouching for a follow-up attack. His right hand was stained with blood from the wound on my back, inflicted with the tiny organic dagger protruding from between his right thumb and forefinger – the pointy root of one of my teeth!

As he rushed toward me, the voice in my ear threw me a lifeline, asking, "Who let Captain Mar-Vell escape capture after the attempted Kree invasion?"

Fighting through the fog in my mind and the blood in my mouth, I answered weakly, "Nick Fury."

A violent gust of wind originating from somewhere in front of my mouth knocked Bat-Seymour to the ground and blew him twenty feet across the platform. It was a simulation of Superman's superbreath, but judging from the fact that Bat-Seymour wasn't instantly frozen into a block of ice, it was the regular variety, not the freezing variety. The only thing that was frozen was the counter over his head. It still read thirty-six. It didn't make any sense. Why in the hell wasn't it changing?

I was hurting bad, and as I watched him get to his feet, I knew if I was going to survive this, I needed to build some momentum. But things went the other way.

The voice in my ear asked, "Who were the Green Lanterns fighting in *Battleground: Oa?*"

As my brain went digging for the answer, Bat-Seymour sprinted toward me, a tooth in each hand. I braced for impact, but he dived to my left, executing a forward roll and coming up with the canister he'd dropped earlier. I understood now his charge had been a ruse, and as he pressed a button on the top of the canister, my stupid brain was too busy not knowing the stupid answer to the stupid Green Lantern question to tell me to shut my stupid mouth. Aerosol spray shot out of the can and rushed into my lungs, expanding into what felt like cotton balls. I collapsed to my knees, helplessly gasping for air.

Bat-Seymour just stood there, watching me thrash around on the ground. He was toying with me now, as Super-Seymour had likely toyed with the others. The aerosol was alarmingly fast acting. It couldn't have been more than three seconds before blackness began to creep in from the periphery of my vision.

Then, at the last possible moment, I heard the voice in my ear ask, "Who exiled J'onn J'onzz and killed most of the Martian population?"

"Commander Blanx," I sputtered with what was nearly my last breath. The effects of the aerosol abated immediately, and I gulped for air as another blast of heat vision was loosed from my eyes. Bat-Seymour cartwheeled across the platform, the blast barely brushing his midsection. I stared at the counter over his head. Still thirty-six. The reality was undeniable. I couldn't keep this up. I was cheating death time after time but making no progress. The adrenaline, the blood loss, the strain of finding answers that felt more elusive every second—it all settled on me like a massive lead blanket.

I didn't even get up from my knees as I watched Bat-Seymour gather himself and trudge toward me. The voice in my ear spoke up, though I barely heard it.

"What small town was home to the fishermen saved by the deaths of the Doom Patrol?"

In my weary state, all I could do was stare at the unchanging number over my opponent's head. Had it been hopeless from the start? Yes, I thought. The whole thing was rigged. No one could triumph here, no matter how well they knew the Scriptures. As Bat-Seymour drew within a dozen yards, a Batarang in one hand and a tooth in the other, the impulse to give up was almost irresistible. Until I thought of Cassie. I couldn't quit on her. I wouldn't quit on her. Then I remembered: there was a version of history where Norman reached the finish line. But how? I asked myself. How could he win when his answers achieved nothing? How could anyone win when the rules ensured no one could win? Suddenly, my Spidey-Sense started ringing in my ears. No one could win. No one could win!

I thought back to the question that had started it all, and suddenly I knew the meaning of the number thirty-six hovering over Bat-Seymour's head. "Who wins in a fight?" It wasn't just fodder for a frivolous Chowderhead trivia debate. It was a quote, taken verbatim from *Batman* #36 (2015)—the refrain of a meditative narrative taking place in Batman's mind during his brutal battle with a Joker-toxin-infused Superman. As Batman spits Kryptonite gum into Superman's eye, ostensibly defeating him, a thought bubble appears above the two titans, asking the question for the last time: "Who wins in a fight?" And Batman finally gives an unexpected answer.

"Neither of us," I whispered. I wasn't sure it had even been audible until Bat-Seymour stopped in his tracks, directly in front of me. He stared down at me for a moment. Then, he vanished, and I knew I'd been right. The system had been waiting for those words and those words alone. The rest of it had all been a detour—I'd thought the answer to the so-called "big question" was to be determined by my victory or death in the showdown. I'd thought wrong.

It was all so clear now. This wasn't about which iconic superhero could win in a fight. This was about the fact that neither of them could win if they were fighting each other. It was about the coming war between humans and superhumans. I'd been cast as Superman because he represented the side of the war I'd land on. This whole thing was a desperate entreaty to prevent our differences from sparking a global conflict in which we would all lose.

I'd assumed the trivia questions were random—part of yet another test to prove we'd done our reading. But looking back, every question had hinted at the point, if not yelled it. Larry Bodine was a kid who had committed suicide when his high school tormentors threatened to out him as a mutant (*New Mutants* #45, 1986). The Evolution Kid tried to create a super race to take over the world (*Fate Force* #89, 2032). The New Men, Gene Nation, and Harbinger were all part of that same chorus: death and destruction, courtesy of humans persecuting superhumans and/or superhumans trying to conquer humanity. And where the questions didn't revolve around that volatile discord, they were commentaries on the ravages of war. Commander Blanx incited a civil war that killed nearly everyone on Mars (*Justice League of America* #71, 1969). "Battleground: Oa" ends with a Guardian of the Universe telling Hal Jordan, "Wars are never won, regardless of who might be the victor. The very act of war is itself a horrible defeat" (*Green Lantern* #127, 1980). And of course, Nick Fury's choice to let Mar-Vell escape capture in *Avengers* #92 (1971) was inspired by his experience of what Japanese-American detainment camps had done to men on "both sides of the barbed wire."

Seymour was imploring us to overcome our fear of one another and do right by one another, no matter how great our differences may seem. I couldn't believe it had taken me so long to see it. There had even been a didactic reference to *Doom Patrol* #121 (1968). The New England town I'd failed to name was home to fourteen fishermen for whom the original Doom Patrol had given their lives. A team of "superfreaks" had seen past the feelings of alienation that had always haunted them to make the ultimate sacrifice for what the evil Captain Zahl called "a handful of stupid, ordinary men."

But where that issue stood out by virtue of how glaringly on the nose it was, another stood out for different reasons: *Spider-Man* #36. Just weeks after the 9/11 attacks in the US, when the country was calling for blood, Marvel called for sanity, depicting Muslims among the victims of the attacks and reminding readers that it was not all of Islam that was responsible but a cabal of deranged extremists. Interestingly, this issue of Spider-Man clashed with a rich irony at work in the vast majority of the source material. In most cases, the messages were shrouded in metaphor. Superpowers had stood in for the real-life things that divided us—as Kitty Pryde had dramatically illustrated in her speech at poor Larry Bodine's memorial, drawing a parallel between the ostracization of "muties" and that of "niggers, spics, wops, slopes, and faggots." The irony was that in the coming war, the metaphors and their meanings would switch places. Life was about to imitate art imitating life, with the real-world prejudices of the past becoming analogs for the comic bookish differences that would drive us to destroy each other.

I saw now that every example cited harbored layers upon layers of meaning. Seymour hadn't been phoning it in at all. He'd given it everything. He'd pulled out all the stops.

This was his Mona Lisa. This was his Beethoven's Third.

And he was an asshole who had killed the girl I loved. I hated him and his game. The self-indulgence. The savagery. All of it.

B.H.C. policy prohibited outright warnings about the future, so I supposed he was trying to give those who entered this chamber an abstract sense of the suffering his message was meant to prevent. But that suffering was nothing compared to the suffering of the broken reality his goddamn scenario had created.

It had taken just seconds for me to reflect on all of this, but I was snapped back into the present as I heard Seymour's Vic Sage voice in my ear again.

"Congratulations," it said, as a door began sliding open to reveal a hidden vault at the other end of the level. "And now, for your prize."

With those last words, I felt my earpiece dissolve, along with my supersuit. Then, to my horror, the force fields above and below my level dropped. Apparently, Seymour had thought there would be no need for containment at this point. If it had been possible for me to hate him more than I already did, I would have.

Norman's telepathically enslaved mob bounded down the stairs toward me. I tried for the vault, but they overtook me like a rushing river and pinned me to the floor. I struggled futilely against a dozen hands. To my right, I caught sight of Arthur being dragged down the stairs by the guards. We'd thought our gambit had put Norman out of the running. We'd thought everything we'd endured had ensured it would be me who welcomed Seymour. We'd been wrong. Now we were both back in our roles as captive audience–witnesses to Norman's ultimate triumph, which was just moments away.

"Well done, kid," Norman said, taking his unexpected good fortune in stride as only the psychotically entitled can.

He walked past me and entered the vault. There, before him, stood an enormous searchlight with Batman's logo affixed to the lens: the Bat-Signal. A small metal box with a toggle switch sat atop a pedestal beside the signal. Norman paused, visibly willing himself to take a moment to appreciate the scene and all the anticipation that had led up to it.

"I haven't been this amped since my old man's 'accidental OD.'"

He made air quotes, and I realized he'd just confessed to his father's murder. Of course. I thought about the reports of his father threatening to disown him. It had been no coincidence that he'd gained control of the company when he had, and he seemed to relish revealing it now. More than ever, he was above the law, beyond consequences.

He stepped forward and flipped the switch beside the Bat-Signal. As expected, the signal lit up, projecting a huge bat symbol onto the wall behind us. Norman frowned impatiently as he waited for something else to happen. Then it did. A swirling blue vortex appeared behind the Bat-Signal and out stepped Seymour in full Cateklysm Catholicon dress. I knew straight away, this was the real McCoy—there was none of the slightly robotic, artificiality of his holo-spawn. I'd find out later that the Bat-Signal emitted a temporal alert beacon that marked the moment someone completed the Challenge, so he could make the leap here right after his speech at Comic-Con to present the worthy champion with his or her prize, in person.

This was it. This was where Norman met Seymour—where he got the Translocator. I had a lot to say to Seymour, but there was only one thing that mattered right now.

I lunged forward and screamed, "Don't let him touch y—" but three hands shot out to cover my mouth, and an arm wrapped around my throat.

I'd failed to convey the details, but it only took a brief glance around for Seymour to know things hadn't gone according to plan. Aside from me and Arthur being suspiciously restrained, from his vantage point, he could see the bodies of Loyd and the other Chowderhead Norman had executed on the stairs leading up to the eighth level. As brutal as his scenario was, there was no explanation for dead bodies up there—none other than foul play.

"Oh, for crying out loud," he groaned, raising both palms in Norman's direction and brandishing the hand blasters he'd used to paralyze the guards during his broadcast.

Norman wasn't ready for this. He'd expected to find Cateklysm's U.A.T. in the vault, not Cateklysm himself. Like most Chowderheads, he'd assumed if Cateklysm was going to step in to rebuff him, he would have done so long ago. Based on the facts Norman had, he was now facing an other-dimensional being who was pissed off at him. He made the safe play, bowing down on both knees and placing his hands flat on the floor in front of Seymour.

I hoped Seymour would just whip out his Translocator and jump back to B.H.C. HQ. But he seemed to need to make sense of his scenario gone wrong. "You're some kind of evil, cheating bastard, aren't you?" He took a step toward Norman, who said nothing in reply.

"I know I said you people were the absolute worst, but even I can't believe this. I mean your species is headed right down the crapper! Do you not get that?" True to B.H.C. protocol, he wasn't breaking character. He stomped closer to Norman, who cringed and recoiled. I took some small pleasure in this and thought maybe our simple presence here had changed things. Despite my feelings for Seymour and his scenario, I had to admit he'd pegged Norman at lightning speed and seemed to have the situation well in hand.

"I thought I was coming here to meet a shining example of the new and improved humanity," he said. "Instead I find this cluster bumble!"

He reached into a compartment on his suit and pulled out a box like the one we'd received on HBBI, though this one was gold. It had to be the grand prize. (It was smaller than I'd expected, but I'd learn later it was a digital record of the plans for the U.A.T. and not the device itself.) I didn't think there was any chance Seymour was actually going to award it to Norman, and I was right. He leaned down, shook it in Norman's face and yelled, "You were supposed to have attained the virtue and strength of character to deserve this!"

Then Norman looked up, and I realized he hadn't been recoiling in fear earlier, he'd been drawing back like a snake, luring Seymour closer as he prepared to strike. And then he did. He lunged up, clasping a hand around Seymour's wrist, and Seymour froze. Norman didn't know what the being before him was, but he'd wagered it was a life-form on which his power would work – and he'd been right. I knew now that our presence here hadn't changed anything. Norman would take control of Seymour, and one way or another the future we feared would unfold.

But as Seymour's jaw went slack and his eyes began to take on a glassy sheen, Norman's control over the others wavered for just a moment, and I felt their grip on me relax slightly. Out of the corner of my eye, I noted the shoulder holster of one of the guards helping restrain me. I was sure the gun inside would have been lasered to dust if he'd entered this level before the Challenge was completed. But now there it was, intact, and it was my last chance. Pro code or no, there was one choice and one choice only. I wrenched my arm free, ripped the gun from the holster, and fired three times at Norman. One shot went wide, but the other two were right on target. Unfortunately, that target became Seymour, as his now remote-controlled body leaped in front of Norman – an extension of

Norman's reflex to shield himself.

The bullets tore into Seymour, spinning him around like a tragic ballet dancer. I felt the guard ripping the gun from my grasp and the horde's claws draw tight around me again as Seymour's body hit the ground. On impact, the gold box flew out of his hand, sliding off the edge of the platform. Norman checked himself for bullet wounds, but his relief at finding none was short lived as he rushed to the edge of the platform and looked down at what I assumed were the ruins of the gold box somewhere far below. Then he looked over at Seymour's dead body, a mask of blind fury hardening his features.

"You . . . little . . . shit!" He turned and glared at me. Then he continued—but not just him—suddenly, all his minions spoke in unison.

"You took it from me!" the sea of enraged voices yelled. "You took everything from me!"

I knew the U.A.T. would have been of limited interest to him, given what it really was. I also knew there was something that would interest him much more still somewhere on Seymour's person. And finally, I knew he would eventually find that something. But he didn't know any of that. No, at the moment, he believed I'd undone his life's work, and he'd snapped. The eleven-year-old psychopath who had tortured uncooperative Chowderheads was at the wheel now. And he had no restraint. None at all. A ferocious, synchronous cry went up from his horde as it pounced.

Punches and kicks flew at me from every direction, and I rolled into a ball, protecting myself as best I could. But it was no good. I felt a rib crack as a foot slammed into my midsection. Then my arms were stretched in either direction as countless fists hammered at my face. My lips split. Another two teeth came loose. Within seconds, I was a bloody, bruised mess.

Through fractured glimpses, I could see them going at Arthur too. I was sure most of his pain receptors had long since shut down, and for that I was thankful. Unlike me, he was not invulnerable to the shock sticks and guns the guards were carrying. Sparks flew, shots rang out, and the mob pushed and shoved to get at him like coyotes fighting over a carcass. I saw his neck severed and his head ripped from his shoulders, just as my own attackers reached a new gear, stomping and kicking me as if they were trying to put out a raging blaze.

And that's when the seizure hit. It was like a bolt of lightning ripping through me, making my previous seizures feel like the hiccups. My body thrashed around so violently my assailants were thrown away in every direction. The world spun so fast it was like I was tied to the top of a pinwheel. I felt blood running out of my nose and realized I was choking on more of it.

I heaved forward, vomiting a spray of crimson, then gasped for air as the seizure consumed me again. I was right back where I'd been in my battle with Bat-Seymour – surrendering to death – when it finally stopped.

Norman's minions paused, as he tried to make sense of what had happened. Then . . . they rushed back toward me. I thought fate just couldn't make up its mind how to kill me. But it turned out fate was on my side. Because as the feet and fists fell upon me, they began rebounding away, crackling like bags of busted pretzels, and I knew what the seizure had done. My vulnerability to organic matter was gone.

Another wave of bodies raced forward, and my instincts kicked in. Staggering to my feet, I lashed out, punching madly in every direction. Everything I hit crumbled under my fists, as did everything that hit me. I knew my attackers were just unwilling hosts to Norman's will. I knew they didn't have a choice here. But neither did I. The stakes were too high to give quarter. I let out a bestial growl as I cut my way through them like a stone-skinned Kronan in a brawl with glass figurines.

It wasn't long before those who were still conscious and ambulatory clawed their way clear of me. In each of their eyes, I could see Norman's comprehension of what had happened, having experienced "upgrade by seizure" himself.

Suddenly, each of the guards ran toward the edge of the platform, drew their guns and shock sticks, and hurled them into the abyss. I looked at Norman.

He smiled in contempt and said, "Your move, kid."

He'd just made it a stalemate. His horde couldn't harm me, but without the guns in play, I couldn't harm him without getting close enough for him to hijack me. Any moment, he'd start ransacking Seymour's body in search of a consolation prize, and logically all I'd be able to do was cower at a safe distance. But now that the area around me was clear, I finally looked down and saw what was left of Arthur. His headless body had just one arm and one leg. The missing pieces lay scattered across the platform. As horrible as it sounds, at that point I'd gotten used to seeing my friends die, and I was all out of shock and sorrow. But I had plenty of anger left. And I could use that. My heart rate redlined, and I heard my teeth grinding. I forgot my broken bones and bloody wounds.

"I'm gonna kill you, you son of a bitch!" I roared.

As I charged toward him, his smile didn't waver and he didn't wilt. In fact, he surged forward, matching my gait. He could see I was enraged. He could see I was hulking the hell out. And that's exactly what I wanted him to see. I wanted him to think my anger had made me reckless. I wanted him to think it had made me stupid. But it hadn't. A split second before I reached him, I dropped to the ground and slid past him, like I was stealing home base, just missing his outstretched hand. After my fake out back on the Charon, I couldn't believe he was so easily duped again. I came to a stop right next to Seymour's body and yanked up one of his hands, aiming the palm-mounted blaster at Norman, whose eyes lit up with panic. He was about to take a nap, and he was probably thinking I'd make sure he never woke up. All I had to do was pull the trigger. But I didn't. I couldn't. There was no trigger. No button. No nothing. Because Seymour's blasters were obviously controlled through his neural implant. I'd known it was a possibility, but I'd hoped for the best.

My face fell. There was no way Norman could know the details, but he could read the defeat in my eyes. His smile returned. Until he heard the thumping sound behind him. Before he could even turn around, something hopped into him with a bloodcurdling scream. He went down hard, and there, on top of him, was Arthur. Well, not all of Arthur, but his torso, a leg, and an arm – an arm holding his own severed and battered head, which he jammed into Norman's horrified face, synthetic blood and saliva streaming out of it as if it were a punctured water balloon.

"F.L.N., M-M-MOTHERFUCKER!" Arthur's head yelled.

Norman flailed around, trying to free himself from the weight of the half body on top of him. It was almost impossible to pull my eyes away from the spectacle. But Arthur had bought me time, and I wasn't about to waste it. I started searching Seymour's body frantically – and there, clipped to the back of his belt, was the Translocator. It was a clunky black glass octagon with a single button. I pressed the button, and a series of menus were projected in the air above it. I thanked God the prototype had been abandoned before it had been configured to interface with neural implants. Then I took back my thanks as I realized I couldn't read anything in the menus I was looking at. The language looked like some insane hybrid of English, Chinese, and emoticons.

"Shit!" I shrieked. Then I started jabbing at the menus desperately. Apparently I got something right because a vortex suddenly sprang open behind me just as Norman gained purchase and hoisted Arthur's bloody and mangled remains off himself, sending Arthur's head hurtling across the platform toward me. It rolled to a stop a few feet away, face up, and the eyes settled on me.

"Time to g-g-go," his head said.

"Fucking A," I agreed.

Then, as Norman scrambled to his feet and started toward me, I grabbed my friend's severed head and jumped into a wormhole to travel to the future and prevent Armageddon. You know, the usual.

CHAPTER 32

"DID YOU THINK THIS THROUGH AT ALL?" I DEMANDED.
I'd been yelling at Seymour for about half an hour.

"I mean setting aside the possibility of an ass hat like Norman ending up with the prize, what if no one could solve your damn puzzles? Or what if they all got killed by your doppelgangers done up as the World's Finest?!"

"Yeah, maybe I made it too hard," he said flatly.

"You think?!"

"Even the Conundrum. Man, it took you people years longer than expected. Plus, you discovered the crystals way late. But sometimes you have to patch it to perfect it, and I figured we'd have the chance. I guess some of those borderline probabilities got us. Something went awfully wonky."

"Wonky? Wonky?! I should kick your time-diddling ass!"

"Wouldn't blame you if you did."

He stood up. "I'm gonna get some coffee. Want some?"

"I hate you," I answered.

He nodded. "I know."

As he headed for the kitchen, I turned and stared out the window at the compound. It was the size of a small college campus. I could see a dozen or so buildings, all less than ten stories, constructed of some unfamiliar steel that gave off a slight copper glow. The streets were packed with greenery—trees half the height of most of the buildings. I saw virtually no activity on the walking paths below, but there were a couple of hover platforms traveling between the top floors of various buildings.

In the distance, I detected the greenish sheen of an energy field that surrounded the place. Through that, I could make out what looked like a scenic vista in Colorado, but that and the clear blue sky above were apparently projections of some sort to bring a little bit of Earth to the otherwise uninhabited alien world where the compound was located.

The room in which I was sitting was Seymour's. There were comics everywhere. He'd been a devoted fan long before the scenario, and his tastes ran to American publishers—hence the focus of the Challenge. But there was more than just comics littering the room. A lot more. The place was packed with crap he'd collected from his vacations throughout history. It looked like an Arabian bazaar and a Manhattan department store had had a baby, and it had exploded. The accommodations were equipped with hard hologram projectors, so the decor, furniture, lighting, etc. could be transformed at the resident's whim. But the really mind-blowing thing was the food, which was produced by honest-to-God matter fabricators. That and much of the other tech I'd seen made the so-called U.A.T. look like a toaster oven. I understood now how small a feat it must have been to create an unhackable website, generate the resources to buy out the comic book industry, and spin up the Danger Room, the Batcave, and all their trimmings.

The door opened and Arthur walked in. I was still getting used to the new synthetic body he'd been issued. He was downright brawny, though not as brawny as you'd expect considering he could now bench press a metric ton. I thought with his superstrength and my indestructibleness, the two of us would make a pretty badass superduo.

"They said we can g-g-go in now," he said.

I nodded and stood up as Seymour returned with his coffee. I looked at him and thought about my lifelong love of the Scriptures. Despite everything, I still believed in them, and always would. But I was overwhelmed by the sur-realism of standing before the man responsible for that enduring belief, as well as all the really miserable stuff that had happened in my life. I was reminded of Spider-Man meeting Stan Lee (*Stan Lee Meets the Amazing Spider-Man*, 2006). While I knew everything I'd been through had made me what I was, I resented it, just like Spidey. However, unlike Spidey, I didn't come away from meeting my creator with a compulsion to heap praise upon him.

I said, "I hope it's a good long while before you get another goddamn sce-nario signed off."

"It will be," he said. "And for what it's worth, I am sorry."

"Well I guess that's something."

Arthur and I walked out of the room and down the hall.

"S-s-still feeling okay?" he asked.

"Yup. Doc says the seizures have run their course."

"That's g-g-great. And no Translocator issues?"

"Nope," I answered. "You?"

"Nope."

Fortunately, it seemed none of our molecules had been scrambled, even though it had taken more than one try to get here. My random menu slapping hadn't actually landed us in the compound. We'd touched down in a field near Freehold, New Jersey, in 1696. Given the enigmatic language in which the

Translocator's menus were inscribed, deciphering them wasn't easy. Hence, I'd spent the creepiest hour of my life in that field, holding Arthur's detached head up in front of the menus while we worked out enough of their meaning to identify Seymour's itinerary and land ourselves in the compound. That had been a week ago.

"'Bout time," Slade grunted as we approached him, Rachit, and Meylene standing by a door at the end of the hall.

We were just getting to know them again because we'd arrived at the compound seconds after Seymour's departure to launch his scenario and minutes before their return from vacation. Being that we were the stone dropped in the pond, the ripples from our trip to the future/past hadn't affected us. Everyone else was a different story because they were still within the one-week window during which the compound's artificial Ripple Resistance field failed.

Of course, as much as our actions had changed things, the current scenario data backed up most of the story we had to tell. But the vote to spare the two of us during the reset had still been less than unanimous. No civilian had been granted the B.H.C.'s temporal protections since Moira McCaffrey's time. So while none of the B.H.C. bigwigs denied we'd saved all of human history and safeguarded the future, there were a good number of traditionalists worried about precedent. And when the time came to vote on our second, more controversial proposal, the holdouts had a lot more company. But we'd come out ahead on that count as well, if only by a single vote.

"Anesthesia's just wearing off now," Rachit said.

"Anesthesia?" Arthur asked.

"Standard protocol for unvetted guests," Slade answered.

He shook his head disdainfully at Rachit and Meylene and added, "Not that any a' you colostomy bags got any respect for protocol." Unlike them, he'd voted against both our proposals. I smiled. He was every bit the asshole he'd warned me about.

Meylene opened the door for us, and as we started into the sterile white room beyond, I noted a furtive glance between her and Arthur. The fledgling sparks I'd witnessed in the previous timeline were flying again.

The B.H.C. had waited a week before making any changes to history, ensuring everyone in the compound would retain all they'd learned since our arrival. In another week, Slade and his team would travel back to reset everything, scrubbing history clean of the Cateklysm Scenario. The change they had just now completed was preliminary – the product of our second proposal that had so narrowly survived the vote. While plucking Seymour from the timeline before his death had been a convenient detour that simplified his debriefing, he wasn't the one we'd lobbied to save.

I took a breath and approached the bed in the middle of the room. Cassie opened her eyes and looked up at me.

"Clayton?" she croaked groggily. "Where am I?"

"It's complicated," I answered.

EPILOGUE

In the years that followed, Cassie's and my dreams of righting wrongs and making the world a better place came true, though not in a way we had ever imagined. There's a lot to tell about our time as B.H.C. agents, but one memory stands out above all the rest.

It was a spring day in 2047, at a comic book store in San Francisco's Sunset District. I'd reviewed the records. I knew the facts. But I still needed to see for myself.

I walked in, and there they were, in maybe the fifth inning of a debate about who would win a race between Superman and the Flash. As always, they argued with the reckless abandon of true love.

"The Flash is aka 'the fastest man alive'!" he cried. "And Superman is a man, who is alive – which puts him in the category of things that are slower than the Flash!"

"Technically, Superman isn't a man," she countered.

"Unbelievable!"

"I'm just saying! He's an alien, not a man."

"Ma and Pa Kent would throw up if they could hear you right now!"

A girl appeared from behind a rack of ninety-nine cent comics. She looked a lot like me when I was eleven or twelve.

"You guys are embarrassing me!" she said. "Especially you, Mom. You know Superman can't access the speed force. You're being ridiculous."

Preventing the events that led to my parents' deaths had changed a lot of things. But they'd still found one another, as I knew they would. After all, their love was like Adamantium.

THE END

APPENDIX A

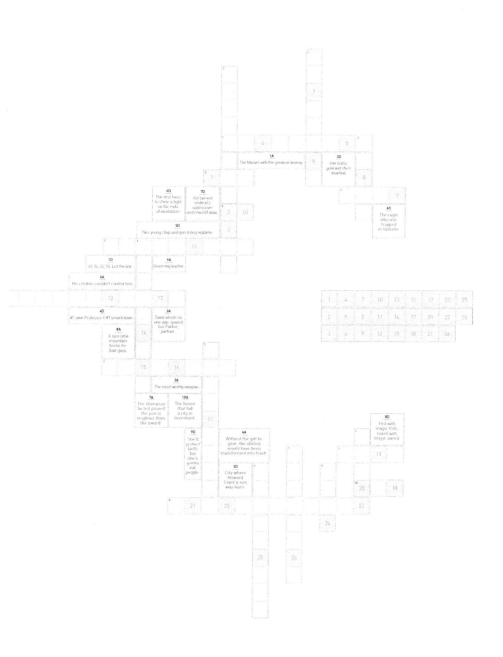

APPENDIX B

3 Across: *Town where none were spared but Parker, partner.*
Answer: Bane. A fair amount of Spider-Man research was wasted here due to the assumption that the answer would have something to do with Peter Parker. But the colloquial Old West term "partner" gives it away. Bane is the town where Al Simmons's great-grandfather Francis Parker was spared by Gunslinger Spawn, who killed everyone else (*Spawn* #174–#175, 2008).

6 Across: *His creators couldn't control him.*
Answer: Adam Warlock. Originally called "Him," Adam was created by the Enclave, who he destroyed (*Marvel Premiere* #1, 1972).

10 Across: *The house that hid a city in Greenland.*
Answer: Lor. The Inhuman royal house of Lor built the hidden city of Orollan in Greenland's Eternal Chasm (*All-New, All-Different Marvel Universe* #1, 2016).

3 Down: *Her dad is gone and she's a sad kid.*
Answer: Sarah. Julie Winters, social worker and deuteragonist of the Maxx, has a young charge named Sarah, whose father is the murdering, raping villain Mr. Gone (*The Maxx* #4, 1993).

5 Down: *Nice young chap and gun-toting vigilante.*
Answer: Bruce Wayne. Commissioner Gordon calls him a "nice young chap" at the end of *Detective Comics* #27 (1939). And despite his rep for abhorring firearms, he sometimes carried a gun in the early days (*Detective Comics* #32, 1939).

6 Down: *The first hero to shine a light on the evils of vandalism.*
Answer: Alan Scott. He was the first to fight Vandal Savage in *Green Lantern* #10, 1943.

ACKNOWLEDGEMENTS

I want to extend my boundless gratitude to my wife and kids for putting up with me during the writing process. There'd be no point to anything without you.

I also want to acknowledge my mom and my sister for inspiring my passion for story-telling – as well as my dad for inspiring me to put in the work demanded by writing and every other area of life. And there is no way this book could have been finished without the support of Matt and the whole team at Iron Creative. There are no words that really get the job done, so I'll have to settle for "thank you." I must also thank my friend Kathy, who inspired my Chowderheadedness during my weekend visits to The Comic Book Box decades ago. And of course, I have to thank the legends that have made such a powerful impact on me from a distance, from Jerry Siegel, to Jack Kirby, to Frank Miller, to Todd McFarlane. But that goes double for Ernest Cline and Grant Morrison because let's face it, this book is in large part a mashup of *Ready Player One* and *Supergods*. If you haven't read them, you have to.

Lastly, for the Scripture faithfuls among you, I want to concede that I've likely botched a comic book reference somewhere that makes me look like a dilettante bonehead. But in the years I spent researching the book, I discovered that that is the beauty of the art form – absolutely no one I interviewed considered themselves an "expert." No one knows it all, because no one wants to. We all identify with the publishers and the titles that speak to us. And speak to us they do, in the most personal, most compelling way.

That said, despite their many flavors, the vast majority of comics do have a common, positive message – a unifying morality. So in looking at the discord and strife humanity sometimes faces, I leave you with one question: was Seymour's plan really such an outrageous idea?

ABOUT THE AUTHOR

J.J. Walsh is a novelist and owner of San Francisco-based advertising agency, Iron Creative Communication. He lives in San Francisco with his wife, two boys, and their Labrador Retriever. So far, his comic book knowledge has not been called upon to save the world. But he is ready.

Made in the USA
Las Vegas, NV
29 November 2024

12870891R00157